I0592385

Flora Annie Webster Steel

On the face of the waters

A tale of the mutiny

Flora Annie Webster Steel

On the face of the waters
A tale of the mutiny

ISBN/EAN: 9783337137861

Printed in Europe, USA, Canada, Australia, Japan

Cover: Foto ©Andreas Hilbeck / pixelio.de

More available books at **www.hansebooks.com**

ON THE FACE OF THE WATERS

ON THE FACE OF
THE WATERS

A TALE OF THE MUTINY

BY

FLORA ANNIE STEEL

AUTHOR OF "MISS STUART'S LEGACY," "THE
FLOWER OF FORGIVENESS," ETC., ETC.

New York
THE MACMILLAN COMPANY
1897

First Edition January, 1897.   Reprinted January 20, January 25, January 30, 1897.

THE MERSHON COMPANY PRESS,
RAHWAY, N. J.

PREFACE.

A WORD of explanation is needed for this book, which, in attempting to be at once a story and a history, probably fails in either aim.

That, however, is for the reader to say. As the writer, I have only to point out where my history ends, my story begins, and clear the way for criticism. Briefly, then, I have not allowed fiction to interfere with fact in the slightest degree. The reader may rest assured that every incident bearing in the remotest degree on the Indian Mutiny, or on the part which real men took in it, is scrupulously exact, even to the date, the hour, the scene, the very weather. Nor have I allowed the actual actors in the great tragedy to say a word regarding it which is not to be found in the accounts of eye-witnesses, or in their own writings.

In like manner, the account of the sham court at Delhi —which I have drawn chiefly from the lips of those who saw it—is pure history; and the picturesque group of schemers and dupes—all of whom have passed to their account—did not need a single touch of fancy in its presentment. Even the story of Abool-Bukr and Newâsi is true; save that I have supplied a cause for an estrangement, which undoubtedly did come to a companionship of which none speak evil. So much for my facts.

Regarding my fiction: An Englishwoman *was* concealed in Delhi, in the house of an Afghan, and succeeded in escaping to the Ridge just before the siege. I have imagined another; that is all. I mention this because it may possibly be said that the incident is incredible.

And now a word for my title. I have chosen it because when you ask an uneducated native of India why the Great Rebellion came to pass, he will, in nine cases out

v

of ten, reply, " God knows! He sent a Breath into the World." From this to a Spirit moving on the face of the Waters is not far. For the rest I have tried to give a photograph—that is, a picture in which the differentiation caused by color is left out—of a time which neither the fair race or the dark race is ever likely to quite forget or forgive.

That they may come nearer to the latter is the object with which this book has been written.

F. A. STEEL.

CONTENTS.

BOOK I.

THISTLEDOWN AND GOSSAMER.

CHAPTER		PAGE
I.	GOING! GOING! GONE!	1
II.	HOME, SWEET HOME,	14
III.	THE GREAT GULF FIXED,	27
IV.	TAPE AND SEALING-WAX,	40
V.	BRAVO!	52
VI.	THE GIFT OF MANY FACES,	67

BOOK II.

THE BLOWING OF THE BUBBLE.

I.	IN THE PALACE,	84
II.	IN THE CITY,	99
III.	ON THE RIDGE,	114
IV.	IN THE VILLAGE,	130
V.	IN THE RESIDENCY,	147
VI.	THE YELLOW FAKIR,	164
VII.	THE WORD WENT FORTH,	179

BOOK III.

FROM DUSK TO DAWN.

I.	NIGHT,	192
II.	DAWN,	208
III.	DAYLIGHT,	222
IV.	NOON,	236
V.	SUNSET,	248
VI.	DUSK,	262

BOOK IV.

"Such Stuff as Dreams are Made of."

CHAPTER		PAGE
I.	The Death-Pledge,	275
II.	Peace! Peace!	290
III.	The Challenge,	306
IV.	Bugles and Fifes,	322
V.	The Drum Ecclesiastic,	338
VI.	Vox Humana,	354

BOOK V.

"There Arose a Man."

I.	Forward!	370
II.	Bits, Bridles, Spurs,	385
III.	The Beginning of the End,	403
IV.	At Last,	419
V.	Through the Walls,	434
VI.	Rewards and Punishments,	449

BOOK VI.

Appendix a,		470
Appendix b,		474

ON THE FACE OF THE WATERS.

BOOK I.

THISTLEDOWN AND GOSSAMER.

CHAPTER I.

GOING! GOING! GONE!

" Going! Going! Gone! "

The Western phrase echoed over the Eastern scene
without a trace of doubt in its calm assumption of finality.
It was followed by a pause, during which, despite the
crowd thronging the wide plain, the only recognizable
sound was the vexed yawning purr of a tiger impatient for
its prey. It shuddered through the sunshine, strangely
out of keeping with the multitude of men gathered together in silent security; but on that March evening of
the year 1856, when the long shadows of the surrounding
trees had begun to invade the sunlit levels of grass by
the river, at Lucknow, the lately deposed King of Oude's
menagerie was being auctioned. It had followed all his
other property to the hammer, and a perfect Noah's Ark
of wild beasts was waiting doubtfully for a change of
masters.

" Going! Going! Gone! "

Those three cabalistic words, shibboleth of a whole
hemisphere's greed of gain, had just transferred the
proprietary rights in an old tusker elephant for the sum
of eighteenpence. It is not a large price to pay for a
leviathan, even if he be lame, as this one was. Yet the

new owner looked at his purchase distastefully, and
even the auctioneer sought support in a gulp of brandy
and water.

"Fetch up them pollies, Tom," he said in a dejected
whisper to a soldier, who, with others of the fatigue party
on duty, was trying to hustle refractory lots into
position. "They'll be a change after elephants—go off
lighter like. Then there's some of them La Martiniery
boys comin' down again as ran up the fightin' rams
this mornin'. Wonder wot the 'ead master said! But
boys is allowed birds, and Lord knows we want to be a
bit brisker than we 'ave bin with *guj-putti*. But there!
it's slave-drivin' to screw bids for beasts as eats hunder-
weights out of poor devils as 'aven't enough for themselves, or a notion of business as business."

He shook his head resentfully yet compassionately
over the impassive dark faces around. He spoke as an
auctioneer; yet he gave expression to a very common
feeling which in the early fifties, when the commercial
instincts of the West met the uncommercial ones of the
East in open market for the first time, sharpened the antagonism of race immensely; that inevitable antagonism
when the creed of one people is that Time is Money, of
the other that Time is Naught.

From either standpoint, however, the auction going
on down by the river Goomtee was confusing; even to
those who, knowing the causes which had led up to it—
the unmentionable atrocities, the crass incapacity on the
one hand, the unsanctioned treaties and craze for
civilization on the other—were conscious of a distinct
flavor of Sodom and Gomorrah, the Ark of the Covenant,
and the Deluge all combined, as they watched the just
and yet unjust retribution going on. But such spectators were few, even in the outer fringe of English onlook-
ers pausing in their evening drive or ride to gratify their
curiosity. The long reports and replies regarding the
annexation of Oude which filled the office boxes of the
elect were unknown to them, so they took the affair as
they found it. The King, for some reason satisfactory
to the authorities, had been exiled, majesty being thus
vested in the representatives of the annexing race: that

is, in themselves. A position which comes naturally to most Englishmen.

To the silent crowds closing round the auctioneer's table the affair was simple also. The King, for some unsatisfactory reason, had been ousted from his own. His goods and chattels were being sold. The valuable ones had been knocked down, for a mere song—just to keep up the farce of sale—to the Huzoors. The rubbish —lame elephants and such like—was being sold to them; more or less against their will, since who could forbear bidding sixpence for a whole leviathan? That this was in a measure inevitable, that these new-come sahibs were bound to supply their wants cheaply when a whole posse of carriages and horses, cattle and furniture was thrown on an otherwise supplied market, did not, of course, occur to those who watched the hammer fall to that strange new cry of the strange new master. When does such philosophy occur to crowds? So when the waning light closed each day's sale and the people drifted back city-ward over the boat-bridge they were no longer silent. They had tales to tell of how much the barouche and pair, or the Arab charger, had cost the King when he bought it. But then Wajeed Ali, with all his faults, had never been a bargainer. He had spent his revenues right royally, thus giving ease to many. So one could tell of a purse of gold flung at a beggar, another a life pension granted to a tailor for inventing a new way of sewing spangles to a waistcoat; for there had been no lack of the insensate munificence in which lies the Oriental test of royalty, about the King of Oude's reign.

Despite this talk, however, the talkers returned day after day to watch the auction; and on this, the last one, the grassy plain down by the Goomtee was peaceful and silent as ever save for the occasional cry of an affrighted hungry beast. The sun sent golden gleams over the short turf worn to dustiness by crowding feet, and the long curves of the river, losing themselves on either side among green fields and mango trees, shone like a burnished shield. On the opposite bank, its minarets showing fragile as cut paper against the sky, rose the Chutter Munzil—the deposed King's favorite palace. Behind it, above the belt of trees dividing the high Residency gardens from the maze of houses and hovels still occupied by the hangers-on to the late Court, the English flag drooped lazily in the calm floods of yellow light.   For the rest, were dense dark groves following the glistening curve of the river, and gardens gravely gay in pillars of white *chum-bacli* creeper and cypress, long prim lines of latticed walls, and hedges of scarlet hibiscus.   Here and there above the trees, the dome of a mosque or the minaret of a mausoleum told that the town of Lucknow, scattered yet coherent, lay among the groves.   The most profligate town in India which by one stroke of an English pen had just been deprived of the *raison-d'être* of its profligacy, and been bidden to live as best it could in cleanly, courtless poverty.

So, already, there were thousands of workmen in it, innocent enough panderers in the past to luxurious vice, who were feeling the pinch of hunger from lack of employment; and there were those past employers also, deprived now of pensions and offices, with a bankrupt future before them.   But Lucknow had a keener grievance than these in the new tax on opium, the drug which helps men to bear hunger and bankruptcy; so, as the auctioneer said, it was not a place in which to expect brisk bidding for wild beasts with large appetites.   But the parrots roused a faint interest, and the crowd laughed suddenly at the fluttering screams of a red and blue macaw, as it was tossed from hand to hand, on its way to the surprised and reluctant purchaser who had bid a farthing for it out of sheer idleness.

" Another mouth to feed, Shumshu! " jeered a fellow butcher, as he literally flung the bird at a neighbor's head.   " Rather he than I," laughed the recipient, continuing the fling.   " *Ari!* Shumshu, take thy baby.   Well caught, brother! but what will thy house say? "

" That I have made a fat bargain," retorted the big, coarse owner coolly, as he wrung the bird's neck, and twirled it, a quivering tuft of bright feathers and choking cries, above his head.   " Thou'lt buy no meat at a farthing a pound, even from my shop, I'll swear, and this bird weighs two, and is delicate as chicken."

The laugh which answered the sally held a faint scream, not wholly genuine in its ring. It came from the edge of the crowd, where two English riders had paused to see what the fun was about.

"Cruel devils, aren't they, Allie?" said one, a tall, fair man whose good looks were at once made and marred by heaviness of feature. "Why! you've turned pale despite the rouge!" His tone was full of not over-respectful raillery; his bold, bloodshot eyes met his companion's innocent looking ones with careless admiration.

"Don't be a fool, Erlton," she replied promptly; and the even, somewhat hard pitch of her voice did not match the extreme softness of her small, childish face. "You know I don't rouge; or you ought to. And it was horrible, in its way."

"Only what your ladyship's cook does to your ladyship's fowls," retorted Major Erlton. "You don't *see* it done, that's all the difference. It is a cruel world, Mrs. Gissing, the sex is the cruelest thing in it, and you, as I'm always telling you, are the cruelest of your sex."

His manner was detestable, but little Mrs. Gissing laughed again. She had not a fine taste in such matters; perhaps because she had no taste for them at all. So, in the middle of the laugh, her attention shifted to the big white cockatoo which formed the next lot. It had a most rumpled and dejected appearance as it tried to keep its balance on the ring which the soldier assistant swung backward and forward boisterously.

"Do look at that ridiculous bird!" she exclaimed, "Did you ever see any creature look so foolish?"

It did, undoubtedly, with its wrinkled gray eyelids closed in agonized effort, its clattering gray beak bobbing rhythmically toward its scaly gray legs. It roused the auctioneer from his depression into beginning in grand style. "Now, then, gentlemen! This is a real treat, indeed! A cockatoo, old as Methusalem and twice as wise. It speaks, I'll be bound. Says 'is prayers—look at 'im gemyflexing! and maybe he swears a bit like the rest of us. Any gentleman bid a rupee!—a eight annas? —a four annas? Come, gentlemen!"

"One anna," called Mrs. Gissing, with a coquettish

nod to the big Major, and a loud aside: " Cruel I may be
to you, sir, but I'll give that to save the poor brute from
having its neck wrung."

" Two annas! "   There was a stress of eagerness in the
new voice which made many in the crowd look whence
it came.   The speaker was a lean old man wearing a faded
green turban, who had edged himself close to the auctioneer's table and stood with upturned eyes watching the
bird anxiously.   He had the face of an enthusiast, keen,
remorseless, despite its look of ascetic patience.

" Three annas! "   Alice Gissing's advance came with
another nod at her big admirer.

" Four annas! "   The reply was quick as an echo.

A vexed surprise showed on the pretty babyish face.
" What an impertinent wretch!   Eight annas—do you
hear?—eight annas! "

The auctioneer bowed effusively.   " Eight annas bid
for a cockatoo as says——" he paused cautiously, for
the bidding was brisk enough without exaggeration.
" Eight annas once—twice—Going! going——"

" One rupee! "

Mrs. Gissing gave a petulant jag to her rein.   " Oh!
come away, Erlton, my charity doesn't run to rupees."

But her companion's face, never a very amiable one,
had darkened with temper.   " D——n the impudent
devil," he muttered savagely, before raising his voice to
call: " Two rupees! "

" Five! "   There was no hesitation still; only an almost
clamorous anxiety in the worn old voice.

" Ten! "   Major Erlton's had lost its first heat, and settled into a dull decision which made the auctioneer turn
to him, hammer in hand.   Yet the echo was not wanting.

" Fifteen! "

The Englishman's horse backed as if its master's hand
lay heavy on the bit.   There was a pause, during which
that shuddering cough of the hungry tiger quavered
through the calm flood of sunshine, in which the crowd
stood silently, patiently.

" Fifteen rupees," began the auctioneer reluctantly, his
sympathies outraged, " Fifteen once, twice——"

Then Alice Gissing laughed. The woman's laugh of derision which is responsible for so much.

" Fifty rupees," said Major Erlton at once.

The old man in the green turban turned swiftly; turned for the first time to look at his adversary, and in his face was intolerant hatred mingled with self-pity; the look of one who, knowing that he has justice on his side, knows also that he is defeated.

"Thank *you*, sir," caught up the auctioneer. " Fifty once, twice, thrice! Hand the bird over, Tom. Put it down, sir, I suppose, with the other things?"

Major Erlton nodded sulkily. He was already beginning to wonder why he had bought the brute. Meanwhile Tom, still swinging the cockatoo derisively, had jumped from the table into the crowd round it as if the sea of heads was non-existent; being justified of his rashness by its prompt yielding of foothold as he elbowed his way outward, shouting for room good-naturedly, and answered by swift smiles and swifter obedience. Yet both were curiously silent; so that Mrs. Gissing's voice, wondering what on earth Herbert was going to do with the creature now that he had bought it, was distinctly audible.

" Give it to you, of course," he replied moodily. " You can wring its neck if you choose, Allie. You are cruel enough for that, I dare say." The thought of the fifty rupees wasted was rankling fiercely; fifty rupees! when he would be hard put to it for a penny if he didn't pull off the next race. Fifty rupees! because a woman laughed!

But Mrs. Gissing was laughing again. " I shan't do anything of the kind. I shall give it to your wife, Major Erlton. I'm sure she must be dull all alone; and then she loves prayers!" the absolute effrontery of the speech was toned down by her indifferent expression. " Here, sergeant! " she went on, " hold the bird up a bit higher, please, I want to see if it is worth all that money. Gracious! what a hideous brute! "

It was, in truth; save for the large gold-circled eyes, like strange gems, which opened suddenly as the swinging ceased. They seemed to look at the dainty little figure taking it in; and then, in an instant, the dejected feathers were afluff, the wings outspread, the flame-colored crest, unseen before, raised like a fiery flag as the bird gave an ear-piercing scream.

"*Deen! Deen! Futteh Mohammed.*" (For the Faith! For the Faith! Victory to Mohammed.)

The war cry of the fiercest of all faiths was unmistakable; the first two syllables cutting the air, keen as a knife, the last with the blare as of a trumpet in them. And following close on their heels came an indescribable sound, like the answering vibration of a church to the last deep organ-note. It was a faint murmur from the crowd till then so silent.

"D——n the bird! Hold it back, man! Loosen the curb, Allie, for God's sake, or the brute will be over with you!"

Herbert Erlton's voice was sharp with anxiety as he reined his own horse savagely out of the way of his companion's, which, frightened at the unexpected commotion, was rearing badly.

"All right," she called; there was a little more color on her child-like face, a firmer set of her smiling mouth: that was all. But the hunting crop she carried fell in one savage cut after another on the startled horse's quarters. It plunged madly, only to meet the bit and a dig of the spur. So, after two or three unavailing attempts to unseat her, it stood still with pricked ears and protesting snorts.

"Well sat, Allie! By George, you can ride! I do like to see pluck in a woman; especially in a pretty one." The Major's temper and his fears had vanished alike in his admiration. Mrs. Gissing looked at him curiously.

"Did you think I was a coward?" she asked lightly; and then she laughed. "I'm not so bad as all that. But look! There is your wife coming along in the new victoria—it's an awfully stylish turn-out, Herbert; I wish Gissing would give me one like it. I suppose she has been to church. It's Lent or something, isn't it? Anyhow, she can take that screaming beast home."

"You're not——" began the Major, but Mrs. Gissing had already ridden up to the carriage, making it impossible for the solitary occupant to avoid giving the order to stop. She was rather a pale woman, who leaned listlessly among the cushions.

" Good evening, Mrs. Erlton," said the little lady, " been, as you see, for a ride. But we were thinking of you and hoping you would pray for us in church."

Kate Erlton's eyebrows went up, as they had a trick of doing when she was scornful. " I am only on my way thither as yet," she replied; " so that now I am aware of your wishes I can attend to them."

The obvious implication roused the aggressor to greater recklessness. " Thanks! but we really deserve something, for we have been buying a parrot for you. Erlton paid a whole fifty rupees for it because it said its prayers and he thought you would like it! "

" That was very kind of Major Erlton,"—there was a fine irony in the title,—" but, as he knows, I'm not fond of things with gay feathers and loud voices."

The man, listening, moved his feet restlessly in his stirrups. It was too bad of Allie to provoke these sparring matches. Foolish, too, since Kate's tongue was sharp when she chose to rouse herself. None sharper, in his opinion.

" If you don't want the bird," he interrupted shortly, " tell the groom to wring its neck."

Mrs. Gissing looked at him, her reproachful blue eyes perfect wells of simplicity. " Wring its neck! How can you, when you paid all that money to save it from being killed! That is the real story, Mrs. Erlton; it is indeed——"

He interrupted his wife's quick glance of interest impatiently. " The main point being that I had, or shall have to pay fifty rupees—which I must get. So I must be off to the racecourse if I don't want to be posted. I ought to have been there a quarter of an hour ago; should have been but for that confounded bird. Are you coming, Mrs. Gissing, or not? "

" Now, Erlton! " she replied, " don't be stupid. As if he didn't know, Mrs. Erlton, that I am every bit as much interested as he is in the match with that trainer man!— what's his name, Erlton? Greyman—isn't it? I have endless gloves on it, sir, so of course I'm coming to see fair play."

Major Erlton shot a rapid glance at her, as if to see what she really meant; then muttered something angrily about chaff as, with a dig of his heels, he swung his horse round to the side of hers.

Kate Erlton watched their figures disappear behind the trees, then turned indifferently to the groom who was waiting for orders with the cockatoo. But she started visibly in finding herself face to face with a semi-circle of spectators which had gathered about the figure of an old man in a faded green turban who stood close beside the groom, and who, seeing her turn, salaamed, and with clasped hands began an appeal of some sort. So much she gathered from his bright eyes, his tone; but no more, and all unconsciously she drew back to the furthest corner of the carriage, as if to escape from what she did not understand, and therefore did not like. That, indeed, was her attitude toward all things native. Yet at times, as now, she felt a dim regret at her own ignorance. What did he want? What were they thinking of, those dark, incomprehensible faces closing closer and closer round her? What could they be thinking of, uncivilized, heathen, as they were? tied to hateful, horrible beliefs and customs, unmentionable thoughts; so the innate repulsion of the alien overpowered her dim desire to be kind.

" Drive on! " she called in her clear, soft voice, " drive on to the church."

The grooms, new taken from royal employ,—for the victoria had been one of the spoils of the auction,—began their arrogant shouting to the crowd; the coachman, treating it also in royal fashion, cut at his horses regardless of their plunging. So after an instant's scurry and flurry, a space was cleared, and the carriage rolled off. The old man, left standing alone, looked after it silently for a moment, then flung his arms skyward.

"O God, reward them! reward them to the uttermost!" The appeal, however, seemed too indefinite for solace, and he turned for closer sympathy to the crowd. " The bird is mine, brothers! I lent it to the King, to teach his the Cry-of-Faith that I had taught it. But the Huzoors would not listen, or they would not understand. It was a little thing to them! So I brought all I had, thinking to buy mine own again. But yonder hell-doomed infidel hath it for nothing—for he paid nothing; and here—here is *my* money!" He drew a little bag from his breast and held it up with shaking hand.

"For nothing!" echoed the crowd, seizing on what interested it most. "For sure he paid nothing."

The murmur, spreading from man to man in doubt, wonder, assertion, was interrupted by a voice with the resonance and calm in it of one accustomed to listeners. "Nay! not for nothing. Have patience. The bird may yet give the Great Cry in the house of the thief. I, Ahmed-oolah, the dust of the feet of the Most High, say it. Have patience. God settles the accounts of men."

"It is the Moulvie," whispered some, as the gaunt, hollow-eyed speaker moved out of the crowd, a good head and shoulders taller than most there. "The Moulvie from Fyzabad. He preaches in the big Mosque to-night, and half the city goes to hear him." The whispering voices formed a background to the recurring cry of the auctioneer, "Going! Going! Gone!" as lot after lot fell to the hammer, while the crowd listened to both, or drifted cityward with the memory of them lingering insistently.

"Going! Going! Gone!" What was going? Everything, if tales were true; and there were so many tales nowadays. Of news flashed faster by wires than any, even the gods themselves, could flash it; of carriages, fire-fed, bringing God knows what grain from God knows where! Could a body eat of it and not be polluted? Could the children read the school books and not be apostate? Burning questions these, not to be answered lightly. And as the people, drifting homeward in the sunset, asked them, other sounds assailed their ears. The long-drawn chant of the call to prayer from the Mohammedan mosques, the clashing of gongs from the Hindoo temples, the solitary clang of the Christian church bell. Diverse, yet similar in this, that each called Life to face Death, not as an end, but as a beginning; called with more insistence than usual in the church, where a special missionary service was being held, at which a well-known worker in the vineyard was to give an address on the duty of a faithful soldier of Christ in a heathen land. With greater authority in the mosque also, where the Moulvie was to lay down the law for each soldier of the faith in an age of unbelief and change. Only in the Hindoo temples the circling lights flickered as ever, and there was neither waxing nor waning of worship as mortality drifted in, and drifted out, hiding the rude stone symbol of regeneration with their chaplets of flowers; the symbol of Life-in-Death, of Death-in-Life. The cult of the Inevitable.

There was no light in these dark shrines, save the circling cresset; none, save the dim reflection of dusk from white marble, in the mosque where the Moulvie's sonorous voice sent the broad Arabic vowels rebounding from dome to dome. But in the church there was a blaze of lamps, and the soldierly figure at the reading desk showed clear to the men and women listening leisurely in the cushioned pews. Yet the words were stirring enough; there was no lack of directness in them. Kate Erlton, resting her chin on her hand, kept her eyes on the speaker closely as his voice rose in a final confession of the faith that was in him.

"I conceive it is ever the hope and aim of a true Christian that his Lord should make him the happy instrument of rescuing his neighbor from eternal damnation. In this belief I find it my duty to be instant in season and out of season, speaking to all, sepoys as well as civilians, making no distinction of persons or place, since with the Lord there are no such distinctions. In the temporal matters I act under the orders of my earthly superior, but in spiritual matters I own no allegiance save to Christ. So, in trying to convert my sepoys, I act as a Christian soldier under Christ, and thus, by keeping the temporal and spiritual capacities in which I have to act clearly under their respective heads, I render unto Cæsar the things that are Cæsar's, to God the things that are God's."*

* From Colonel W. Wheler's defense.

There was a little rustle of satisfaction and relief from the pews, the hymn closing the service went with a swing, and the congregation, trooping out into the scented evening air, fell to admiring the address.

" And he looked so handsome and soldierly, didn't he? " said one voice with a cadence of sheer comfortableness in it as the owner nestled back in the barouche.

" Quite charming! " assented another. " And to think of a man like that, brave as a lion, submitting to be hustled off his own parade ground because his sepoys objected to his preaching. It is an example to us all! "

" I wouldn't give much for the discipline of his regiment," began Kate Erlton impulsively, then paused, certain of her hearers, uncertain of herself; for she was of those women who use religion chiefly as an anodyne for the heartache, leaving her intellect to take care of itself. With the result that it revenged itself, as now, by sudden flashes of reason which left her helpless before her own common sense.

" My dear Mrs. Erlton! " came a shocked coo, " discipline or no discipline, we are surely bound to fight the good—— Gracious heavens! what *is* that? "

It was the cockatoo. Roused from a doze by the movement of Kate's carriage toward the church-door, it had dashed at once into the war-cry—" *Deen! Deen! Futteh Mohammed!* "

The appositeness of the interruption, however, was quite lost on the ladies, who were too ignorant to recognize it; so their alarm ended in a laugh, and the suggestion that the bird would be a noisy pet.

Thus, with worldly gossip coming to fill the widening spaces in their complacent piety, they drove homeward together where the curving river shimmered faintly in the dark, or through scented gardens where the orange-blossom showed as faintly among the leaves, like star-dust on a dark sky.

But Kate Erlton drove alone, as she generally did. She was one of those women whose refinement stands in their way; who are *gourmets* of life, failing to see that the very fastidiousness of their palate argues a keener delight in its pleasures than that of those who take them more simply, perhaps more coarsely. And as she drove, her mind diverted listlessly to the semicircle of dark faces she had left unanswered. What had they wanted? Nothing worth hearing, no doubt! Nothing was worth much in this weary land of exile where the heart-hunger for one little face and voice gnawed at your vitality day and night. For Kate Erlton set down all her discontent to the fact that she was separated from her boy. Yet she had sent him home of her own free will to keep him from growing up in the least like his father. And she had stayed with that father simply to keep him within the pale of respectability for the boy's sake. That was what she told herself. She allowed nothing for her own disappointment; nothing for the keen craving for sentiment which lay behind her refinement. All she asked from fate was that the future might be no worse than the past; so that she could keep up the fiction to the end.

And as she drove, a sudden sound made her start, for —soldier's wife though she was—the report of a rifle always set her heart a-beating. Then from the darkness came a long-drawn howl; for over on the other side of the river they were beginning to shoot down the hungry beasts which all through the long sunny day had found no master.

The barter of *their* lives was complete. The last " Going! Going! Gone! " had come, and they had passed to settle the account elsewhere. So, amid this dropping fire of kindly meant destruction, the night fell soft and warm over the shimmering river and the scented gardens with the town hidden in their midst.

CHAPTER II.

HOME, SWEET HOME!

" You sent for me, I believe, Mrs. Erlton."

" Yes, Mr. Greyman, I sent for you."

Both voices came reluctantly into the persistent cooing of doves which filled the room, for the birds were perched among a coral begonia overhanging the veranda. But the man had so far the best of it in the difficult interview which was evidently beginning, in that he stood with his back to the French window through which he had just entered; his face, therefore, was in shadow. Hers, as she paused, arrested by surprise, faced the light. For Kate Erlton, when she sent for James Greyman in the hopes of bribing him to silence regarding the match which had been run the evening before between his horse and her husband's, had not expected to see a gentleman in the person of an ex-jockey, trainer, and general hanger-on to the late King's stables. The diamonds with which she had meant to purchase honor lay on the table, but this man would not take diamonds. What would he take? She scanned his face anxiously, yet with a certain relief in her disappointment; for the clean-shaven contours were fine, if a trifle stern; and the mouth, barely hidden by a slight mustache, was thin-lipped, well cut.

"Yes! I sent for you," she continued—and the even confidence of her own voice surprised her. "I meant to ask how much you would want to keep this miserable business quiet; but now——" She paused, and her hand, which had been resting on the center table, shifted its position to push aside the jewel-case; as if that were sufficient explanation.

"But now?" he echoed formally, though his eyes followed the action. She raised hers to his, looking him full in the face. They were beautiful eyes, and their cold gray blue, with the northern glint of steel in it, gave James Greyman an odd thrill. He had not looked into eyes like these for many a long year. Not since, in a room just like this one, homely and English in every twist and turn of foreign flowers and furniture, he had ruined his life for a pair of eyes, as coldly pure as these, to look at. He did not mean to do it again.

"But now I can only ask you to be kind, and generous, Mr. Greyman! I want you to save my husband from the disgrace your claim must bring—if you press it."

Once more the monotonous cooing from the outside filled the darkness and the light of the large, lofty room.

For it was curiously dark in the raftered roof and the distant corners; curiously light in the great bars of golden sunshine slanting across the floor.   In one of them James Greyman stood, a dark silhouette against an arch of pale blue sky, wreathed by the climbing begonia.   He was a man of about forty, looking younger than his age, taller than his real height, by reason of his beardless face and the extreme ease and grace of his figure.   He was burned brown as a native by constant exposure to the sun; but as he stooped to pick up his glove which had slipped from his hold, a rim of white showed above his wrist.

"So I supposed; but why should I save him?" he said briefly.   The question, thus crudely put, left her without reply for a minute; during which he waited. Then, with a new tinge of softness in his voice, he went on: "It was a mistake to send for me.   I thought so at the time, though, of course, I had no option.   But now——"

" But now?" she echoed in her turn.

" There is nothing to be done save to go away again." He turned at the words, but she stopped him by a gesture.

" Is there not?" she asked.   " I think there is, and so wil' you if you understand—if you will wait and let me speak."   His evident impatience made her add quickly, " You can at least do so much for me, surely?" There was a quiver in her voice now, and it surprised her as her previous calm had done; for what was this man to her that his unkindness should give pain?

" Certainly," he said, pausing at once, " but I understand too much, and I cannot see the use of raking up details.   You know them—or think you do.   Either way they do not alter the plain fact that I cannot help—because I would not if I could.   That sounds brutal; but, unfortunately, it is true.   And it is best to tell the truth, as far as it can be told."

A faint smile curved her lips.   " That is not far.   If you will wait I will tell you the truth to the bitter end."

He looked at her with sudden interest, for her pride attracted him.   She was not in the least pretty; she might be any age from five-and-twenty to five-and-thirty. And she—well! she was a lady.   But would she tell the

truth? Women, even ladies, seldom did; still he must
wait and hear what she had to say.

" I sent for you," she began, " because, knowing you
were an adventurer, a man who had had to leave the
army under a cloud—in disgrace——"

He stared at her blankly. Here was the truth about
himself at any rate!

" I thought, naturally, you would be a man who would
take a bribe. There are diamonds in that case; for
money is scarce in this house." She paused, to gain
firmness for what came next. " I was keeping them for
the boy. I have a son in England and he will have to go
to school soon; but I thought it better to save his father's
reputation instead. They are fine diamonds"—she
drew the case closer and opened it—the sunshine, streaming in, caught the facets of the stones, turning them to
liquid light. " You needn't tell me they are no use," she
went on quickly, as he seemed about to speak; " I am not
stupid; but that has nothing to do with the question. I
want you to save my husband—don't interrupt me, please,
for I do want you to understand, and I will tell you the
truth. You asked me why? and you think, no doubt,
that he does not deserve to be saved. Do you think I
do not know that? Mr. Greyman! a wife knows more of
her husband than anyone else can do; and I have known
for so many years."

A sudden softness came into her hearer's eyes. That
was true at any rate. She must know many things of
which she could not speak; a sort of horror at what she
must know, with a man like Major Erlton as her husband, held him silent.

" Yet I have saved him so far," she went on, " but if
what happened yesterday becomes public property all my
trouble is in vain. He will have to leave the regiment——"

" He is not the first man, as you were kind enough to
mention just now," interrupted James Greyman, " who
has had to leave the army under a cloud. He would sur-
vive it—as others have done."

" I was not thinking of him at all," she replied quietly.
" I was thinking of my son; my only son."

" There are other only sons also, Mrs. Erlton," he retorted. " I was my mother's, but I don't think the fact was taken into consideration by the court-martial. Why should I be more lenient? You have come to the wrong person when you come to me for charity or consideration. None was shown to me."

" Perhaps because you did not need it," she said quickly.

" Not need it? "

" Many a man falls under the shadow of a cloud blamelessly. What do they want with charity? "

He rose swiftly and so, facing the light again, stood looking out into it. " I am obliged to you," he said after a pause. " Whether you are right or wrong doesn't affect the question from which we have wandered. Except—" he turned to her again with a certain eagerness —" Mrs. Erlton! You say you are prepared to tell the truth to the bitter end; then for Heaven's sake let us have it for once in our lives. You never saw me before, nor I you. It is not likely we shall ever meet again. So we can speak without a past or a future tense. You ask me to save your husband from the consequences of his own cheating. I ask why? Why should I sacrifice myself? Why should I suffer? for, mark you, there were heavy bets——"

" There are the diamonds," she interrupted, pointing to them; their gleam was scarcely brighter than her scornful eyes.

He gave a half smile. " Doubtless there are the diamonds! I can have my equivalent, so far, if I choose; but I don't choose. It does not suit me personally; so that is settled. I can't do this thing, then, to please myself. Now, let us go on. You are a religious woman, I think, Mrs. Erlton—you have the look of one. Then you will say that I should remember my own frailty, and forgive as I would be forgiven. Mrs. Erlton! I am no better than most men, no doubt, but I never remember cheating at cards or pulling a horse as your husband does—it is the brutal truth between us, remember. And if you tell me I'm bound to protect a man from the natural punishment of a great crime because I've stolen a pin, I say you are wrong. That theory won't hold water. If our own faults, even our own crimes, are to make us tender over these things in others, there must be —what, if I remember right, my Colenso used to call an arithmetical progression in error until the Day of Judgment; for the odds on sin would rise with every crime. I don't believe in mercy, Mrs. Erlton. I never did. Justice doesn't need it. So let us leave religion alone too, and come to other things—altruism—charity—what you will. Now who will benefit by my silence? Will you? You said just now that a wife knows more of her husband than a stranger can. I well believe it. That is why I ask you to tell me frankly, if you really think that a continuance of the life you lead with him can benefit you?" He leaned over the table, resting his head on his hand, his eyes on hers, and then added in a lower voice, " The brutal truth, please. Not as a woman to man, or, for the matter of that, woman to woman; but soul to soul, if there be such a thing."

She turned away from him and shook her head. " It is for the boy's sake," she said in muffled tones. " It will be better for him, surely."

" The boy," he echoed, rising with a sense of relief. She had not lied, this woman with the beautiful eyes; she had simply shut the door in his face. " You have a por-trait of him, no doubt, somewhere. I should like to see it. Is that it, over the mantelpiece? "

He walked over to a colored photograph, and stood looking at it silently, his hands—holding his hunting crop—clasped loosely behind his back. Kate noticed them even in her anxiety; for they were noticeable, nervous, fine-cut hands, matching the figure.

" He is not the least like you. He is the very image of his father," came the verdict. " What right have you to suppose that anything you or I can do now will overcome the initial fact that the boy is your husband's son, any more than it will ease you of the responsibility of having chosen such a father for the boy? "

She gave a quick cry, more of pain than anger, and hid her face on the table in sudden despair.

" You are very cruel," she said indistinctly.

He walked back toward her, remorseful at the sight of

her miserable self-abasement. He had not meant to hit so hard, being accustomed himself to facing facts without flinching.

" Yes! I am cruel; but a life like mine doesn't make a man gentle. And I don't see how this trivial concealment of fact—for that is all it would be—can change the boy's character or help him. If I did——" he paused. " I should like to help you if I could, Mrs. Erlton, if only because you—you refused me charity! But I cannot see my way. It would do no one any good. Begin with me. I'm not a religious man, Mrs. Erlton. I don't believe in the forgiveness of sins. So my soul—if I have one—wouldn't benefit. As for my body? At the risk of you offering me diamonds again,"—he smiled charmingly,—I must mention that I should lose—how much is a detail—by concealment. So I must go out of the question of benefit. Then there is you——"

He broke off to walk up and down the room thoughtfully, then to pause before her. " I wish you to believe," he said, " that I want really to understand the truth, but I can't, because I don't know one thing. I don't know if you love your husband—or not."

She raised her head quickly with a fear behind the resentment of her eyes. " Put me outside the question too. I have told you that already. It is the simplest, the best way."

He bowed cynically. She came no nearer to truth than evasion.

" If you wish it, certainly. Then there is the boy. You want to prevent him from realizing that his father is a—let us twist the sentence—what his father is. You have, I expect, sent him away for this purpose. So far good. But will this concealment of mine suffice? Will no one else blab the truth? Even if concealment succeeds all along the line, will it prevent the boy from following in his father's steps if he has inherited his father's nature as well as his face? Wouldn't it be a deterrent in that case to know early in life that such instincts can't be indulged with impunity in the society of gentlemen? You will never have the courage to keep the boy out of your life altogether as you are doing now. Sooner or

later you will bring him back, he will bring himself back,
and then, on the threshold of life, he will have an example
of successful dishonesty put before him.   Mrs. Erlton!
you can't keep up the fiction always; so it is better for
you, for me, for him, to tell the truth—and I mean to
tell it."

She rose swiftly to her feet and faced him, thrusting
her hair back from her forehead passionately, as if to
clear away aught that might obscure her brain.

"And for my husband?" she asked.   "Have you no
word for him?   Is he not to be thought of at all?   You
asked me just now if I loved him, and I was a coward.
Well!   I do not love him—more's the pity, for I can't
make up the loss of that to him anyhow.   But there is
enough pity in his life without that.   Can't you see it?
The pity that such things should be in life at all.   You
called me a religious woman just now.   I'm not, really.
It is the pity of such things without a remedy that drives
me to believe, and the pity of it which drives me back
again upon myself, as you have driven me now.   For
you are right!   Do you think I can't see the shame?
Do you think I don't know that it is too late—that I
should have thought of all this before I called my boy's
nature out of the dark?   And yet——" her face grew
sharp with a pitiful eagerness, she moved forward and
laid her hand on his arm.   "It is all so dark!   You said
just now that I couldn't keep up the fiction; but need it
be a fiction always?   What do we know?   God gives
men a chance sometimes.   He gives the whole world a
chance sometimes of atoning for many sins.   A Spirit
moves on the Waters of life bringing something to
cleanse and heal.   It may be moving now.   Give my
husband his chance, Mr. Greyman, and I will pray that,
whatever it is, it may come quickly."

He had listened with startled eyes; now his hand
closed on hers in swift negation.

"Don't pray for that," he said, in a quick low voice,
"it may come too soon for some of us, God knows—too
soon for many a good man and true!"   Then, as if
vexed at his own outburst, he drew back a step, looking
at her with a certain resentment,

" You plead your cause well, Mrs. Erlton, and it is a stronger argument than you perhaps guess. So let him have this chance that is coming. Let us all have it, you and I into the bargain. No! don't be grateful, please, for he may prove himself a coward, among other things. So may I, for that matter. One never knows until the chance comes for being a hero—or the other thing."

" When the chance comes we shall see," she said, trying to match his light tone. " Till then, good-by—you have been very kind." She held out her hand, but he did not take it.

" Pardon me! I have been very rude, and you——" he paused in his half-jesting words, stooped over her outstretched hand and kissed it.

Kate stood looking at the hand with a slight frown after his horse's hoofs died away; and then with a smile she shut the jewel case. Not that she closed the incident also; for full half an hour later she was still going over all the details of the past interview. And everything seemed to hinge on that unforeseen appeal of hers for a chance of atonement, on that unpremeditated strange suggestion that a Spirit might even then be moving on the face of the waters; until, in that room gay with English flowers, and peaceful utterly in its air of security, a terror seized on her body and soul. A causeless terror, making her strain eyes and ears as if for a hint of what was to come and make cowards or heroes of them all.

But there was only the flowerful garden beyond the arched veranda, only the soft gurgle of the doves. Yet she sat with quivering nerves till the sight of the gardener coming as usual with his watering pot made her smile at the unfounded tragedy of her imaginings.

As she passed into the veranda she called to him, in the jargon which served for her orders, not to forget a plentiful supply to the heartsease and the sweet peas; for she loved her poor clumps of English annuals more than all the scented and blossoming shrubs which in those late March days turned the garden into a wilderness of strange perfumed beauty. But her cult of home was a religion with her; and if a visitor remarked that anything in her environment was reminiscent of the old country, she rejoiced to have given another exile what was to her as the shadow of a rock in a thirsty land.

So, her eye catching something barely up to western mark in the pattern of a collar her tailor was cutting for her new dress, she crossed over to where he squatted in the further corner of the veranda.

" That isn't right. Give me something to cut—here! this will do."

She drew a broad sheet of native paper from the bundle of scraps beside him, and began on it with the scissors; too full of her idea to notice the faint negation of the man's hand. " There! " she said after a few deft snippings, " that is new fashion."

" Huzoor! " assented the tailor submissively as, apparently from tidiness, he put away the remainder of the paper, before laying the new-cut pattern on the cloth.

His mistress looked down at it critically. There was a broad line of black curves and square dots right across the pattern suggestive of its having been cut from a title-page. But to her ignorance of the Persian character they were nothing but the curves and dots, though the tailor's eyes read clearly in them " The Sword is the Key of Heaven."

For he, in company with thousands of other men, had been reading the famous pamphlet of that name; reading it with that thrill of the heart-strings which has been the prelude to half the discords and harmonies of history. Since, quaintly enough, those who may hope to share your heaven are always friends, those who can with certainty be consigned to hell, your enemies.

" That is all right," she said. " Cut it well on the bias, so that it won't pucker."

As she turned away, she felt the vast relief of being able to think of such trivialities again after the strain and stress of the hours since her husband had come home from the race course, full of excited maledictions on the mean, underhand bribery and spying which might make it necessary for him to send in his papers—if he could. Kate had heard stories of a similar character before; since Major Erlton knew by experience that she had his reputation more at heart than he had himself, and that her brain was clearer, her tact greater than his. But she had never heard one so hopeless. Unless this jockey Greyman, who, her husband said, was so mixed up with native intrigue as to have any amount of false evidence at his command, could be silenced, her labor of years was ruined. So long after her husband had gone off to his bed to sleep soundly, heavily, after the manner of men, Kate had lain awake in hers after the manner of women, resolving to risk all, even to a certain extent honesty, in order to silence this man, this adventurer; who no doubt was not one whit better than her husband.

And now? As her mind flashed back over that interview the one thing that stood out above all others was the bearing, the deference of the man as he had stooped to kiss her hand. For the life of her, she—who protested even to herself that such things had no part in her life—could not help a joy in the remembrance; a quick recognition that here was a man who could put romance into a woman's life. The thought was one, however, from which to escape by the first distraction at hand. This happened to be the cockatoo, which, after a bath and plentiful food, looked a different bird on its new perch.

"Pretty, pretty poll," she said hastily, with tentative white finger tickling its crest. The bird, in high good humor, bent its head sideways and chuckled inarticulately; yet to an accustomed ear the sound held the cadence of the Great Cry, and the tailor, who had heard it given wrathfully, looked up from his work.

"Oh, Miffis Erlton! what a boo'ful new polly," came a silvery lisp. She turned with a radiant smile to greet her next door neighbor's little boy, a child of about three years old, who, pathetically enough, was a great solace to her child-bereft life.

"Yes, Sonny, isn't it lovely?" she said, her slim white hand going out to bring the child closer; "and it screams splendidly. Would you like to hear it scream?"

Sonny, clinging tightly to her fingers, looked doubtful. "Wait till muvver comth, muvver's comin' to zoo esectly. Sonny's always flightened wizout hith muvver,"

At which piece of diplomacy, Kate, feeling lighthearted, caught the little white-clad golden-curled figure
in her arms and ran out with it into the garden, smothering the laughing face with kisses as she ran.

" Sonny's a little goose to be ' flightened,' " came her
glad voice between the laughs and the kisses. " He
ought never to be ' flightened ' at all, because no one in
all the wide, wide world would ever hurt a good little
childie like Sonnykins—No one! No one! No one! "

She had sat the little fellow down among the flowers
by this time, being, in good sooth, breathless with his
weight; and now, continuing the game, chased him with
pretense booings of " No one! No one! " about the
pansy bed, and so round the sweet peas; until in
delicious terror he shrieked with delight, and chased her
back between her chasings.

It was a pretty sight, indeed, this game between the
woman and the child. The gardener paused in his watering, the tailor at his work; and even the native orderly
going his rounds with the brigade order-book grinned
broadly, so adding one to the kindly dark faces watching the chasing of Sonny.

" My dear Kate! How can you? " The querulous
voice broke in on the booings, and made Mrs. Erlton
pause and think of her loosened hair pins. The speaker
was a fair, diaphanous woman, the most solid-looking
part of whose figure, as she dawdled up the path, was
the large white umbrella she carried. " Here am I melting with the heat! What I shall do next year if George
is transferred to Delhi, I don't know. He says we shan't
be able to afford the hills. And he has the dogcart at
some of those eternal court-martials. I wonder why the
sepoys give so much trouble nowadays. George says
they're spoiled. So I came to see if you'll drive me to the
band; though I'm not fit to be seen. I was up half the
night with baby. She is so cross, and George will have
it she must be ill; as if children didn't have tempers!
Lucky you, to have your boy at home. And yet you go
romping with other people's. I wouldn't; but then I
look horrid when I'm hot!"

Kate laughed. She did not, and as she rearranged her

hair seemed to have left years of life behind her. " I can't
help it," she said. " I feel so ridiculously young myself
sometimes—as if I hadn't lived at all, as if nothing belonged to me, and I was really somebody else. As
if——" She paused abruptly in her confidences, and,
to change the subject, turned to the group behind Mrs.
Seymour:—an ayah holding a toddler by the hand, a
tall orderly in uniform carrying a year-old baby in his
arms; such a languid little mortal as is seldom seen out
of India, where the swift, sharp fever of the changing
seasons seems to take the very life from a child in a few
hours. The fluffy golden head in its limp white sun-
bonnet rested inert against the orderly's scarlet coatee,
the listless little legs drooped helplessly among the burnished belts and buckles.

" Poor little chick! Let me have her a bit, orderly,"
said Kate, laying her hand caressingly on the slack
dimpled arm; but baby, with a fretful whine, nestled her
cheek closer into the scarlet. A shade of satisfaction
made its owner's dark face less impassive, and the small,
sinewy, dark hands held their white burden a shade
tighter.

" She *is* so cross," complained the mother. " It has
been so all day. She won't leave the man for an instant.
He must be sick of her, though he doesn't show it. And
she used to go to the ayah; but do you know, Kate, I
don't trust the woman a bit. I believe she gives opium
to the child, so that she may get a little rest."

Kate looked at the ayah's face with a sudden doubt.
" I don't know," she said slowly. " I think they believe
it is a good thing. I remember when Freddy was a
baby——"

" Oh, I don't believe they ever think that sort of
thing," interrupted Mrs. Seymour. " You never can
trust the natives, you know. That's the worst of India.
Oh! how I wish I was back in dear old England with a
real nurse who would take the children off my hands."

But Kate Erlton was following up her own doubt.
" The children trust them——" she began.

" My dear Kate! you can't trust children either.
Look at baby! It gives me the shudders to think of

touching Bij-rao, and see how she cuddles up to him," replied Mrs. Seymour, as she dawdled on to the house; then, seeing the bed of heartsease, paused to go into raptures over them. They were like English ones, she said.

The puzzled look left Kate's face. " I sent some home last mail," she replied in a sort of hushed voice, " just to show them that we were not cut off from everything we care for; not everything."

So, as if by one accord, these two Englishwomen raised their eyes from the pansy bed, and passing by the flowering shrubs, the encircling tamarind trees framing the cozy, home-like house, rested them on the reddening gold of the western sky. Its glow lay on their faces, making them radiant.

But baby's heavy lids had fallen at last over her heavy eyes as she lay in the orderly's arms, and he glanced at the ayah with a certain pride in his superior skill as a nurse.

CHAPTER III.

THE GREAT GULF FIXED.

It was a quaint house in the oldest quarter of the city of Lucknow, where odd little groves linger between the alleys, so that men pass, at a step, from evil-smelling lanes to cool, scented retreats, dark with orange and mango trees; where birds flutter, and squirrels loll yawning through the summer days, as if the great town were miles away.

It was in the furthest corner of such a flowerless, shady garden that the house reared its lessening stories and projecting eaves above its neighbors. The upper half of it was not unlike an Italian villa in its airiness, its balustraded roof, its green jalousies; but the lower portion was unmistakably Indian. It was a perfect rabbit warren of dark cells, crushed in on each other causelessly; the very staircase, though but two feet wide, hav-

ing to fold itself away circumspectly so as to find space
to creep upward.

But no one lived below, and the dark twists and turns
of the brick ladder mattered little to Zora *bibi*, who lived
in the pleasant pavilions above; for she had scarcely
ever left them since the day, nearly eight years past,
when James Greyman had installed her there with all
the honor possible to the situation. Which was, briefly,
that he had bought the slip of a girl from a house of ill-
fame, as he would have bought a horse, or a flower-pot,
or anything else which he thought would make life
pleasanter to him. He had paid a long price for her, not
only because she was beautiful, but because he pitied the
delicate-looking child—for she was little more—just
about to enter a profession to which she was evidently a
recruit kidnaped in early infancy; as so many are in
India. Not that his pity would have led him to buy her
if she had been ugly, or even dark; for the creamy ivory
tint of her skin satisfied his fastidiousness quite as much
as did the hint of a soul in her dark, dreamy eyes.
Romance had perhaps had more to do with his purchase
than passion; restless, reckless determination to show
himself that he had no regrets for the society which had
dispensed with his, had had more than either. For he
had begun to rent the pleasant pavilions after a few
years of adventurous roving had emphasized the gulf
fixed between him and his previous life, and forced his
pride into leading his present one as happily as he could.

As for the girl, those eight years of pure passion on
the housetops had been a dream of absolute content.
It was so even now, when she lay dying, as so many
secluded women do, of a slow decline. To have flowers
and fruit brought to her, to find no change in his tenderness because she was too languid to amuse him, to have
him wait upon her and kiss away her protests; all this
made her soft warm eyes softer, warmer. It was so
unlike anything she had ever heard or dreamed of; it
made her blind to the truth, that she was dying. How
could this be so when there was no hint of change, when
life still gave her all she cared for? She did not, to be

sure, play tricks with him like a kitten, as she used to; but that was because she was growing old—nearly one and twenty!

" She is worse to-day. I deem her close to freedom, Soma, so I have warned the death-tender," said a tall woman, as she straightened the long column of her throat to the burden of a brass water-pot, new-poised on her head, and stepped down from the low parapet of the well which stood in one corner of the shady grove. Sometimes its creaking Persian wheel moaned over the task of sending runnels of water to the thirsty trees; but to-day it was silent, save for an intermittent protest when the man—who was lazily leaning his back against the yoke—put out his strength so as to empty an extra water can or two into the trough for the woman's use. He was in the undress uniform of a sepoy, and as he also straightened himself to face the speaker the extraordinary likeness between them in face and figure stamped them as twins. It would have been difficult to give the palm to either for superior height or beauty; and in their perfection of form they might have stood as models of the mythical race-founders whose names they bore. For Tara Devi and Soma Chund were Rajpoots of the single Lunar or Yadubansi tribe. She was dressed in an endless scarf of crimson wool, which with its border of white and yellow embroidery hung about her in admirable folds. The gleam of the water-pot matched the dead gold circlets on the brown wrists and ankles; for Tara wore her savings thus, though she had no right to do so, being a widow. But she had been eight years in James Greyman's service; more than eight bound to him by the strangest of ties. He had been the means of saving her from her husband's funeral pyre; in other words of preventing her from being a saint, of making her outcaste utterly. Since none, not even other widows, would eat or drink with a woman rejected by the very gods on the threshold of Paradise. Such a mental position is well-nigh incomprehensible to western minds. It was confusing even to Tara herself;

and the mingling of conscious dignity and conscious degradation, gratitude, resentment, attraction, repulsion, made her a puzzle even to herself at times.

" The master will grieve," replied Soma; his voice was far softer than his sister's had been, but it had the effect of hardening hers still more.

" What then?" she asked; " man's sorrow for a woman passes; or even if it pass not, bears no fruit here, or hereafter.   But I, as *thou knowest, Soma,* would have burned with my love.   *But for thee,* as thou knowest, I would have been *suttee* (*lit.* virtuous).   *But for thee* I should have found, ay! and given salvation."

She passed on with a sweep of full drapery, bearing her water-pot as a queen might her crown, leaving Soma's handsome face full of conscious-stricken amaze. His sister—from whom, despite her degradation, he had not been able to dissociate himself utterly—had never before rounded on him for his share in her misfortune; but in his heart of hearts he had admitted his responsibility at one moment, scorned it the next.   True, he had told his young Lieutenant that his brother-in-law was going to be burned, as an excuse for not accompanying him after black-buck one morning; but who would have dreamed that this commonplace remark would rouse the Huzoor's curiosity to see the obsequies of a high-caste Rajpoot, and so lead, incidentally, to a file of policemen and the neighboring magistrate dragging the sixteen-year old widow from the very flames?— when she was drugged, too, and quite happy—when the wrench was over, even for him, and she, to all intents, was a saint scattering salvation on seven generations of inconstant males!   Much as he loved Tara, the little twin sister who, so the village gossips loved to tell, had left the Darkness for the Light of Life still clasping his hand, how could he have done her such an injury?   As a Rajpoot how could he have brought such a scandalous dishonor on any family?

But being also a soldier, as his fathers had been before him, and so leavened unconsciously by much contact with Europeans, he could not help admiring Tara's pluck in refusing to accept the life of a dog, which was all that

was left to her among her own people. And he had been
grateful to the Huzoor, as she was, for giving her good
service where he could see her; though he would not
for worlds have touched the hand which had lain in his
from the beginning of all things. It was unclean now.

Still he could not forget the gossip's story any more
than he could forget that James Greyman had been his
Lieutenant, and that together they had shot over half
Hurreeana. So when he passed through Lucknow on
his way to spend his leave in his wife's village, he always
gave a day or two of it to the quaint garden-house.

And now Tara had definitely accused him of ruining
her life! Anger, born of a vague remorse, filled him as
he watched her disappear up the plinth. If it was anybody's fault it was the Huzoor's; or rather of the *Sirkar*
itself who, by high-handed interference with venerable
customs, made it possible for a poor man, by a mere slip
of the tongue, to injure one bound to him by the closest
of ties.

"It will leave us naught to ourselves soon," he muttered sulkily as he went out to the doorstep to finish
polishing the master's sword; that being a recognized
office during these occasional visits, which, as it occurred
to him in his discontent, would be still more occasional
if among other things the *Sirkar*, now that Oude was
was annexed, took away the extra leave due to foreign
service. They had said so in the regiment; and though
he was too tough to feel pin-pricks in advance, he had
sneered with others in the current jest that the maps
were tinted red—*i. e.*, shown to be British territory—by
savings stolen from the sepoy's pocket.

It was very quiet on the paved slope leading up from
the alley to the carved door beyond the gutter. The
lane was too narrow for wheeled traffic, the evening not
sufficiently advanced for the neighbors to gather in it
for gossip. But every now and again a veiled figure
would sidle along the further wall, passing good-looking
Soma with a flurried shuffle. Whereat, though he knew.
these ghostly figures to be old women on their way to
market, he cocked his turban more awry, and curled his
mustachios nearer his eyes; from no set purpose of

playing the gay Lothario, but for the honor of the regiment, and because War and Women go together, East and West.

After a time, however, the workmen began to dawdle past from their work, and some of them, remembering Soma, paused to ask him the latest news; a stranger in a native city being equivalent to an evening paper. And, of course, there were questions as to what the regiment thought of this and that. But Soma's replies were curt. He never relished being lumped in as a simple Rajpoot with the rest of the Rajpoots, for he was inordinately proud of his tribe. That was one reason why he stood aloof, as he did, from much that went on among his comrades. He drilled, it is true, between two of them who were entered as he was—that is to say, as a Rajpoot—on the roster. But the three were in reality as wide apart as the Sun, the Moon, and the Fire from which they respectively claimed descent. They would not have intermarried into each other's families for all the world and its wealth. A causeless differentiation which makes, and must make, a people who cling to it incomprehensible to a race which boasts as a check to pride or an encouragement to humility that all men are born of Adam, and which seeks no hall-mark for its descendants save the stamp of the almighty dollar.

Soma, therefore, polishing his master's sword sulkily, grew irritable also; especially when the frequenters of the opium and hemp shops began, with wavering steps and lack-luster eyes, to loaf homeward for the evening meal which would give them strength for another dose. There were many such habitual drug-takers in the quarter; for it was largely inhabited by poor claimants to nobility who, having nothing to do, had time for dreams. That was why people from other quarters flocked to this one at sundown for gossip; since it is to be had at its best from the opium-eater, whose imagination is stimulated, his reason dulled, beyond the power of discriminating even his own truth or falsehood. One of these, a haggard, sallow fellow in torn muslin and ragged embroidery, stopped with a heavy-lidded leer beside Soma.

"So, brother, back again!" he said with the maudlin

gravity of a hemp-smoker; "and thou lookest fat. The bone dust must agree with thee."

It was as if a bomb had fallen. The Hindoo bystanders, recognizing the rumor that ground bones were mixed with commissariat flour, drew back from the Rajpoot instinctively; the Mohammedans smiled on the sly. Soma himself had in a moment one sinewy hand on the half-drunk creature's throat, the other brandishing the fresh-polished sword.

"Bone dust thyself, and pigs meat too, foul-mouthed slayer of sacred kine!" he gasped, carrying the war into the enemy's country. "Thou beast! Unsay the lie!"

His indignation, showing that he appreciated the credence some might be disposed to give to the accusation, only made the Hindoos look at each other. The Mohammedans, however, dragged him from the swaying figure of the accuser, who, after all, was one of themselves.

"Heed him not!" they chorused appeasingly. "'Tis drug-shop talk, and every sane man knows that for dreams. Lo! his sense is clean gone as horns from a donkey! Sure, thy mother ate chillies in her time for thou to be so hot-blooded. It is not morning, brother, because a hen crows, and a snake is but a snake, and goes crooked even to his own home!"

These hoarded saws, with physical force superadded, left Soma reduced to glaring, and renewed claims for a retraction of the insult.

The hemp-smoker looked at him mournfully. "Wouldst have me deny God's truth?" he hiccuped. "Lo! I say not thou didst eat it. Thou sayst not, and who am I to decide between a man and his stomach, even though he looks fat? Yet this all know, that as a bird fattens his tail shrinks, and honor is nowhere nowadays. But this I say for certain. Let him eat who will, there is bone dust in the flour—there is bone dust in the flour——"

He lurched from a supporter's hold and drifted down the lane, half-chanting the words.

Soma glared, now, at those doubtful faces which remained. "'Tis a lie, brothers! But there, 'tis no use wearing the red coat nowadays when all scoff at it. And why not? when the *Sirkar* itself mocks our rights. I tell thee at the father-in-law's village, but now, a man who titled me sahib last year puffed his smoke in my face this. And wherefore not? May not every scoundrel nowadays drag us to court and set us a-bribing underlings as the common herd have to do? We, soldiers of Oude, who had a Resident of our own always, and——"

"Nothing lasts for always, save God," said a long-bearded bystander, interrupting Soma's parrot roll of military grievances, "as the Moulvie said last night at our mosque, it is well he remains ever the same, giving the same plain orders once and for all. So none of the faithful can mistake. God is Might and Right. All the rest is change."

"*Wah! wah!*" murmured some respectfully; but the Rajpoot's scowl lost its fierceness in supercilious indifference.

"That may suit the Moulvie. It may suit thee and thine, *syyed-jee,*" he replied, with a shrug of the shoulders. "It suits not me nor mine, being of a different race. We are Rajpoots, and there is no change possible to that. We are ever the same."

The pride in his voice and manner reflected but faintly the inconceivable pride in his heart. Yet he was on the alert, salaaming cheerfully, as James Greyman came riding with a clatter down the alley, and without drawing bridle, passed through the low gateway into the dark garden heavy with the perfume of orange-blossom. His arrival ended the incident, for Soma followed him quickly, and in obedience to his curt order to see the groom rub down the horse while it waited, as it had been a breather round the race course, walked off with it toward the well. It was such an opportunity for ordering other men about as natives dearly love; so that the more autocratic a master is, the better pleased they are to gain dignity by serving him.

James Greyman, meanwhile, had paused on the plinth

to give a low whistle and look upward to the terraced roof. And as he did so his face was full of weariness, and yet of impatience. He had been telling himself that he was a fool ever since he had left Kate Erlton's drawing room half an hour before, and even his mad gallop round the steeple-chase course had not effaced the curious sense of compulsion which had made him promise to let her husband go scot-free. Even now, when he waited with that dread at his heart, which of late had been growing stronger day by day, for the answer which Zora loved to make to his signal, his fear lest the Great Silence had fallen between them was lost in the recollection that, if it were so, his freedom had come too late. He hated himself for thus bracketing death and freedom together, but for all that he would not blind himself to its truth. Now that his profession had gone with the King's exile, Zora was, indeed, the only tie to a life which had grown distasteful to him, and when the Great Silence came, as come it must, he had made up his mind to leave James Greyman behind, and go home to England. He was nearing forty, and though the spirit of reckless adventure was fading, the ambitions of his youth seemed to be returning; as they so often do when the burden and heat of passion passes. He was tired of perpetual sunshine; the thought of the cold mists on the hilltops, the wild storms on the west coast, haunted him. He wanted to see them again. Above all, he wanted to hear himself called by his own familiar name, not by the one he had assumed. It had seemed brutal to dream of all this sometimes, while little Zora still lay in his arms smiling contentedly; but it was inevitable. And so, while he waited, watching with the dread growing at his heart for the flutter of the tinsel veil, the half-heard whisper " *Khush amud-eed* " (welcome), it was inevitable also that the remembrance of his promise to Kate Erlton should invade, and as it were desecrate, his real regret for the silence that seemed to grow deeper every second. It had come too late— too late! There could be no solace in freedom now. That other silence in regard to Major Erlton's misdeeds meant the loss of every penny he had scraped together for England. He might have to sell up almost everything he possessed in order to pay his bets honorably; and that he must do, or he gave away his only hope of recouping his bad luck. Why had he promised? Why had he given up a certainty for that vague chance of which he had spoken, he scarcely knew why, to these cold blue northern eyes with the glint of steel. The remembrance brought a passionate anger at himself. Was there anything in the world worth thinking of now, with that silence new-fallen upon him, except the soft warm eyes which were perhaps closed forever? So, with a quick step, he passed up the stairs and gave his signal knock at the door which led on to the terraced roof.

Tara, opening it, answered his look with finger to her lip, and a warning glance to the low string-bed set close to the arches of the summer-house so as to catch the soft-scented breeze. He stepped over to it lightly and looked down on the sleeper; but the relief passed from his face at what he saw there. It could only be a question of hours now.

"Why didst not send before?" he asked in a low voice. "I bid thee send if she were worse and she needed me." Once more the anger against that other woman came uppermost. What was she to him that she should filch even half an hour from this one who loved him? He might so easily have come earlier; and then the promise would not have been made. Was he utterly heartless, that this thought would come again and again?

"She slept," replied Tara coldly. "And sleep needs naught. Not even Love's kisses. It is nigh the end though, master, as thou seest; so I have warned mother Jewuni, the death tender." She had spoken so far as if she desired to make him wince; now the pain on his face made her add hurriedly: "She hath not suffered, Huzoor, she hath not complained. Had it been so I would have sent. But sleep is rest."

She passed on to a lower roof softening her echoing steps with a quaint crooning lullaby:

> " My breast is rest
> And rest is Death.
> Ye who have breath
> Say which is best ?
> Death's Sleep is rest ! "

Was it so? As he stood, still looking down on the
sleeper, something in the lack of comfort, of all the re-
finements and luxuries which seem to belong by right
to the sickness of dear ones in the West, smote him
suddenly with a sense of deprivation, of division. And
though he told himself that Death came in far more
friendly fashion out there in the sunlight, where you
could hear the birds, watch the squirrels, and see the
children's kites go sailing overhead in the blue sky; still
the bareness of it seemed somehow to reveal the great
gulf between his complexity, his endless needs and
desires, and the simplicity of that human creature drifting to death, almost as the animals drift, without complaint, without fears, or hopes. It seemed so pitiful.
The slender figure, still gay in tinsel and bright draperies, all cuddled up on the quilt, its oval face resting hardly
on the thin arm where the bracelets hung so loosely, had
an uncared-for look. It seemed alone, apart; as far from
Death in its nearness to Life, as it was from Life in its
closeness to Death. In swift pity he stooped to risk an
awakening by gathering it into his warm friendly arms.
It would at least feel the beating of another human heart
when it lay there. It would at least be more comfortable than on the bare, hard, pillowless bed.

But he paused. How could he judge? How dare he
judge even for that wasted body, which, despite its softness, had never known half the luxuries his claimed?
So he left her lying as he had often seen her sleep, all
curled up on herself like a tired squirrel, and passing to
the parapet leaned over it looking moodily down into
the darkening orange trees. Their heavy perfume floated
upward, reminding him of many another night in spring-
time spent with Zora upon this terraced roof.

And suddenly his hand fell in a gesture of sheer anger.

Before God! it had been unfair; this idyl on the housetops. The world had held no more for her save her ·pas-

sion for him, pure in its very perfection. His for her had been but a small part of his life. It never was more than that to a man, in reality, and so this sort of thing must always be unfair. That she had been content made it worse, not better. Poor little soul! drifting away from the glow and the glamour.

A resentment for her, more than for himself, made him go to where Tara sat gossiping with her fellow-servant on the other roof and bid them wait downstairs. If the silence were indeed about to fall, if the glow and the glamour were going, then she and he might at least be alone once more beneath the coming stars; alone in the soft-scented darkness which had so often seemed to clasp them closer to each other as they sat in it like a couple of children whispering over a secret.

Closer! As he leaned over the parapet his keen eyes stared down into the half-seen city spreading below him. Wide, tree-set, full of faint sounds of life; the wreaths of smoke from thousands of hearths rising to obscure it from his view. Obscuring it hopelessly with their tale of a life utterly apart from any he could lead. Even there on the housetop he had only pretended to lead it. It was not she, drifting to death so contentedly, who was alone! It was he. Yet some men he had known had seemed able to combine the two lives. They had been content to think half-caste thoughts, to rear up a tribe of half-caste children; while he? How many years was it since he had seen Zora weeping over a still little morsel of humanity, his child and hers, that lay in her tinseled veil? She had wept, mostly because she was afraid he might be angry because his son had never drawn breath; and he had comforted her. He had never told her of the relief it was to him, of the vague repulsion which the thought of a child had always brought with it. One could not help these things; and, after all, she had only cared because she was afraid he cared. She did not crave for motherhood either. It was the glow and glamour that had been the bond between them; nothing else. And, thank Heaven! she had never tired of it, had never seen him tire of it—for Death would come before that now.

A chiming clash of silver made him turn quickly. She had awakened, and seeing him by the parapet, had set her small feet to the ground, and now stood trying to steady herself by her thin, wide-spread arms.

" Zora! wait! I am coming," he cried, starting forward. Then he paused, speech and action arrested by something in her look, her gesture.

" Let me come," she murmured, her breath gone with the effort. " I can come. I must be able to come. My lord is so near—so near."

A fierce pity made him stand still. " Surely thou canst come," he answered. " I will stay here."

As she stood, with parted lips, waiting for a glint of strength ere she tried to walk, her swaying figure, the brilliance of her eyes, the heaving of her delicate throat, cut him to the very heart for her sake more than for his own. Then the jingle of her silver anklets rose again in irregular cadence, to cease at the next pillar where she paused, steadying herself against the cold stone to regain her breath.

" Surely, I can come; arid he so near," she murmured wistfully, half to herself.

" Thou art in too great a hurry, sweetheart. There is plenty of time. The stars are barely lit, and star-time is ever our time."

He set his teeth over the words; but the glow and the glamour should not fail her yet. He would take her back with him while he could to the past which had been so full of it.

" Come slower, my bird, I am waiting," he said again as the jingling cadence ceased once more.

" It is so strange," she gasped; " I feel so strange." And even in the dim light he could see a vague terror, a pitiful amaze in her face. That must not be. That must be stopped. " And it is strange," he answered quickly. " Strange, indeed, for me to wait like a king, when thou art my queen! "

A faint smile drove the wonder away, a faint laugh mingled with the chiming and clashing. She was like a wounded bird, he thought, as he watched her; a wounded bird fluttering to find shelter from death.

"Take care! Take care of the step!" he cried, as a stumble made him start forward; but when she recovered herself blindly he stood still once more, waiting. Let her come if she could. Let her keep the glamour.

Keep it! She had done more than that. She had given it back to him at its fullest, as, close at hand he saw her radiant face, and his outstretched hands met hers warm and clasping. The touch of them made him forget all else; he drew her close to him passionately. She gave a smiling sob of sheer content, raising her face to meet his kisses.

"I have come," she whispered. "I have come to my king." Her voice ended like a sigh. Then there was silence, a fainter sigh, then silence again.

"Zora!" he called with a sudden dread at his heart. "What is it? Zora! Zora!'

Half an hour afterward, Tara Devi, obeying her master's summons, found him standing beside the bed, which he had dragged out under the stars, and flung up her arms to give the wail for what she saw there.

"Hush!" he said sternly, clutching at her shoulder. "I will not have her disturbed."

Tara looked at him wonderingly. "There is no fear of that," she replied clearly, loudly, "none shall disturb Zora again. She hath found *that* freedom in the future. For the rest of us, God knows! The times are strange. So let her have her right of wailing, master. She will feel silent in the grave without the voices of her race."

He drew his hand away sharply; even in death a great gulf lay between him and the woman he had loved.

So the death wail rang out clamorously through the soft dark air.

CHAPTER IV.

TAPE AND SEALING-WAX.

"I CAN'T think," said a good-looking middle-aged man as he petulantly pushed aside a pile of official papers, "where Dashe picks these things up. I never come across them. And it is not as if he were in a big station or—or in the swim in any way." He spoke fretfully, as one might who, having done his best, has failed. And he had grounds for this feeling, since the fact that the diffident district-officer named Dashe was not in the swim, must clearly have been due to his official superiors; the speaker being one of them.

Fortunately, however, for England, these diffident sons of hers cannot always hide their lights under bushels. As the biographies of many Indian statesmen show, some outsider notices a gleam of common sense amid the gloom, and steers his course by it. Now Mr. Dashe's intimate knowledge of a certain jungle tract in this district had resulted in a certain military magnate bagging three tigers. From this to a reliance on his political perceptions is not so great a jump as might appear; since a man acquainted with the haunt of every wild beast in his jurisdiction may be credited with knowledge of other dangerous inhabitants. So much so that the military magnate, being impressed by some casual remarks, had asked Mr. Dashe to put down his views on paper, and had passed them on to a great political light.

It was he who sat at the table looking at a broadsheet printed in the native character, as if it were a personal affront. The military magnate, who had come over to discuss the question, was lounging in an easy-chair with a cheroot. They were both excellent specimens of Englishmen. The civilian a trifle bald, the soldier a trifle gray; but one glance was sufficient to judge them neither knaves nor fools.

" That's the proclamation you're at now, isn't it? " asked the military magnate, looking up, " I'm afraid I could only make out a word here and there. That's the worst of Dashe. He's so deuced clever at the vernaculars himself that he imagines other people——"

The political, who had earned his first elevation from the common herd to the Secretariat by a nice taste in Persian couplets suitable for durbar speeches, smiled compassionately.

" My dear sir! This is not even *shikust* [broken character]. It is lithographed, and plain sailing to anyone not a fool—I mean to anyone on the civil side, of course—you soldiers have not to learn the language. But I have a translation here.   As this farrago of Dashe's must go to Calcutta in due course, I had one made for the Governor General's use."

He handed a paper across the table, and then turned to the next paragraph of the jeremiad. .

The military magnate laid down his cigar, took up the document and glanced at it apprehensively, resumed his cigar, and settled himself in his chair.   It was a very comfortable one and matched the office-room, which, being in the political light's private house, was under the supervision of his wife, who was a notable woman.   Her portrait stood in the place of honor on the mantelpiece and it was flanked by texts; one inculcating the virtue of doing as you would be done by, the other the duty of doing good without ceasing.   Both rather dangerous maxims when you have to deal with a different personal and ethical standard of happiness and righteousness.   There was also a semicircle of children's photographs—of the kind known as positives—on the table round the official ink-pot.   When the sun shone on their glasses, as it did now through a western window, they dazzled the eyes.   Maybe it was their hypnotizing influence which inclined the father of the family toward treating every problem which came to that office-table as if the first desideratum was their welfare, their approbation; not, of course, as his children, but as the representative Englishmen and women of the future.   Yet he was filled with earnest desires to do his duty by those over whom he had been set to rule, and as he read, his sense of responsibility was simply portentous, and his pen, scratching fluently in comments over the half margin, was full of wisdom.   This sound was the only one in the room save, occasionally, voices raised eagerly in the rehearsal going on in the drawing room next door. It was a tragedy in aid of an orphan asylum in England which the notable wife was getting up; and once her voice could be heard distinctly, saying to her daughter, " Oh, Elsie, I'm sure you could die better than that! "

Meanwhile the military magnate was reading:

" I, servant of God, the all-powerful, and of the

prophet Mohammed—to whom be all praise. I, Syyed Ahmed-Oolah, the dust of the feet of the descendants of *Huzrut Ameer-Oolah-Moomereen-Ali-Moortuza, the Holy."* He shifted uneasily, looked across the table, appeared discouraged by that even scratching, and went on:

" I, Syyed Ahmed, after preferring my salaams and the blessings of Holy War, to all believers of the sect of Sheeahs or the sect of Sunnees alike, and also to all those having respectful regards to the Faith, declare that I, the least of servants in the company of those waiting on the Prophet, did by the order of God receive a Sword of Honor, on condition that I should proclaim boldly to all the duty of combining to drive out Infidels. In this, therefore, is there great Reward; as is written in the Word of God, since His Gracious Power is mighty for success. Yea! and if any fail, will they not be rid of all the ends of this evil world, and attain the Joys and Glories of Martyrdom? So be it. A sign is ever sufficient to the intelligent, and the Duty of a servant is simply to point the way."

When he had finished he laid the document down on the table, and for a minute or so continued to puff at his cigar. Then he broke silence with that curious constraint in his tone which most men assume when religious topics crop up in general conversation. " I wonder if this—this paper is to be considered the sign, or "—he hesitated for a moment, then the cadence of the proclamation being suggestive, he finished his sentence to match—" or look we for another? "

" Another! " retorted his companion irritably. " According to Dashe the whole of India is one vast sign-post! He seems to think we in authority are blind to this. On the contrary, there is scarcely one point he mentions which is not, I say this confidentially of course, under inquiry. I have the files in my confidential box here and can show them to you now. No! by the way, the head clerk has the key—that proclamation had to be translated, of course. But, naturally, we don't proclaim this on the housetops. We might hurt people's feelings, or give rise to unfounded hopes. As for these bazaar rumors Dashe retails with such zest, I confess I think it undignified for a district-officer to give any heed to them. They are inevitable with an ignorant population, and we, having the testimony of a good conscience,"—he glanced almost unconsciously at the mantelpiece,— " should disregard these ridiculous lies. Of course every-one—everyone in the swim, that is—admits that the native army is most unsettled. And as Sir Charles Napier declared, mutiny is the most serious danger in the future; in fact, if the first symptoms are not grappled with, it may shake the very foundations. But we are grappling with it, just as we are grappling, quietly, with the general distrust. That was a most mischievous paragraph, by the way, in the *Christian Observer*, jubilant over the alarm created by those first widow re-marriages the other day. So was that in *The Friend of India*, calling attention to the fact that a regular prayer was offered up in all the mosques for the Restoration of the Royal Family. We don't want these things *noticed*. We want to create a feeling of security by ignoring them. That is our policy. Then as for Dashe's political news, it is all stale! That story, for instance, of the Embassy from Persia, and of the old King of Delhi having turned a Sheeah——"

" That has something to do with saying Amen, hasn't it?" interrupted the military magnate, with the air of one determined to get at the bottom of things at all costs to himself.

The political light smiled in superior fashion. " Par-tially; but politically—as a gauge, I mean, to probable antagonism—Sheeahs and Sunnees are as wide apart as Protestants and Papists. The fact that the Royal Family of Oude are Sheeahs, and the Delhi one Sunnees, is our safeguard. Of course the old King's favorite wife, Zeenut Maihl, is an Oude woman, but I don't credit the rumors. I had it carefully inquired into, however, by a man who has special opportunities for that sort of work. A very intelligent fellow, Greyman by name. He has a black wife or—or something of that sort, which of course helps him to understand the natives better than most of us who—er—who don't—you understand——"

The military magnate, having a sense of humor, smiled to himself. "Perfectly," he replied, "and I'm inclined to think that perhaps there is something to be said for a greater laxity." In his turn he glanced at the mantelpiece, and paused before that immaculate presence. "The proclamation, however," he went on hurriedly, "appears to me a bit dangerous. (Holy War is awkward, and a religious fanatic is a tough subject even to the regulars." He had seen a rush of Ghâzees once and the memory lingered.

"Undoubtedly. And as we have pointed out again and again to your Department, here and at home, the British garrisons are too scattered. These large accessions of territory have put them out of touch with each other. But that again is being grappled with. In fact, personally, I believe we are getting on as well as can be expected." He glanced here at the semicircle of children as if the phrase were suggestive. "We are doing our best for India and the Indians. Now here, in Oude, things are wonderfully ship-shape already. Despite Jackson and Gubbins' tiffs over trifles they are both splendid workers, and Lucknow was never so well governed as it is to-day."

"But about the proclamation," persisted his hearer. "Couldn't you get some more information about it? That Greyman, for instance."

"I'm afraid not. He refused some other work I offered him not long ago. Said he was going home for good. I sometimes wish I could. It is a thankless task slaving out here and being misunderstood, even at home. Being told in so many words that the very system under which we were recruited has failed. Poor old Haileybury! I only hope competition will do as well, but I doubt it; these new fellows can never have the old *esprit de corps*; won't come from the same class! One of the Rajah's people was questioning me about it only this morning—they read the English newspapers, of course. 'So we are not to have sahibs to rule over us,' he said, looking black as thunder. 'Any *krani's* (*lit.* low-caste English) son will do, if he has learned enough.' I tried

to explain——" Here a red-coated orderly entering
with a card, he broke off into angry inquiries why he was
being disturbed contrary to orders.

"The sahib bade me bring it," replied the man, as if
that were sufficient excuse, and his master, looking at
the card, tossed it over the table to the soldier, who exclaimed: "Talk of the devil! He may as well come in, if
you don't mind."

So James Greyman was ushered in, and remained
standing between the civilian and the soldier; for it is
not given to all to have the fine perceptions of the native.
The orderly had unhesitatingly classed the visitor as a
"gentleman to be obeyed"; but the Political Department knew him only as a reliable source of information.

"Well, Greyman! Have you brought any more
news?" asked the civilian, in a tone intended to impress
the Military Department with the fact that here was one
grapnel out of the many which were being employed
in bringing truth to the surface and securing safety. But
the soldier, after one brief look at the newcomer, sat up
and squared his own shoulders a bit.

"That depends, sir," replied James Greyman quietly,
"whether it pays me to bring it or not. I told you last
month that I could not undertake any more work, because I was leaving India. My plans have changed; and
to be frank, I am rather hard up. If you could give me
regular employment I should be glad of it." He spoke
with the utmost deliberation, but the incisive finality of
every word, taking his hearers unprepared, gave an impression of hurry and left the civilian breathless. James
Greyman, however, having said what he had come to say,
said no more. During the past week he had had plenty
of time to make up his mind, or rather to find out that it
was made up. For he recognized frankly that he was
acting more on impulse than reason. After he had buried poor little Zora away in accordance with the customs of her people, and paid his racing bets and general
liabilities,—to do which he had found it necessary to sell
most things, including the very horse he had matched
against Major Erlton's,—he had suddenly found out,
rather to his own surprise, that the idea of starting

again on the old lines was utterly distasteful to him. In
a lesser degree this second loss of his future and severing
of ties in the past had had the same effect upon him as
the previous one. It had left him reckless, disposed to
defy all he had lost, and prove himself superior to ill-
luck. Then being, by right of his Celtic birth, imagina-
tive, in a way superstitious, he had again and again found
himself thrown back, as it were, upon Kate Erlton's
appeal for that chance, to bring which the Spirit might
be, even now, moving on the waters. It was that, that
only, with its swift touch on his own certainty that a
storm was brewing, which had made him yield his point;
which had forced him into yielding by an unreasoning
assent to her suggestion that it might bring a chance of
atonement with it. And now, in calm deliberation, he
confessed that he might find his chance in it also; a better
chance, maybe, than he would have had in England. His
only one, at any rate, for some time to come. Those
gray-blue northern eyes with the glint of steel in them
had, by a few words, changed the current of his life. The
truth was unpalatable, but as usual he did not attempt to
deny it. He simply cast round for the best course in
which to flow toward that tide in the affairs of men
which he hoped to take at its flood. Political employment—briefly, spy's work—seemed as good as any for the
present.

" Regular employment," echoed the civilian, recovering from his sense of hurry. " You mean, I presume,
as a news-writer."

" As a spy, sir," interrupted James Greyman.

The political light disregarded the suggestion. " Your
acquirements, of course, would be suitable enough; but
I fear there are no native courts without one. And the
situation hardly calls for excess expenditure. But of
course, any isolated *douceur*——"

His hearer smiled. " Call it payment, sir. But I think
you must find job-work in secret intelligence rather ex-
pensive. It produces such a crop of marc's-nests; at
least so I have found."

The suspicion of equality in the remark made the official mount his high horse, deftly.

" Really, we have so many reliable sources of information, Mr. Greyman," he began, laying his hand as if casually on the papers before him.   The action was followed by James Greyman's keen eyes.

" You have the proclamation there, I see," he said cheerfully.   " I thought it could not be much longer before the police or someone else became aware of its existence.   The Moulvie himself was here about a week ago."

" The Moulvie—what Moulvie? " asked the military magnate eagerly.   The civilian, however, frowned.   If confidential work were to be carried out on those lines, something, even if it were only ignorance, must be found out.

" The Moulvie of Fyzabad——" began James Greyman.

" And who——? "

" My dear sir," interrupted the other pettishly.   " We really know all about the Moulvie of Fyzabad.   His name has been on the register of suspects for months." He rose, crossed to a bookshelf, and coming back processionally with two big volumes, began to turn over the pages of one.

" M—Mo—Ah! Ma, no doubt.   That is correct, though transliteration is really a difficult task—to be consistent yet intelligible in a foreign language is——   No. It must be under F in the first volume.   F; Fy. Just so! Here we are. 'Fyzabad, Moulvie of—fanatic, tall, medium color, mole on inside of left shoulder.'   This is the man, I think? "

" I was not aware of the mole, sir," replied James Greyman dryly, " but he is a magnificent preacher, a consistent patriot, a born organizer; and he is now on his way to Delhi."

" To Delhi? " echoed the civilian pettishly.   " What can a man of the stamp you say he is want with Delhi? A sham court, a miserable pantaloon of a king, the prey of a designing woman who flatters his dotage.   I admit he is the representative of the Moghul dynasty, but its record for the last hundred and fifty years is bad enough surely to stamp out sentiment of that sort."

" Prince Charles Edward was not a very admirable person, nor the record of the Stuarts a very glorious one, and yet my grandfather——" James Greyman pulled himself up sharply, and seeing an old prayer-book lying on the table, which, with the alternatives of a bottle of Ganges water and a copy of the *Koran*, lay ready for the discriminate swearing of witnesses, finished his sentence by opening the volume at a certain Office, and then placing the open book on the top of the proclamation. " It will be no news to you, sir, that prayers of that sort are being used in all the mosques. Of course here, in Lucknow, they are for my late master's return. But if anything comparable to the '15 or the '45 were to come, Delhi must be the center. It is the lens which would focus the largest area, the most rays; for it appeals to greed as well as good, to this world as well as the next."

" Do you think it a center of disaffection now, Mr. Greyman?" asked the military magnate with an emphasis on the title.

" I do not know, sir. Zeenut Maihl, the Queen, has court intrigues, but they are of little consequence."

" I disagree," protested the Political. " You require the experience of a lifetime to estimate the enormous influence——"

" What do you consider of importance, then?" interrupted the soldier rather cavalierly, leaning across the table eagerly to look at James Greyman. There was an instant's silence, during which those voices rehearsing were clearly audible. The tragedy had apparently reached a climax.

" That; and this." He pointed to the Proclamation, and a small fragment of something which he took from his waistcoat pocket and laid beside the paper. The civilian inspected it curiously, the soldier, leaving his chair, came round to look at it also. The sunny room was full of peace and solid security as those three Englishmen, with no lack of pluck and brains, stood round the white fragment.

" Looks like bone," remarked the soldier.

" It is bone, and it was found, so I heard in the bazaar to-day, at the bottom of a Commissariat flour-sack——"

James Greyman was interrupted by a relieved pshaw! from the Political.

"The old story, eh, Greyman! I wonder what next these ignorant fools——"

"When the ignorant fools happen to be drilled soldiers, and, in Bengal, outnumber our English troops by twenty-four to one," retorted James Greyman sharply, "it seems a work of supererogation to ask what they will do next. If I were in their place—— However, if I may tell you how that came into my hands you will perhaps be able to grasp the gravity of the situation."

"Won't you take a chair?" asked the soldier quickly.

James Greyman glanced at the Political. "No, thanks, I won't be long. There is a class of grain carriers called Bunjârahs. They keep herds of oxen, and have carried supplies for the Royal troops since time immemorial. They have a charter engraved on a copper breastplate. I've only seen a copy, for the original Jhungi and Bhungi lived ages ago in Rajpootana. It runs so:

> "While Jhungi Bhungi's oxen
> Carry the army's corn,
> House-thatch to feed their flocks on,
> House-water ready drawn.
> Three murders daily shriven,
> These rights to them are given,
> While Jhungi Bhungi's oxen
> Carry the army's corn."

"Preposterous," murmured the civilian. "That's at an end, anyhow."

"Naturally; for they no longer carry the corn. The method is too slow, too Eastern for our Commissariat. But the Oude levies used to employ them. So did I at the stables. This is over also, and when I last saw my *tanda*—that's a caravan of them, sir—they were sub-contracting under a rich Hindoo firm which was dealing direct with the Department. They didn't like it."

"Still you can't deny that the growth of a strong, contented commercial class with a real stake in the country——" began the civilian hurriedly.

"That sounds like the home-counties or a vestry

board," interrupted his hearer dryly. " The worst of it, in this case, being that you have to get your content out of the petty dealers like these Bunjârahs. I came upon one yesterday telling a circle of admirers, in the strictest confidence of course, lest the *Sirkar* should kill him for letting the cat out of the bag, that he had found that bit of bone at the bottom of a Commissariat sack he bought to mend his own. The moral being, of course, that it was safer to buy from him. But he was only half through when I, knowing the scoundrel, fell on him and thrashed him for lying. The audience approved, and assented to his confession that it was a lie; but only to please me, the man with the stick. And as for Jhungi, he will tell the tale with additional embellishments in every village to which the caravan goes; unless someone is there to thrash him if he does."

" Scoundrel," muttered the soldier angrily.

" Or saint," added James Greyman. " He will be that when he comes to believe his own story of having burned the sack rather than use it. That won't be long. Then he will be much more dangerous. However, if there is no place vacant for me, sir——"

" If you would not mind waiting a minute——" began the military magnate, with a hasty look at the Political.

James Greyman bowed, and retired discreetly to the window. It looked out upon just such another garden as Kate Erlton's, and the remembrance provoked the cynical question as to what the devil he was doing in that galley. Racing was a far safer way of making money than acting as a spy; to no purpose possibly, at least so far as his own chance was concerned.

Yet five minutes after, when the Political was writing him out a safe conduct in the event of his ever getting into difficulties with the authorities, he interrupted the scratching of the pen to say, suddenly:

" If you would make it out in my own name, sir, I should prefer it. James Sholto Douglas, late of the ——th Regiment."

" Hm!" said the military magnate thoughtfully when the new employee in the Secret Intelligence Department left the room. " So that is Jim Douglas, is it? I

thought he was a service man by the set of his shoulders.
Jim Douglas. I remember his case when I was in the
A.-G.'s office."

" What was it? " asked the civilian curiously.

" Oh, a woman, of course. I forget the details, she
was the wife of his major, a drunken beast. There was
something about a blow, and she didn't back him up;
saved her reputation, you understand. But he was an
uncommonly smart officer, I know that."

CHAPTER V.

BRAVO!

THE Gissings' house stood in a large garden; but
though it was wreathed with creepers, and set with
flowers after the manner of flowerful Lucknow, there was
no cult of pansies or such like English treasures here.
It was gay with that acclimatized tangle of poppies and
larkspur, marigold, mignonette, and corn cockles which
Indian gardeners love to sow broadcast in their cartwheel
mud-beds; " powder of flowers " they call the mixed
seeds they save for it from year to year.

In the big dark dining room also—where Alice Gissing, looking half her years in starch, white muslin, and
blue ribbons, sat at the head of the table—there was no
cult of England. Everything was frankly, stanchly of
the nabob and pagoda-tree style; for the Gissings preferred India, where they were received into society, to
England, where they would have been out of it.

It had been one those heavy luncheons, beginning
with many meats and much bottled beer, ending with
much madeira and many cigars, which sent the insurance
rate for India up to war risks in those days.

And there was never any scarcity of the best beer at
the Gissings', seeing that he had the contract for supply-
ing it to the British troops. His wife, however, preferred
solid-looking porter with a creamy head to it, and a
heavy odor which lingered about her pretty smiling lips.

It was a most incongruous drink for one of her appearance; but it never seemed to affect either her gay little
body or gay little brain; the one remained youthful, slender, the other brightly, uncompromisingly clear.

She had been married twice. Once in extreme youth
to a clerk in the Opium Department, who owed the good
looks which had attracted her to a trace of dark blood.
Then she had chosen wealth in the person of Mr. Gissing.
Had he died, she would probably have married for
position; since she had a catholic taste for the amenities
of life. But he had not died, and she had lived with him
for ten years in good-natured toleration of all his claims
upon her. As a matter of fact, they did not affect her in
the least, and in her clear, high voice, she used to wonder
openly why other women worried over matrimonial
troubles or fussed over so slight an encumbrance as a
husband. In a way she felt equal to more than one,
provided they did not squabble over her. That was unpleasant, and she not only liked things to be pleasant,
but had the knack of making them so; both to the man
whose name she bore, and whose house she used as a
convenient spot wherein to give luncheon parties, and
to the succession of admirers who came to them and
drank her husband's beer.

He was a vulgar creature, but an excellent business
man, with a knack of piling up the rupees which made
the minor native contractors, whose trade he was gradually absorbing, gnash their teeth in sheer envy. For
the Western system of risking all to gain all was too
much opposed to the Eastern one of risking nothing to
gain little for the hereditary merchants to adopt it at once.
They have learned the trick of fence and entered the
lists successfully since then; but in 1856 the foe was new.
So they fawned on the shrewd despoiler instead, and
curried favor by bringing his wife fruits and sweets, with
something costlier hidden in the oranges or sugar drops.
Alice Gissing accepted everything with a smile; for her
husband was not a Government servant. The contracts,
however, being for Government supplies, the givers did
not discriminate the position so nicely. They used to
complain that the *Sirkar* robbed them both ways, much

to Mr. Gissing's amusement, who, as a method of self-glorification, would allude to it at the luncheon parties where many men used to come. Men who, between the intervals of badinage with the gay little hostess, could talk with authority on most affairs. They did not bring their wives with them, but Alice Gissing did not seem to mind; she did not get on with women.

"So they complain I rob them, do they?" he said loudly, complacently, to the men on either side of him. "My dear Colonel! an Englishman is bound to rob a native if that means creaming the market, for they haven't been educated, sir, on those sound commercial principles which have made England the first nation in the world. Take this flour contract they are howling about. I'm beer by rights, of course, and, by George, I'm proud of it. Your men, Colonel, can't do without beer; England can't do without soldiers; so my business is sound. But why shouldn't I have my finger in any other pie which holds money? These hereditary fools think I shouldn't, and they were trying a ring, sir. Ha! ha! an absurd upside-down d——d Oriental ring based on utterly rotten principles. You can't keep up the price of a commodity because your grandfather got that price. They ignored the facility of transport given by roads, etc., ignored the right of government to benefit—er—slightly—by these outlays. Commerce isn't ·a selfish thing, sir, by gad. If you don't consider your market a bit, you won't find one at all. So I stepped in, and made thousands; for the Commissariat, seeing the saving here, of course asked me to contract for other places. It serves the idiots uncommon well right; but it will benefit them in the end. If they're to face Western nations they must learn—er—the—the morality of speculation." He paused, helped himself to another glass of madeira, and added in an unctuous tone, "but till they do, India's a good place."

"Is that Gissing preaching morality?" asked his wife, in her clear, high voice. The men at her end of the table had had their share of her; those others might be getting bored by her husband.

"Only the morality of business," put in a coarse-look-

ing fellow who, having been betwixt and between the
conversations, had been drinking rather heavily.
" There's no need for you to join the ladies as yet, Mrs.
Gissing."

Major Erlton, at her right hand, scowled, and the boy
on her left flushed up to the eyes. He was her latest admirer, and was still in the stage when she seemed an
angel incarnate. Only the day before he had wanted
to call out a cynical senior who had answered his
vehement wonder as to how a woman like she was could
have married a little beast like Gissing, with the irrever-
ent suggestion that it might be because the name rhymed
with kissing.

In the present instance she heeded neither the scowl
nor the flush, and her voice came calmly. " I don't intend to, doctor. I mean to send you into the drawing
room instead. That will be quite as effectual to the
proprieties."

Amid the laugh, Major Erlton found opportunity for
an admiring whisper. She had got the brute well above
the belt that time. But the boy's flush deepened; he
looked at his goddess with pained, perplexed eyes.

" The morality of speculation or gambling," retorted
the doctor, speaking slowly and staring at the delighted
Major angrily, " is the art of winning as much money
as you can—conveniently. That reminds me, Erlton;
you must have raked in a lot over that match."

A sudden dull red showed on the face whose admiration Alice was answering by a smile.

" I won a lot, also," she interrupted hastily, " thanks
to your tip, Erlton. You never forget your friends." •

" No one could forget you—there is no merit——" began the boy hastily, then pausing before the publicity of
his own words, and bewildered by the smile now given to
him. Herbert Erlton noted the fact sullenly. He
knew that for the time being all the little lady's personal
interest was his; but he also knew that was not nearly so
much as he gave her. And he wanted more, not understanding that if she had had more to give she would
probably have been less generous than she was; being
of that class of women who sin because the sin has no

appreciable effect on them. It leaves them strangely, inconceivably unsoiled. This imperviousness, however, being, as a rule, considered the man's privilege only, Major Erlton failed to understand the position, and so, feeling aggrieved, turned on the lad.

"I'll remember you the next time if you like, Mainwaring," he said, "but someone has to lose in every game. I'd grasped that fact before I was your age, and made up my mind it shouldn't be me."

"Sound commercial morality!" laughed another guest. "Try it, Mainwaring, at the next *Gymkhâna*. By the way, I hear that professional, Greyman, is off, so amateurs will have a chance now; he was a devilish fine rider."

"Rode a devilish fine horse, too," put in the unappeased doctor. "You bought it, Erlton, in spite——"

"Yes! for fifteen hundred," interrupted the Major, in unmistakable defiance. "A long price, but there was hanky-panky in that match. Greyman tried fussing to cover it. You never can trust professionals. However, I *and my friends* won, and I shall win again with the horse. Take you evens in gold *mohurs* for the next——"

There was always a sledge-hammer method in the Major's fence, and the subject dropped.

The room was heavy with the odors of meats and drinks. Dark as it was, the flood of sunshine streaming into the veranda outside, where yellow hornets were buzzing and the servants washing up the dishes, sent a glare even into the shadows. Neither the furniture nor appointments of the room owed anything to the East— for Indian art was, so to speak, not as yet invented for English folk—yet there was a strange unkennedness about their would-be familiarity which suddenly struck the latest exile, young Mainwaring.

"India is a beastly hole," he said, in an undertone— "things are so different—I wish I were out of it." There was a note of appeal in his young voice; his eyes, meeting Alice Gissing's, filled with tears to his intense dismay. He hoped she might not see them; but she did, and leaned over to lay one kindly be-ringed little hand on the table quite close to his.

" You've got liver," she said confidentially. " India is quite a nice place. Come to the assembly to-night, and I will give you two extras—whole ones. And don't drink any more madeira, there is a good boy. Come and have coffee with me in the drawing room instead; that will set you right."

Less has set many a boy hopelessly wrong. To do Alice Gissing justice, however, she never recognized such facts; her own head being quite steady. But Major Erlton understood the possible results perfectly, and commented on them when, as a matter of course, his long length remained lounging in an easy-chair after the other guests had gone, and Mr. Gissing had retired to business. People, from the Palais Royale playwrights, downward —or upward—always poke fun at the husbands in such situations; but no one jibes at the man who succeeds to the cut-and-dried necessity for devotion. Yet there is surely something ridiculous in the spectacle of a man playing a conjugal part without even a sense of duty to give him dignity in it, and the curse of the commonplace comes as quickly to Abelard and Heloise as it does to Darby and Joan. So Major Erlton, lounging and commenting, might well have been Mrs. Gissing's legal owner. " Going to make a fool of that lad now, I suppose, Allie. Why the devil should you when you don't care for boys? "

She came to a stand in front of him like a child, her hands behind her back, but her china-blue eyes had a world of shrewdness in them. \" Don't I? Do you think I care for men either? I don't. You just amuse me, and I've got to be amused. By the way, did you remember to order the cart at five sharp? I want to go round the Fair before the Club."

If they had been married ten times over, their spending the afternoon together could not have been more of a foregone conclusion; there seemed, indeed, no choice in the matter. And they were prosaically punctual, too; at " five sharp " they climbed into the high dog-cart boldly, in face of a whole posse of servants dressed in the nabob and pagoda-tree style, also with silver crests in their pith turbans and huge monograms on their breastplates; old-fashioned servants with the most antiquated notions as to the needs of the sahib *logue*, and a fund of passive resentment for the least change in the inherited routine of service. Changes which they referred to the fact that the new-fangled sahibs were not real sahibs. But the heavy, little and big breakfasts, the unlimited beer, the solid dinners, the milk punch and brandy *pâni*, all had their appointed values in the Gissings' house; so the servants watched their mistress with approving smiles. And on Mondays there was always a larger posse than usual to see the old Mai, who had been Alice Gissing's ayah for years and years, hand up the bouquet which the gardener always had ready, and say, " My salaams to the missy-baba." Mrs. Gissing used to take the flowers just as she took her parasol or her gloves. Then she would say, " All right," partly to the ayah, partly to her cavalier, and the dog-cart, or buggy, or mail-phaeton, whichever it happened to be, would go spinning away. For the old Mai had handed the flowers into many different turn-outs and remained on the steps ready with the authority of age and long service, to crush any frivolous remarks newcomers might make. But the destination of the bouquet was always the same; and that was to stand in a peg tumbler at the foot of a tiny white marble cross in the cemetery. Mrs. Gissing put a fresh offering in it every Monday, going through the ceremony with a placid interest; for the date on the cross was far back in the years. Still, she used to speak of the little life which had come and gone from hers when she was yet a child herself, with a certain self-possessed plaintiveness born of long habit.

" I was barely seventeen," she would say, " and it was a dear little thing. Then Saumarez was transferred, and I never returned to Lucknow till I married Gissing. It was odd, wasn't it, marrying twice to the same station. But, of course, I can't ask him to come here, so it is doubly kind of you; for I couldn't come alone, it is so sad."

Her blue eyes would be limpid with actual tears; yet as she waited for the return of the tumbler, which the watchman always had to wash out, she looked more like some dainty figure on a cracker than a weeping Niobe. Nevertheless, the admirers whom she took in succession into her confidence thought it sweet and womanly of her never to have forgotten the dead baby, though they rather admired her dislike to live ones. Some of them, when their part in the weekly drama came upon them, as it always did in the first flush of their fancy for the principal actress in it, began by being quite sentimental over it. Herbert Erlton did. He went so far once as to bring an additional bouquet of pansies from his wife's pet bed; but the little lady had looked at it with plaintive distrust. " Pansies withered so soon," she said, " and as the bouquet had to last a whole week, something less fragile was better." Indeed, the gardener's bouquets, compact, hard, with the blossoms all jammed into little spots of color among the protruding sprigs of privet, were more suited to her calm permanency of regret, than the passionate purple posy which had looked so pathetically out of place in the big man's coarse hands. She had taken it from him, however, and strewn the already drooping flowers about the marble. They looked pretty, she had said, though the others were best, as she liked everything to be tidy; because she had been very, very fond of the poor little dear. Saumarez had never been kind, and it had been so pretty; dark, like its father, who had been a very handsome man. She had cried for days, then, though she didn't like children now. But she would always remember this one, always! The old Mai and she often talked of it; especially when she was dressing for a ball, because the gardener brought bouquets for them also.

Major Erlton, therefore, gave no more pansies, and his sentiment died down into a sort of irritable wonder what the little woman would be at. The unreality of it all struck him afresh on this particular Monday, as he watched her daintily removing the few fallen petals; so he left her to finish her task while he walked about. The cemetery was a perfect garden of a place, with rectangular paths bordered by shrubs which rose from a tangle of annual flowers like that around the Gissings' house. This blossoming screen hid the graves for the most part;

but in the older portions great domed erections—generally safeguarding an infant's body—rose above it more like summer-houses than tombs. Herbert Erlton preferred this part of the cemetery. It was less suggestive than the newer portion, and he was one of those wholesome, hearty animals to whom the very idea of death is horrible. So hither, after a time, she came, stepping daintily over the graves, and pausing an instant on the way to add a sprig of mignonette to the rosebud she had brought from a bush beside the cross; it was a fine, healthy bush which yielded a constant supply of buds suitable for buttonholes. She looked charming, but he met her with a perplexed frown.

"I've been wondering, Allie," he said, "what you would have been like if that baby had lived. Would you have cared for it?"

Her eyes grew startled. " But I do care for it! Why should I come if I didn't? It isn't amusing, I'm sure; so I think it very unkind of you to suggest——"

" I never suggested anything," he protested. " I know you did—that you do care. But if it had lived——" he paused as if something escaped his mental grasp. " Why, I expect you would have been different somehow; and I was wondering——"

" Oh! don't wonder, please, it's a bad habit," she replied, suddenly appeased. " You will be wondering next if I care for you. As if you didn't know that I do."

She was pinning the buttonhole into his coat methodically, and he could not refuse an answering smile; but the puzzled look remained. " I suppose you do, or you wouldn't——" he began slowly. Then a sudden emotion showed in face and voice. " You slip from me somehow, Allie—slip like an eel. I never get a real hold—— Well! I wonder if women understand themselves? They ought to, for nobody else can, that's one comfort." Whether he meant he was no denser than previous recipients of rosebuds, or that mankind benefited by failing to grasp feminine standards, was not clear. And Mrs. Gissing was more interested in the fact that the mare was growing restive. So they climbed into the high dog-cart again, and took her a quieting spin down the road. The fresh wind of their own speed blew in their faces, the mare's feet scarcely seemed to touch the ground, the trees slipped past quickly, the palm-squirrels fled chirruping. He flicked his whip gayly at them in boyish fashion as he sat well back, his big hand giving to the mare's mouth. Hers lay equably in her lap, though the pace would have made most women clutch at the rail.

" Jolly little beasts; aint they, Allie? "

" Jolly altogether; jolly as it can be," she replied with the frank delight of a girl. They had forgotten themselves innocently enough; but one of the men in a dog-cart, past which they had flashed, put on an outraged expression.

" Erlton and Mrs. Gissing again! " he fussed. " I shall tell my wife to cut her. Being in business ourselves we have tried to keep square. But this is an open scandal. I wonder Mrs. Erlton puts up with it. I wouldn't."

His companion shook his head. " Dangerous work, saying that. Wait till you are a woman. I know more about them than most, being a doctor, so I never venture on an opinion. But, honestly, I believe most women— that little one ahead into the bargain—don't care a button one way or the other. And, for all our talk, I don't believe we do either, when all is said and done."

" What is said and done? " asked the other peevishly.

There was a pause. The lessening dog-cart with its flutter of ribbons, its driver sitting square to his work, showed on the hard white road which stretched like a narrowing ribbon over the empty plain. Far ahead a little devil of wind swept the dust against the blue sky like a cloud. Nearer at hand lay a cluster of mud hovels, and—going toward it before the dog-cart—a woman was walking along the dusty side of the road. She had a bundle of grass on her head, a baby across her hip, a toddling child clinging to her skirts. The afternoon sun sent the shadows conglomerately across the white metal.

" Passion, Love, Lust, the attractions of sex for sex— what you will," said the doctor, breaking the silence. " Nothing is easier knocked out of a man, if he is worth calling one—a bugle call, a tight corner—— God

Almighty!—they're over that child! Drive on like the devil, man, and let me see what I can do."

There is never much to do when all has been done in an instant. There had been a sudden causeless leaving of the mother's side, a toddling child among the shadows, a quick oath, a mad rear as the mare, checked by hands like a vise for strength, snapped the shafts as if they had been straws. No delay, no recklessness; but one of these iron-shod hoofs as it flung out had caught the child full on the temple, and there was no need to ask what that curved blue mark meant, which had gone crashing into the skull.

Alice Gissing had leaped from the dog-cart and stood looking at the pitiful sight with wide eyes.

"We couldn't do anything," she said in an odd hard voice, as the others joined her. "There was nothing we could do. Tell the woman, Herbert, that we couldn't help it."

But the Major, making the still plunging mare a momentary excuse for not facing the ghastly truth, had, after one short, sharp exclamation—almost of fear, turned to help the groom. So there was no sound for a minute save the plunging of hoofs on the hard ground, the groom's cheerful voice lavishing endearments on his restless charge, and a low animal-like whimper from the mother, who, after one wild shriek, had sunk down in the dust beside the dead child, looking at the purple bruise dully, and clasping her living baby tighter to her breast. For it, thank the gods! was the boy. That one with the mark on its forehead only the girl.

Then the doctor, who had been busy with deft but helpless hands, rose from his knees, saying a word or two in Hindustani which provoked a whining reply from the woman.

"She admits it was no one's fault," he said. "So Erlton, if you will take our dog-cart——"

But the Major had faced the position by this time. "I can't go. She is a camp follower, I expect, and I shall have to find out—for compensation and all that. If you

would take Mrs. Gissing——" His voice, steady till
then, broke perceptibly over the name; its owner looked
up sharply, and going over to him laid her hand on his
arm.

" It wasn't your fault," she said, still in that odd hard
voice. " You had the mare in hand; she didn't stir an
inch. It is a dreadful thing to happen, but "—she
threw her head back a little, her wide eyes narrowed
as a frown puckered her smooth forehead—" it isn't as if
we could have prevented it. The thing had to be."

She might have been the incarnation of Fate itself as
she glanced down at the dead child in the dust, at the
living one reaching from its mother's arms to touch its
sister curiously, at the slow tears of the mother herself
as she acquiesced in the eternal fitness of things; for a
girl more or less was not much in the mud hovel, where
she and her man lived hardly, and the Huzoors would
doubtless give rupees in exchange, for they were just.
She wept louder, however, when with conventional wailing the women from the clustering huts joined her, while
the men, frankly curious, listened to the groom's spirited
description of the incident.

" You had better go, Allie; you do no good here," said
the Major almost roughly. He was anxious to get
through with it all; he was absorbed in it.

So the man who had said he was going to tell his wife
to cut Mrs. Gissing had to help her into the dog-cart.

" It was horrible, wasn't it? " she said suddenly when,
in silence, they had left the little tragedy far behind them.
" We were going an awful pace, but you saw he had the
mare in hand. He is awfully strong, you know." She
paused, and a reflectively complacent smile stole to her
face. " I suppose you will think it horrid," she went on;
" but it doesn't feel to me like killing a human being,
you know. I'm sorry, of course, but I should have been
much sorrier if it had been a white baby. Wouldn't
you? "

She set aside his evasion remorselessly. " I know all
that! People say, of course, that it is wicked not to feel
the same toward people whether they're black or white.

But we don't. And they don't either. They feel just the same about us because we are white. Don't you think they do?"

" The antagonism of race——" he began sententiously, but she cut him short again. This time with an irrelevant remark.

" I wonder what your wife would say if she saw me driving in your dog-cart?"

He stared at her helplessly. The one problem was as unanswerable as the other.

" You had better drive round the back way to the Fair," she said considerately. " Somebody there will take me off your hands. Otherwise you will have to drive me to the Club; for I'm not going home. It would be dreadful after that horrid business. Besides, the Fair will cheer me up. One doesn't understand it, you know, and the people crowd along like figures on a magic lantern slide. I mean that you never know what's coming next, and that is always so jolly, isn't it?"

It might be, but the man with the wife felt relieved when, five minutes afterward, she transferred herself to young Mainwaring's buggy. The boy, however, felt as if an angel had fluttered down from the skies to the worn, broken-springed cushion beside him; an angel to be guarded from humanity—even her own.

" How the beggars stare," he said after they had walked the horse for a space through the surging crowds. " Let us get away from the grinning apes." He would have liked to take her to paradise and put flaming swords at the gate.

" They don't grin," she replied curtly, " they stare like Bank-holiday people stare at the wild beasts in the Zoo. But let us get away from the watered road, the policemen, and all that. That's no fun. See, go down that turning into the middle of it; you can get out that way to the river road afterward if you like."

The bribe was sufficient; it was not far across to peace and quiet, so the turn was made. Nor was the staring worse in the irregular lane of booths and stalls down which they drove. The unchecked crowd was strangely silent despite the numberless children carried shoulder

high to see the show, and though the air was full of throb-
bings of tomtoms, twanging of *sutaras*, intermittent pop-
pings and fizzings of squibs. But it was also strangely
insistent; going on its way regardless of the shouting
groom.

"Take care," said Mrs. Gissing lightly, "don't run
over another child. By the way, I forgot to tell you—
the Fair was so funny—but Erlton ran over a black baby.
It wasn't his fault a bit, and the mother, luckily, didn't
seem to mind; because it was a girl, I expect. Aren't
they an odd people? One really never knows what will
make them cry or laugh."

Something was apparently amusing them at that moment, however, for a burst of boisterous merriment
pealed from a dense crowd near a booth pitched in an
open space.

"What's that?" she cried sharply. "Let's go and
see."

She was out of the dog-cart as she spoke despite his
protest that it was impossible—that she must not venture.

"Do you imagine they'll murder me?" she asked with
an *insouciant*, incredulous laugh. "What nonsense!
Here, good people, let me pass, please!"

She was by this time in the thick of the crowd, which
gave way instinctively, and he could do nothing but follow; his boyish face stern with the mere thought her
idle words had conjured up. Do her any injury? Her
dainty dress should not even be touched if he could
help it.

But the sightseers, most of them peasants beguiled
from their fields for this Festival of Spring, had never
seen an English lady at such close quarters before, if,
indeed, they had ever seen one at all. So, though they
gave way they closed in again, silent but insistent in their
curiosity; while, as the center of attraction came nearer,
the crowd in front became denser, more absorbed in the
bursts of merriment. There was a ring of license in them
which made young Mainwaring plead hurriedly:

"Mrs. Gissing!—don't—please don't."

"But I want to see what they're laughing at," she replied. And then in perfect mimicry of the groom's

familiar cry, her high clear voice echoed over the heads in front of her: " *Hut! Hut! Ari bhaiyan! Hut!* "

They turned to see her gay face full of smiles, joyous, confident, sympathetic, and the next minute the cry was echoed with approving grins from a dozen responsive throats.

" Stand back, brothers!   Stand back! "

There were quick hustlings to right and left, quick nods and smiles, even broad laughs full of good fellow-ship; so that she found herself at the innermost circle with clear view of the central space, of the cause of the laughter.   It made her give a faint gasp and stand trans-fixed.   Two white-masked figures, clasped waist to waist, were waltzing about tipsily.   One had a curled flaxen wig, a muslin dress distended by an all too visible crino-line, giving full play to a pair of prancing brown legs. The other wore an old staff uniform, cocked hat and feather complete.   The flaxen curls rested on the tar-nished epaulet, the unembracing arms flourished brandy bottles.

It was a vile travesty; and the Englishwoman turned instinctively to the Englishman as if doubtful what to do, how to take it.   But the passion of his boy-ish face seemed to make things clear—to give her the clew, and she gripped his hand hard.

" Don't be a fool! " she whispered fiercely.   " Laugh. It's the only thing to do."   Her own voice rang out thrill above the uncertain stir in the crowd, taken aback in its merriment.

But something else rose above it also.   A single word:

" Bravo! "

She turned like lightning to the sound, her cheeks for the first time aflame, but she could see no one in the cir-cle of dark faces whom she could credit with the exclama-tion.   Yet she felt sure she had heard it.

" Bravo! "   Had it been said in jest or earnest, in mockery or—— Young Mainwaring interrupted the problem by suggesting that as the maskers had run away into a booth, where he could not follow and give them the licking they deserved because of her presence, it might be as well for her to escape further insult by returning to the buggy. His tone was as full of reproach as that of a lad in love could be, but Mrs. Gissing was callous. She declared she was glad to have seen it. Englishmen did drink and Englishwomen waltzed. Why, then, shouldn't the natives poke fun at both habits if they chose? They themselves could laugh at other things. And laugh she did, recklessly, at everything and everybody for the remainder of the drive. But underneath her gayety she was harping on that " Bravo! " And suddenly as they drove by the river she broke in on the boy's prattle to say excitedly: " I have it! It must have been the one in the Afghan cap who said ' Bravo! ' He was fairer than the rest. Perhaps he was an Englishman disguised. Well! I should know him again if I saw him."

" Him? who—what? Who said bravo? " asked the lad. He had been too angry to notice the exclamation at the time.

She looked at him quizzically. " Not you—you abused me. But someone did—or didn't "—here her little slack hands resting in her lap clasped each other tightly. " I rather wish I knew. I'd rather like to make him say it again. Bravo! Bravo! "

And then, as if at her own mimicry, she returned to her childish unreasoning laugh.

CHAPTER VI.

THE GIFT OF MANY FACES.

MRS. GISSING had guessed right. The man in the Afghan cap was Jim Douglas. who found the disguise of a frontiersman the easiest to assume, when, as now, he wanted to mix in a crowd. And he would have said " Bravo " a dozen times over if he had thought the little lady would like to hear it; for her quick denial of the possibility of insult had roused his keenest admiration. Here had spoken a dignity he had not expected to find in one whom he only knew as a woman Major Erlton delighted to honor. A dignity lacking in the big brave

boy beside her; lacking, alas! in many a big brave
Englishman of greater importance. So he had risked
detection by that sudden " Bravo! " Not that he dreaded
it much. To begin with, he was used to it, even when he
posed as an out-lander, for there was a trick in his gait,
not to be Orientalized, which made policemen salute
gravely as he passed disguised to the tent. Then there
was ignorance of some one or another of the million
shibboleths which divide men from each other in India;
shibboleths too numerous for one lifetime's learning,
which require to be born in the blood, bred in the bone.
In this case, also, he had every intention of asserting his
race by licking one at least of the offenders when the
show was over. For he happened to know one of them;
having indeed licked him a few days before over a certain
piece of bone. So, as the crowd, accepting the finale of
one amusement placidly, drifted away to see another, he
walked over to the tent in which the discomforted
caricaturists had found refuge. It was a tattered old
military bell-tent, bought most likely at some auction
with the tattered old staff uniform. As he lifted the flap
the sound of escaping feet made him expect a stern chase;
but he was mistaken. Two figures rose with a start of
studied surprise and salaamed profoundly as he entered.
They were both stark naked save for a waistcloth, and
Jim Douglas could not resist a quick glance round for the
discarded costumes. They were nowhere to be seen;
being hidden, probably, under the litter of properties
strewing the squalid green-room. Still of the identity of
the man he knew Jim Douglas had no doubt, and as this
one was also the nearest, he promptly seized him by the
both shoulders and gave him a sound Western kick,
which would have been followed by others if the recipient had not slipped from his hold like an eel. For Jhungi,
Bunjârah, and general vagrant, habitually oiled himself from head to foot after the manner of his profession
as a precaution against such possible attempts at capture.

His assailant, grasping this fact, at any rate, did not
risk dignity by pursuit; though the man stood salaaming again within arm's length.

" You scoundrel! " said Jim Douglas with as much

severity as he could command before the mixture of
deference and defiance, innocence and iniquity, in the
sharp, cunning face before him. " Wasn't the licking I
gave you before enough? "

Jhungi superadded perplexity to his other show of
emotions. " The Huzoor mistakes," he said, with sudden cheerful understanding. " It was the miscreant
Bhungi, my brother, whom the Huzoor licked. The
misbegotten idler who tells lies in the bazaar about bones
and sacks. So his skin smarts, but my body is whole.
Is it not so, Father Tiddu? "

The appeal to his companion was made with curious
eagerness, and Jim Douglas, who had heard this tale of
the ill-doing double before, looked at the witness to it
with interest. That this man was or was not Jhungi's
co-offender he could not say with certainty, for there was
a remarkable lack of individuality about both face and
figure when in repose. But the nickname of Tiddu, or
cricket, was immediately explained by the jerky angu-
larity of his actions,. Save for the faint frostiness of
sprouting gray hairs on a shaven cheek and skull he
might have been any age.

" Of a truth it was Bhungi," he said in a well-modu-
lated but creaky voice. " Time was when liars, such as
he, fell dead. Now they don't even catch fevers, and if
they do, the Huzoors give them a bitter powder and start
them lying again. So, since one dead fish stinks a whole
tank, virtuous Jhungi, being like as two peas in a pod,
suffers an ill-name. But Bhungi will know what it
means to tell lies when he stands before his Creator.
Nevertheless in this world the master being enraged——"

" Not so, Father Tiddu," interrupted Jhungi glibly,
" the Huzoor is but enraged with Bhungi. And rightly.
Did not we hide our very faces with shame while he mimicked the noble people? Did we not try to hold him
when he fled from punishment—as the Huzoor no doubt
heard——"

Jim Douglas without a word slipped his hand down
the man's back. The wales of a sound hiding were
palpable; so was his wince as he dodged aside to
salaam again.

"The Huzoor is a male judge," he said admiringly.
"No black man could deceive him. This slave has certainly been whipped. He fell among liars who robbed
him of his reputation. Will the Huzoor do likewise?
On the honor of a Bunjârah 'tis Bhungi whom the
Huzoor beats. He gives Jhungi bitter powders when
he gets the fever. And even Bhungi but tries to earn a
stomachful as he can when the Huzoors take his trade
from him."

"The world grows hollow, to match a man's swallow,"
quoted Tiddu affably.

The familiar by-word of poverty, the quiet mingling of
truth and falsehood, daring and humility in Jhungi's plea,
roused both Jim Douglas' sense of humor, and the
sympathy—which with him was always present—for the
hardness and squalidness of so many of the lives around
him.

"But you can surely earn the stomachful honestly,"
he said, anger passing into irritation. "What made you
take to this trade?" He kicked at a pile of properties,
and in so doing disclosed the skeleton of a crinoline.
Jhungi with a shocked expression stooped down and
covered it up decorously.

"But it is my trade," he replied; "the Huzoor must
surely have heard of the Many-Faced tribe of Bunjârahs?
I am of them.'

"Lie not, Jhungi!" interrupted Tiddu calmly, "he is
but my apprentice, Huzoor, but I——" he paused, caught
up a cloth, gave it one dexterous twirl round him, squatted
down, and there he was, to the life, a veiled woman
watching the stranger with furtive, modest eye. "But
I," came a round feminine voice full of feminine inflec-
tions, "am of the thousand-faced people who wander to
a thousand places. A new place, a new face. It makes
a large world, Huzoor, a strange world." There was a
melancholy cadence in his voice, which added interest to
the sheer amaze which Jim Douglas was feeling. He had
heard the legend of the Many-Faced Tribe, had even seen
clever actors claiming to belong to it, and knew how the
Stranglers deceived their victims, but anything like this

he had never credited, much less seen. He himself, though he knew to the contrary, could scarcely combat the conviction, which seemed to come to him from that one furtive eye, that a woman sat within those folds.

" But how? " he begun in perplexity. " I thought the Baharupas [*Lit.* many-faced] never went in caravans."

Tiddu resumed the cracked voice and let the smile become visible, and, as if by magic, the illusion disappeared. " The Huzoor is right. We are wanderers. But in my youth a woman tied me to one place, one face; women have the trick, Huzoor, even if they are wanderers themselves. This one was, but I loved her; so after we had burned her and her fellow-wanderer together hand-in-hand, according to the custom, so that they might wander elsewhere but not in the tribe, I lingered on. He was the father of Jhungi, and the boy being left destitute I taught him to play; for it needs two in the play as in life. The man and the woman, or folks care not for it. So I taught Jhungi——"

" And brother Bhungi? " suggested his hearer dryly.

A faint chuckle came from the veil. " And Bhungi. He plays well, and hath beguiled an old rascal with thin legs and a fat face like mine into playing with him. Some, even the Huzoor himself, might be beguiled into mistaking Siddu for Tiddu. But it is a tom-cat to a tiger. So being warned, the Huzoor will give no unearned blows. Yet if he did, are not two kicks bearable from the milch-cow? " As he spoke he angled out a hand impudently for an alms with the beggars' cry of " *Alakh,*" to point his meaning.

It was echoed by Jhungi, who, envious of Tiddu's holding the boards, as it were, had in sheer devilry and desire not to be outdone, taken up the disguise of a mendicant. It was a most creditable performance, but Tiddu dismissed it with a waive of the hand.

" *Bullah!* " he said contemptuously, " 'tis the refuge of fools. There is not one true beggar in fifty, so the forty-and-nine false ones go free of detention as the potter's donkey. Even the Huzoor could do better—had I the teaching of him."

He leaned forward, dropping his voice slightly, and

Jim Douglas narrowed his eyes as men do when some unbidden idea claims admittance to the brain.

" You? " he echoed; " what could you teach me? "

Tiddu rose, let fall the veil to decent dignified drapery, and fixed his eyes full on the questioner. They were luminous eyes, differing from Jhungi's beady ones as the fire-opal differs from the diamond.

" What could I teach? " he re-echoed, and his tone, monotonously distinct to Jim Douglas, was inaudible to others, judging by Jhungi's impassive face. " Many things. For one, that the Baharupas are not mimics only. They have the Great Art. What is it? God knows. But what they will folk to see, that is seen. That and no more."

Jim Douglas laughed derisively. Animal magnetism and mesmerism were one thing: this was another.

" The Huzoor thinks I lie; but he must have heard of the doctor sahib in Calcutta who made suffering forget to suffer."

" You mean Dr. Easdale. Did you know him? Was he a pupil of yours? " came the cynical question.

Tiddu's face became expressionless. " Perhaps; but this slave forgets names. Yet the Huzoors have the gift sometimes. The Baharupas have it not always; though the father's hoard goes oftenest to the son. Now, if, by chance, the Huzoor had the gift and could use it, there would be no need for policemen to salute as he passes; no need for the drug-smokers to cease babbling when he enters. So the Huzoor could find out what he wants to find out; what he is paid to find out."

His eyes met Jim Douglas' surprise boldly.

" How do you know I want to find out anything? " said the latter, after a pause.

Tiddu laughed. " The Huzoor must find a turban heavy, and there is no room for English toes in a native shoe; folk seek not such discomfort for naught."

Jim Douglas paused again; the fellow was a charlatan, but he was consummately clever; and if there was anything certain in this world it was the wisdom of forgetting Western prejudices occasionally in dealing with the East.

"Send that man away," he said curtly, "I want to talk to you alone."

But the request seemed lost on Tiddu. He folded up the veil impudently, and resumed the thread of the former topic. "Yet Jhungi plays the beggar well, for which Fate be praised, since he must ask alms elsewhere if the Huzoor refuses them. For the purse is empty "—here he took a leathern bag from his waistband and turned it inside out—"by reason of the Huzoor's dislike to good mimics. So thou must to the temples, Jhungi, and if thou meetest Bhungi give him the sahib's generous gift; for blows should not be taken on loan."

Jhungi, who all this time had been telling his beads like the best of beggars, looked up with some perplexity; whether real or assumed Jim Douglas felt it was impossible to say, in that hotbed of deception.

"Bhungi?" echoed the former, rising to his feet. "Ay! that will I, if I meet him. But God knows as to that. God knows of Bhungi——"

"The purse is empty," repeated Tiddu in a warning voice, and Jhungi, with a laugh, pulled himself and his disguise together, as it were, and passed out of the tent; his beggar's cry, "*Alakh! Alakh!*" growing fainter and fainter while Tiddu and Jim Douglas looked at each other.

"Jhungi-Bhungi—Bhungi-Jhungi," jeered the Baharupa, suddenly, jingling the names together. "Which be which, as he said, God knows, not man. That is the best of lies. They last a body's lifetime, so the Huzoor may as well learn old Tiddu's——"

"Or Siddu's?"

"Or Siddu's," assented the mountebank calmly. "But the Huzoor cannot learn to use his gift from that old rascal. He must come to the many-faced one, who is ready to teach it."

"Why?"

Tiddu abandoned mystery at once.

"For fifty rupees, Huzoor; not a *pice* less. Now, in my hand."

Was it worth it? Jim Douglas decided instantly that

it might be. Not for the gift's sake; of that he was incredulous. But Tiddu was a consummate actor and could teach many tricks worth knowing. Then in this roving commission to report on anything he saw and heard to the military magnate, it would suit him for the time to have the service of an arrant scoundrel. Besides, the pay promised him being but small, the wisdom of having a second string to the bow of ambition had already decided him on combining inquiry with judicious horse-dealing; since he could thus wander through villages buying, through towns selling, without arousing suspicion; and this life in a caravan would start him on these lines effectively. Finally, this offer of Tiddu's was unsought, unexpected, and, ever since Kate Erlton's appeal, Jim Douglas had felt a strange attraction toward pure chance. So he took out a note from his pocket-book and laid it in the Baharupa's hand.

"You asked fifty," he said, "I give a hundred; but with the branch of the neem-tree between us two."

Tiddu gave him an admiring look. "With the sacred '*Lim ke dagla*' between us, and Mighty Murri-am herself to see it grow," he echoed. "Is the Huzoor satisfied?"

The Englishman knew enough of Bunjârah oaths to be sure that he had, at least, the cream of them; besides, a hundred rupees went far in the purchase of good faith. So that matter was settled, and he felt it to be a distinct relief; for during the last day or two he had been casting about for a fair start rather aimlessly. In truth, he had underrated the gap little Zora's death would make in his life, and had been in a way bewildered to find himself haunting the empty nest on the terraced roof in forlorn, sentimental fashion. The sooner, therefore, that he left Lucknow the better. So, as the Bunjârah had told him the caravan was starting the very next morning, he hastily completed his few preparations, and having sent Tara word of his intention, went, after the moon had risen, to lock the doors on the past idyl and take the key of the garden-house back to its owner; for he himself had always lodged, in European fashion, near the Palace.

The garden, as he entered it, lay peaceful as ever; so utterly unchanged from what he remembered it on many balmy moonlit nights, that he could not help looking up once more, as if expectant of that tinsel flutter, that soft welcome, "*Khush-âmud-und Huzrut.*" Strange! So far as he was concerned the idyl might be beginning; but for her? All unconsciously, as he paused, his thought found answer in one spoken word—the Persian equivalent for " it is finished," which has such a finality in its short syllables:

" KHUTM."

" Khutm." The echo came from Tara's voice, but it had a ring in it which made him turn, anticipating some surprise. She was standing not far off, below the plinth, as he was, having stepped out from the shadow of the trees at his approach, and she was swathed from head to foot in the white veil of orthodox widowhood, which encircled her face like a cere-cloth.• Even in the moonlight he could see the excitement in her face, the glitter in the large, wild eyes.

" Tara! " he exclaimed sharply, his experience warning him of danger, " what does this mean? "

" That the end has come; the end at last! " she cried theatrically; every fold of her drapery, though she stood stiff as a corpse, seeming to be instinct with fierce vitality.

He changed his tone at once, perceiving that the danger might be serious. " You mean that your service is at an end," he said quietly. " I told you that some days ago. Also that your pay would be continued because of your goodness to her—to the dead. I advised your returning north, nearer your own people, but you are free to go or stay. Do you want anything more? If you do, be quick, please, for I am in a hurry."

His coolness, his failure to remark on the evident meaning of her changed dress, calmed her somewhat.

" I want nothing," she replied sullenly. " A *suttee* wants nothing in this world, and I am *suttee*. I have been the master's servant for gratitude's sake—now I am the servant of God for righteousness' sake." So far she had spoken as if the dignified words had been pre-arranged;

now she paused in a sort of wistful anger at the indifference on his face. The words meant so much to her,
and, as she ceased from them, their controlling power
seemed to pass also, and she flung out her arms wildly,
then brought them down in stinging blows upon her
breasts.

"I am *suttee*. Yes! I am *suttee!* Reject me not again,
ye Shining Ones! reject me not again."

The cry was full of exalted resolve and despair. It
made Jim Douglas step up to her, and seizing both
hands, hold them fast.

"Don't be a fool, Tara!" he said sternly. "Tell me,
sensibly, what all this means. Tell me what you are
going to do."

His touch seemed to scorch her, for she tore herself
away from it vehemently; yet it seemed also to quiet
her, and she watched him with somber eyes for a minute
ere replying: "I am going to Holy Gunga. Where else
should a *suttee* go? The Water will not reject me as the
Fire did, since, before God! I am *suttee*. As the master
knows,"—her voice held a passionate appeal,—"I have
been *suttee* all these long years. Yet now I have given
up all—all!"

With a swift gesture, full of womanly grace, but with
a sort of protest against such grace in its utter abandon-
ment and self-forgetfulness, she flung out her arms once
more. This time to raise the shrouding veil from her
head and shoulders. Against this background of white
gleaming in the moonlight, her new-shaven skull showed
death-like, ghastly. Jim Douglas recoiled a step, not
from the sight itself, but because he knew its true meaning; knew that it meant self-immolation if she were left
to follow her present bent. She would simply go down
to the Ganges and drown herself. An inconceivable
state of affairs, beyond all rational understanding; but
to be reckoned with, nevertheless, as real, inevitable.

"What a pity!" he said, after a moment's pause had
told him that it would be well to try and take the starch
out of her resolution by fair means or foul, leaving its
cause for future inquiry. "You had such nice hair. I
used to admire it very much,"

Her hands fell slowly, a vague terror and remorse came to her eyes; and he pursued the advantage remorselessly. "Why did you cut it off?" He knew, of course, but his affected ignorance took the color, the intensity from the situation, by making her feel her *coup de theatre* had failed.

"The Huzoor must know," she faltered, anger and disappointment and vague doubt in her tone, while her right hand drew itself over the shaven skull as if to make sure there was no mistake. "I am *suttee*——" The familiar word seemed to bring certainty with it, and she went on more confidentially. "So I cut it all off and it lies there, ready, as I am, for purification."

She pointed to the upper step leading to the plinth, where, as on an altar, lay all her worldly treasures, arranged carefully with a view to effect. The crimson scarf she had always worn was folded—with due regard to the display of its embroidered edge—as a cloth, and at either end of it lay a pile of trumpery personal adornments, each topped and redeemed from triviality by a gold wristlet and anklet. In the center, set round by fallen orange-blossoms, rose a great heap of black hair, snakelike in glistening coils. The simple pomposity of the arrangement was provocative of smiles, the wistful eagerness of the face watching its effect on the master was provocative of tears. Jim Douglas, feeling inclined for both, chose the former deliberately; he even managed a derisive laugh as he stepped up to the altar and laid sacrilegious hands on the hair. Tara gave a cry of dismay, but he was too quick for her, and dangled a long lock before her very eyes, in jesting, but stern decision.

"That settles it, Tara. You can go to Gunga now if you like, and bathe and be as holy as you like. But there will be no Fire or Water. Do you understand?"

She looked at the hand holding the hair with the oddest expression, though she said obstinately, "I shall drown if I choose."

"Why should you choose?" he asked. "You know as well as I that it is too late for any good to you or others. The Fire and Water should have come twelve years ago. The priests won't say so of course. They

want fools to help them in this fuss about the new law.
Ah! I thought so! They have been at you, have they?
Well, be a fool if you like, and bring them pennies at
Benares as a show. You cannot do anything else. You
can't even sacrifice your hair really, so long as I have
this bit." He began to roll the lock round his finger,
neatly.

"What is the Huzoor going to do with it?" she
asked, and the oddness had invaded her voice.

"Keep it," he retorted. "And by all these thirty
thousand and odd gods of yours, I'll say it was a love-
token if I choose. And I will if you are a fool." He
drew out a small gold locket attached to the Brah-
minical thread he always wore, and began methodically
to fit the curl into it, wondering if this cantrip of his—
for it was nothing more—would impress Tara. Possibly. He had found such suggestions of ritual had
an immense effect, especially with the womenkind who
were for ever inventing new shackles for themselves; but
her next remark startled him considerably.

"Is the *bibi's* hair in there too?" she asked. There
was a real anxiety in her tone, and he looked at her
sharply, wondering what she would be at.

"No," he answered. In truth it was empty; and had
been empty ever since he had taken a fair curl from it
many years before; a curl which had ruined his life.
The memory making him impatient of all feminine
subtleties, he added roughly, "It will stay there for the
present; but if you try *suttee* nonsense I swear I'll tie it
up in a cowskin bag, and give it to a sweeper to make
broth of."

The grotesque threat, which suggested itself to his
sardonic humor as one suitable to the occasion, and
which in sober earnest was terrible to one of her race,
involving as it did eternal damnation, seemed to pass
her by. There was even, he fancied, a certain relief in
the face watching him complete his task; almost a smile
quivering about her lips. But when he closed the locket
with a snap, and was about to slip it back to its place,
the full meaning of the threat, of the loss—or of something beyond these—seemed to overtake her; an un-

mistakable terror, horror, and despair swept through her. She flung herself at his feet, clasping them with both hands.

" Give it me back, master," she pleaded wildly. " Hinder me not again! Before God I am *suttee!* I am *suttee!* "

But this same Eastern clutch of appeal is disconcerting to the average Englishman. It fetters the understanding in another sense, and smothers sympathy in a desire to be left alone. Even Jim Douglas stepped back from it with something like a bad word. She remained crouching for a moment with empty hands, then rose in scornful dignity.

" There was no need to thrust this slave away," she said proudly. " Tara, the Rajputni, will go without that. She will go to Holy Gunga and be purged of inmost sin. Then she will return and claim her right of *suttee* at the master's hand. Till then he may keep what he stole."

" He means to keep it," retorted the master savagely, for he had come to the end of his patience. " Though what this fuss about *suttee* means I don't know. You used to be sensible enough. What has come to you? "

Tara looked at him helplessly, then, wrapping her widow's veil round her, prepared to go in silence. She could not answer that question even to herself. She would not even admit the truth of the old tradition, that the only method for a woman to preserve constancy to the dead was to seek death itself. That would be to admit too much. Yet that was the truth, to which her despair at parting pointed even to herself. Truth? No! it was a lie! She would disprove it even in life if she was prevented from doing so by death. So, without a word, she gathered up the crimson drapery and what lay on it. Then, with these pathetic sacrifices of all the womanhood she knew tight clasped in her widow's veil, she paused for a last salaam.

The incomprehensible tragedy of her face irritated him into greater insistence.

" But what *is* it all about? " he reiterated. " Who has been putting these ideas into your head? Who has been telling you to do this? Is it Soma, or some devil of a priest?"

As he waited for an answer the floods of moonlight threw their shadows together to join the perfumed darkness of the orange trees. The city, half asleep already, sent no sound to invade the silence.

" No! master. It was God."

Then the shadow left him and disappeared with her among the trees. He did not try to call her back. That answer left him helpless.

But as, after climbing the stairs, he passed slowly from one to another of the old familiar places in the pleasant pavilions, the mystery of such womanhood as Tara Devi's and little Zora's oppressed him. Their eternal cult of purely physical passion, their eternal struggle for perfect purity and constancy, not of the soul, but the body; their worship alike of sex and He who made it seemed incomprehensible. And as he turned the key in the lock for the last time, he felt glad to think that it was not likely the problem would come into his life again; even though he carried a long lock of black hair with him. It was an odd keepsake, but if he was any judge of faces his cantrip had served his purpose; Tara would not commit suicide while he held that hostage.

So, having scant leisure left, he hurried through the alleys to return the key. They were almost deserted; the children at this hour being asleep, the men away lounging in the bazaars. But every now and again a formless white figure clung to a corner shadow to let him pass. A white shadow itself, recalling the mystery he had been glad to leave unsolved; for he knew them to be women taking this only opportunity for a neighborly visit. Old or young, pretty or ugly? What did it matter? They were women, born temptresses of virtuous men; and they were proud of the fact, even the poor old things long past their youth. There was a chink in a door he was about to pass. A chink an inch wide with a white shadow behind it. A woman was looking out. What sort of a woman, he wondered idly? Suddenly the chink widened, a hand crept through it, beckoning. He could see it clearly in the moonlight. An old wrinkled hand, delicately old, delicately wrinkled, inconceivably thin, but with the pink henna stain of the temptress still on palms and fingers. A hand with the whole history of seclusion written on it. He crossed over to it, and heard a hurried breathless whisper.

"If the Huzoor would listen for the sake of any woman he loves."

It was an old voice, but it sent a thrill to his heart. " I am listening, mother," he replied, " for the sake of the dead."

" God send her grave peace, my son! " came the voice less hurriedly. " It is not much for listening. I am pensioner, Huzoor. The King gave me three rupees, but now he is gone and the money comes not. If the Huzoor would tell those who send it that Ashrâf-un-Nissa-Zainub-i-Mahal—the Huzoor may know my name, being as my father and mother—wants it. That is all, Huzoor."

It was not much, but Jim Douglas could supplement the rest. Here was evidently a woman who had lived on bounty, and who was starving for the lack of it. There were hundreds in her position, he knew, even among those whose pensions had been guaranteed; for they had not been paid as yet. The papers were not ready, the tape not tied, the sealing-wax not sealed.

" It will not be for long, Huzoor, and it is only three rupees. I was watching for a neighbor to borrow corn, if I could, and seeing the Huzoor——"

" It is all right, mother," he interrupted reassuringly. " I was coming to pay it. Hold the hand straight and I will count it in. Three rupees for three months; that is nine."

The chink of the silver had a background of blessings, and Jim Douglas walked on, thinking what a quaint commentary this little incident was on his puzzle. " Ashrâf-un-Nissa-Zainub-i-Mahal." " Honor-of-women and Ornament-of-Palaces." If the King's paymaster had thought twice about such things, the poor old lady might not have been starving. He was the real culprit. And three months' delay was not long for sanctions, references, for all the paraphernalia and complex machinery of our Government. But a case like this? He looked up into the star-sprinkled riband of sky between the narrowing housetops, and wondered from how many unseen hearths and unheard voices the cry, " How long, O Lord! How long!" was rising. But even to his listening ear there was no sign, no sound. And as he went on through the bazaars, the crowds were passing and repassing contentedly upon the trivial errands of life, and the twinkling cressets in the shops showed faces eager only after a trivial loss or gain.

And the world of Lucknow was apparently awakening contentedly to a new day, when, before dawn, he passed out of it disguised by Tiddu as a deaf-and-dumb driver to the bullock which carried the tattered bell-tent and the tattered staff uniform. It was still dark, but there was a sense of coming light in the sky, and the hum of the housewives' querns, early at work over the coming day's bread, filled the air like swarming bees. The spectral white shadows of widow-drudges were already at work on the creaking well-gear, and the swish of their reed brooms could be heard behind screening walls.

But on the broad white road beyond the bazaars the fresh perfume of the dew-steeped gardens drifted with the faint breeze which heralds the dawn. And down the road, heard first, then dimly seen against its whiteness, came a band of chanting pilgrims to the Holy River.

"*Hurri Gunga! Hurri Gunga! Hurri Gunga!*"

Jim Douglas, swerving his bullock to give them room, wondered if Tara were among them. What if she were? That lock of hair went with *him*. So, with a smile, he swerved the bullock back again. There was a hint of a gleaming river-curve through the lessening trees now, and that big black mass to his left must be the Bailey-guard gate. He could see a faint white streak like a sentry beside it; so it must be close on gunfire. Even as the thought came, a sudden rolling boom filled the silence, and seemed to vibrate against the archway. And hark! From within the Residency, and from far Dilkhusha, the clear glad notes of the reveille answered the challenge; while close at hand the clash of arms told they were changing guards. Then, though he could not see it, the English flag must be rising beyond the trees to float over the city during the coming day.

For one day more, at least.

BOOK II.

THE BLOWING OF THE BUBBLE.

CHAPTER I.

IN THE PALACE.

IT was a day in late September. Nearly six months, therefore, had gone by since Jim Douglas had passed the Bailey-guard at gunfire, and the English flag had risen behind the trees to float over Lucknow. It floated there now, serenely, securely, with an air of finality in its folds; for folk were becoming accustomed to it. At least so said the official reports, and even Jim Douglas himself could trace no waxing in the tide of discontent. It neither ebbed nor flowed, but beat placidly against the rocks of offense.

But at Delhi there was one corner of the city over which the English flag did not float. It lay upon the eastern side above the river where four rose-red fortress walls hemmed in a few acres of earth from the march of Time himself, and safe-guarded a strange survival of sovereignty in the person of Bahâdur Shâh, last of the Moghuls. An old man past eighty years of age, who dreamed a dream of power among the golden domes, marble colonnades, and green gardens with which his ancestors had crowned the eastern wall.

The sun shone hotly, steamily, within those four inclosing walls, save on that eastern edge, where the cool breezes from the plains beyond blew through open arches and latticed balconies. For the rest, the palace-fort—shut in from all outside influence—was like some tepid, teeming breeding-place for strange forms of life unknown to purer, clearer atmospheres.

It was at the Lahore gate of this Delhi palace that on

this late September day a tawdry palanquin, followed by a few tawdry retainers, paused before a cavernous arch, ending the quaint, lofty vaulted tunnel which led inward for some fifty yards or more to another barrier. Here an old man in spectacles sat writing hurriedly.

"Quick, fool, quick! Read, and let me sign," called the huge unwieldy figure in the palanquin, as the bearers, panting under their gross burden, shifted shoulders. Mahboob Ali, Chief Eunuch and Prime Minister, groaned under the jolt; it was a foretaste of many to be endured ere he reached the Resident's house, miles away on the northern edge of the river. Yet he had to endure them, for important negotiations were on foot between the Survival and Civilization. The heir-apparent to those few acres where the sun stood still had died, had been poisoned some said; and another had to be recognized. There was no lack of claimants; there never was a lack of claimants to anything within those walls, where everyone strove to have t¹e first and last word with the Civilization which supported the Survival. And here was he, Mahboob, Prime Minister, being delayed by a miserable scrivener.

"Read, pig! read," he reiterated, laying his puffy hand on his jeweled sword-hilt; for he was still within the gate, therefore a despot. A few yards further he would be a dropsical old man; no more.

"Your slave reads!" faltered the editor of the Court Journal. "Mussamât Hâfzan's record of the women's apartments being late to-day, hath delayed——"

"'Twas in time enough, uncle, if thou wouldst make fewer flourishes," retorted a woman's voice; it was nothing but a voice by reason of the voluminous Pathan veil covering the small speaker.

"Curse thee for a misbegotten hound!" bawled Mahboob. "Am I to lose the entrance fee I paid Gâmu, the Huzoor's orderly, for first interview—when money is so scarce too! Read as it stands, idiot—'tis but an idle tale at best."

The last was an aside to himself as he lay back in his cushions; for, idle though the tale was undoubtedly, it suited him to be its Prime Minister. The editor laid

down his pen hurriedly, and the polished Persian poly-
syllables began to trip over one another, while their
murmurous echo—as if eager to escape the familiar
monotony—sped from arch to arch of the long tunnel,
which was lit about the middle by side arches on the
guards' quarters, and through which the sunlight
streamed in a broad band of gold across the red stone
causeway.

The attributes of the Almighty having come to an end
the reader began on those of Bahâdur Shâh, Father of
Victory, Light of Religion, Polestar and Defender of
the Faith——

" Faster, fool, faster," came the fat voice.

The spectacled old man swallowed his breath, as it
were, and went on at full gallop through the uprisal and
bathing of Majesty, through feelings of pulses and recep-
tion of visitors, then slowed down a bit over the recital
of dinner; for he was a *gourmet*, and his tongue loved
the very sound of dainty dishes.

" May your grave be spat upon! " shouted the Chief
Eunuch. " So none were poisoned by it what matters
the food? Pass on——"

" The Most Exalted then said his appointed prayers,"
gasped the reader. " The Light-of-the-World then
slept his usual sleep. On awakening, the physician
Ahsan-Oolah——"

Mahboob sat up among his cushions. " Ahsan-
Oolah! he felt the Royal pulse at dawn also——"

" The Most Noble forgets," interrupted a voice with
the veiled venom of a partisan in its suavity. " The
King—may his enemies die!—took a cooling draught
yesterday and requires all the care we can give him."

" The King, Meean-sahib, needs nothing save the
prayers of the holy priest, who has piously made over
long years of his own life to prolong his Majesty's," retorted Mahboob, scowling at the speaker, who wore the
Moghul dress, proclaiming him a member of the royal
family. There was no lack of such in the palace-fort,
for though Bahâdur Shâh himself, being more or less
of a saint, had contented himself with some sixty children, his ancestors had sometimes run to six hundred,

The Meean-sahib laughed scornfully as he passed inward, and muttered that those who went forth with the dog's trot might return with the cat's slink, since the great question had yet to be settled. Mahboob's scowl deepened; the very audacity of the interruption rousing a fear lest the king's eldest son, Mirza Moghul, whose partisan the speaker was, might have some secret understanding with Civilization. All the more need for haste.

" Read on, fool! Who told thee to stop? "

" The Princess Farkhoonda Zamâni entered by the Delhi gate."

Mahboob gave a scornful laugh in his turn. " To visit the Mirza's house, no doubt. Let her come—a pretty fool! Yet she had wiser stay where she hath chosen to live, instead of being princess one day and plain Newâsi the next. There are enough women without her in the palace! "

So it seemed, to judge by the stream of female names and titles belonging to the curtained dhoolies, which had passed and repassed the barriers, upon which the editor launched his tongue. But Mahboob, as Chief Eunuch, knew the value of such information and cut it short with a sneer.

" If that be all! quick! the pen, and I will sign."

A bystander, also in the Moghul dress, laughed broadly at the well-worn inuendo on the possibilities of curtained dhoolies in intrigue. " Thou art right, Mahboob," he said, " God only knows."

" His own work," chuckled the Keeper of Virtue. " And the Devil made most of the women here. Now pigs! Canst not start? Am I to be kept here all day? "

As the litter went swaying out between the presented arms of the sentries, the white chrysalis of a Pathan veil stepped lamely down into the causeway. " That, seeing there is no news, will be something to amuse the Queen withal," came the sharp voice.

" There may be news enough, when that fat pig returns, to make it hard to amuse thy mistress, Mussamât Hâfzan," suggested another bystander.

The chrysalis paused. " My mistress! Nay, sahib! Hâfzan is that to herself only. I am for no one save

myself. I carry news, and the more the better for my
trade. Yet I have not had a real good day for gifts of
gratitude from my hearers, since Prince Fukrud-deen,
the heir-apparent, died." There was a reckless cynicism
in her voice, and he of the Moghul dress broke in hotly.

" Was poisoned, thou meanest, by——"

Hâfzan's shrill laugh rang through the arches.

" No names, Mirza sahib, no names! And 'tis no
news surely to have folk poisoned in the fort; as thou
wouldst know ere long, may be, if Hâfzan were spiteful.
But I name no names—not I! I carry news, that is all."

So, with a limp, showing that the woman within was a
cripple, the formless figure passed along the tunnel
through the inner barrier, and so across the wide courtyard where the public hall of audience stood blocking
the eastern end. It was a massive, square, one-storied
building, with a remorseless look in its plain expanse of
dull red stone, pierced by toothed arches which yawned
darkly into a redder gloom, like monstrous mouths
agape for victims. Past this, with its high-set fretted
marble *baldequin* showing dimly against the end wall—
whence a locked wicket gave sole entrance from the
palace to this seat of justice or injustice—the Pathan
veil flitted like a ghost; so, through a narrow passage
guarded by the King's own body-guard, into a different
world; a cool breezy world of white and gold and blue,
clasping a garden set with flowers and fruit. Blue sky,
white marble colonnades, and golden domes vaulting
and zoning the burnished leaves of the orange trees,
where the green fruit hung like emeralds above a tangle
of roses and marigolds, chrysanthemums and crimson
amaranth. Hâfzan paused among them for a second;
then, all unchallenged by any, passed on up the steps of
the marble platform, which lies between the Baths and
the Private Hall of Audience. That marvelous building
where the legend, cunningly circled into the decorations,
still tells the visitor again and again that, " If earth holds
a haven of bliss, It is this, it is this, it is this."

Here, on the platform, Hâfzan paused again to look
over the low parapet. The wide eastern plains stretched
away to the pale blue horizon before her, and the curv-

ing river lay at her feet edging the high bank, faced with
stone, which forms the eastern defense of the palace-fort.
Thus the levels within touch the very top of the wall;
so that the domes, and colonnades, and green gardens,
when seen from the opposite side of the stream, cut clear
upon the sky, like a castle in the air at all times; but
in the sunsettings, when they show in shades of pale lilac,
with the huge dome of the great mosque bulging like
a big bubble into the golden light behind them as a
veritable Palace of Dreams.

She looked northward, first; along the sheer face of
the rosy retaining wall to its trend westward at the
Queen's favorite bastion, which was crowned by a bal-
conied summer-house overhanging the moat between the
fort itself and the isolated citadel of Selimgarh; which,
jutting out into the river, partially hid the bridge of
boats spanning the stream beyond. Then she looked
southward. Here was the sheer face of rosy wall again,
but it was crowned, close at hand, by the colonnade and
projecting eaves of the Private Hall of Audience. Further on it was broken by the carved *corbeilles* of the
King's balcony, and it ended abruptly at a sudden eastward turn of the river, so giving a view of rolling rocky
hillocks sweeping up to the horizon where, faint and far
like a spear-point, the column of the Kutb showed on a
clear day. The Kutb! that splendid promise, never ful-
filled,—that first minaret of the great mosque that never
was, and never will be built; symbol of the undying
dream of Mohammedan supremacy that never came,
that never can come to pass.

As she paused, a troop of women laden with cosmetics
and combs and quaint baskets containing endless aids to
beauty, came shuffling out of the baths, gossiping and
chattering shrilly, and clanking heavy anklets as they
came. And with them, a heavy perfumed steam suggestive of warm indolence, luxury, sensuality, passed
out into the garden.

" What! done already? " called Hâfzan in surprise.

" Already! " echoed a bold-faced trollop pertly, " *Ari*,
sister. Art grown a loose-liver? Sure this is Friday,
and the King, good man, bathes apart, religiously! So

we be religious too, matching his humor. That is the
way with us women."

An answering giggle met the sally.

" Thou art an impudent hussy, Goloo!" said Hâfzan
angrily. "And the Queen—where is she?"

" In the mosque praying for patience—in the summer-
house playing games—in the King's room coaxing him
to belief—in the vestibule feeding her son with lollipops
—he likes them big, and sweet, and lively, and of his own
choosing, does the prince, as I know to my cost." Here
a general titter broke in on the unabashed recital.

" *Loh!* leave Hâfzan to find out what the Queen does
elsewhere," suggested another voice. "We speak not
of such things."

" Then speak lower of others," retorted Hâfzan.
" Walls have echoes, sister, and thy mistress would fare
no better than others if thy talk reached Zeenut Maihl's
ears."

" Tell her, spy! if thou wilt," replied the woman carelessly. "We have friends on our side now, as thou
mayst understand mayhap ere nightfall, when the answer
comes."

Hâfzan laughed. "Thou hast more faith in friends
than I. *Loh!* I trust none within these four walls. And
out of them but few."

So saying she limped back into the garden, giving a
glance as she passed it into the Pearl Mosque, which
showed like a carven snowdrift against the blue of the
sky, the green of the trees. Finding none there, she
went straight to the Queen's favorite summer-house on
the northern bastion.

It was a curious fatality which made Zeenut Maihl
choose it, since all her arts, all her cunning, could scarcely
have told her that it would ere long be a watch-tower,
whence the chance of success or failure could be counted.
For the white road beyond the bridge of boats, and
trending eastward to the packed population of Oude,
to Lucknow, to all that remained of the vitality in the
Mohammedan dream, was to be ere long like a living,
growing branch to which she, the spider, hung by an
invisible thread, spinning her cobwebs, seemingly in
mid-air.

" Hush!" The whispered monition made Hâfzan pause in the screened archway till the game was over. It was a sort of dumb-crambo, and a most outrageous *double entendre* had just brought a smile to the broad heavy face of a woman who lay among cushions in the alcoved balcony. This was Zeenut Maihl, who for nearly twenty years had kept her hold upon the King, despite endless rivals. She was dark-complexioned, small-eyed, with a curious lack of eyebrows which took from her even vivacity of expression. But it was a man with experience in many wives who remarked that favor is deceitful and beauty is vain; he knew, no doubt, that in polygamy, the victory must go to the most unscrupulous fighter. Zeenut Maihl, at any rate, secured hers by ever-recurring promises of another heir to her octogenarian husband; a flattery to which his other wives either could not or would not stoop. But the trick served the Queen's purpose in more ways than one. Her oft-recurring disappointments could have but one cause: witchcraft. So on such occasions, with her paid priest, Hussan Askuri, saying prayers for those *in extremis* at her bedside, Zeenut Maihl's enemies went down like nine-pins, and she rose from her bed of sickness with a board cleared of dangerous rivalry. For none in the hot-bed of shams felt secure enough to get into grips with her. Ahsan-Oolah, the physician, might have; she had cried quarter from his keen fence before now; but he did not care to take the trouble. For he was a philosopher, content to let his world go to the devil its own way, so long as it did not interfere with his passionate greed of gold. And this master-passion being shared by Zeenut Maihl they hoisted the flag of truce for the most part against mutual spoliations. So the Queen played her game unmolested, as she played dumb-crambo; at which her servants, separated like their betters into cliques, tried to outdo each other.

" *Wâh!* " said the set, jubilant over the *double entendre.* " That is the best to-day."

" If you like it, a clod is a betel nut," retorted the leader of another set. " I'll wager to beat it easily."

The Queen frowned. There was too much freedom in this speech of Fâtma's to suit her.

" And I will be the judge," she said with a cruel smile. " Fâtma must be taught better manners."

Fâtma—a woman older than the rest—salaamed calmly; and the fact made the other clique look at each other uneasily. What certainty gave her such confidence as she plucked a gray hair from her own head and placed it on the black velvet cushion which lay at the Queen's feet?

" That is my riddle," she said. " Let the world guess it, and honor the real giver of it."

What could it be? Even the Queen raised herself in curiosity; a sign in itself of commendation.

" Sure I know not," she began musingly, when Fâtma sprang to her feet in theatrical appeal.

" Not so! Ornament of Palaces," she cried. " This may puzzle the herd; it is plain to the mother of Princes. It lies too lowly now for recognition, but in its proper place——" She snatched the hair from the cushion, and, with a flourish, laid it on the head of a figure which appeared as if by magic behind her. A figure dressed as a young Moghul Prince, and wearing all the crown jewels.

" My son, Jewun!" cried the Queen, starting angrily. And the adverse clique, taking their cue from her tone, shrieked modestly, and scrambled for their veils.

Fâtma salaamed to the very ground.

" No! Mother of Princes, 'tis but my riddle—the heir-apparent."

Zeenut Maihl paused, bewildered for an instant; then in the figure recognized the features of a favorite dancing girl, saw the pun, and laughed uproariously, delightedly. The English sentry on the drawbridge leading to Selim-gurh might have heard her had there been one; but within the last month the right to use the citadel as a private entry to the palace had been given to the King. It enabled him to cross the bridge of boats without the long circuit by the Calcutta gate of the city.

" A gold mohur for that to Fâtma!" she cried, " and a post nearer my person. I need such wits sorely." As she spoke she rose to her feet, the smiles fading from her face as she looked out along that white eastward

streak; for the jest had brought her back to earnest, to
that mixture of personal ambition for her son and real
patriotism for her country which kept her a restless in-
triguer. " I need men, too," she muttered. " Not dissolute, idle weathercocks or doting old pantaloons! There
are plenty of them yonder." So she stood for a second,
then turned like lightning on her attendants. " What
time——" she began, then seeing Hâfzan, who had unveiled at the door, she gave a cry of pleasure. " 'Tis well
thou hast come," she said, beckoning to her, " for thou
must know God! if I were free to come and go, what could
I not compass? But here, in this smothering veil——"
She flung even the gauze apology for one which she
wore from her, and stood with smooth, bare head, and
fat, bare arms, her quaint little pigtail dangling down her
broad back. Not a romantic figure truly, but one in its
savage temper, strength, obstinacy, to be reckoned with.
" What time "—she went on rapidly—" does the King
receive his initiates? "

" At five," replied Hâfzan. Seen without its veil, also,
her figure showed more shrunk than ill-formed, and her
pale, thin face would have been beautiful but for its look
of permanent ill-health. " The ceremony of saintship
begins then."

" Saints! " echoed the Queen, with a hard laugh. " I
would make them saints and martyrs, too, were I free.
Quick, woman! pen and ink! And stay! Fâtma's puzzle hath driven all else from my head. What time was't
that Hussan Askuri was bidden to come? "

" The saintborn comes at four," replied Hâfzan ceremoniously, " so as to leave leisure ere the Chief Eunuch's
return with the answer."

Zeenut Maihl's face was a study. " The answer! My
answer lies there in Fâtma's riddle; take two gold mohurs
for it, woman, it hath given me new life. Write, Hâfzan,
to the chamberlain, that the disciples must pass the
southern window of the King's private room ere they
leave the palace. And call my litter; I must see Hussan
Askuri ere I meet him at the King's."

An hour afterward, with bister marks below her eyes,
and delicate hints of causeful, becoming languor in face

and figure, she was waiting the King's return from the latticed balcony overhanging the river, where he always spent the heats of the day; waiting in the cluster of small, dark rooms which lie behind it, on the other side of the marble fountain-set aqueduct which flows under a lace-like marble screen to the very steps of the Hall of Audience.

"Is all prepared?" she asked anxiously, as a glint of light from a lifted curtain warned her of the King's approach.

"All is prepared," echoed a hollow, artificial voice. The speaker was a tall, heavily built man with long gray beard, big bushy gray eyebrows, and narrow forehead. A dangerous man, to judge by the mixed spirituality and sensuality in his face; a man who could imagine evil, and make himself believe it good. It was Hussan Askuri, the priest and miracle-monger, who led the last of the Moghuls by the nose. It was not a difficult task, for Bahâdur Shâh, who came tottering across the intervening sunlit space, was but a poor creature. The first impression he gave was of extreme old age. It was evident in the sparse hair, the high, hollow checks, the waxy skin, the purple glaze over the eyes. The next was of a feeble-ness beyond even his apparent years. He seemed fiber-less, mind and body. Yet released at the door of privacy, from the eunuch's supporting hands, he ambled gayly enough to a seat, and exclaimed vivaciously:

"A moment! A moment! good priest and physician. My mind first; my body after. The gift is on me. I feel it working, and the historian must write of me more as poet than king."

"As the king of poets, sire," suggested Hussan Askuri pompously.

Bahâdur Shâh smiled fatuously. "Good! Good! I will weave that thought with mine into perfumed poesy." He raised one slender hand for silence, and with the fingers of the other continued counting feet laboriously, until with a sigh of relief, he declaimed:

"Bahâdur Shâh, sure all the world will know it,
Was poet more than king, yet king of poets."

Zeenut Maihl gave a cry of admiration. "Quick! *Pir*-sahib, quick!" she exclaimed. "Such a gem must not be lost."

"But 'tis yet to be polished," began the King complacently.

"That is the office of the scribe," replied Hussan Askuri, as he drew out his ink-horn. He was by profession an ornamental writer, and gained great influence with the old poetaster by gathering up the royal fragments and hiding their lameness amid magnificent curves and flourishes.

"And now, *Pir*-sahib," continued the Queen, with a look of loving anxiety at her lord, "for this strange ailment of which I spoke to you——"

The King's face lost its self-importance as if he had been suddenly recalled to unpleasant memory. "'Tis naught of import," he said hastily. "The Queen will have it I start and sweat of nights. But this is but the timorous dread of one in her condition. I am well enough."

"My lord, *Pir*-sahib, hath indeed renewed his youth through thy pious breathing of thy own life into his mouth—as time will show," murmured the Queen with modest, downcast look. "But last night he muttered in his sleep of enemies——"

Bahâdur Shâh gave a gasp of dismay. "Of enemies! Nay!—did I truly? Thou didst not tell me this."

"I would not distress my lord, till fear was over. Now that the pious priest, who hath the ear of the Almighty——"

Hussan Askuri, who had stepped forward to gaze at the King, began to mutter prayers. "'Tis that cooling draught of Ahsan-Oolah's stands in the way," he gasped, his hands and face working as if he were in deadly conflict with an unseen foe. "No carnal remedy—Ah! God be praised! I see, I see! The eye of faith opens—*Hai!* venomous beast, I have you!" With these words he rushed to the King's couch, and, scattering its cushions, held up at arm's length a lizard. Held by the tail, it seemed in semi-darkness to writhe and wriggle.

"*Ouée! Umma!*" yelled the Great Moghul, shrinking

to nothing in his seat, and using after his wont the woman's cry—sure sign of his habits.

"Fear not!" cried the priest. "The mutterings are stilled, the sweats dried! And thus will I deal also with those who sent it." He flung his captive on the ground and stamped it under foot.

"Was it—was it a bis-cobra, think you?" faltered the King. He had hold of Zeenut Maihl's hand like a frightened child. The priest shook his head. "It was no carnal creature," he said in a hollow, chanting voice. "It was an emissary of evil made helpless by prayer. Give Heaven the praise." Bahâdur Shâh began on his creed promptly, but the priest frowned.

"Through his servant," he went on. "For day and night, night and day, I pray for the King. And I see visions, I dream dreams. Last night, while my lord muttered of enemies, Hussan Askuri saw a flood coming from the West, and on its topmost wave, upon a raft of faithful swords, as on a throne, sate——"

"With due respect," came voices from the curtained door. "The disciples await initiation in the Hall of Audience."

Hussan Askuri and the Queen exchanged looks. The interruption was unwelcome, though strangely germane to the subject.

"I will hear thee finish the dream afterward," fussed the King, rising in a bustle; for he prized his saintship next to his poetry. "I must not keep my pupils from grace. Hast the kerchiefs ready, Zeenut?" There was something almost touching in the confidence of his appeal to her. It was that of a child to its mother, certain of what it demanded.

"All things are ready," she replied tartly, with a meaning and vexed look at the miracle-monger; for they had meant to finish the dream before the initiation.

"A goodly choice," said the royal saint, as he looked over the tiny silk squares, each embroidered with a text from the *Koran*, which she took out of a basket. "But I need many, *Pir*-sahib. Folk come fast, of late, to have the way of virtue pointed by this poor hand. And thou hast more in the basket, I see, Zeenut, ready against——"

" They are but begun," put in the Queen, hastily covering the basket. " Nor will they, likely, be needed, since
the leave season passes, and 'tis the soldiers who come
most to be disciples to the defender of their faith."

" I am the better pleased," replied the King with edify-
ing humility. " This summer hath too many pupils as
it is. Come! *Pir*-sahib, and support me through mine
office with real saintship."

As the curtain fell behind them Zeenut Maihl crossed
swiftly to the crushed lizard and raised it gingerly.

" No carnal creature," she repeated. It was not; only
a deft piece of patchwork. Yet it, or something else,
made her shiver as she dropped the tell-tale remains into
the basket. This man Hussan Askuri sometimes seemed
to her own superstition a saint, sometimes to her clear
head a mere sinner. She was not quite certain of anything about him save that his delusions, his dreams, his
miracles, suited her purpose equally, whether they were
false or true.

So she crossed over again to a marble lattice and
perred through a convenient peephole toward the
Audience Hall, which rose across an intervening stretch
of platform in white shadow, and whiter light. She could
not see or hear much; but enough to show her that
everything was going on the same as usual. The disciples, most of them in full uniform, went up and down the
steps calmly, and the wordy exordium on the cardinal
virtues went on and on. How different it might be, she
thought, if she had the voice. She would rouse more
than those faint " *Wâh! Wâhs.*" She would make the
fire come to men's eyes. In a sort of pet with her own
helplessness, she moved away and so, through another
room, went to stand at another lattice. It looked south
over a strip of garden, and there was an open square
left in the tracery through which a face might look, a
hand might pass. And as she stood she counted the remaining kerchiefs in the basket she still held. They were
all of bright green silk and bore the same lettering. It
was the Great Cry: " *Deen! Deen! Futteh Mohammed!* "
As dangerous a woman this, as Hussan Askuri was a
man; as dangerous, both of them, to peaceful life, as the

fabled bis-cobra, at the idea of which the foolish old King had cried, "*Ouée, Umma!*" like any woman.

And now at last that wordy exordium must be over, for, along the garden path, came the clank of accouterments. Zeenut Maihl's listless figure seem galvanized to sudden life, there was a flutter of green at the open square, and her voice followed the shower of silk.

" These banners from the Defender to his soldiers."

But as she spoke, a stir of excitement, a subdued murmur of expectation reached her ear from outside, and, leaning forward, she caught a glimpse of a swinging litter coming along the path. Mahboob returned already! Vexatious, indeed, when she had turned and planned everything so as to be sure of having the King in her apartments when the answer arrived. None others would know it before she did—unless!—the thought obliterated all others, and she flew back to the further lattice. The King, returning from the initiation, had paused in the middle of the platform at the sight of the approaching litter, and his courtiers, as if by instinct, had grouped themselves round him, leaving him the central figure. The cruel sunlight streamed down on the tawdry court, on the worn-out old man.

It seemed interminable to the woman behind the lattice, that pause while the fat eunuch was helped from his litter. She could have screamed to him for the answer, could have had at his fat carcass with her hands for its slowness. But the old King had better blood in his veins. He stood quietly, his tawdry court around him; behind him the marble, and gold, and mosaics of his ancestors.

" What news, slave? " he asked boldly.

" None, Light of the Faithful," replied the Chief Eunuch.

" None! " The semi-circle closed in a little, every face full of disappointed curiosity.

" I have a letter for the Lord of the World with me. Its substance is this. The *Sirkar* will recognize no heir. During the lifetime of our Great Master, whose life be prolonged forever, the *Sirkar* will make no promise of any kind, either to his majesty, or to any other member of the royal family. It is to remain as if there were no succession."

No succession! Above the sudden murmur of universal surprise and dissent, a woman's cry of inarticulate rage came from behind the lattice. The King turned toward the sound instinctively. "I must to the Queen," he murmured helplessly, "I must to the Queen."

CHAPTER II.

IN THE CITY.

"Come, beauty, rare, divine,
   Thy lover like a vine
   With tendril arms entwine ;
   Lay rose red lips to mine,
   Bewildering as wine."

THE song came in little insistent trills and quaverings, and quaint recurring cadences, which matched the insistency of the rhymes. The singer was a young man of about three-and-twenty, and as he sang, seated on a Persian rug on the top of a roof, he played an elaborate symphony of trills and cadences to match upon a tinkling *saringi.* He was small, slight, with a bright, vivacious face, smooth shaven, save for a thin mustache trimmed into a faint fine fringe. His costume marked him as a dandy of the first water, and he smelled horribly of musk.

The roof on which he sat was a secluded roof, protected from view, even from other roofs, by high latticed walls; its only connection with the world below it being by a dizzy brick ladder of a stair climbing down fearlessly from one corner. Across the further end stretched a sort of veranda, inclosed by lattice and screens. But the middle arch being open showed a blue and white striped carpet, and a low reed stool. Nothing more. But a sweet voice came from its unseen corner.

"Art not ashamed, Abool, to come to my discreet house among godly folk and sing lewd songs? Will they not think ill of me? And if thou comest drunken horribly with wine, as thou didst last week, claiming audience of me, thine aunt, not all that title will save me from aspersion. And if I lose this calm retreat, whither shall poor Newâsi go?"

"Nay, kind one!" cried Prince Abool-Bukr, "that shall never be." So saying, he cast away the tinkling *saringi* and from the litter of musical instruments around him laid impulsive hands on a long-necked fiddle with a 'cello tone in it. "I would sing psalms to please mine aunt," he went on in reckless gayety, "but that I know none. Will pious Saadi suit your sober neighbors, since lovelorn Hafiz shocks them? But no! I can never stomach his sentimental sanctity, so back we go to the wisest of all poets."

The high, thin tenor ran on without a break into a minor key, and a stanza of the Great Tentmakers. And as it quivered and quavered over the illusion of life, a woman's figure came to lean against the central arch, and look down on the singer with kindly eyes.

They were the most beautiful eyes in the world. Such is the consensus of opinion among all who ever saw them. Judged, indeed, by this standard, the Princess Farkhoonda Zamâni, alias Newâsi Begum, the widow of one of the King's younger sons, must have had that mysterious charm which is beyond beauty. But she was beautiful also, though smallpox had left its marks upon her. Chiefly, however, by a thickening of the skin, which brought an opaque pallor, giving her oval face a look of carved ivory. In truth, this memento of the past tragedy, which at the age of thirteen had brought her, the half-wedded bride, to death's door, and sent her fifteen-year-old bridegroom from the festival to the grave, enhanced, rather than detracted from her beauty. Her lips were reddened after the fashion of court women, her short-sighted hazel eyes were heavily blackened with antimony; but she wore no jewels, and her graceful, sweeping Delhi dress was of deadest, purest white, embroidered in finest needlework round hems and seams, and relieved only by the lighter folds of her white, lacelike veil. For she had forsworn colors when she fled from court-life and its many intrigues for an alliance with the charming widow; and, on the plea of a call to a religious and celibate life, had taken up her abode in the Mufti's Alley. This was a secluded little lane off the bazaar, which lies to the south of the Jumma Mosque, where a score or two of the Mohammedan families connected with the late chief magistrate of the city lived, decently, respectably, respectedly. To do this, having sometimes to close the gate at the entrance of the alley, and so shut out the wicked world around them. But that whole quarter of the city held many such learned, well-born, well-doing folk. Hussan Askari's house lay within a stone's throw of the Mufti's Alley; Ahsan-Oolah's not far off, and, all about, rose tall, windowless buildings, standing sentinel blindly over the naughtiness around them; but they had eyes within, and ears also. So the hands belonging to them were held up in horror over the doings of the survival, and—despite race and religion— an inevitably reluctant, yet inevitably firm adherence was given to civilization. Even the womenfolk on the high roofs knew something of the mysterious woman across the sea, who reigned over the Huzoors and made them pitiful to women. And Farkhoonda Zamâni read the London news, with great interest, in the newspaper which Abool-Bukr used to bring her regularly. Hers was the highest roof of all, save one at the back of her veranda room; so close to it indeed that the same *neem* tree touched both.

It was not a quarter, therefore, in which the leader of the fastest set in the palace might have been expected to be a constant visitor. But he was. And the decorous alley put up with his songs patiently. Partly, no doubt, for his aunt's sake; more for his own charm of manner, which always gained him a consideration better men might have lacked. Being the late heir-apparent's eldest son, he was certain of succeeding to the throne if he outlived all his uncles; for the claims of the elder generation are, by Moghul law, paramount over those of the younger. Now, the inevitable harking back to the eldest branch, after years of power enjoyed by the junior ones, which this plan necessitates, being responsible for half the wars and murders which mark an Indian succession, some of these learned progressive folk admitted tentatively that the Western plan was better; and that if Prince Abool-Bukr were only other than he was, he might as well succeed now as later on.

The idea roused a like ambition in the young idler, now and again, but as a rule he was content to be the best musician in Delhi, the boldest gambler, the fastest liver. Yet through all, he kept his hold on one kind woman's hand; and those who knew the prince and princess have never a word to say against the friendship which led to that singing of Omar Khayyam upon the latticed roof.

" Life could be better than that for thee, nephew, didst thou but choose," said her soft voice, interrupting the cynicism, while her delicate fingers, touching the singer's shoulder as if in reproof, lingered there tenderly. He bent his smooth cheek impulsively to caress the hand so close to it, with a frank, boyish action. The next moment, however, he had started to his feet; the minor tone changed to a dance measure, then ended in a wild discord, and a wilder laugh. Her use of the word nephew was apt to rouse his recklessness, for she was but a month or two older than he.

" Thou canst not make me other than I was born——" he began; but she interrupted him quickly.

" Thou wast born of good parts enough, God knows."

" But my father deemed me fool, therefore I was brought up in a stable, mine aunt; and sang in brothels ere I knew what the word meant. So 'tis sheer waste time to interview my scandalized relations as thou dost, and beg them to take me serious. By all the courtesans in the Thunbi Bazaar, Newâsi, I take not myself so. Nor am I worse than the holy, pious aunt: I take paradise now, and leave hell to the last. They choose the other way. And make a better bargain for pleasure than I, seeing that the astrologers give me a short life, a bloody death."   •

Newâsi caught her hand back to another resting place above her heart. "A—a bloody death!" she echoed; " who—who told the lie?"

Prince Abool-Bukr shook his head with a kindly smile. " Oh! heed it not, kind lady. Such is the fashion with soothsayers nowadays. The heavens are black with portents. Someone's cow hath three calves, someone's child hath ten noses and a tail. Fire hath come from heaven—thou thyself didst tell me some such wind-sucker's tale—or from hell more likely——"

" Nay! but it is true," she interrupted eagerly; " I had it from the milkwoman, who comes from the village where the *suttee*——"

" The mouse began to gnaw the rope. The rope began to bend the ox. The ox began——" hummed the prince irreverently.

Newâsi stamped her foot. " But it *is* true, scoffer! There is a festival of it to-day in some idol temple—may it be defiled! The widow would have burned, after sin-ful custom, but was prevented by the Huzoors. And rightly. Yet, God knows—seeing the poor soul had to burn sometime through being an idolater—they might have let her burn with her love——"

Abool laughed softly. " And yet thou wilt have naught of Hafiz—Hafiz the love-lorn! Verily, Newâsi, thou art true woman."

She ignored the interruption. " So being hindered she went to Benares, and there this fire fell on her through prayer, and burned hands and feet——"

" But not her face," cried Prince Abool, thrumming the muted strings and making them sound like a tom-tom. " I'll wager my best pigeon, not her face, if she be a good-looking wench! And since fire follows on other things besides prayer, she was a fool not to get it, like me, through pleasure instead. To burn a virgin! What a dreary tale! Look not so shocked, Newâsi! a man must enjoy these presents, when folk around him waste half the time in dreaming of a future—of some-thing better to come—as thou dost——" He paused, and a soft eager ring came to his voice. " If thou couldst only forget all that—forget who I might be in the years to come—forget what thou wouldst have been had my respected uncle not preferred peace to pleasure—for it never came to pass, remember, it never came to pass

—then we two, you and I——" He paused again, perhaps at the sudden shrinking in her eyes, and gave a restless laugh. "As 'tis, the present must suffice," he added lightly, "and even so thou dost mourn for what I might be if the grace of God took me unawares. Thou hast caught the dreaming trick, mayhap, from the Prince of Dreamers yonder."

He moved over to the outer parapet and waved his hand toward Hussan Askuri's house. Then his vagrant attention turned swiftly to something which he could see in a peep of bazaar visible from this new point of view.

"Three, four, five trays of sweetstuffs! and one of milk and butter," he cried eagerly, "and by my corn-merchant's bill—which I must pay soon or starve—the carriers are palace folk! Is there, by chance, a marriage in the clan? Why didst not tell me before, Newâsi? then I could have gone as musician and earned a few rupees."

He gave a flourish of his bow, so drawing forth a lugubrious wail from the long-necked fiddle.

"No marriage that I wot of," she replied, smiling fondly over his heedless gayety. "The trays will be going to the *Pir*-sahib's house. They have gone every Thursday these few weeks past, ever since the Queen took ill on hearing the answer about the heirship. She vowed it then every week, so that the holy man's prayer might bring success to our cousin of Persia in this war. God save the very dust of it from the winds of misfortune so long as dust and wind exist," she added piously.

Prince Abool-Bukr turned round on her sharply with anxiety in his face.

"So! Thou too canst quote the proclamation like other fools—a fool's message to other fools. Where didst thou see it?"

Newâsi looked at him disdainfully. "Can I not read, nephew, and are there many in Delhi as heedless as thou? Why, even the Mufti's people discuss such things."

He shrugged his shoulders. "Ay! they will talk. Gossip hath a double tongue and wings too, nowadays. In old time the first tellers of a tale had half forgot it, ere

the last hearer heard it; now the whole world is agog
in half an hour. But it means naught. Even his heirship. Who cares in Delhi? None!—out of the palace,
none! Not even I. Yet mischief may come of it; so
have naught to do with dreamings, Newâsi, if only for
my sake. Remember the old saw, ' Weevils are ground
with the corn.' "

" Thou canst scarce call thyself that, Abool, and thou
so near the throne," she said, still more coldly.

" Have me what pleaseth thee, kind one," he replied,
a trifle impatiently; " but remember also that ' the body
is slapped in the killing of mosquitoes.' " Then, suddenly, an odd change came to his mobile face. It grew
strained, haggard; his voice had a growing tremor in it.
" Lo! I tell thee, Newâsi, that Sheeah woman, Zeenut
Maihl, in her plots for that young fool, her son, will hang
the lot of us. I swear I feel a rope around my neck each
time I think of her. I who only want to be let live as I
like—not to die before my time—die and lose all the love
and the laughter; die mayhap in the sunlight; die when
there is no need; I seem to see it—the sunlight—and I
helpless—helpless! "

He hid his face in his shuddering hands as if to shut
out some sight before his very eyes.

" Abool! Abool! What is't, dear? Look not so
strange," she cried, stretching out her hand toward him,
yet standing aloof as if in vague alarm. Her voice
seemed to bring him back to realities; he looked up with
a reckless laugh.

" 'Tis the wine does it," he said. " If I lived sober—
with thee, mine aunt—these terrors would not come.
Nay! be not frightened. Hanging is a bloodless death,
and that would confound the soothsayer; so it cuts both
ways. And now, since I must have more wine or weep,
I will leave thee, Newâsi."

" For the bazaar? " she asked reproachfully.

" For life and laughter. Lo! Newâsi, thou thyself
wouldst laugh at those new-come Bunjârah folk I told
thee of, who imitate the sahibs so well. But for their
eyes," here he nodded gayly to someone below, " they

should get one of Mufti's folk to play," he added, his
attention as usual following the first lead. "Saw you
ever such blue ones as the boy has yonder?"

Newâsi, drawing her veil tighter, stepped close to
his side and peered gingerly.

"His sister's are as blue, his cousin's also. It runs in
the blood, they say. I cannot like them. Dost thou
not prefer the dark also?"

She raised hers to his innocently enough, then shrank
back from the sudden passion of admiration she saw blazing in them. Shrank so that her arm touched his no
longer. The action checked him, made him savage.

"I like black ones best," he said insolently; "big, black,
staring eyes such as my mother swears my betrothed
has to perfection. Thou hast not seen her yet, Newâsi;
so thou canst keep me company in imagining them lan-
guishing with love. They will not have to languish long
for—hast thou heard it? The King hath fixed the wedding." He paused, then added in a low, cruel voice,
"Art glad, Newâsi?"

But her temper could be roused too, and her heart had
beat in answer to his look in a way which ended calm.
"Ay! It will stop this farce of coming thither for study
and learning—as to-day—without a line scanned."

"Thou dost study enough for both, as thou art virtuous enough for both," he retorted. "I am but flesh and
blood, and my small brain will hold no more than it can
gather from bazaar tongues."

"Of lies, doubtless."

"Lies if thou wilt. But they fill the mind as easily as
truth, and fit facts better. As the lie the courtesans tell of
my coming hither fits fact better than thy reason. Dost
know it? Shall I tell it thee?"

"Yea! tell it me," she answered swiftly, her whole face
ablaze with anger, pride, resentment. His matched it,
but with a vast affection and admiration added which
increased his excitement. "The lie, did I say?" he
echoed, "nay, the truth. For why do I come? Why
dost let me come? Answer me in truth?" There was
an instant's silence, then he went on recklessly: "What
need to ask? We both know. And why, in God's name,

having come—come to see thy soft eyes, hear thy soft voice, know thy soft heart, do I go away again like a fool? I who take pleasure elsewhere as I choose. I will be a fool no longer. Nay! do not struggle. I will but force thee to the truth. I will not even kiss thee—God knows there are women and to spare for that—there is but one woman whom Abool-Bukr cares to——" he broke off, flung the hands he had seized away from him with a muttered curse, and stepped back from her, calming himself with an effort. "That comes of making Abool-Bukr in earnest for once. Did I not warn thee it was not wise?" he said, looking at her almost reproachfully, as she stood trying to be calm also, trying to hide the beating of her heart.

"'Tis not wise, for sure, to speak foolishness," she murmured, attempting unconsciousness. "Yet do I not understand——"

He shook his delicate hand in derisive denial. "Why, the Princess Farkhoonda refuses to marry! Nay, Newâsi, we are two fools for our pains. That is God's truth between us. So now for lies in the bazaar."

"Peace go with thee." There was a sudden regret, almost a wistful entreaty in the farewell she sent after him. There was none in his reply, given with a backward look as his gay figure went downward dizzily. "Nay! Peace stays ever with thee."

It was true. Those other women of whom he had spoken gave him kisses galore, but this one? It was a refinement of sensuality, in a way, to go as he had come. But Newâsi went back to her books with a sigh, telling herself that her despondency was due to Abool's hopeless lack of ambition. If he would only show his natural parts, only let these new rulers see that he had the makings of a king in him! As for the other foolishness, if the old King would give his consent—if it were made clear that she was not really—— She pulled herself up with a start, said a prayer or two, and went on with *The Mirror of Good Behavior*, through which she was wading diligently. The writer of it had not been a beautiful woman, widowed before she was a wife, but his ideals were high.

Abool-Bukr meanwhile was already in a house with a wooden balcony. There were many such in the Thunbi Bazaar, giving it an airiness, a cleanliness, a neatness it would otherwise have lacked. But Gul-anâri's was the biggest, the most patronized; not only for the tired heads which looked out unblushingly from it, but for the news and gossip always to be had there. The lounging crowds looked up and asked for it, as they drifted backward and forward aimlessly, indifferently, among the fighting quails in their hooded cages, the dogs snarling in the filth of the gutters, while a mingled scent of musk, and drains, and humanity steamed through the hot sunshine. Sometimes a corpse lay in the very roadway awaiting burial, but it provoked no more notice than a passing remark that Nargeeza or Yasmeena had been a good one while she lasted. For there was a hideous, horrible lack of humanity about the Thunbi Bazaar; even in the very women themselves, with their foreheads narrowed by plastered hair to a mere wedge above a bar of continuous eyebrow, their lips crimsoned in unnatural curves, their teeth reddened with *pân* or studded with gold wire, their figures stiffened to artificial prominence. It was as if humanity, tired of its own beauty, sought the lack of it as a stimulant to jaded sensuality.

" Allâh! the old stale stories," yawned Gul-anâri from the broad sheet of native newspaper whence, between the intervals of some of Prince Abool-Bukr's worst songs, she had been reading extracts to her illiterate clients; that being a recognized attraction in her trade. " Persia! Persia! nothing but Persia! Who cares for it? I dare swear none. Not even the woman Zeenut herself, for all her pretense of sympathy with Sheeahs, who——"

" Have a care, mistress! " interrupted an arrogant looking man, who showed the peaked Afghan cap below a regimental turban. He was a sergeant in a Pathan company of the native troops cantoned outside Delhi on the Ridge, and had been bickering all the afternoon with a Rajpoot of the 38th N. I., who had ousted him in his hostess' easy affections, being therefore in an evil

temper, ready to take offense at a word. " I am of the
north—a Sheeah myself, and care not to hear them mis-
called. And I have those who would back me," he continued, glaring at the Rajpoot, who sat in the place of
honor beside the stout siren; "for yonder in the corner is another hill-tiger." He pointed to a man who had
just thanked one of the girls in Pushtoo for a glass of
sherbet she handed him.

" Hill-cat, rather! " giggled Gul-anâri. " He brought
me this one, but yesterday, from a caravan new-come to
the serai,"—she stroked the long fur of a Persian
kitten on her lap,—" and when I asked for news could
not give them. He scarce knew enough Urdu for the
settling of prices."

A coarse joke from the Rajpoot, suggesting that he
had found few difficulties of that sort in the Thunbi
Bazaar, made the sergeant scowl still more and swear
that he would get Mistress Gul-anâri the news for mere
love. Whereat he called over, in Pushtoo, to the man
in the corner, who, however, took no notice.

" He is as deaf as a lizard! " giggled Gul-anâri, enjoying the rejected one's discomfiture. " Get my friend
the corporal here to yell at him for thee, sergeant. His
voice goes further than thine! "

The favored Rajpoot squeezed the fat hand nearest to
him. " Go up and pluck him by the beard," he suggested vaingloriously, " then we might see a Pathan
fight for once."

" Thou wouldst see a fair one, which is more than thou
canst among thine own people."

" Peace! Peace! " cried the courtesan, smiling to
see both men look round for a weapon. " I'll have no
bloodshed here. Keep that for the future." She dwelt
on the last word meaningly, and it seemed to have a
soothing effect, for the sepoys contented themselves
with scowls again.

" The future? " echoed a graybeard who had been
drinking cinnamon tea calmly. " God knows there will
be wars enough in it. Didst hear, *Meean* sahib? I
have it on authority—that Jarn Larnce is to give Pesha-

wur to Dost Mohammed and take Rajpootana instead. Take it as Oude was taken and Sambalpore, and Jhansi, and all the others."

" Even so," assented a quiet looking man in spectacles. " When the last *Lât*-sahib went, he got much praise for having taken five kingdoms and given them to the Queen. The new one was told he must give more. This begins it."

" Let us see what we Rajpoots say first," cried the corporal fiercely. " 'Tis we have fought the *Sirkar's* battles, and we are not sheep to be driven against our own."

Gul-anâri leered admiringly at her new lover. " Nay! the Rajpoots are men! and 'twas his regiment, my masters, who refused to fight over the sea, saying it was not in the bond. Ay! and gained their point."

" That drop has gone over the sea itself," sneered a third soldier. " The bond is altered now. Go we must, or be dismissed. The Thakoor-*jee* would not be so bold now, I warrant."

The Rajpoot twirled his mustache to his very eyes and cocked his turban awry.

" Ay, would I! and more, if they dare touch our privilege."

Gul-anâri leered again, rousing the Pathan sergeant to mutter curses, and—as if to change the subject—cross over to the man in the corner, lay insolent hands on his shoulder, and shout a question in his ear. The man turned, met the arrogant eyes bent on him calmly, and with both hands salaamed profusely but slowly with a sort of measured rhythm. Apparently he had not caught the words and was deprecating impatience. His hands were fine hands, slender, well-shaped, and he wore a metal ring on the seal-finger. It caught the light as he salaamed.

" Louder, man, louder!" gibed the corporal. But the sergeant did not repeat the question; he stood looking at the upturned face awaiting an answer.

" Maybe he is Belooch, his speech not mine," he said suddenly, yet with a strange lack of curiosity in his tone. There was a faint quiver, as if some strain were over in the face below, and the silence was broken by a rapid sentence.

"Yea! Belooch!" he went on in a still more satisfied tone, "I know it by the twang. So there is small use in bursting my lungs."

Here Prince Abool-Bukr, who had been dozing tipsily, his head against his fiddle, woke, and caught the last words. "Ay, burst! burst like the royal kettle-drums of mine ancestors. Yet will I do my poor best to amuse the company and—and instruct them in virtue." Whereupon, with much maudlin emotion, he thrummed and thrilled through a lament on the fallen fortunes of the Moghuls written by that King of Poets his Grandpapa. Being diffuse and didactic, it was met with acclamations, and Abool, being beyond the stage of discrimination, was going on to give an encore of a very different nature, when a wild clashing of cymbals and hooting of conches in the bazaar below sent everyone to the balcony. Everyone save Abool, who, deprived of his audience, dozed off against his fiddle again, and the man from the corner who, as he took advantage of the diversion to escape, looked down at the handsome drunken face as he passed it and muttered, "Poor devil! He rode honest enough always." Then the Rajpoot's arrogant voice rising from the crush on the balcony, he paused a second in order to listen—that being his trade.

"'Tis the holy Hindu widow to whom God sent fire on her way to the festival. A saint indeed! I know her brother, one Soma, a Yadubansi Rajpoot in the 11th, new-come to Meerut."

The clashings and brayings were luckily loud enough to hide an irrepressible exclamation from the man behind. The next instant he was halfway down the dark stairs, tearing off cap, turban, beard, and pausing at the darkest corner to roll his baggy northern drawers out of sight, and turn his woolen green shawl inside out, thus disclosing a cotton lining of ascetic ochre tint. It was the work of a second, for Jim Douglas had been an apt pupil. So, with a smear of ashes from one pocket, a dab of turmeric and vermilion from another—put on as

he finished the stairs—he emerged into the street disguised as a mendicant; the refuge of fools, as Tiddu had
called it. The easiest, however, to assume at an instant's
notice; and in this case the best for the procession
Jim Douglas meant to join. Careless and hurried
though his get-up was, he set the very thought of detection from him as he edged his way among the streaming crowd. For in that, so he told himself, lay the
Mysterious Gift. To be, even in your inmost thoughts,
the personality you assumed was the secret. Somehow
or another it impressed those around you, and even if a
challenge came there was no danger if the challenger
could be isolated—brought close, as it were, to your own
certainty. To this, so it seemed to him—the many-
faced one vehemently protesting—came all Tiddu's
mysterious instructions, which nevertheless he followed
religiously. For, be they what they might, they had
never failed him during the six months, save once, when,
watching a horse-race, he had lost or rather recovered
himself in the keen interest it awakened. Then his
neighbors had edged from him and stared, and he had
been forced into slipping away and changing his personality; for it was one of Tiddu's maxims that you should
always carry that with you which made such change
possible. To be many-faced, he said, made all faces
more secure by taking from any the right of perma-
nence. Jim Douglas therefore joined the procession
and forced his way to the very front of it, where the red-
splashed figure of Durga Devi was being carried shoulders high. It was garlanded with flowers and censed
by swinging censers, and behind it with widespread
arms to show her sacred scars walked Tara. She was
naked to the waist, and the scanty ochre-tinted cloth
folded about her middle was raised so as to show the
scars upon her lower limbs. The sunlight gleaming on
the magnificent bronze curves showed a seam or two
upon her breast also. No more. As Abool-Bukr had
prophesied, her face, full of wild spiritual exaltation,
was unmarred and, with the shaven head, stood out bold
and clear as a cameo.

Jai! Jai! Durga mai ke jai (Victory to Mother
Durga).

The cry came incessantly from her lips, and was
echoed not only by the procession, but by the spectators.
So from many a fierce throat besides the corporal's, who
from Gul-anâri's balcony shouted it frantically, that
appeal to the Great Death Mother—implacable, athirst
for blood—came to light the sordid life of the bazaar
with a savage fire for something unknown—horribly
unknown, that lay beyond life. Even the Mohammedans, though they spat in the gutter at the idol, felt
their hearts stir; felt that if miracles were indeed abroad
their God, the only true One, would not shorten His
Hand either.

Jai! Jai! Durga mai ke jai.

The cry met with a sudden increase of volume as, the
procession passing into the wider space before the big
mosque, it was joined by a band of widows, who in rap-
turous adoration flung themselves before Tara's feet so
that she might walk over them if need be, yet somehow
touch them.

" Pigs of idolators! " muttered one of a group standing on the mosque steps; a group of men unmistakable
in their flowing robes and beards.

" Peace, *Kazi*-sahib! " came a mellow voice. " Let
God judge when the work is done. ' The clay is base,
and the potter mean, yet the pot helps man to wash and
be clean.' "

The speaker, a tall, gaunt man, rose a full head above
the others, and Jim Douglas' keen eyes, taking in everything as they passed, recognized him instantly. It was
the Moulvie of Fyzabad. It was partly to hear what he
had to say when he was preaching, partly to find out
how the people viewed the question of the heirship, which
had brought Jim Douglas to Delhi, so he was not surprised.

And now the procession, reaching the Dareeba, that
narrowest of lanes hedged by high houses, received a
momentary check. For down it, preceded by grooms
with waving yak tails, came the Resident's buggy. He
was taking a lady to see the picturesque sights of the
city. This was one, with a vengeance, as the red-
splashed figure of the Death-Goddess jammed itself in the

gutter to let the aliens pass, so getting mixed up with a Mohammedan sign-board. And the crowd following it,—an ignorant crowd agape for wonders,—stood for a minute, hemmed in, as it were, between the buggy in front and the mosque behind, with that group of Moulvies on its steps.

> " Fire worship for a hundred years,
> A century of Christ and tears,
> Then the True God shall come again
> And every infidel be slain,"

quoted he of Fyzabad under his breath, and the others nodded. They knew the prophecy of Shah N'amut-Oolah well. It was being bandied from mouth to mouth in those days; for the Mohammedan crowd was also agape for wonders.

CHAPTER III.

ON THE RIDGE.

" A MELLY Klistmus to zoo, Miffis Erlton! An' oh! they's suts a lot of boo'ful, boo'ful sings in a velanda."

Sonny's liquid lisp said true. On this Christmas morning the veranda of Major Erlton's house on the Ridge of Delhi was full of beauties to childish eyes. For, he being on special duty regarding a scheme for cavalry remounts and having Delhi for his winter headquarters, there were plenty of contractors, agents, troopers, dealers, what not, to be remembered by one who might probably have a voice in much future patronage. So there were trays on trays of oranges and apples, pistachios, almonds, raisins, round boxes of Cabul grapes, all decked with flowers. And on most of them, as the surest bid for recognition, lay a trumpery toy of some sort for the Major sahib's little unknown son, whose existence could, nevertheless, not be ignored by these gift-bringers, to whom children are the greatest gift of all.

And so, as they waited, with a certain child-like com-

placency in their own offerings, for the recipients' tardy
appearance, they had smiled on little Sonny Seymour as
he passed them on his way to give greeting to his dearest
Mrs. Erlton. For the Seymours had had the expected
change to Delhi, and Sonny's mother was now· com-
plaining of the climate, and the servants, and the babies,
in one of the houses within the Cashmere gate of the
city; a fact which took from her the grievance regarding
dog-carts, since it lay within a walk of her husband's
office.

So some of the smiles had not simply been given to a
child, but to a child whose father was a sahib known to
the smiler; and one broad grin had come because Sonny
had paused to say, with the quaint precision with which
all English children speak Hindustani.

"*Ai! Bij Rao! tu kyon aie?*" (Oh, Bij Rao, why
are you here?) The orderly's face, which Mrs. Seymour had said gave her the shivers, had beamed over the
recognition; he had risen and saluted, explaining gravely
to the *chota* sahib that he came from Meerut, because the
Major sahib was now his sahib for the time. Sonny had
nodded gravely as if he understood the position perfectly, and passed on to the drawing room, where Kate
Erlton was sticking a few sprigs of holly and mistletoe
round the portrait of another fair-haired boy; these same
sprigs being themselves a Christmas offering from the
Parsee merchant, who had a branch establishment at a
hill station. He sent for them from the snows every
year for his customers as a delicate attention. And this
year something still more reminiscent of home had
come with them: a real spruce fir for the Christmas tree
which Kate Erlton was organizing for the school children. The tree in itself was new to India, and she had
suggested a still greater innovation; namely, that all
children of parents employed in Government offices or
workshops should be invited, not only those with pretensions to white faces. For Kate, being herself far
happier and more contented than she had been nine
months before, when she begged that last chance from
Jim Douglas, had begun to look out from her own
life into the world around her with greater interest. In

a way, it seemed to her that the chance had come. Not tragically, as Jim Douglas had hinted, but easily, naturally, in this special duty which had removed her husband both from Alice Gissing and his own past reputation.

It had sent him to Simla, where people are accepted for what they are; and here his good looks, his good-natured, devil-may-care desire for amusement had made him a favorite in society, and his undoubted knowledge of cavalry requirements stood him in good stead with the authorities. So he had come down for the winter to Delhi on a new track altogether. To begin with, his work interested him and made him lead a more wholesome life. It took him away from home pretty often, so lessening friction; for it was pleasant to return to a well-ordered house after roughing it in out-stations. Then it took him into the wilds where there was no betting or card-playing. He shot deer and duck instead, and talked of caps and charges, instead of colors and tricks. To his vast improvement; for though the slaying instinct may not be admirable in itself, and though the hunter may rightly have been branded from the beginning with the mark of Cain, still the shooter or fisher generally lives straighter than his fellows, and murder is not the most heinous of crimes. Not even in regard to the safety and welfare of the community.

So Kate had begun to have those pangs of remorse which come to women of her sort at the first symptom of regeneration in a sinner. Pangs of pitiful consideration for the big, handsome fellow who could behave so nicely when he chose, vague questionings as to whether the past had not been partly her fault; whether if this were the chance, she ought not to forget and forgive— many things.

He looked very handsome as he lounged in, dressed spick and span in full uniform for church parade. And she, poised on a chair, her dainty ankles showing, looked spick and span also in a pretty new dress. He noticed the fact instantly.

"A merry Christmas, Kate! Here! give me your hand and I'll help you down."

How many years was it since he had spoken like that, with a glint in his eyes, and she had had that faint flush in her cheek at his touch? The consciousness of this stirring among the dry bones of something they had both deemed dead, made her set to shaking some leaves from her dress, while he, with an irrelevantly boisterous laugh, stooped to swing Sonny to his shoulder. " You here, jackanapes! " he cried. " A merry Christmas! Come and get a sweetie—you come too, Kate, the beggars will like to see the *mem*. By Jove! what a jolly morning! "

A foretaste of the winter rains had fallen during the night, leaving a crisp new-washed feeling in the air, a heavy rime-like dew on the earth; the sky of a pale blue, yet colorful, vaulted the wide expanse cloudlessly. And from the veranda of the Erltons' house the expanse was wide indeed; for it stood on the summit of the Ridge at its extreme northern end—the end, therefore, furthest from the city, which, nearly three miles away, blocked the widening wedge of densely wooded lowland lying between the rocky range and the river. The Ridge itself was not unlike some huge spiny saurian, basking in the sunlight; its tail in the river, its wider, flatter head, crowned by Hindoo Rao's house, resting on the groves and gardens of the Subz-mundi or Green Market, a suburb to the west of the town. It is a quaint, fanciful spot, this Delhi Ridge, even without the history of heroism crystallized into its very dust. A red dust which might almost have been stained by blood. A dust which matches that history, since it is formed of isolated atoms of rock, glittering, perfect in themselves, like the isolated deeds which went to make up the finest record of pluck and perseverance the world is ever likely to see. Perseverance and pluck which sent more Englishmen to die cheerfully in that red dust than in the defenses and reliefs of Lucknow, Cawnpore, and the subsequent campaigns all combined. Let the verdict on the wisdom of those months of stolid endurance be what it may, that fact remains.

And the quaintness of the Ridge lies in its individuality. Not eighty feet above the river, its gradients so slight that a driver scarce slackens speed at its steepest, there is never a mistake possible as to where it begins or ends. Here is the river bed, founded on sand; there, cleaving the green with rough red shoulder, is the ridge of rock.

From the veranda, then, its stony spine split by a road like a parting, it trended southwest, so giving room between it and the river for the rose-lit, lilac-shaded mass of the town, with the big white bubble of the Jumma mosque in its midst; the delicate domes fringing the palace gateways showing like strings of pearls on the blue sky. And beyond them, a dazzle of gold among the green of the Garden of Grapes, marked that last sanctuary of a dead dynasty upon the city's eastern wall.

The cantonments lay to the back of the house on the western slope of the Ridge and on the plain beyond. This also was a widening wedge of green wooded land cut off from the rest of the plain by a tree-set overflow canal. The Ridge, therefore, formed the backbone of a triangle protected by water on two sides. On the third was the city and its suburbs. But—to carry out the image of the lizard—a natural outwork lay like a huge paw on either side of the head; on the river side the spur of Ludlow Castle, on the canal side the General's mound.

A brisk breeze was fluttering the flag on the tower cresting the ridge, a few hundred yards from the house, and as Major Erlton stepped into the veranda, a puff of white smoke curled cityward, and the roll of the time-gun reverberated among the rocks.

" By Jingo! I must hurry up if I'm to have breakfast before church," he exclaimed, as the circle of gift-bringers, who had been waiting nearly half an hour, rose simultaneously with salaams and good wishes. The sudden action made a white cockatoo perched in the corner raise its flame-colored crest and begin to prance.

" Naughty Poll! Bad Poll! " came Sonny's mellifluous lisp from the Major's shoulder. " Zoo mufn't make a noise and interrupt."

The admonition made the bird smooth its ruffled temper and feathers. Not that there was much to interrupt; the Major's halting acknowledgments being of the briefest; partly because of breakfast, partly from lack of Hindustani, mostly from the inherent insular horror of a function.

"Thank God! that's over," he said piously, when the last tray had been emptied on the miscellaneous pile, round which the servants were already hovering expectantly, and the last well-wisher had disappeared. "Still it was nice of them to remember Freddy," he added, looking at the toys—"Wasn't it, wife?"

She looked up almost scared at the title. "Very," she replied, with a faint quiver in her voice. "We must send some home to him, mustn't we?"

The pronoun of union made the Major, in his turn, feel embarrassed. He sought refuge once more in Sonny.

"You must have your choice first, jackanapes!" he said, swinging the child to the ground again. "Which is it to be? A box of soldiers or a monkey on a stick?"

"Fanks!" replied Sonny with honest dignity, "but I'se gotted my plesy already. She's give-ded me the polly—be-tos it 'oves me dearly."

Kate answered her husband's look with a half-apology. "He means the cockatoo. I thought you wouldn't mind, because it was so dreadfully noisy. And it never screams at him. Sonny! give Polly an apple and show Major Erlton how it loves you."

The child, nothing loth to show off, chose one from the heap and went over fearlessly to the vicious bird; the servants pausing to look admiringly. The cockatoo seized it eagerly, but only as a means to draw the little fellow's arm within reach of its clambering feet. The next moment it was on the narrow shoulder dipping and sidling among the golden curls.

"See how it 'oves me," cried Sonny, his face all smiles.

Major Erlton laughed good-temperedly at the pretty sight and went in to breakfast.

Then the dog-cart came round. It was the same one in which the Major had been used to drive Alice Gissing. But this Christmas morning he had forgotten the fact, as he drove Kate instead, with Sonny, who was to be taken to church as a great treat, crushing the flounces of her pretty dress.

Yet the fresh wind blew in their faces keenly, and the Major, pointing with his whip to the scudding squirrels, said, " Jolly little beasts, aren't they, Kate," just as he had said it to Alice Gissing. What is more, she replied that it was jolly altogether, with much the same enjoyment of the mere present as the other little lady had done. For the larger part of life is normal, common to all.

So they sped past the rocks and trees swiftly, down and down, till with a rumble they were on the drawbridge, through the massive arch of the Cashmere gate. into the square of the main-guard. The last clang of the church bell seemed to come from the trees overhanging it, and in the ensuing silence a sharp click of the whip sounded like a pistol crack. The mare sped faster through the wooden gate into the open. To the left the Court House showed among tall trees, to the right Skinner's House. Straight ahead, down the road to the Calcutta gate and the boat bridge, stood the College, the telegraph office, a dozen or so of bungalows in gardens, and the magazine shouldering the old cemetery. Quite a colony of Western ways and works within the city wall, clinging to it between the water-bastion and the Calcutta gate.

Close at hand in a central plot of garden, circled by roads, was the church, built after the design of St. Paul's; obtrusively Occidental, crowned by a very large cross.

As the mare drew up among the other carriages, the first notes of the Christmas hymn pealed out among the roses and the pointsettias, the glare and the green. Not a Christmas environment; but the festival brings its own atmosphere with it to most people, and Major Erlton, admiring his wife's rapt face, remembered his own boyhood as he sang a rumbling Gregorian bass of two tones and a semi-tone:

" Oh come, all ye faithful !   Joyful and triumphant."

The words echoed confidently into the heart of the great Mohammedan stronghold, within earshot almost of the rose-red walls of the palace; that survival of all the vices Christianity seeks to destroy.

"They have a new service to-night," yawned the chaplain's groom to others grouped round a common pipe. "I, who have served *padrés* all my life—the pay is bad but the kicks less—saw never the like. 'Tis a queer tree hung with lights, and toys to bribe the children to worship it. They wanted mine to go, but their mother is pious and would not. She says 'tis a spell."

"Doubtless!" assented a voice. "The spell Kali's priest, who came from Calcutta seeking aid against it, warned us of—the spell which forces a body to being Christian against his will."

A scornful cluck came from a younger, smarter man. "Trra! a trick that for offerings, Dittu. The priest came to me also, but I told him my master was not that sort. He goes not to church except on the big day."

"But the *mem?*" asked a new speaker enviously. "'Tis the *mems* do the mischief to please the *padres;* just as our women do it to please the priests. My *mem* reads prayers to her ayah."

"Paremeshwar be praised!" ejaculated the man to whom the pipe belonged. "My master keeps no *mem*, but the other sort. Though as for the ayah it matters not, she has no caste to lose."

There was a grunt of general assent. The remark crystallized the whole question to unmistakable form. So long as a man could get a pull from his neighbor's pipe and have a right to one in return, the master might say and do what he chose. If not; then——?

An evil-faced man who still smarted from a righteous licking, given him that morning for stealing his horse's grain, put his view of what would happen in that case plainly.

"Bullah!" sneered a bearded Sikh orderly waiting to carry his master's prayer-book. "You Poorbeahs can talk glibly of change. And why not? seeing it is but a change of masters to born slaves. Oil burns to butter! butter to oil!"

' The evil face scowled. " Thou wilt have to shave
under thy master, anyhow, Gooroo-jee! Ay! and dock
thy pigtail too."

This allusion to a late ruling against the Nazarene customs of the newly raised Sikh levies might have led to
blows—the bearded one being a born fighter—if, the
short service coming to an end, the masters had not
trooped out, pausing to exchange Christmas greetings
ere they dispersed.

" Never saw Mrs. Erlton looking so pretty," remarked
Captain Seymour to his wife, as, with the restored Sonny
between them, they moved off to their own house, which
stood close by, plumb on the city wall. He spoke in a
low voice, but Major Erlton happened to be within earshot. He turned complacently to identify the speaker,
then looked at his wife to see if the remark was true.
Scarcely; to Herbert Erlton's quickened recollection of
the girl he had married. Yet she looked distinctly
creditable, desirable, as she stood, the center of a little
group of men and women eager to help her with the
Christmas tree. It struck him suddenly, not in the least
unpleasantly, that of late his wife had had no lack of
aids-de-camp, and that one, Captain Morecombe, the
pick of the lot, seemed to have little else to do. A symptom which the Major could explain from his own experience, and which made him smile; he being of those
who admire women for being admired.

" I have arranged about the conjuror, Mrs. Erlton,"
said Captain Morecombe, who was, indeed, quite ready
to do her behests; " that sweep, Prince Abool-bukr,—
who is coming, by the way, to see the show,—has promised me the best in the bazaar. And some Bunjârah
fellows who act, and that sort of business."

" Better find out first what they do act," put in young
Mainwaring, who chafed under the superior knowledge
which the Captain claimed as interpreter to the Staff.
" I saw some of those brutes in Lucknow last spring,
and——"

" Oh! there is no fear," retorted the other with a con-
descending smile. " The Prince is no fool, and he is
responsible. It will most likely be something extremely

instructive. Now, Mrs. Erlton, I will drive you round
to the College and you can show me anything else you
want done. I can drive you home afterward."

" Don't think we need trouble you, thanks, Morecombe," said a voice behind. " I'll drive my wife. I'll
stay as long as you like, Kate; and I can stick things
high up, you know."

There was no appeal in his tone, but Kate, looking up
at his great height, felt one; and with it came a fresh
spasm of that self-reproach. As she had knelt beside
him in church she had been asking herself if she was
not unforgiving; if it was not hard on him.

" That will be a great help," she said soberly.

So Mrs. Seymour, coming in daintily when the hard
work was over to put a Father Christmas on the topmost
shoot, wondered plaintively how she could have managed it without Major Erlton, and put so much soft
admiration into her pretty eyes, that he could scarcely
fail to feel a fine fellow. He was in consequence a
better one for the time being. So that he insisted on returning in the afternoon to hand the tea and cake, when
he made several black-and-tan matrons profusely apologetic and proud at having the finest gentleman there to
wait upon them. For the Major was a very fine animal,
indeed. As Alice Gissing had told him frankly, over and
over again, his looks were his strong point.

The larger portion of the guests were of this black-
and-tan complexion. Of varying shades, however, from
the unmistakably pure-blooded native Christian, to the
pasty-faced baby with all the yellow tones of skin due to
its pretty, languid mother, emphasized by the ruddiness
of the English father who carried it.

They came chiefly from Duryagunj, a quarter of the
city close to the Palace, between the river and the Thunbi
Bazaar. It had once been the artillery lines, and now
its pleasant garden-set houses were occupied by clerks,
contractors, overseers, and such like. Then later on,
for the sports and games, came a contingent of College
lads, speaking English fluently, and younger boys
clinging affrightedly to their father's hand as he smirked
and bowed to the special master for whose favor he had

perhaps braved bitter tears of opposition from the women at home. The mission school sent orderly bands, and there was a ruck of servants' children, who would have gone to the gates of hell for a gift.

"You will tire yourself to death, Kate," called her husband, as, quite in his element, he handicapped the boys for the races. He spoke in a half-satisfied, half-dissatisfied tone, for though her success pleased him, he fancied she looked less dainty, less attractive.

"Come and see the play," suggested Captain Morecombe, who did not seem to notice anything amiss. "It will be rest, and we needn't light up yet a while."

"I'm going wis zoo," said Sonny confidently, escaping from his ayah as they passed; so, with the child's hand in hers, Kate went on into the long narrow veranda which had been inclosed by tent-walls as a theater. Open to the sunlight at the entrance, it was dark enough to make a swinging lamp necessary at the further end. There was no stage, no scenery, only a coarse cotton cloth with indistinguishable shadows and lights on it hung over a rope at the very end. The place was nearly empty. A few native lads squatted in front, a bench or two held a sprinkling of half-castes, and at the entrance a group of English ladies and gentlemen waited for the performance to begin, laughing and talking the while.

"You look quite done," said Captain Morecombe tenderly, as Kate sank back in the armchair he placed for her halfway down, where a chink of light and air came through a slit in the canvas.

"I didn't feel tired before," she replied dreamily. "I suppose it is the quiet, and the giving in. Tell me about the play, please," she went on more briskly. "If I don't know something of the plot before it begins, I shall not understand."

"I expect you will," he began; but at that moment a cry for Captain Morecombe arose, and to his infinite anger he had to go off and interpret for the Colonel and Prince Abool-Bukr, who had just arrived. Kate, to tell truth, felt relieved. After the clamor outside, and the constant appeals to her, the peace within was delightful. She leaned back, with Sonny in her arms, feeling so disposed for sleep that her husband's loud voice coming through the chink startled her.

"Can't possibly take that into consideration. The race must be run on the runners' own merits only."

He was only, she knew, laying down the law of handicaps to some dissentient; but the words thrilled her. Poor Herbert! What had *his* merits been? And then she wondered how long it had been since she had thought of him thus by his Christian name, as it were. Would it be possible——

"It's a story of Fate, really," said one of the spectators at the entrance, to the ladies who were with him; his voice clearly audible in a sudden hush which had come to the dim veranda that grew dimmer and dimmer to the end, despite the swinging lamp. "A sort of miracle play, called 'The Lord of Life, and the Lord of Death.' Yama and Indra of course. I saw it two days ago, and one of the actors is the best pantomimist— That's the man—now."

Kate turned her eyes instinctively to the open space which was to do duty as a stage. The play had begun; must have been going on while she was thinking, for a scene was in full swing. A scene? A misnomer that, surely! when there was no scenery, nothing but that strange dim curtain with its indefinite lights and shadows. Or was there some meaning in the dabs and splashes after all? Was that a corn merchant's shop? Yes, there were the gleaming pots, the cavernous shadows, the piled baskets of flour and turmeric and pulse, the odd little strings of dried cocoanuts and pipe cups, the blocks of red rock-salt. And that—she gave an odd little sigh of certainty—was the corn merchant himself selling flour, with a weighted balance, to a poor widow. What magnificent pantomime it was!. And what a relief that it was pantomime; so leaving her no whit behind anyone in comprehension; but the equal of all the world, as far as this story was concerned. And it was unmistakable. She seemed to hear the chink of money, to see the juggling with the change, the substitution of inferior flour for that chosen; the whole give and take of cheating, till the ill-gotten gain was clutched tight, and the robbed woman turned away patiently, unconsciously.

An odd, doubtful murmur rose among the squatting boys, checked almost as it began; for the shadowy curtain behind wavered, seemed to grow dimmer, to curve in cloud-like festoons, and then disclosed a sitting figure.

There was a burst of laughter from the entrance. "Rum sort of God, isn't he?" came the voice again. But from the front rose an uneasy whisper. "Yama! Sri Yama himself; look at his nose!"

Viewed without reference to either remark, the figure, if quaint, almost ludicrous, did not lack dignity. There was impassiveness in the pea-green mask below the miter-like gilt tiara, and impressiveness in the immovability of the pea-green hands folded on the scarlet draperies.

"He answers to Charou, you know," went on the voice again. "I suppose it means that the *buniya-jee* will need all his ill-gotten gain to pay fare to Paradise."

Did it mean that? Kate wondered, as she leaned back clasping Sonny tighter in her arms, or was it only to show that Fate lay behind the daily life of every man. Then what a farce it was to talk of chance! Yet she had pleaded for it, till she had gained it. " Let him have his chance. Let us all have our chance. You and I into the bargain. You and I!" What made her think of that now?

A snigger from the lads in front roused her to a new scene; a serio-comic dispute, evidently, between a termagant of a mother-in-law and a tearful daughter. Kate found herself following it closely enough, even smiling at it, but Sonny shifted restlessly on her knee. " I 'ikes a funny man," he said plaintively. " Tell a funny man to come again, Miffis Erlton."

" I expect he will come soon, dear," she replied, conscious of a foolish awe behind her own words. Fate lay there also, no doubt.

It did, but as the termagant triumphed and the dutiful daughter-in-law wept over her baking, the figure

that showed wore a white mask, the rainbow-hued garments were hung with flowers, and the white hands
held a parti-colored bow.

The boys nodded and smiled. " Sri Indra himself,"
they said. " Look at his bow! "

" Who is Indra, Mr. Jones? " asked a feminine voice
from behind.

" Lord of Paradise. And that is the whole show. It
goes on and on. Some of the scenes are awfully funny,
but they wouldn't act the funniest ones here. And they
all end with the green or white dummy; so it gets a bit
monotonous. Shall we go and look at the conjurors
now? "

The voices departed; once more to Kate's relief. She
felt that the explanation spoiled the play. And that was
no dummy! She could see the same eyes through the
mask; curious, steady, indifferent eyes. The eyes of a
Fate indifferent as to what mask it wore. So the play
went on and on. Some of the Eurasians slipped away,
but the boys remained ready with awe or rejoicing, while
Kate sat by the chink through which the light came
more and more dimly as the day darkened. She scarcely
noticed the actors; she waited dreamily for the Lord of
Life or the Lord of Death; for there was never any
doubt as to which was coming. But the child in her
lap waited indiscriminately for the funny man. The
thought of the contrast struck her, making her smile.
Yet, after all, the difference only lay in the way you
looked at life. There was no possibility of change to it;
the Great Handicap was run on its own merits. And
then, like an unseen hand brushing away the cobwebs
which of late had been obscuring the unalterable facts,
like a wave collapsing her house of sand, came the
memory of words which at the time they were spoken
had made her cry out on their cruelty. " What possible
right have you or I to suppose that anything you or I can
do now will alter the initial fact? " If he—that stranger
who had stepped in and laid rude touch on her very soul,
had been the Lord of Life or Death himself, could he have
been more remorseless? And what possessed her that

she should think of him again and again; that she should wonder what his verdict would be on those vague thoughts of compromise?

"Mrs. Erlton! Mrs. Erlton, everything is ready. Everybody is waiting! I have been hunting for you everywhere. It never occurred to me you would be here after all this time. Why, you are almost alone!" Captain Morecombe's aggrieved regret was scarcely appeased by her hurried excuse that she believed she had been half-asleep. For the Christmas tree was lit to its topmost branch, the guests admitted, the drawings begun.

Perhaps it was the sudden change from dark to light, silence to clamor, which gave Kate Erlton the dazed look with which she came into that circle of radiant faces where Prince Abool-Bukr was clapping his hands like a child and thinking, as he generally did when his pleasures could be shared by virtue, of how he would describe it all to Newâsi Begum on her roof. He drew a spotless white lamb as his gift; Major Erlton its fellow, and the two men compared notes in sheer laughter, broken English, and shattered Hindustani. And through the fun and the pulling of crackers, Kate, who recovered herself rapidly, flitted here and there, arranging, deciding, setting the ball a-rolling. There was a flush on her cheek, a light in her eyes which forced other eyes to follow her, even among the packed, prying faces, peeping from every door and window at the strange sight, the strange spell. One pair of eyes in particular, belonging to a slight, clean-shaven man standing beside two others who carried bundles in their hands, and who, having come from the inside veranda, had found space to slip well to the front, They were the actors in the now forsaken drama of Life and Death. One of them, however, had evidently seen a Christmas tree before, since he suddenly called out in the purest English:

"The top branch on the left has caught! Put it out, someone!"

The sound seemed to discomfit him utterly. He looked round him quickly, then realizing that the crowd was too dense for the voice to be accurately located save by his immediate neighbors, gave a half apologetic sign to the older of his two companions and slipped away. They followed obediently, but once outside Tiddu shook his head at his pupil.

" The Huzoor will never remember to forget. He will get into trouble some day," he said reproachfully.

" Not if I stick to playing Yama and Indra," replied Jim Douglas with a shrug of his shoulders. " The Mask of Fate is apt to be inscrutable." He made the remark chiefly for his own benefit; for he was thinking of the strange chance of meeting those cold blue-gray eyes again in that fashion. Beautiful eyes, brilliant eyes! Then he smiled cynically. The chance he had given had evidently borne fruit. She seemed quite happy, and there was no mistaking the look on her owner's heavy face. So the heroics had meant nothing, and he had given up his chance for a vulgar kiss-and-make-it-up-again!

It was too dark to see that look on Major Erlton's face, but it was there, as, carrying Kate off with a certain air of proprietorship from the compliments which had grown stale, they went to find the dog-cart, which, in deference to the mare's nerves, had been told to await them in a quiet corner of the compound.

" You did it splendidly, Kate! "

His voice came contentedly through the soft darkness which hid the easy arm which slipped to her waist, the easy smiling face which bent to kiss hers.

" Oh, don't! Please don't! " The cry, almost a sob, was unmistakable. So was the start which made her stumble over an unseen edging to the path. Even Herbert Erlton with his blunted delicacy could not misjudge it. He stood silent for a moment, then gave a short hard laugh.

" You haven't hurt yourself, I expect," he said dryly, " so there's no harm done. I'll call that fellow with the lantern to give us a light."

He did, and the vague shadow preceded by a swinging light turned out to be young Mainwaring on his pony, with the groom carrying a lantern.

" Mrs. Erlton," cried the lad, slipping to the ground, " what luck! The very person I wanted. I was going round by your house on the chance of catching you, as it was useless trying to get in a quiet word this afternoon. I want to ask if you know of any houses to let! I had a letter this morning from Mrs. Gissing asking me to look out one for her."

" For her?" The echo came in a dull voice. Kate had scarcely recovered from her own recoil, from a vague doubt of what she had done.

" Yes! Her husband had to go home on business and won't be out till May. So, as the new people at Lucknow seem a poor lot, and she has old friends at Delhi——" A remembrance that some of these old friendships must be an unwelcome memory to his hearer made the boy pause. But the man, smarting with resentment, had no such scruples—what was the use of them?

" Coming here, is she?" he echoed. " Then we may hope to have some fun in this deadly-lively stuck-up place. I say, Mainwaring, would you mind driving my wife home and lending me your pony to gallop round to the mess. I must go there, and as it is getting late there is no use dragging Mrs. Erlton all that way. And she has a big Christmas dinner on, haven't you, Kate?"

As the young fellow climbed up into the dog-cart beside her, Kate Erlton knew that one chance had gone irretrievably, irrevocably. Would there be another? Suddenly in the darkness she clasped her hands tight and prayed that there might be—that it might come soon!

And round them as they drove slowly to gain the city gate, the half-seen crowd which had gathered to see the strange spell were drifting homeward to spread the tale of it from hearth to hearth.

CHAPTER IV.

IN THE VILLAGE.

THE winter rains had come and gone, leaving a legacy of gold behind them. Promise of future gold in the emerald sea of young wheat, guerdon of present gold in the mustard blossom curving on the green, like the crests of waves curving upon a wind-swept northern sea. Far and near, wide as the eye could reach, there was nothing to be seen save this—a waving sea of green wheat crested by yellow mustard. But in the center, whence the eye looked, stood a human ant-hill; for the congeries of mud alleys, mud walls, mud roofs, forming the village, looked from a little distance like nothing else. Viewed broadly, too, it was simply Earth made plastic by the Form-bringer, Water, hardened again by the Sun-fire. The triple elements combined into a shell for laboring life. Like most villages in Northern India this one stood high on its own ruins, girt round by shallow glistening tanks which were at once its cradle and its grave. From them the mud for the first and last house had been dug, to them the periodical rains of August washed back the village bit by bit.

There was scarcely a sign of life in the sky-encircled plain. Scarcely a tree, scarcely a landmark. Nothing far or near to show that aught lay beyond the pale hori-zon. The crisp, cold air of a mid-January dawn held scarcely a sound, for the village was still asleep. Here and there, maybe, someone was stirring; but with that deliberate calm which comes to those who by virtue of early rising have the world to themselves. Here and there, too, in the high stone inclosures serving at once as a protection to the village and a cattlefold, some goat, impatient to be roaming, bleated querulously; but these sights and sounds only seemed to increase the still-ness, the silence surrounding them. It is a scene which to most civilized eyes is oppressive in its self-centered isolation, its air of remoteness. The isolation of a community, self-supporting, self-sufficing, the re-moteness of a place which cares not if, indeed, there be a world beyond its boundaries. And this one, type of many alike in most things—above all, in steadfast self-absorption—shall be left nameless. We are in the vil-lage, that is enough.

Suddenly an odd, clamorous wail rang from among the green corn, and a band of gray cranes which had been standing knee-deep in the wheat rose awkwardly and headed, arrow-shaped, for the great Nujjufgurhjheel

which they wotted of below the horizon: in this display-
ing a wider outlook than the villagers who toiled and
slept within sight of those fields, while the birds left them
at dawn for the sedgy stretches of another world.

At the sound a man, who had been crouching half-
asleep against a mud wall, rose to his feet and peered
drowsily over the fields. Something, he knew, must have
startled the gray cranes; and he was the village watchman. As his father had been before him, as his son, please
God, would be after him. He carried a short spear hung
with jingles as his badge of office, and he leaned upon it
lazily as he looked out into the gray dawn. Then he
wrapped his blanket closer round him, and walked
leisurely to meet the solitary figure coming toward him,
threading its way by an invisible path through the dew-
hung sea of wheat.

" *Ari*, brother," he called mildly when he reached earshot, " is it well? "

" It is well," came the answer. So he waited, leaning
on his spear, until the newcomer stood beside him, his
bare legs glistening and the folds of his drooping blanket
frosted with the dew. In one hand he, also, held a watchman's spear; in the other one of those unleavened cakes,
round and flat like a pancake, which form the daily bread
alike of rich and poor. This he held out, saying briefly:

" For the elders. From the South to the North.
From the East to the West."

" Wherefore? " The brief reply held vague curiosity;
no more. The cake had already changed hands, unchallenged.

" God knows. It came to us from Goloowallah with
the message as I gave it. Thy folk will pass it on? "

" Likely; when the day's work is done. How go the
crops thy way? Here, as thou seest, 'tis God's dew on
God's grain."

" With us also. There will be marriages galore this
May."

" Ay! if this bring naught." The speaker nodded
toward the cake which now lay on the ground between
them, for they had inevitably squatted down to take alter-
nate pulls at a pipe. " What can it bring? "

"God knows," replied the host in his turn. So the two, with that final reference in their minds, sat looking dully at the *chupatti* as if it were some strange wild fowl. Sat silently, as men will do over a pipe, till a clinking of anklets and a chatter of feminine voices came round the corner, and the foremost woman of the troop on their way to the tank drew her veil close swiftly at sight of a stranger. Yet her voice came as swiftly. "What news, brother? What news?"

"None for thee, Mother Kirpo," answered the resident watchman tartly. "'Tis for the elders."

The titterings and tossings of veiled heads at this snub to the worst gossip in the village, ended in an expectant pause as a very old woman, with a fine-cut face which had long since forsworn concealment, stepped up to the watchman, and squatting down beside them, raised the cake in her wrinkled hands.

"From the North to the South or the South to the North. From the East to the West or the West to the East. Which?" she asked, nodding her old head.

"Sure it was so, mother," replied the stranger, surprised. "Dost know aught?"

"Know?" she echoed; "I know 'tis an old tale—an old tale."

"What is an old tale, mother?" asked the women eagerly, as, emboldened by the presence of the village spey-wife, they crowded round, eying the cake curiously.

She gave a scornful laugh, let the *chupatti* drop, and, rising to her feet, passed on to the tank. It suited her profession to be mysterious, and she knew no more than this, that once, or at most twice in her long life, such a token had come peacefully into the village, and passed out of it as peacefully with its message.

"Mai Dhunnoo knows something, for sure," commented a deep-bosomed mother of sons as the troop followed their "chaperone's" lead, closer serried than before, full of whispering surmise. "The gods send it mean not smallpox. I will give curds and sugar to thee, Mâta jee, each Friday for a year! I swear it for safety to the boys."

"He slipped in a puddle and cried 'Hail to the Ganges,'" retorted her neighbor, an ill-looking woman blind of one eye. She had been the richest heiress in the village, and was in consequence the wife of the handsomest young man in it; a childless wife into the bargain. "Boys do not fill the world, Veru; not even thine! Their welfare will not set tokens a-going. It needs some real misfortune for that."

"Then thy life is safe for sure," began the other hotly, when a peacemaker intervened.

"Wrangle not, sisters! All are naked when their clothes are gone; and the warning may be for us all. Mayhap the Toorks are coming once more—Mai Dhunnoo said 'twas an old tale. God send we be not all reft from our husbands."

"That would I never be," protested the heiress, provoking uproarious titterings among some girls.

"No such luck for poor Ramo," whispered one. "And she sonless too!"

"He shaved for the heat, and then the hail fell on his bald pate," quoted the prettiest callously. "Serve him right, say I. He, at least, had two eyes."

The burst of laughter following this sally made the peacemaker, who, as the wife of the headman, had authority, turn in rebuke. 'Twas no laughing matter to Jâtnis, as they were, who did so much of the field work, that a token, maybe of ill, should come to the village when the harvest promised so well. The revenue had to be paid, smallpox or no smallpox, Toork or no Toork. And was not one of the Huzoors in camp already giving an eye to the look of the crops, and the other to the shooting of wild things? Could they not hear the sound of his gun for themselves if they listened instead of chattering? And truly enough, in the pause which came to mirth, there echoed from the pale northern horizon, beyond which lay the big jheels, a shot or two, faint and far; for all that dealing death to some of God's creatures. And these listeners dealt death to none; their faith forbade it.

"Think you they will come our way and kill our deer as they did once?" asked a slender slip of a girl anxiously. Her tame fawn had lately taken to joining the wild ones when they came at dawn to feed upon the wheat.

"God knows," replied one beside her. "They will come if they like, and kill if they like. Are they not the masters?"

So the final reference was in the women's minds also, as, while the muddy water strained slowly into their pots through a filtering corner of their veils, they raised their eyes curiously, doubtfully, to the horizon which held the master. It had held him always. To the north or to the south, the east or the west. Mohammedan, Mahratta, Christian. But always coming over the far horizon and slaying something. In old days husbands, brothers, fathers. Nowadays the herds of deer which the sacredness of life allowed to have their full of the wheat unchecked, or the peacocks who spread their tails, securely vainglorious, on the heaps of corn upon the threshing floors.

So the unleavened cake stayed in the village all day long, and when the slant shadows brought leisure, the headman's wife baked two cakes, one for the north the other for the west, and Dittu the old watchman, and the embryo watchman his son, set off with them to the next village west and north, since that was the old custom. So much must be done because their fathers had done it; for the rest, who could tell?

Nevertheless, as the messengers passed through the village street where the women sat spinning, many paused to look after them, with a vague relief that the unknown, unsought, had gone out of their life. Then the moon rose peacefully, and one by one the sights and sounds of that life ceased. The latest of all was the hum of a mill in one of the poorest houses, and a snatch of a harvest-song in murmuring accompaniment:

> "When the sickle meets the corn,
> From their meeting joy is born ;
> When the sickle smites the wheat,
> Care is conquered, sorrow beat."

"Have a care, sister, have a care!" came that rebuking voice from the headman's house close by. "Wouldst bring ill-luck on us all, that grinding but millet thou singest the song of wheat?"

And thereinafter there was no song at all, and sleep settled on all things peacefully. The token had come and gone, leaving the mud shell and the laboring life within it as it had been before. Curiously impassive, impassively curious. There was one more portent in the sky, one more mist on the dim horizon. That was all.

So through the dew-hung fields the mysterious message sped west and south.

Sent by whom? And wherefore?

The question was being asked by the masters in desultory fashion as they sat round a bonfire, which blazed in the center of the Resident's camp, on the banks of the great jheel. It was a shooting camp, a standing camp, lavish in comfort. The white tents were ranged symmetrically on three sides of a square, and, in the moonlight, shone almost as brightly as the long levels of water stretching away on the fourth side to the sedgy brakes and isolated palms of the snipe marshes. Behind rose a heavy mass of burnished foliage, and in front of the big mess-tent the English flag drooped from its mast in the still night air. Nearer the jheel again the bonfire flashed and crackled, sending a column of smoke and sparks into the star-set sky. The ground about it was spread with carpets and Persian rugs, and here, in luxurious arm-chairs, the comfortably-tired sportsmen were lounging after dinner, some of them in mess uniform, some in civilian black, but all in decorous dress; for not only was the Brigadier present, but also a small sprinkling of ladies wrapped in fur cloaks above their evening fineries. Briefly, a company more suitable to the *foyer* of a theater than this barbaric bonfire. But the whole camp, with its endless luxury, stood out in keen contrast with the sordid savagery of a wretched hamlet which lay half-hidden behind the trees.

The contrast struck Jim Douglas, who for that evening only, happened to be the Resident's guest; for, having been on the jheel in a very different sort of camp when the Resident had invaded his solitude, the usual invitation to dine had followed as a matter of course; as

it would have followed to any white face with pretensions
to be considered a gentleman's. He had accepted it, because, every now and again, a desire "to chuck" as he
expressed it, and go back to the ordinary life of his class
came over him. This mood had been on him persistently ever since the Yama and Indra incident, so that,
for the time being, he had dismissed his scoundrels and
given up spying in disgust. He had, he told himself,
wasted his time, and the military magnate was justified
in politely dispensing with his further services. There
was, in truth, no need for them so far as he could see.
There was plenty of talk, plenty of discontent, but nothing more. And even that anyone could observe and
gauge; for there was no mystery, no concealment. The
whole affair was invertebrate utterly, except every now
and again when you came upon the track of the Moulvie
of Fyzabad. It was conceivable that the aspect might
change, but for the present he was sick of the whole
thing, ambition and all. Horse-dealing was better. So
he had established himself in a small house in Duryagunj,
started a stable, and then taken a holiday in a shooting
pâl among the jheels and jungles, where in his younger
days he had spent so much of his time.

Thus, after eating a first-class dinner, he was smoking
a first-class cigar, and, being a stranger to everyone
there, thinking his own thoughts, when the Resident's
voice came from the other side of the fire which, with its
dancing flame-light distorting every feature in myriad
variation, disguised rather than revealed the faces seen
by it.

"You have bagged one or two in your district, haven't
you, Ford?"

"What, sir? Bustard?" inquired the Collector of the
next district, who had come over his border for a day or
two's shoot, and who had been engrossed in sporting
talk with his neighbor. There was a laugh from the
other side of the fire.

"No! these *chupatties*. The Brigadier was asking me
if they were as numerous as they are further south, and
Fraser, here, said none had come into the Delhi district
as yet."

"One came to-day into the hamlet behind the tents," said Jim Douglas quietly. "I met the man bringing it. A watchman from over the border in Mr. Ford's district."

Half a dozen faces turned to the voice which spoke so confidently, and then asked in whispers who the man was? But there was nothing in the whispered replies to warrant that tone of imparting information to others, and a man in black clothes seemed to resent it, for he appealed to the Resident rather fulsomely.

"It will be in the reports to-morrow, no doubt, sir. For myself I attach no importance to it. The custom is an old one. I remember observing it in Muttra when smallpox was bad. But I should like to have your opinion. You ought to know if anyone does."

The compliment was no idle flattery. None had a better right to it than Sir Theophilus Metcalfe, whose illustrious name had been a power in Delhi for two generations, and whose uncle had been one of India's most distinguished statesmen. So there was a hush for his reply.

"I can't say," he answered deliberately. "Personally I doubt the dissatisfaction ever coming to a head. There is a good deal, of course, but of late, so it has seemed to me, it is quieting down. People are getting tired of fermenting. As for the causes of the disaffection it is patent. We can't, simply, do the work we are doing without making enemies of those whose vested interests we have to destroy. We may have gone ahead a little too fast; but that is another question. As for the army, I've no right to speak of it, but it seems to me it has been allowed to get out of hand, out of touch. It will need care to bring it into discipline, but I don't anticipate trouble. Its mixed character is our safeguard. It would be hard for even a good leader to hit on a general grievance which would touch both the army and the civil population, Hindoos and Mohammedans—and as a matter of fact they have no leader at all."

"Have you ever come across the Moulvie of Fyzabad, sir?" remarked Jim Douglas again. "If I had the power I would shoot him like a mad dog. But for the rest I quite agree."

Here a stir behind them distracted both his attention and the attention of those who were listening to this authoritative voice with bated breath.

" Is that the post? Oh, how delightful! " chorused the ladies, and more than one added plaintively, " I wonder if the English mail is in."

" Let's bet on it. Sir Theophilus to hold the stakes," cried a young fellow who had been yawning through the discussion. But the subject was too serious for such light handling, to judge by the eager faces which crowded round, while the red-coated *chuprassies* poured the contents of the bags into a heap on the carpet at their master's feet. There is always a suspense about that moment of search among the bundles of official correspondence, the files, the cases which fill up the camp mail, for the thin packet of private letters which is the only tie between you and the world; but when hopes of home news is superadded, the breath is apt to come faster. And so a scene, trivial in itself, points an inexorable finger to the broad fact underlying all our Indian administration, that we are strangers and exiles.

" Not in! " announced the Resident, studiously cheerful. " But there are heaps of letters for everybody. Did the mem-sahib come in the carriage, Gâmu? " he added as he sorted out the owners.

" Huzoor! " replied the head orderly, who was also his master's factotum, thrusting the remainder back in the bags. " And the Major sahib also. According to order, refreshments are being offered."

" Glad Erlton could come," remarked a voice to its neighbor. " We want another good shot badly."

" And Mrs. Gissing is awfully good company too," assented the neighbor. Jim Douglas, who was sitting on the other side, looked up quickly. The juxtaposition of the names surprised him after what he had seen, or thought he had seen at Christmas time.

" Is that Mrs. Gissing from Lucknow? " he asked.

" I believe so. She is a stranger here. Seems awfully jolly, but the women don't like her. Do you know anything of her? "

Jim Douglas hesitated. He could have easily satisfied

the ear evidently agog for scandal; but what, after all, did he know of her? What did he know of his own experience? It seemed to him as if she stood there, defiantly dignified, asking him the question, her china-blue eyes flashing, the childish face set and stern.

" Personally I know little," he replied, " but that little is very much to her credit."

As he relapsed into silence and smoke he felt that she had once more walked boldly into his consciousness and claimed recognition. She had forced him to acknowledge something in her which corresponded with something in him. Something unexpected. If Kate Erlton's eyes with their cold glint in them had flashed like that, he would not have wondered; but they had not. They had done just the reverse. They had softened; they had only looked heroic. Underneath the glint which had sent him on a wild-goose chase had lain that commonplace indefinable womanhood, sweet enough, but a bit sickly, which could be in any woman's eyes if you fancied yourself in love with her. It had lain in the eyes belonging to the golden curl, in poor little Zora's eyes, might conceivably lie in half a dozen others.

" By George!" came an eager voice from the group of men who were reading their letters by the light of a lamp held for the purpose by a silent bronze image of a man in uniform. " I have some news here which will interest you, sir. There has been a row at Dum-Dum about the new Enfield cartridges."

" Eh! what's that?" asked the Brigadier, looking up from his own correspondence. " Nothing serious, I hope."

" Not yet, but it seems curious by the light of what we were discussing, and what Mr.—er—Capt——"

" Douglas," suggested the owner of the name, who at the first words had sat up to listen intently. His face had a certain anticipation in it; almost an eagerness.

" Thanks. It's a letter from the musketry depôt. Shall I read it, sir?"

The Brigadier nodded, one or two men looked up to listen, but most went on with their letters or discussed the chances of slaughter for the morrow.

"There is a most unpleasant feeling abroad respecting these new cartridges, which came to light a day or two ago in consequence of a high-caste sepoy refusing to let a lower caste workman drink out of his cup. The man retorted that as the cartridges being made in the Arsenal were smeared with pig's grease and cow's fat there would soon be no caste left in the army. The sepoy complained, and it came out that this idea is already widely spread. Wright denied the fact flatly at first, but found out that large quantities of beef-tallow *had* been indented for by the Ordnance. And that, of course, made the men think he had lied about it. Bontein, the chief, has wisely suggested altering the drill, since the men say they will not bite the cartridges. If they do, their relations won't eat with them when they go home on leave. You see, with this new rifle it is not really necessary to bite the cartridge at all, so it would be a quite natural alteration, and get us out of the difficulty without giving in. The suggestion has been forwarded, and if it could be settled sharp would smother the business; but what with duffers and——" The reader broke off, and a faint smile showed even on the Brigadier's face as the former skipped hurriedly to find something safer—"Old General Hearsey, who knows the natives like a book, says there is trouble in it. He declares that the Moulvie of Fyzabad—whoever that may be——"

The faces looked at Jim Douglas curiously, but he was too eager to notice it.

"Is at the bottom of the *chupatties* we hear are being sent round up-country; but that he is in league also with the Brahmins in Calcutta—especially the priests at Kali's shrine—over *suttee* and widow re-marriage and all that. However, all I know is that both Hindoos and Mohammedans in my classes are in a blue funk about the cartridges, and swear even their wives won't live with them if they touch them."

"The common grievance," said Jim Douglas, in the silence that ensued. "It alters the whole aspect of affairs."

"Prepare to receive cavalry!" yawned the man who had suggested betting on the chance of the home-mail.

What was the use of a week's leave on the best snipe
jheel about, if it was to be spent in talking shop?

"No!" cried the man in black, not unwilling to
change the subject of which he had not yet official cognizance. "Prepare to receive ladies. There is Mrs.
Gissing, looking as fresh as paint!"

She looked fresh, indeed, as she came forward; her
curly hair, rough when fashionable heads were smooth,
glistening in the firelight, the fluffy swansdown on her
long coat framing her childish face softly. Behind her,
heavy, handsome, came Major Erlton with the half-
sheepish air men assume when they are following a
woman's lead.

"Here I am at last, Sir Theophilus," she began, in a
gay artificial voice as she passed Jim Douglas, who stood
up, pushing his chair aside to give more room. "I'm *so*
glad Major Erlton managed to get leave. I'm such a
coward! I should have died of fright all by myself in
that long, lonely——"

"Keep still!" interrupted a peremptory voice behind
her, as a pair of swift unceremonious arms seized her
round the waist, and by sheer force dragged her back a
step, then held her tight-clasped to something that beat
fast despite the calm tone. "Kill that snake, someone!
There, right at her feet! It isn't a branch. I saw it
move. Don't stir, Mrs. Gissing, it's all right."

It might be, but the heart she felt beat hard; and the
one beneath his hand gave a bound and then seemed to
stand still, as the sticks and staves, hastily caught up,
smote furiously on her very dress, so close did certain
death lie to her. There was a faint scent of lavender
about that dress, about her curly hair, which Jim Douglas never forgot; just as he never forgot the passionate
admiration which made his hands relax to an infinite
tenderness, when she uttered no cry, no sound; when
there was no need to hold her, so still did she stand, so
absolutely in unison with the defiance of Fate which
kept him steady as a rock. Surely no one in all his life,
he thought, had ever stood so close to him, yet so
far off!

"God bless my soul! My dear lady, what an escape!"

The hurried faltering exclamation from a bystander heralded the holding up of a long limp rope of a thing hanging helplessly over a stick. It was the signal for a perfect babel. Many had seen the brute, but had thought it a branch, others had similar experiences of drowsy snakes scorched out of winter quarters in some hollow log, and all crowded round Mrs. Gissing, loud in praise of her coolness. Only she turned quickly to see who had held her; and found Major Erlton.

"The brute hasn't touched you, has he?" he began huskily, then broke into almost a sob of relief, "My God! what an escape!"

She glanced at him with the faint distaste which any expression of strong emotion showed toward her by a man always provoked, and gave one of her high irrelevant laughs.

"Is it? I may die a worse death. But I want *him*—where is he?"

"Slipped away from your gratitude, I expect," said the Collector. "But I'll betray him. It was the man who knew about the *chupatties*, Sir Theophilus; I don't know his name."

"Douglas," said the host. "He is in camp a mile or two down the jheel. I expect he has gone back. He seemed a nice fellow."

Mrs. Gissing made a *moue*. "I would not have been so grateful as all that! I would only have said 'Bravo' to him."

Her own phrase seemed to startle her, she broke off with a sudden wistful look in her wide blue eyes.

"My dear Mrs. Gissing, have a glass of wine; you must indeed," fussed the Brigadier. But the little lady set the suggestion aside.

"Douglas!" she repeated. "I wonder where he comes from? Does anyone know a Douglas?"

"James Sholto Douglas," corrected the host. "It's a good name."

"And I knew a good fellow of that name once; but he went under," said an older man.

"About what?" Alice Gissing's eyes challenged the speaker, who stood close to her.

"About a woman, my dear lady."

"Poor dear! Erlton, you must fetch him over to see me to-morrow morning." She said it with infinite verve, and her hearers laughed.

"Him!" retorted someone. "How do you know it's the same man?"

She nodded her head gayly. "I've a fancy it is. And I am bound to be nice to him anyhow."

She had not the chance, however. Major Erlton, riding over before breakfast to catch him, found nothing but the square-shaped furrow surrounding a dry vacant spot which shows where a tent has been.

For Jim Douglas was already on his way back to Delhi, on his way back to more than Delhi if he succeeded in carrying out a plan which had suggested itself to him when he heard of General Hearsey's belief that the priests conducting the agitation against widow remarriage and the abolition of *suttee* were leagued with the Mohammedan revival. Tara, the would-be saint, was still in Delhi. He had not sought her out before, being in truth angry with the woman's duplicity, and not wanting to run the risk of her chattering about him. Now, as he had said, the whole position was changed. He had no common hold upon her, and might through her get some useful hints as to the leading men in the movement. She must have seen them when the miracle took place at Benares. The thought made him smile rather savagely. Decidedly she would not care to defy his tongue; from saint to sinner would be too great a fall.

So at dusk that very evening he was back in his mendicant's disguise, begging at a doorway in one of the oldest parts of Delhi. An insignificant doorway in an insignificant alley. But there was a faded wreath of yellow marigolds over the architrave, a deeper hollow in the stone threshold; sure signs, both, that something to attract worshiping feet lay within. Yet at first sight the court into which you entered, after a brief passage barred by blank wall, was much as other courts. It was set round with high irregular houses, perfect rabbit-warrens of tiny rooms, slips of roof, and stairs; all conglomerate,

yet distinct. Some reached from within, some from
without, some from neighboring roofs, and some, Heaven
knows how! possibly by wings, after the fashion of the
purple pigeons cooing and sidling on the purple brick
cornices. In one corner, however, stood a huge *peepul-
tree*, and partly shaded by this, partly attached to an
arcaded building of two stories, was a small, squalid-
looking, black stone Hindoo temple. It was not more
than ten feet square, triply recessed at each corner, and
with a pointed spire continuing the recesses of the base.
A sort of hollow monolith raised on a plinth of three
steps. In its dark windowless sanctuary, open to the
outside world by a single arch, stood a polished black
stone, resting on a polished black stone cup, like a large
acorn. For this was the oldest Shivâla in Delhi, and in
the rabbit-warrens surrounding this survival of Baal
worship lived and lodged *yogis*, beggars, saints, half the
insanity and sacerdotalism of Delhi. It was not a place
into which to venture rashly. So Jim Douglas sat at the
gate begging while the clashings and brayings and drum-
ings echoed out into the alley. For the seven fold
circling of the Lamps was going on, and if Tara did not
pass to this evening service from outside, she most likely
lived within; that she lodged near the temple he knew.

So as he sat waiting, watching, the light faded, the
faint smell of incense grew fainter, the stream of wor-
shipers coming to take the holy water in which the god
had been washed slackened. Then by twos and threes
the Brahmins and *yogis*—the Dean and Chapter, as it
were—passed out clinking half-pennies, and carrying
the offertory in kind, tied up in handkerchiefs.

The service was over, and Tara must therefore live in
a lodging reached from within. And now, when the
coast was clearing, he might still have opportunity of
tracing her. So he rose and walked in boldly, disappointed to find the courtyard was almost empty already.
There were only a few stragglers, mostly women, and
they in the white shroud of widows; but even in the
gloom and shadow he could see the tall figure he sought
was not among them, and he was about to slip away
when, following their looks, he caught sight of another

figure crouching on the topmost step of the plinth, right
in front of the sanctuary door, so that it stood faintly
outlined against the glimmer of the single cresset, which,
raised on the heap of half-dead flowers within, showed
them and nothing more—nothing but the shadows.

He drew back hastily into the empty arcade, and
waited for the widows' lingering bare feet—scarcely
heard even on those echoing stones—to pass out and
leave him and Tara alone. For it was Tara. That he
knew though her face was turned from him.

The feet lingered on, making him fear lest some of the
mendicants who must lodge in these arcades should return, after almsgiving time, and find him there. And
as they lingered he thought how he had best make himself known to the devotee, the saint. It must be something dramatic, something to tie her tongue at once,
something to bring home to her his hold upon her. The
locket! He slipped it from his neck and stood ready.
Then, as the last flutter of white disappeared, he stepped
noiselessly across the court.

And so, suddenly, between the rapt face and the dim
light on which its eyes were fixed, hung a dangling gold
oval, and the Englishman, bending over the woman's
shoulder from behind, could see the amaze flash to the
face. And his other hand was ready with the clutch of
command, his tongue with a swift threat; but she was too
quick for him. She was round at his feet in an instant,
clasping them.

"Master! Master!"

Jim Douglas recoiled from that touch once more; but
with a half-shamed surprise, regret, almost remorse. He
had meant to threaten this woman, and now——

She was up again, eager, excited. "Quick! The
Huzoor is not safe here. They may return any moment.
Quick! Quick! Huzoor, follow me."

And as, blindly, he obeyed, passing rapidly through a
low doorway and so up a dark staircase, he slipped the
locket back to its place with a sort of groan. Here was
another woman to be reckoned with, and though the discovery suited his purpose, and though he knew himself
to be as safe as her woman's wit could make him, he

wondered irritably if there was anything in the world into which this eternal question of sex did not intrude. And then, suddenly, he seemed to feel Alice Gissing's heart beat beneath his hand; there had been no womanhood in that touch.

So he passed on. And next morning he was on his way southward. Tara had told him what he wanted to know.

CHAPTER V.

IN THE RESIDENCY.

"STRAWBERRIES! Oh, how delightful!"

Kate Erlton looked with real emotion at a plate of strawberries and cream which Captain Morecombe had just handed to her. "They are the first I have ever seen in India," she went on in almost pathetic explanation of her apparent greed. "Where could Sir Theophilus have got them?"

"Meerut," replied her cavalier with a kindly smile. "They grow up-country. But they put one in mind of home, don't they?" He turned away, almost embarrassed, from the look in her eyes; and added, as if to change the subject, "The Resident does it splendidly, does not he?"

There could be no two opinions as to that. The park-like grounds were kept like an English garden, the house was crammed from floor to ceiling with works of art, the broad verandas were full of rare plants, and really valuable statuary. That toward the river, on the brink of which Metcalfe House stood, gave on a balustraded terrace which was in reality the roof of a lower story excavated, for the sake of coolness, in the bank itself. Here, among others, was the billiard room, from the balcony of which you could see along the curved stone embankment of the river to the Koodsia garden, which lay between Metcalfe Park and the rose-red wall of the city. It was an old pleasure-ground of the Moghuls, and a ruined palace, half-hidden in creepers, half lost in

sheer luxuriance of blossom, still stood in its wilderness
of forest trees and scented shrubs; a very different style
of garden from that over which Kate Erlton looked, as it
undulated away in lawns and drives between the Ridge
and the river.

"Yes!" she said, "it always reminds me of England;
but for that——" She pointed to the dome of a Mohammedan tomb which curved boldly into the blue sky close
to the house.

"Yet that is the original owner," replied her companion. "There is rather an odd story about that tomb,
Mrs. Erlton. It is the burial place of the great Akhbar's
foster-brother. Most likely he was a cowherd by caste,
for their women often go out as nurses, and the land
about here all belonged to these Goojers, as they are
called. But when we occupied Delhi, a civilian—one
Blake—fancied the tomb as a house, added to it, and
removed the good gentleman's grave-stone to make room
for his dining-table—a hospitable man, no doubt, as the
Resident is now. But the Goojers objected, appealed to
the Government agent. In vain. Curiously enough
both those men were, shortly afterward, assassinated."

"You don't mean to connect——" began Kate in a
tone of remonstrance.

Captain Morecombe laughed. "In India, Mrs.
Erlton, it is foolish to try and settle which comes first, the
owl or the egg. You can't differentiate cause and effect
when both are incomprehensible. But if I were Resident
I should insure myself and my house against the act of
God and the Queen's enemies."

"But this house?" she protested.

"Is built on the site of a Goojer village, and they were
most unwilling to sell. One could hardly believe it now,
could one? Come and see the river terrace. It is the
prettiest place in Delhi at this time of the year."

He was right; for the last days of March, the first ones
of April are the crown and glory of a Northern Indian
garden. Perhaps because there is already that faint hint
of decay which makes beauty more precious. Another
short week and the flower-lover going the evening round
will find many a sun-weary head in the garden. But on

this glorious afternoon, when the Resident was entertaining Delhi in right residential fashion, there was not a leaf out of place, a blade of grass untrimmed. Long lines of English annuals in pots bordered the broad walks evenly, the scentless gardenia festooned the rows of cypress in disciplined freedom, the roses had not a fallen petal, though the palms swept their long fringes above them boldly, and strange perfumed creepers leaped to the branches of the forest trees. In one glade, beside an artificial lake, some ladies in gay dresses were competing for an archery prize. On a brick dais close to the house the band of a native regiment was playing national airs, and beside it stood a gorgeous marquee of Cashmere shawls with silver poles and Persian carpets; the whole stock and block having belonged to some potentate or another, dead, banished, or annexed. Here those who wished for it found rest in English chairs or Oriental divans; and here, contrasting with their host and his friends, harmonizing with the Cashmere shawl marquee, stood a group of guests from the palace. A perfect bevy of princes, suave, watchful, ready at the slightest encouragement to crowd round the Resident, or the Commissioner, or the Brigadier, with noiseless white-stockinged feet. Equally ready to relapse into stolid indifference when unnoticed. Here was Mirza Moghul, the King's eldest son, and his two supporters, all with lynx eyes for a sign, a hint, of favor or disfavor. And here—a sulky, sickly looking lad of eighteen—was Jewun Bukht, Zeenut Maihl's darling, dressed gorgeously and blazing with jewels which left no doubt as to who would be the heir-apparent if she had her way. Prince Abool-Bukr, however, scented, effeminate, watched the proceedings with bright eyes; giving the ladies unabashed admiration and after a time actually strolling away to listen to the music. Finally, however, drifting to the stables to gamble with the grooms over a quail fight. Then there were lesser lights. Ahsan-Oolah the physician, his lean plausible face and thin white beard suiting his black gown and skull-cap, discussed the system of Greek medicine with the Scotch surgeon, whose fluent, trenchant Hindustani had an Aberdonian twang. Then there was Elahi Buksh, whose daughter was widow of the late heir-apparent; a wily man, dogging the Resident's steps with persistent adulation, and watched uneasily by all the other factions. A few rich bankers curiously obsequious to the youngest ensign, and one or two pensioners owing their invitations to loyal service, made up the company, which kept to the Persian carpets so as to avoid the necessity for slipping on and off the shoes which lay in rows under Gâmu the orderly's care, and the consequent necessity for continual fees. For Gâmu piled up the shekels until his master, after the mutiny, had reluctantly to hang him for extorting blood-, as well as shoe-money.

They were a curious company, these palace guests, aliens in their own country, speaking to none save high officials, caring to speak to none, and waiting with ill-concealed yawns for the blunt dismissal or the ceremonious leave-taking after a decent space of boredom due to their rank.

" I wonder they come," said Mrs. Erlton, passing on rapidly to escape from the loud remarks of two of her countrywomen who were discussing Jewun Bukht's jewels as if the wearer, standing within a yard of them, was a lay figure: as indeed he was to them.

" Why does anyone come? " asked Captain Morecombe airily, as he followed her across the terrace, and, leaning over the balustrade, looked down at the sandbanks and streams below. " So far as I am concerned," he went on, " the reason is palpable. I came because I knew you would be here, and I like to see my friends."

He was in reality watching her to see how she received the remark, and something in her face made him continue casually. " And there, I should say, are some other people who have similar excuse for temporary aberration." He pointed to the figures of a man and woman who were strolling toward the Koodsia along a narrow path which curved below the embanking wall, and his sentence ended abruptly. He turned hastily to lean his back on the parapet and look parkward, adding lightly, " And there are two more, and two more! In fact most people really come to see other people."

But Kate Erlton was proud. She would have no evasion, and the past three months since Christmas Day had forced her to accept facts.

" It is my husband and Mrs. Gissing," she said, looking toward the strolling figures. " I suppose he is seeing her home. I heard her say not long ago she was tired. She hasn't been looking strong lately."

The indifference, being slightly overdone, annoyed her companion. No man likes having the door slammed in his sympathetic face. " She is looking extremely pretty, though,' he replied coolly. " It softens her somehow. Don't you agree with me? "

There was a pause ere Kate Erlton replied; and then her eyes had found the far horizon instead of those lessening figures.

" I do. I think she looks a better woman than she did—somehow." She spoke half to herself with a sort of dull wonder in her voice. But the keenness of his, shown in his look at her, roused her reserve instantly. To change the subject would be futile; she had gone too far to make that possible if he wished otherwise, without that palpable refusal which would in itself be confession. So she asked him promptly if he would mind bringing her a glass of iced water, cup, anything, since she was thirsty after the strawberries; and when he went off reluctantly, took her retreat leaning over the balustrade, looking out to the eastern plains beyond the river; to that far horizon which in its level edge looked as if all or nothing might lie behind it. A new world, or a great gulf!

Three months! Three months since she had given up that chance, such as it was, on Christmas Day. And now her husband was honestly, truly in love with Alice Gissing. Would he have been as honestly, as truly in love with her if—if she could have forgotten? Had this really been his chance, and hers? Had it come, somehow? She did not attempt to deny facts; she was too proud for that. It seemed incredible, almost impossible; but this was no Lucknow flirtation, no mere sensual *liaison* on her husband's part. He was in love. The love which she called real love, which, given to her, would, she admitted, have raised her life above the mere compromise from which she had shrunk. But he had never given it to her. Never. Not even in those first days. And now, if that chance had gone, what remained? What disgrace might not the future hold for her boy's father with a man like Mr. Gissing, in a country where the stealing of a man's wife from him was a criminal offense? Thank Heaven! Herbert was too selfish to risk—she turned and fled, as it were, from that cause for gratitude to find refuge in the certainty that Alice Gissing, at least, would not lose her head. But the chance! the chance was gone.

"Miffes Erlton," came a little silvery voice behind her. "Oh, Miffes Erlton! He's giv-ded me suts a boo'ful birdie."

It was Sonny clasping a quail in both dimpled hands. His bearer was salaaming in rather a deprecatory manner, and a few paces off, strolling back from the stables with a couple of young bloods like himself, was Prince Abool-Bukr. All three with a furtive eye for Kate Erlton's face and figure.

"He giv-ded it to me be-tos it tumbled down, and everybody laughed," went on Sonny confidently. "And so I is do-ing to comfit birdie, and 'ove it."

"Sonny," exclaimed Kate, suddenly aghast, "what's that on your frock—down your arm?"

It was blood. Red, fresh-spilled blood! She was on her knees beside him in instant coaxing, comforting, unclasping his hands to see where they were hurt. The bird fell from them fluttering feebly, leaving them all scarlet-stained with its heart's blood, making Sonny shriek at the sight, and hide face and hands in her muslin skirts. She stood up again, her cheeks ablaze with anger, and turned on the servant.

"How dare you! How dare you give it to the *chota-sahib*? How dare you!"

The man muttered something in broken English and Hindustani about a quail fight, and not knowing the bird was dying when the Mirza gave it; accompanying his excuses with glances of appeal to Prince Abool-Bukr, who, at Sonny's outburst, had paused close by. Kate's eyes, following the bearer's, met those bright, dark, cruel ones, and her wrath blazed out again. Her Hindustani, however, being unequal to a lecture on cruelty to animals, she had to be content with looks. The Prince returned them with an indifferent smile for a moment, then with a half-impatient shrug of his shoulders, he stepped forward, lifted the dying quail gingerly between finger and thumb, and flung it over the parapet into the river.

"*Ab khutm piyâree tussulli rukhiye!*" (Now is it finished, dear one; take comfort!) he said consolingly, looking at Sonny's golden curls. The liquid Urdu was sheer gibberish to the woman, but the child turning his head half-doubtfully, half-reassured, Abool-Bukr's face softened instantly.

"*Mujhe muaâf. Murna sub ke hukk hai*" (Excuse me. Death is the right of all), he said with a graceful salaam as he passed on.

So the water Captain Morecombe brought back was used for a different purpose than quenching pretended thirst; and the bringer, hearing Kate's version of the story, hastily asked Sonny—who by this time was holding out chubby hands cheerfully to be dried and prattling of dirty birdies—what the Prince had said. The child, puzzled for an instant, smiled broadly.

"He said it was deaded all light."

Kate shivered. The incident had touched her on the nerves, taking the color from the flowers, the brightness from the sunshine.

"Come and have a turn," suggested Captain Morecombe; " they have began dancing in the saloon. It will change the subject."

But as she took his arm, she said in rather a tremulous voice, "There is such a thing as a Dance of Death, though."

"My dear lady," he laughed, "it is a most excellent pastime. And one can dance anywhere, on the edge of a volcano even, if one doesn't smell brimstone."

Kate, however, found otherwise, and when the waltz was over, announced her intention of going off to take Sonny home, and see, Mrs. Seymour and the new baby. But in this her cavalier saw difficulties. The mare was evidently too fresh for a lady to drive, and Major Erlton,

returning, might need the dog-cart.   It would be far
better for him to drive her in his, so far, and afterward let
the Major know he had to call for her.   Kate assented
wearily.   Such arrangements were part of the detail of
life, with a woman neglected as she was by her husband.
She could not deliberately avoid them, and yet keep the
unconsciousness her pride claimed.   How could she,
when there were twenty men in society to one woman?
Twenty—for the most part—gentlemen, quite capable of
gauging a woman's character.   So Captain Morecombe
drove her to the Seymour's house on the city wall by the
Water Bastion.   There were several houses there, set so
close to the rampart that there was barely room for a
paved pathway between their back verandas and the
battlement.   In front of them lay a metaled road and
shady gardens; and at the end of this road stood a small
bungalow toward which Kate Erlton looked involuntarily.   There was a horse waiting outside it.   It was
her husband's charger.   He must have arranged to
have it sent down, arranged, as it were, to leave her in
the lurch, and a sudden flash of resentment made her
say, as she got down at the Seymours' house, " You had
better call for me in half an hour; that will be best."
    Captain   Morecombe   flushed   with   sheer   pleasure.
Kate was not often so encouraging.   But as he drove
round to wait for her at a friend's house, close to the
Delhi Gazette press, he, too, noticed the Major's charger,
and swore under his breath.   Before God it was too bad!
But if ever there were signs of a coming smash they were
to be seen here.   Erlton, after years of scandal, had lost
his head—it seemed incredible, but there was a Fate in
such things from which mortal man could not escape.
    And as he told himself this tale of Fate—the man's
excuse for the inexcusable which will pass current gayly
until women combine in refusing to accept it for themselves—another man, at the back of the little house past
which he was driving, was telling it to himself also.   For
a great silence had fallen between Major Erlton and Alice
Gissing after she had told him something, to hear which
he had arranged to come home with her for a quiet talk.
And, in the silence, the hollow note of the wooden bells

upon the necks of the cattle grazing below the battlement, over which he leaned, seemed to count the slow
minutes. Quaintest, dumbest of all sounds, lacking
vibration utterly, yet mellow, musical, to the fanciful ear,
with something of the hopeful persistency of Time in its
recurring beat.

Alice Gissing was not a fanciful woman, but as she lay
back in her long cane chair, her face hidden in its pillows
as if to shut out something unwelcome, her foot kept
time to the persistency on the pavement, till, suddenly,
she sat up and faced round on her silent companion.

" Well," she said impatiently. " Well! what have you
got to say? "

" I—I was thinking," he began helplessly, when she
interrupted him.

" What *is* the use of thinking? That won't alter facts.
As I told you, Gissing will be back in a month or so;
and then we must decide."

Major Erlton turned quickly. " You can't go back to
him, Allie; you weren't considering that, surely. You
can't—not—not now." His voice softened over the last
words; he turned away abruptly. His face was hidden
from her so.

She looked toward him strangely for a second, covered her face with her hands for another, then, changing
the very import of the action, used them to brush the hair
back from her temples; so, clasping them behind her
head, leaned back on the pillows, and looked toward him
again. There was a reckless defiance in her attitude and
expression, but her words did not match it.

" I suppose I can't," she said drearily, " and I suppose
you wouldn't let me go away by myself either."

Once more he turned. " Go! " he echoed quickly.
" Where would you go? "

" Somewhere! "—the recklessness had invaded her
voice now—" Anywhere! Wherever women do go in
these cases. To the devil, perhaps."

He gave a queer kind of laugh; this spirited effrontery
had always roused his admiration. " I dare say," he replied, " for I'm not a saint, and you have got to come
with me, Allie. You must. I shall send in my papers,

and by and by, when all the fuss is over "—here he gave
a fierce sigh—" for I expect Gissing will make a fuss,
we can get married and live happily ever after."

She shook her head. " You'll regret it. I don't see
how you can help regretting it!"

He came over to her, and laid his big broad hand very
tenderly on her curly hair. " No! I shan't, Allie," he
replied in a low, husky voice, " I shan't, indeed. I never
was a good hand at sentiment and that sort, but I love
you dearly—dearly. All the more—for this that you've
told me. I'd do anything for you, Allie. Keep straight
as a die, dear, if you wanted it. And I wasn't regretting
—it—just now. I was only thinking how strange——"

" Strange!" she interrupted, almost fiercely. " If it
is strange to you, what must it be to me? My God! I
wonder if any man will ever understand what this means
to a woman? All the rest seems to pass her by, to leave
no mark—I—I—never cared. But this! Herbert! I
feel sometimes as if I were Claude's wife again—Claude's
wife, so full of hopes and fears. And I dream of him too.
I haven't dreamed of him for years, and I learned to hate
him before he died, you know. I have gone back to that
old time, and nothing seems different. Nothing at all!
Isn't that strange? And the old Mai—she has gone
back, too—sees no difference either. She treats me just
as she did in those old, old days. She fusses round, and
cockers me up, and talks about it. There! she is coming now with smelling-salts or sal-volatile or something!
Oh! Go away, do, Mai, I don't want anything except to
be left alone!"

But the old ayah's untutored instincts were not to be
so easily smothered. Her wrinkled face beamed as she
insisted on changing the dainty laced shoes for easy
slippers, and tucked another pillow into the chair. The
mem was tired, she told the Major with a respectful
salaam, after her long walk; the faint resentment in her
tone being entirely for the latter fact.

" You see, don't you?" said Mrs. Gissing, with bright
reckless eyes, when they were alone once more. " She
doesn't mind. She has forgotten all the years between,
forgotten everything. And I—I don't know why—but

there! What is the use of asking questions? I never can answer even for myself. So we had better leave it alone for the present. We needn't settle yet a while, and there is always a chance of something happening."

"But you said your husband would be back——" he began.

"In a month—but we may all be dead and buried in a month," she interrupted. "I only told you now, because I thought you ought to know soon, so as not to be hurried at the last. It means a lot, you see, for a man to give up his profession for a woman; and it isn't like England, you know——" She paused, then continued in an odd half-anxious voice, her eyes fixed on him inquiringly as he stood beside her. "I shouldn't be angry, remember, Herbert, if—if you didn't."

"Allie! What do you mean? Do you mean that you don't care?" His tone was full of pained surprise, his hand scarcely a willing agent as she drew it close to caress it with her cheek.

"Care? of course I care. You are very good to me, Herbert, far nicer to me than you are to other people. And I can't say 'no' if you decide on giving up for me. I *can't* now. I see that. Only don't let us be in a hurry. As that big fat man in the tight satin trousers said to the Resident to-day, when he was asked what the people in the city thought of the fuss down country, '*Delhi dur ust.*'"

"*Delhi dur ust?* What the devil does that mean?" asked the Major, his brief doubt soothed by the touch of her soft cheek. "You are such a clever little cat, Allie! You know a deuced sight more than I do. How you pick it up I can't think."

She gave one of her inconsequent laughs. "Don't have so many men anxious to explain things to you as I have, I expect, sir! But if you ever spoke to a native here—which you don't—you'd know *that*. Even my old Mai says it—they all say it when they don't want to tell the truth, or be hurried, and that is generally. 'Delhi is far,' they say. Dr. Macintyre translates it as 'It's a far cry to Lochawe'; but I don't understand that; for it was an old King of Delhi who said it first. People came and told him an enemy had crossed his border. '*Delhi dur ust,*' says he. Can't you see him, Herbert? An old Turk of a thing with those tight satin trousers! Then they told him the enemy was in sight. '*Delhi dur ust,*' said he. And he said it when they were at the gate—he said it when their swords——" the dramatic instinct in her was strong, and roused her into springing to her feet and mimicking the thrust. '*Delhi dur ust.*'"

Her gay mocking voice rang loud. Then she laid her hand lightly on his arm. " Let us say it too, dear," she said almost sharply. " I won't think—yet. '*Delhi dur ust.*'"

The memory of the phrase went with him when he had said good-by, and was pacing his charger toward the Post Office. But it only convinced him that the Delhi of his decision was reached; he would chuck everything for Allie.

It was by this time growing dusk, but he could see two figures standing in the veranda of the Press Office, and one of them called him by name. He turned in at the gate to find Captain Morecombe reading a proof-sheet by the light of a swinging lamp; for Jim Douglas drew back into unrecognizable shadow as he approached. He had purposely kept out of Major Erlton's way during his occasional returns to Delhi, and as he stepped back now he asked himself if he hated the big man most for his own sake, or for Kate's, or for that other little woman's. Not that it mattered a jot, since he hated him cordially on all three scores.

" Bad news from Barrackpore, Erlton," said the Captain, " and as I have to drive Mrs. Erlton home I thought you might take it round to the Brigadier's. At least if you have no objection, Douglas? "

" None. The telegram is all through the bazaar by now. You can't help it if you employ natives."

" ' Through the medium of a private telegram,' " read Captain Morecombe, " ' the following startling news has reached our office. On Sunday (the 29th of March) about 4.30 P. M., a Brahmin sepoy of the 34th N. I.'— that's the missionary fellow's regiment, of course— ' went amuck, and rushing to the quarter-guard with his

musket, ordered the bugler to sound the assembly to all
who desired to keep the faith of their fathers. The
guard, ordered to arrest him, refused. The whole regiment being, it is said, in alarm at the arrival that morning of the first detachment of British troops, detailed to
keep order during the approaching disbandment of the
19th for mutiny; rumor having it that all sepoys then
refusing to become Christians would be shot down at
once. The mutineer, who had been drinking hemp,
actually fired at Sergeant-major Hewson, providentially
missing him; subsequently he fired at the Adjutant, who,
after a hand-to-hand scuffle with the madman, in which
Hewson joined, only escaped with his life through the
aid of a faithful Mohammedan orderly. Until, and, indeed, after Colonel Wheler the Commandant arrived on
the parade ground, the mutineer marched up and down
in front of the guard, flourishing his musket and calling
for his comrades to join him. The Colonel therefore
ordered the guard to advance and shoot the man down.
The men made show of obedience, but after a few steps
they refused to go on, unless accompanied by a British
officer. On this, Colonel Wheler, considering the risk
needless with an unreliable guard already half-mutinous,
rode off to report his failure to the Brigadier, who had
halted on the further side of the parade ground. At this
juncture (about 5.30 P. M.) matters looked most serious.
The 43d N. I. had turned out, and were barely restrained
from rushing their bells of arms by the entreaties of their
native officers. The 34th, beyond control altogether,
were watching the mutineer's unchecked defiance with
growing sympathy. Fortunately at this moment General
Hearsey, commanding the Division, rode up, followed
by his two sons as *aides.* Hearing what had occurred
from the group of officers awaiting further developments,
he galloped over to the guard, ordered them to follow
him, and made straight for the mutineer; shouting back,
" D——n his musket, sir!" to an officer who warned
him it was loaded. But seeing the man kneel to take
aim he called to his son, " If I fall, John, rush in and put
him to death somehow." The precaution was, providentially, unnecessary, for the mutineer, seeing the re-

maining officers join in this resolute advance, turned his
musket on himself.   He is not expected to live.   Adjutant Baugh, a most promising young officer, is, we
regret to say, dangerously wounded.' "

" Treacherous black devils!   I'd shoot 'em down like
dogs—the lot of them," said Major Erlton savagely.
He had slipped from his horse and now stood in the
veranda overlooking the proof, his back to Jim Douglas.
Perhaps it was the closer sight of his enemy's face which
roused the latter's temper.   Anyhow he broke into the
conversation with that nameless challenge in his voice
which makes a third person nervous.

" It is a pity you were not at Barrackpore.   They seem
to have been in need of a good pot-shot—even of an
officer to be potted at—till Hearsey came to the front."

Captain Morecombe turned quickly to put up his sword
as it were.   " By the way, Erlton," he said hastily, " I
don't think you know Douglas, though you tried to see
him at Nujjufghur after he saved Mrs. Gissing from
that snake."

But Jim Douglas' temper grew, partly at his own
fatuity in risking the now inevitable encounter; and he
had a vile, uncontrollable temper when he was in the
wrong.

" Major Erlton and I have met before," he interrupted,
turning to go; " but I doubt if he will recognize me.
Possibly his horse may."

He paused as he spoke before the Arab which stood
waiting.   It whinnied instantly, stretching its head toward its old master.   Major Erlton muttered a startled
exclamation, but regained his self-possession instantly.
" I beg your pardon—Mr.—er—Douglas, I think you
said, Morecombe; but I did not recognize you."

The pause was aggressive to the last degree.

" Under that name, you mean," finished Jim Douglas,
white with anger at being so obviously at a disadvantage.
" The fact is, Captain Morecombe, that as the late King
of Oude's trainer I called myself James Greyman.   I sold
that Arab to Major Erlton under that name, and under—
well—rather peculiar circumstances.   I am quite ready
to tell them if Major Erlton thinks them likely to interest
the general public."

His eyes met his enemy's, fiercely getting back now full measure of sheer, wild, vicious•temper.   Everything else had gone to the winds, and they would have been at each other's throats gladly; scarcely remembering the cause of quarrel, and forgetting it utterly with the first grip, as men will do to the end of time.

Then the Major, being less secure of his ground since fighting was out of the question, turned on his heel. "So far as I'm concerned," he said, "the explanation is sufficient.   Give the devil his due and every man his chance."

The innuendo was again unmistakable; but the words reminded Jim Douglas of an almost-forgotten promise, and he bit his lips over the necessity for silence.   But in that—as he knew well—lay his only refuge from his own temper; it was silence, or speech to the uttermost.

"If you have quite done with the proof, Captain Morecombe," he said very ceremoniously.

"Certainly, certainly.   Thanks for letting me see it," interrupted the Captain, who had been looking from one to the other doubtfully, as most men do even when their dearest friends are implicated, if the cause of a quarrel is a horse.   "It is a serious business," he went on hurriedly to help the diversion.   "After all the talk and fuss, this cutting down of an officer——"

"Is first blood," put in Jim Douglas.   "There will be more spilled before long."

"Disloyal scoundrels!" growled Major Erlton wrathfully.   "Idiots!   As if they had a chance!"

"They have none.   That's the pity of it," retorted his adversary as he rode off quickly.

Ay! that was the pity of it!   The pity of blood to be spilled needlessly.   The thought made him slacken speed, as if he were on the threshold of a graveyard; though he could not foresee the blood to be spilled so wantonly in that very garden-set angle of the city, so full now of the scent of flowers, the sounds of security.   From far came the subdued hum which rises from a city in which there is no wheeled traffic, no roar of machinery; only the feet of men, their tears, their laughter, to assail the irresponsive air.   Nearer, among the scattered houses hidden by trees, rose children's voices playing about the servants' quarters.   Across the now empty playground of the College the outlines of the church showed faintly among the fret of branches upon the dull red sky, which a cloudless sunset leaves behind it.   And through the open arch of the Cashmere gate, the great globe of the full moon grew slowly from the ruddy earth-haze, then loud and clear came the chime of seven from the mainguard gong, the rattle of arms dying into silence again.   The peace of it all seemed unassailable, the security unending.

" *Delhi dur ust!* "

The words were called across the road in a woman's voice, making him turn to see a shadowy white figure outlined against the dark arches of a veranda close upon the road. He reined up his horse almost involuntarily, remembering as he did so that this was Mrs. Gissing's house.

" I beg your pardon——" he began.

" I beg yours," came the instant reply.   " I mistook you for a friend.   Good-night! "

" Good-night! "

As he paced his horse on, choosing the longer way to Duryagunj, by the narrow lanes clinging to the city wall, the remembrance of that frank good-night lingered with him. *For a friend!* What a name to call Herbert Erlton! Poor little soul! The thought, by its very intolerableness, drove him back to the other, roused by her first words:

" *Delhi dur ust.* "

True!   Even this Delhi lying before his very eyes was far from him.   How would it take the news which by now, as he had said, must have filtered through the bazaar?   He could imagine that.   He knew, also, that the Palace folk must be all discussing the Resident's garden party, with a view to their own special aims and objects.   But what did they think of the outlook on the future?   Did they also say *Delhi dur ust?*

One of them was saying it on a roof close by.   It was Abool-Bukr, who, on his way home, had given himself the promised pleasure of retailing his virtuous afternoon's experiences to Newâsi; for his two-months-wed bride had not broken *him* of his habit of coming to his kind one, though it had made *her* graver, more dignified. Still she broke in on his thick assertion—for he had drunk brandy in his efforts to be friendly with the sahibs—that he had seen an Englishwoman of her sort, with the quick query:

" Like me! How so? "

He laughed mischievously. " And thou art not jealous of my wife!—or sayest thou art not! She was but like thee in this, aunt, that she is of the sort who would have men better than God made them——"

" No worse, thou meanest," she replied.

He shook his head. " Women, Newâsi, are as the ague. A man is ever being made better or worse till he knows not if he be well or ill. And both ways God's work is marred, a man driven from his right fate——"

" But if a man mistakes his fate as thou dost, Abool," she persisted. " Sure, if Jewun Bukht with that evil woman, Zeenut——"

He started to his feet, thrusting out lissome hands wildly, as if to set aside some thought. " Have a care, Newâsi, have a care! " he cried. " Talk not of that arch plotter, arch dreamer. Nay! not arch dreamer! 'tis thou that dreamest most. Dreamest war without blood, men without passion, me without myself! Was there not blood on my hands ere ever I was born—I, Abool-Bukr, of the race of Timoor—kings, tyrants, by birth and trade? The blood of those who stood in my father's way and my father's fathers. I tell thee there is too much tinder yonder——" He pointed to where, across the flat chequers of moonlit roofs, inlaid by the shadows of the intersecting alleys the cupolas of the Palace gates rose upon the sky. " There is too much tinder here," he struck his own breast fiercely, " for such fiery thoughts. Why canst not leave me alone, woman? "

She drew back coldly. " Do I ask thee to come thither? Thy wife——"

He gave a half-maudlin laugh. " Nay, I mean not that! Sure thou art very woman, Newâsi! That is why I love mine aunt! That is why I come to see her—that——"

She interrupted him hastily; but her eyes grew soft, her voice trembled.

"And I do but goad thee for thine own good, Abool. These are strange times. Even the Mufti sahib——"

"Ah! defend me from his wise saws. I know the ring of them too well as 'tis. Even that I endure—for mine aunt's sake. Though, by the faith, if he and others of his kidney waylay me as they do much longer, I will have a rope ladder to thy roof and scandalize them all. I can stomach thy wisdom, dear; none else. So tell them that Abool-Bukr can quote saws as well as they. Tell them he lives for Pleasure, and Pleasure lives in the present. For the rest, *Delhi dur ust! Delhi dur ust!*"

His reckless, unrestrained voice rang out over the roofs, and into the alley below where Jim Douglas was telling himself, that with his finger on the very pulse of the city he had failed to count its heart beats.

He looked up quickly. "*Delhi dur ust!*" All the world seemed to be saying it that night; though the first blood had been shed in the quarrel.

CHAPTER VI.

THE YELLOW FAKIR.

THE days passed to weeks, the weeks to a month, after that shedding of first blood, and no more was spilled, save that of the shedders. Two of them were hanged, the regiment ordered to be disbanded. For the rest, though causeless fires broke out in every cantonment, though a Sikh orderly divulged to his master some tale of a concerted rising, though the dread of the greased cartridge grew to a perfect panic, even Jim Douglas, with his eyes wide open, was forced to admit that, so far as any chance of action went, the reply might still be "*Delhi dur ust.*" The sky was dark indeed, there were mutterings on the horizon; but he and others remembered how often in India, even when rain is due, the clouds creep up and up day by day, darker and more lowering, until the yellowing crops seem to grow greener in sheer hope of the purple pall above them. And then some unseen hand juggles those portentous rain-clouds into the daily darkness of night, and some dawn rises clear and dry to show, in its fierce blaze of sunlight, how the yellow has gained on the green.

So, day by day, the impression grew among the elect that the storm signals would pass; that the best policy was to tide over the next few months somehow. In pursuance of which a sepoy who ventured to draw attention to the state of feeling in one regiment was publicly told he need expect no promotion.

But there were dissentients to this policy, apparently. Anyhow, in the end of April, Colonel Carmichael Smyth, commanding the 3d Bengal Cavalry at Meerut, returned from leave one evening, and ordered fifteen men from each troop to be picked out to learn the use of the new cartridge next morning, and then went to bed comfortably. The men, through their native officers, appealed to their captain for delay. They were neither prepared to take nor refuse the cartridges, old or new. No answer was given them. They marched to the parade obediently at sunrise, and eighty-five of the ninety men picked from a picked regiment for smartness and intelligence refused to take the cartridges, even from their Colonel's or their Adjutant's hand. Their own troop officers were not present. They were at once tried by a court-martial of native officers, some of whom came from the regiments at Delhi; but thirty odd miles off along a broad, level driving road. They were sentenced to ten years' penal servitude, and a parade of all troops was ordered for sunrise on the 9th of May, to put the sentence into force.

So the night of the 8th found Jim Douglas riding over from Delhi in the cool to see something which, if anything could, ought to turn mere talk into action. It had brought a new sound into the air already. The clang of cold iron upon hot, rising from the regimental smithy, where the fetters for the eighty-five were being forged. A cruel sound at best, proclaiming the indubitable advantage of coolness and hardness over glow and plasticity. Cruel indeed when the hardness and insistency goes to the forging of fetters for emotion and ignorance.

Clang! Clang! Clang!

The sound rang out into the hot airless night, rang out into the gusty dawn; for it takes time to forge eighty-five pairs of shackles.   Rang out to where a mixed guard of the 11th and 20th Regiments of Native Infantry were waiting round the tumbrils for the last fetter.   The gray of dawn showed the rest piled on the tumbrils, showed two English officers on horseback talking to each other a little way off, showed the faces of the guard dark and lowering like the dawn itself.

" *Loh!* sergeant *jee!* there is the last," said the master-armorer cheerfully.   His task was done, at any rate.

Soma took it from him silently, and flung it on the others almost fiercely; it settled among them with a clank.   His regiment, the 11th, had but newly come to Meerut, and therefore had as yet no ties of personal comradeship with the eighty-five, but fetters for any sepoys were enough to make the pulse beat full and heavy.

" The last, thank Heaven! " said the Captain, giving his bridle rein a jag.   " All right forward, Jones!   Then fall in, men.   Quick march!   We are late enough as it is."

The disciplined feet fell in without a waver; the tumbrils moved on with a clank and a creak.

Quick march!   Soma's mind, fair reflection of the minds of all about him, was full of doubt.   Was that indeed the last fetter, or did Rumor say sooth when it told of others being secretly forged?   Who could say in these days, when the Huzoors themselves had taken to telling lies.   Not his Huzoors as yet; his Colonels and Captains and Majors, even the little sahib, who. laughed over his own mistakes on parade, told the truth still.   But the others lied.   Lied about enlistment, about prize-money and leave, about those cartridges.   At least, so the men in the 20th said; the sergeant marching next to him behind the tumbril most of all.

" 'Tis but three weeks longer, comrade," said this man suddenly in a low whisper.   They were treading the dim, deserted outskirts of the cantonment bazaar, and Soma looked round nervously at the officers behind.   Had they heard?   He frowned at the speaker and made no reply,

He gave a deaf ear, when he could, to the talk in the 20th; but that was not always, for its sepoys were a part of the Bengal army. That army which was not—as a European army is—a mere chance collection of men divided from each other in the beginning and end of life, associated loosely with each other in its middle, and using military service as a make-shift; but, to a great extent, a guild, following the profession of arms by hereditary custom from the cradle to the grave.

Quick march! A woman, early astir, peered at the little procession through the chink of a door, and whispered to an unseen companion behind. What was she saying? What, by implication, would other women, who peeped virtuously—women he knew—say of his present occupation? That he was a coward to be guarding his comrades' fetters? No doubt; since others with less right would say it too. All the miserable, disreputable riff-raff, for instance, which had drifted in from the neighborhood to see the show. The bazaar had been full of it these three days past. Even the sweepers, pariahs, outcastes, would snigger over the misfortunes of their betters—as those two ahead were doubtless sniggering already as they drew aside from their slave's work of sweeping the roadway, to let the tumbrils pass. Drew aside with mock deference, leaving scantiest room for the twice-born following them. So scant, indeed, that the outermost tip of a reed broom, flourished in insolent salaam, touched the Rajput's sleeve. It was the veriest brush, no more than a fly's wing could have given; but the half-stifled cry from Soma's lips meant murder— nothing less. His disciplined feet wavered, he gave a furtive glance at his companions. Had they seen the insult? Could they use it against him?

"Eyes front, there; forward!" came the order from behind, and he pulled himself together by instinct and went on.

"Only three weeks longer, brother!" said that voice beside him meaningly; and a dull rage rose in Soma's heart. So it had been seen. It might be said of him, Soma, that he had tamely submitted to a defiling touch. He did not look round at his officers this time.

They might hear if they chose, the future might hold what it chose. Mayhap they had seen the insult and were laughing at it. They were not his Huzoors; they belonged to the man at his side, who had the right to taunt him. As a matter of fact, they were discussing the chances of their ponies in next week's races; but Soma, lost in a great wrath, a great fear, made it, inevitably, the topic of the whole world.

Hark! The bugle for the Rifles to form; they were to come to the parade loaded with ball cartridge. And that rumble was the Artillery, loaded also, going to take up their position. By and by the Carabineers would sweep with a clatter and a dash to form the third side of the hollow square, whereof the fourth was to be a mass of helpless dark faces, with the eighty-five martyrs and tumbrils in the middle. Soma had seen it all in general orders, talked it over with his dearest friend, and called it tyranny. And now the tumbrils clanked past a little heap of smoldering ashes, that but the day before had been a guard-house. The lingering smoke from this last work of the incendiary drifted northward, after the fetters, making one of the officers cough. But he went on talking of his ponies. True type of the race which lives to make mistakes, dies to retrieve them. Quick march!

Streams of spectators bound for the show began to overtake them, ready with comments on what Soma guarded. And on the broad white Mall, dividing the native half of the cantonments and the town of Meerut from the European portion, more than one carriage with a listless, white-faced woman in it dashed by, on its way to see the show. The show!

Quick march! Whatever else might be possible in the future, that was all now, midway between the barracks of the Rifles and the Carabineers, with the church—mute symbol of the horror which, day by day, month by month, had been closing in round the people—blocking the way in front. So they passed on to the wide northern parade ground, with that hollow square ready; three sides of it threatening weapons, the fourth of unarmed men, and in the center the eighty-five picked men of a picked regiment.

The knot of European spectators round the flag

listened with yawns to the stout General's exordium. The eighty-five being hopelessly, helplessly in the wrong by military law, there seemed to be no need to insist on the fact. And the mass of dark faces standing within range of loaded guns and rifles, within reach of glistening sabers, did not listen at all. Not that it mattered, since the units in that crowd had lost the power of accepting facts. Even Soma, standing to attention beside the tumbrils, only felt a great sense of outrage, of wrong, of injustice somewhere. And there was one Englishman, at least, rigid to attention also before his disarmed, dismounted, yet loyal troop, who must have felt it also, unless he was more than human. And this was Captain Craigie, who, when his men appealed to him to save them, to delay this unnecessary musketry parade, had written in his haste to the Adjutant, " Go to Smyth at once! Go to Smyth! " and Smyth was his Colonel! Incredible lack of official etiquette. Repeated hardily, moreover. " Pray don't lose a moment, but go to Smyth and tell him." What? Only " that this is a most serious matter, and we may have the whole regiment in open mutiny in half an hour if it is not attended to." Only that! So it is to be hoped that Captain Craigie had the official wigging for his unconventional appeal in his pocket as he shared his regiment's disgrace, to serve him as a warning—or a consolation.

And now the pompous monotone being ended, the silence, coming after the clankings, and buglings, and trampings which had been going on since dawn, was almost oppressive. The three sides of steel, even the fourth of faces, however, showed no sign. They stood as stone while the eighty-five were stripped of their uniforms. But there was more to come. By the General's orders the leg-irons were to be riveted on one by one; and so, once more, the sound of iron upon iron recurred monotonously, making the silence of the intervals still more oppressive. For the prisoners at first seemed stunned by the isolation from even their as yet unfettered comrades. But suddenly from a single throat came that cry for justice, which has a claim to a hearing, at least, in the estimation of the people of India.

" *Dohai! Dohai! Dohai!* "

Soma gave a sort of sigh, and a faint quiver of expectation passed over the sea of dark faces.

Clang! Clang! The hammers, going on unchecked, were the only answer. Those three sides of stone had come to see a thing done, and it must be done; the sooner the better. But the riveting of eighty-five pairs of leg-irons is not to be done in a moment; so the cry grew clamorous. Dohai! Dohai! Had they not fought faithfully in the past? Had they not been deceived? Had they had a fair chance?

But the hammers went on as the sun climbed out of the dust-haze to gleam on the sloped sabers, glint on the loaded guns, and send glittering streaks of light along the rifles.

So the cry changed. Were their comrades cowards to stand by and see this tyranny and raise no finger of help? Oh! curses on them! 'Tis they who were degraded, dishonored. Curses on the Colonel who had forced them to this! Curses on every white face!—curses on every face which stood by!

One, close to the General's flag, broke suddenly into passionate resentment. Jim Douglas drew out his watch, looked at it, and gathered his reins together. "An hour and forty-five minutes already. I'm off, Ridgeway. I can't stand this d——d folly any more."

" My dear fellow, speak lower! If the General——"

" I don't care who hears me," retorted Jim Douglas recklessly as he steered through the crowd, followed by his friend, " I say it is d——d inconceivable folly and tyranny. Come on, and let's have a gallop, for God's sake, and get rid of that devilish sound."

The echo of their horses' resounding hoofs covered, obliterated it. The wind of their own swiftness seemed to blow the tension away. So after a spin due north for a mile or two they paused at the edge of a field where the oxen were circling placidly round on the threshing-floors and a group of women were taking advantage of the gustiness to winnow. Their bare, brown arms glistened above the falling showers of golden grain, their unabashed smiling faces showed against the clouds of golden chaff drifting behind them.

Jim Douglas looked at them for a moment, returned the salaam of the men driving the oxen and forking the straw, then turned his horse toward the cantonment again.

"It is nothing to them; that's one comfort," he said. "But they will have to suffer for it in the end, I expect. Who will believe when the time comes that this "—he gave a backward wave of his hand—" went on unwittingly of that?"

His companion, following his look ahead, to where, in the far distance, a faint cloud of dust, telling of many feet, hung on the horizon, said suddenly, as if the sight brought remembrance: "By George! Douglas, how steady the sepoys stood! I half expected a row."

"Steadier than I should," remarked the other grimly. "Well, I hope Smyth is satisfied. To return from leave and drive your regiment into mutiny in twelve hours is a record performance."

His hearer, who was a civilian, gave a deprecating cough. "That's a bit hard, surely. I happen to know that he heard while on leave some story about a concerted rising later on. He may have done it purposely, to force their hands."

Jim Douglas shrugged his shoulders. "Did he warn you what he was about to do? Did he allow time to prepare others for his private mutiny? My dear Ridgeway, it was put on official record two months ago that an organized scheme for resistance existed in every regiment between Calcutta and Peshawur; so Smyth might at least have consulted the colonels of the other two regiments at Meerut. As it is, the business has strained the loyalty of the most loyal to the uttermost; and we deserve to suffer, we do indeed."

"You don't mince matters, certainly," said the civilian dryly.

"Why should anybody mince them? Why can't we admit boldly—the C.-in-C. did it on the sly the other day—that the cartridges are suspicious? that they leave the muzzle covered with a fat, like tallow? Why don't we admit it *was* tallow at first. Why not, at any rate, admit we are in a hole, instead of refusing to take the common precaution of having an ammunition wagon loaded up for fear it should be misconstrued into alarm? Is there no medium between bribing children with lollipops and torturing them—keeping them on the strain, under fire, as it were, for hours, watching their best friends punished unjustly?"

"Unjustly?"

"Yes. To their minds unjustly. And you know what forcible injustice means to children—and these are really children—simple, ignorant, obstinate."

They had come back to cantonments again and were rapidly overtaking the now empty tumbrils going home, for the parade was over. Further down the road, raising a cloud of dust from their shackled feet, the eighty-five were being marched jailward under a native escort.

"Well," said the civilian dryly, "I would give a great deal to know what those simple babes really thought of us."

"Hate us stock and block for the time. I should," replied Jim Douglas. They were passing the tumbrils at the moment, and one of the guard, in sergeant's uniform, looked up in joyful recognition.

"Huzoor! It is I, Soma."

The civilian looked at his companion oddly when, after a minute or two spent in answering Soma's inquiries as to where and how the master was to be found, Jim Douglas rode alongside once more.

"Out a bit, eh?" he said dryly.

"Very much out; but they are a queer lot. Do you remember the story of the self-made American who was told his boast relieved the Almighty of a great responsibility? Well, he is only responsible for one-half of the twice-born. The other is due to humanity, to heredity, what you will! That is what makes these high-caste men so difficult to deal with. They are twice born. Yes! they are a queer lot."

He repeated the remark with even greater fervor twelve hours later, when, about midnight, he started on his return ride to Delhi. For though he had spent the whole day in listening, he had scarcely heard a word of blame for the scene which had roused him to wrath that morning. The sepoys had gone about their duties as if nothing had happened; and despite the undoubted presence of a lot of loose characters in the bazaar, there had been no disturbance. He laughed cynically to himself at the waste of a day which would have been better spent in horse dealing. This, however, settled it. If this intolerable tyranny failed to rouse action there could be no immediate danger ahead. To a big cantonment like Meerut, the biggest in Northern India, with two thousand British troops in it, even the prospect of a rising was not serious; at Delhi, however, where there were only native troops, it might have been different. But now he felt that a handful of resolute men ought to be able to hold their own anywhere against such aimless invertebrate discontent. He felt a vague disappointment that it should be so, that the pleasant cool of night should be so quiet, so peaceful. They were a poor lot who could do nothing but talk!

As he rode through the station the mess-houses were still alight, and the gay voices of the guests who had been dining at a large bungalow, bowered in gardens, reached his ears distinctly.

" It's the Sabbath already," said one. " Ought to be in our beds! "

" Hooray! for a Europe morning," came a more boyish one breaking into a carol, " of all the days within the week I dearly love——"

" Shut up, Fitz! " put in a third, " you'll wake the General! "

" What's the odds? He can sleep all day. I'm sure his buggy charger needs a rest."

" Do shut up, Fitz! The Colonel will hear you."

" I don't care. It's Scriptural. Thou and thy ox and thy ass——"

"You promised to come to evening church, Mr. Fitzgerald,". interrupted a reproachful feminine voice; " you said you would sing in the choir."

" Did I? Then I'll come. It will wake me up for dinner; besides, I shall sit next you."

The last words came nearer, softer. Mr. Fitzgerald was evidently riding home beside someone's carriage.

Pleasant and peaceful indeed! that clank of a sentry, here and there, only giving a greater sense of security. Not that it was needed, for here, beyond cantonments, the houses of the clerks and civilians lay as peaceful, as secure. In the veranda of one of them, close to the road, a bearer was walking up and down crooning a patient lullaby to the restless fair-haired child in his arms.

No! truly there could be no fear. It was all talk! He set spurs to his horse and went on through the silent night at a hand-gallop, for he had another beast awaiting him halfway, and he wished to be in Delhi by dawn. There was a row of tall trees bordering the road on either side, making it dark, and through their swiftly passing boles the level country stretched to the paler horizon like a sea. And as he rode, he sat in judgment in his thoughts on those dead levels and the people who lived in them.

Stagnant, featureless! A dead sea! A mere waste of waters without form or void! Not even ready for a spirit to move over them; for if that morning's' work left them apathetic, the Moulvie of Fyzabad himself need preach no voice of God. For *this*, surely—this sense of injustice to others, must be the strongest motive, the surest word to conjure with. That dull dead beat of iron upon the fetters of others,—which he still seemed to hear,—the surest call to battle.

He paused in his thought, wondering if what he fancied he heard was but an echo from memory or real sound! Real; undoubtedly. It was the distant clang of the iron bells upon oxen. That meant that he must be seven or eight miles out, halfway to the next stage, so meeting the usual stream of night traffic toward Meerut. He passed two or three strings of large, looming, half-seen wains without drawing bridle, then pulled up almost involuntarily to a trot at the curiously even tread of a drove of iron-shod oxen, and a low chanted song from behind it. Bunjârah folk! The rough voice, the familiar rhythm of the hoofs, reminded him of many a pleasant night-march in their company.

"A good journey, brothers!" he called in the dialect. The answer came unerringly, dark though it was.

" The Lord keep the Huzoor safe!"

It made him smile as he remembered that of course a lone man trotting a horse along a highroad at night was bound to be alien in a country where horses are ambled and travelers go in twos and threes. So the rough, broad faces would be smiling over the surprise of a sahib knowing the Bunjârah talk; unless, indeed, it happened to be—— The possibility of its being the *tanda* he knew had not occurred to him before. He pulled up and looked round. A breathless shadow was at his stirrup, and he fancied he saw a shadow or two further behind.

" The Huzoor has mistaken the road," came Tiddu's familiar creak. " Meerut lies to the north."

Breathless as he was, there was the pompous mystery in his voice which always prefaced an attempt to extort money. And Jim Douglas, having no further use for the old scoundrel, did not intend to give him any, so he simulated an utter lack of surprise.

" Hello, Tiddu!" he said. " I had an idea it might be you. So you recognized my voice?"

The old man laughed. " The Huzoor is mighty clever. He knows old Tiddu has eyes. They saw the Huzoor's horse—a bay Wazeerie with a white star none too small, and all the luck-marks—waiting at the fifteenth milestone, by Begum-a-bad. But the Huzoor, being so clever, is not going to ride the Wazeerie to-night. He is going to ride the Belooch he is on back to Meerut, though the star on her forehead is too small for safety; my thumb could cover it."

" It's a bit too late to teach me the luck-marks, Tiddu," said Jim Douglas coolly. " You want money, you ruffian; so I suppose you have something to sell. What is it? If it is worth anything, you can trust me to pay, surely."

Tiddu looked round furtively. The other shadow, Jhungi or Bhungi, or both, perhaps—the memory made Jim Douglas smile—had melted away into the darkness. He and Tiddu were alone. The old man, even so, reached up to whisper.

" 'Tis the yellow fakir, Huzoor! He has come."

"The yellow fakir!" echoed his hearer; "who the devil is he? And why shouldn't he come, if he likes?"

Tiddu paused, as if in sheer amaze, for a second. "The Huzoor has not heard of the yellow fakir? The dumb fakir who brings the speech that brings more than speech. *Wâh!*"

"Speech that is more than speech," echoed Jim Douglas angrily, then paused in his turn; the phrase reminded him, vaguely, of his past thoughts.

Tiddu's hand went out to the Belooch's rein; his voice lost its creak and took a soft sing-song to which the mare . seemed to come round of her own accord.

"Yea! Speech that is more than speech, though he is dumb. Whence he comes none know, not even I, the Many-Faced. But I can see him when he comes, Huzoor! The others, not unless he wills to be seen. I saw him to-night. He passed me on a white horse not half an hour agone, going Meerutward. Did not the Huzoor see him? That is because he has learned from old Tiddu to make others see, but not to see himself. But the old man will teach him this also if he is in Meerut by dawn. If he is there by dawn he will see the yellow fakir who brings the speech that brings more than speech."

The sing-song ceased; the Belooch was stepping briskly back toward Meerut.

"You infernal old humbug!" began Jim Douglas.

"The Huzoor does not believe, of course," remarked Tiddu, in the most matter-of-fact creak. "But Meerut is only eight miles off. His other horse can wait; and if he does not see the yellow fakir there is no need to open the purse-strings."

The Englishman looked at his half-seen companion admiringly. He was the most consummate scoundrel! His blending of mystery and purely commercial commonplace was perfect—almost irresistible. There was no reason why he should go on; the groom, halfway, had his usual orders to stay till his master came. For the rest, it would be pleasant to renew the old pleasant memory—pleasant even to renew his acquaintance with Tiddu's guile, which struck him afresh each time he came across it.

He slipped from his horse without a word, and was about to pull the reins over her head so as to lead her, when Tiddu stopped short.

"Jhungi will take her to the rest-house, Huzoor, or Bhungi. It will be safer so. I have a clean cotton quilt in the bundle, and the Huzoor can have my shoes and rub his legs in the dust. That will do till dawn."

He gave a jackal's cry, which was echoed from the darkness.

"Leave her so, Huzoor! She is safe," said Tiddu; and Jim Douglas, as he obeyed, heard the mare whinny softly, as if to a foal, as a shadow came out of the bushes. Junghi or Bhungi, no doubt.

Five minutes after, with a certain unaccountable pleasure, he found himself walking beside a laden bullock, one arm resting on its broad back, his feet keeping step with the remittent clang of its bell. A strange dreamy companionship, as he knew of old. And once more the stars seemed, after a time, to twinkle in unison with the bell, he seemed to forget thought, to forget everything save the peaceful stillness around, and his own unresting peace.

So, he and the laden beast went on as one living, breathing mortal, till the little shiver of wind came, which comes with the first paling of the sky. It was one of those yellow dawns, serene, cloudless, save for a puff or two of thin gray vapor low down on the horizon, looking as if it were smoke from an unseen censer swinging before the chariot of the Sun which heads the procession of the hours. He was so absorbed in watching the yellow light grow to those clouds no bigger than a man's hand; so lost in the strange companionship with the laden beast bound to the wheel of Life and Death as he was, yet asking no question of the future, that Tiddu's hand and voice startled him.

"Huzoor!" he said. "The yellow fakir!"

They were close on the city of Meerut. The road, dipping down to cross a depression, left a bank of yellow dust on either side. And on the eastern one, outlined against the yellow sunrise, sat a motionless figure. It was naked, and painted from head to foot a bright yellow color. The closed eyes were daubed over so as to hide them utterly, and on the forehead, as it is in the image of Siva, was painted perpendicularly a gigantic eye, wide, set, stony. Before it in the dust lay the beggar's bowl for alms.

"The roads part here, Huzoor," said Tiddu. "This to the city; that to the cantonments."

As he spoke, a handsome young fellow came swaggering down the latter, on his way evidently to riotous living in the bazaar. Suddenly he paused, his hand went up to his eyes as if the rising sun were in them. Then he stepped across the road and dropped a coin into the beggar's bowl. Tiddu nodded his head gravely.

"That man is wanted, Huzoor. That is why he saw. Mayhap he is to give the word."

"The word?" echoed Jim Douglas. "You said he was dumb?"

"I meant the trooper, Huzoor. The fakir wanted him. To give the word, mayhap. Someone must always give it."

Jim Douglas felt an odd thrill. He had never thought of that before. Someone, of course, must always give the word, the speech which brought more than speech. What would it be? Something soul-stirring, no doubt; for Humanity had a theory that an angel must trouble the waters and so give it a righteous cause for stepping in to heal the evil.

But what a strange knack the old man had of stirring the imagination with ridiculous mystery! He felt vexed with himself for his own thrill, his own thoughts. "He is a very ordinary *yogi*, I should say," he remarked, looking toward the yellow sunrise, but the figure was gone. He turned to Tiddu again, with real annoyance. "Well! Whoever he is, he cannot want me. And I certainly saw him."

"I willed the Huzoor to see!" replied Tiddu with calm effrontery.

Jim Douglas laughed. The man was certainly a consummate liar; there was never any possibility of catching him out.

CHAPTER VII.

THE WORD WENT FORTH.

THE Procession of the Hours had a weary march of it between the yellow sunrise and the yellow sunset of the 10th of May, 1857; for the heavens were as brass, the air one flame of white heat. The mud huts of the sepoy lines at Meerut looked and felt like bricks baking in a kiln; yet the torpor which the remorseless glare of noon brings even to native humanity was exchanged for a strange restlessness. The doors stood open for the most part, and men wandered in and out aimlessly, like swarming bees before the queen appears. In the bazaar, in the city too, crowds drifted hither and thither, thirstily, as if it were not the fast month of Rumzân, when the Mohammedans are denied the solace of even a drop of water till sundown. Drifted hither and thither, pausing to gather closer at a hint of novelty, melting away again, restless as ever.

Mayhap it was but the inevitable reaction after the stun and stupefaction of Saturday, the sudden awakening to the result—namely, that eighty-five of the best, smartest soldiers in Meerut had been set to toil for ten years in shackles because they refused to be defiled, to become apostate. On the other hand, the old Baharupa may have been right about the yellow fakir: the silent, motionless figure might have set folk listening and waiting for the word. It was to be seen by all now sitting outside the city; at least Jim Douglas saw it several times. Saw, also, that the beggar's bowl was fuller and fuller; but the impossibility of asserting that all the passers-by saw it, as he did, haunted him, once the idea presented itself to his mind. It was always so with Tiddu's mysteries; they were no more susceptible to disproof than they were to proof. You could waste time, of course, in this case by waiting and watching, but in the natural course of events half the passers-by would go on as if they saw nothing, and only one in a hundred or so would give an alms. So what would be the good?

No one else, however, among the masters troubled himself to find a cause for the restlessness; no one even knew of it. To begin with, it was a Sunday, so that even the bond of a common labor was slackened between the dark faces and the light. Then a mile or more of waste deserted land and dry watercourse lay on either side of the broad white road which split the cantonment into halves. So that the North knew nothing of what was going on in the South, and while men were swarming like bees in the sun on one side, on the other they were shut up in barracks and bungalows gasping with the heat, longing for the sun to set, and thanking their stars when the chaplain's memo came round to say that the evening service had been postponed for half an hour to allow the seething, glowing air to cool a little.

It was not the heat, however, which prevented Major Erlton from taking his usual *siesta*. It was thought. He had come over from Delhi on inspection duty a few days before and had intended returning that evening; but the morning's post had brought him a letter which upset all his plans. Alice Gissing's husband had come out a fortnight earlier than they had expected, and was already on his way up-country. The crisis had come, the decision must be made. It was not any hesitation, however, which sent the heavy handsome face to rest in the big strong hands as he rested his elbows on a sheet of blank paper. He had made up his mind on the very day when Alice Gissing had first told him why she could not go back to her husband. The letter forwarding his papers for resignation was already sealed on the table beside him; and the surprise was rather a gain than otherwise. Alice could join him at Meerut now, and they could slip away together to Cashmere or any out of the way place where there was shooting. That would save a lot of fuss; and the fear of fuss was the only one which troubled the Major, personally. He hated to know that even his friends would wonder—for the matter of that those who knew him best would wonder most— why he was chucking everything for a woman he had been mixed up with for years. Yet he had found no difficulty in writing that official request; none in telling little Allie to join him as soon as she could. It was this third letter which could not be written. He took up the pen more than once, only to lay it down again. He began, "My dear Kate," once, only to tear the sheet to pieces. How could he call her his when he was going to tell her that she was his no longer; that the best thing she could do was to divorce him and marry some other chap to be a father to the boy.

The thought sent the head into the hands again; for Herbert Erlton was a healthy animal and loved his offspring by instinct. He had, in truth, a queer upside-down notion of his responsibilities toward them. If the fates had permitted it he would have done his best by Freddy. Shown him the ropes, given him useful tips, stood by his inexperience, paid his reasonable debts—always supposing he had the wherewithal.

Then how was he to tell Kate all the ugly story. He had left her in his thoughts so completely, she had been so far apart from him for so many years now, that he hesitated over telling her the bare facts, just as—being conventionally a perfectly well-bred man—he would have hesitated how to tell them to any innocent woman of his acquaintance. Rather more so, for Kate—though she was sentimental enough, he told himself, for two—had never been sensible and looked things in the face. If she had, it might all have been different. Then with a rush came the remembrance that Allie did—that she knew him every inch and was yet willing to come with him. While he? He would stick through thick and thin to little Allie, who never made a man feel a fool or a beast. Something in the last assertion seemed to harden his heart; he took up his pen and began to write:

"My DEAR KATE: I call you that because I can't think of any other beginning that doesn't seem foolish; but it means nothing, and I only want to tell you that circumstances over which we had no control (he felt rather proud of this circumlocution for a circumstance due entirely to his volition) make it necessary for me to leave you. It is the only course open to me as a gentle-

man. Besides I want to, for I love Alice Gissing dearly.
I am going to marry her, D. V., as soon as I can. Mr.
Gissing may make a fuss—it is a criminal offense, you
see, in India—but we shall tide over that. Of course
you could prevent me too, but you are not that sort. So
I have sent in my papers. It is a pity, in a way, because
I liked this work. But it is only a two-year appointment, and I should hate the regiment after it. For the
rest, I am not such a fool as to think you will mind;
except for the boy. It is a pity for him too, but it isn't
as if he were a girl, *and the other may be.* It will do no
good to say I'm sorry. Besides, I don't think it is all
my fault, and I know you will be happier without me.

> " Yours sincerely,
> " Herbert Erlton.

" P. S.—It's no use crying over spilled milk. I believe
you used to think I would get the regiment some day,
but they would never have given it to me. I made a bit
of a spurt lately, but it couldn't have lasted to the finish,
and after all, that is the win or the lose in a race.

> " H. E."

The postscript was added after re-reading the rest with
an uncomfortable remembrance that it was the last letter
he meant to write to her. Then he threw it ready for the
post beside the others, and lay down feeling that he had
done his duty. And as he dozed off his own simile
haunted him. From start to finish! How few men
rode straight all the way; and the poor beggars who
came to grief over the last fence weren't so far behind
those who came in for the clapping. It was the finish
that did it; that was the win or the lose. But he would
run straight with little Allie—straight as a die! So he
lost consciousness in a glow of virtuous content with the
future, and joined the whole of the northern half of
Meerut in their noontide slumbers; for the future outlook, if not exactly satisfying, was not sufficiently
dubious to keep it awake.

But in the southern half, humanity was still swarming
in and out, waiting, listening. In one of the mud-huts,

however, a company of men gathered within closed doors had been listening to some purpose. Listening to an eloquent speaker, the accredited agent of a down-country organization. He had arrived in Meerut a day or two before, and had held one meeting after another in the lines, doing his utmost to prevent any premature action; for the fiat of the leaders was that there should be patience till the 31st of May. Then, not until then, a combined blow for India, for God, for themselves, might be struck with chance of success.

"Ameen!" assented one old man who had come with him. An old man in a huge faded green turban with dyed red hair and beard, and with a huge green waistband holding a curved scimitar. Briefly, a Ghâzee or Mohammedan fanatic. "Patience, all ye faithful, till Sunday, the 31st of May. Then, while the hell-doomed infidels are at their evening prayer, defenseless, fall on them and slay. God will show the right! This is the Moulvie's word, sent by me his servant. Give the Great Cry, brothers, in the House of the Thief! Smite ye of Meerut, and we of Lucknow will smite also." His wild uncontrolled voice rolled on in broad Arabic vowels from one text to another.

"And we of Delhi will smite also," interrupted the wearer of a rakish Moghul cap impatiently. "We will smite for the Queen."

"The Queen?" echoed an older man in the same dress. "What hath the Sheeah woman to do with the race of Timoor?"

"Peace! peace! brothers," put in the agent with authority. "These times are not for petty squabbles. Let who be the heir, the King must reign."

A murmur of assent rose; but it was broken in upon by a dissentient voice from a group of troopers at the door.

"Then our comrades are to rot in jail till the 31st? That suits not the men of the 3d Cavalry."

"Then let the 3d Cavalry suit itself," retorted the agent fearlessly. "We can stand without them. Can they stand without us? Answer me, men of the 20th; men of the 11th."

" There be not many of us here," muttered a voice from a dark corner; " and maybe we could hold our own against the lot of you." It was Soma's, and the man beside him frowned. But the agent who knew every petty jealousy, every private quarrel of regiment with regiment, went on remorselessly. " Let the 3d swagger if it choose. The Rajpoots and Brahmins know how to obey the stars. The 31st is the auspicious day. That is the word. The word of the King, of the Brahmins, of India, of God! "

" The 31st! Then slay and spare not! It is *jehad! Deen! Deen! Futteh Mohammed!* " said the Ghâzee.

The cry, though a mere whisper, electrified the Mohammedans, and an older man in the group of dissentients at the door muttered that he could hold his troop—if others who had risen to favor quicker than he—could hold theirs.

" I'll hold mine, Khân sahib, without thine aid," retorted a very young smart-looking native officer angrily. " That is if the women will hold their tongues. But, look you, my troop held the hardest hitters in the 3d. And Nargeeza's fancy is of those in jail. Now Nargeeza leads all the other town-women by the nose; and that means much to men who be not all saints like Ghâzee-*jee* yonder, who ties the two ends of life with a ragged green turban and a bloody banner! "

" And I see not why our comrades should stay yonder for three weeks, when there is but a native guard to hold them, and I and mine have made the *Sirkar* what it is," put in a man with arrogance and insolence written on him from top to toe; a true type of the pampered Brahmin sepoy.

" Rescue them if thou wilt, Havildar-*jee*," sneered the agent. " But the man who risks our plot will be held traitor by the Council. And the men of the 11th," he added sharply, turning to the corner whence Soma's voice had come, " may remember that also. They have had the audacity to stipulate for their Colonel's life."

" For our officers lives, *baboo-jee*," came the voice again, bold as the agent's. " We of the 11th kill not men who have led us to victory. And if this be not understood I, Soma, Yadubansi, go straight to the Colonel and tell him. We are not butchers in the 11th: Oh, priest of Kâli!"

The agent turned a little pale. He did not care to have his calling known, and he saw at a glance that his challenger had the reckless fire of hemp in his eyes. He had indeed been drinking as a refuge from the memory of the sweeper's broom and from the taunts and threats which had been used to force him to join the malcontents. Such a man was not safe to quarrel with, nor was the audience fit for a discussion of that topic; there was already a stir in it, and mutterings that butchery was one thing, fighting another.

"Pay thy Colonel's journey home if thou likest, Rajpoot-*jee*," he said with a sneer. "Ay! and give him pension, too! All we want is to get rid of them. And there will be plenty of loot left when the pension is paid, for it is to be each man for himself when the time comes. Not share and share alike with every coward who will not risk his life in looting, as it is with the *Sirkar*."

It was a deft red-herring to these born mercenaries, and no more was said. But as the meeting dispersed by twos and threes to avoid notice, the agent stood at the door giving the word in a final whisper:

"Patience till the 31st."

"Willst take a seat in our carriage, Ghâzee-*jee*," said a fat native officer as he passed out. " 'Tis at thy service since thou goest to Delhi and we must return to-night. God knows we have done enough to damn us at Meerut over this court-martial! But what would you? If we had not given the verdict for the Huzoors there would have been more of us in jail. So we bide our time like the rest. And to-morrow there is the parade to hear the sentence on the martyrs at Barrackpore. Do the sahibs think us cowards that they drive us so? God smite their souls to hell!"

"He will, brother, he will. The Cry shall yet be heard in the House of the Thief," said the Ghâzee fiercely, his eyes growing dreamy with hope. He was thinking of a sunset near the Goomtee more than a year ago, when he had bid every penny he possessed for his own, in vain.

"Well, come if thou likest," continued the native officer. "That camel of thine yonder is lame, and we have room. 'Twas Erlton sahib's dâk by rights, but he goes not; so we got it cheap instead of an *ekka*."

"Erlton sahib's!" echoed the fanatic, clutching at his sword. "Ay! Ay!" he went on half to himself. "I knew he was at Delhi, and the mem who laughed, and the other mem who would not 'listen. Nay! Soubadar-*jee!* I travel in no carriage of Erlton sahib's. My camel will serve me."

" 'Tis the vehicle of saints," sneered the owner of the rakish Moghul cap. "Verily, when I saw thee mounted on it, Ghâzee-*jee*, I deemed thee the Lord Ali."

"Peace! scoffer," interrupted the fanatic, "lest I mistake thee for an infidel."

The Moghul ducked hastily from a wild swing of the curved sword, and moved off swearing such firebrands should be locked up; they might set light to the train ere wise men had it ready.

"No fear!" said the smart young troop-sergeant of the 3d. "Who listens to such as he save those whose blood has cooled, and those whose blood was never hot? The fighters listen to women who can make their flame."

Soma, who was drifting with them toward the drug-shops of the city, scowled fiercely. "That may suit thee, Mussulman-*jee*, who art casteless, and can sup shares with sweeper women in the bazaar; but the Rajpoot needs no harlot to teach him courage. The mothers of his race have enough and to spare."

"*Loh!* hark to him!" jibed the corporal of the 20th, who was sticking to his prey like a leech. "Ask him, Havildar-*jee*, if he prefers a sweeper's broom to a sweeper's lips."

There was a roar of laughter from the group.

Soma gave a beast-like cry, looked as though he were about to spring, then—recognizing his own helplessness—flung himself away from all companionship and walked home moodily. They had driven him too far; he would not stand it. If that tale was spread abroad, he would side with the Huzoors who did not believe such things—with the Colonel who understood, like the Colo-

nel before him who had gone home on pension; for the
11th had a cult of their officers. And these fools, his
countrymen, thought to make him a butcher by threats;
sought to make him take revenge for what deserved
revenge. For it was the *Sirkar's* fault—it was the
Sirkar's fault.

In truth a strange conflict was going on in this man's
mind, as it was in many another such as his, between
inherited traditions, making alike for loyalty and disloyalty. There was the knowledge of his forbears' pride
in their victories, in their sahibs who had led them to
victory, and the knowledge of their pride in the veriest
jot or tittle of ceremonial law. A dull, painful amaze filled
him that these two broad facts should be in conflict; that
those, whom in a way he felt to be part of his life, should
be in league against him. All the more reason, that,
for showing them who were the better men; for standing
up fairly to a fair fight. By all the delights of Swarga!
he would like to stand up fair, even to the master—the
man who, in his presence, had shot three tigers on foot
in half an hour—the demi-god of his hunting yarns for
years.

And then, suddenly, he remembered that this hero of
his might be shot like a dog on the 31st at Delhi—would
be shot, since he was certain to be in the front of anything. Soma's heat-fevered, hemp-drugged brain seized
on the thought fiercely, confusedly. That must not be!
The master, at any rate, must be warned. He would go
down when the sun set, and see if he were still where
he had been the day before; and if not?—Why! then it
must be two days leave to Delhi! He was not going to
butcher the master for all the sweepers' brooms in the
world. Fools! those others, to think to drive him,
Soma, Chundrabansi! So he flung himself on his string
bed to sleep till the sunset came, and the tyranny of heat
be overpast.

But there was one, close by in the cantonment bazaar,
who waited for sunset with no desire for it to bring coolness. She meant it to bring heat instead. And this was
Nargeeza the courtesan. She was past the prime of
everything save vice, a woman who, once all-powerful,

could not hope for many more lovers; and hers, a man rich beyond most soldiers, lay in jail for ten years. No wonder, then, that as she lay half-torpid among a heap of tawdry finery in the biggest house of the lane set apart by regulation for such as she, there was all the venom of a snake in her drowsy brain. The air of the low room was deadly with a scent of musk and roses and orange-blossom-oil. The half-dozen girls and women who lounged in it, or in the balcony, were half undressed, their bare brown arms flung carelessly upon dirty mats and torn quilts. Their harvest time was not yet; that would come later when sunsetting brought the men from the lines. This, then, was the time for sleep. But Nargeeza, recognized head of the recognized regimental women, sat up suddenly and said sharply:

"Thou didst not tell me, Nasiban, what Gulâbi said. Is she of us?"

A drowsy lump of a girl stirred, yawned, and answered sullenly, "Yea! Yea! she is of us. She claims our right to kiss no cowards—no cowards."

The voice tailed off into sleep again, and Nargeeza lay back with a smile of content to wait also. So, after a time, folk began to stir in the bungalows. First in the rest-house, where, oddly enough, Jim Douglas occupied one end of the long low barrack of a place, and Herbert Erlton the other. The former having come back from the city in an evil temper to get something to eat before starting for Delhi, had found his horse, the Belooch, unaccountably indisposed; Jhungi, who had brought her there safely, professing entire ignorance of the cause, or, on pressure, suggesting the nefarious Bhungi. Tiddu asserting—with a calm assumption of superior knowledge, for which Jim Douglas could have kicked him— that the mare had been drugged. As if anybody could not tell that? And that the drug had been opium. To which the old scoundrel had replied affably that in that case the effects would pass off during the night, and the mare be none the worse; no one be any the worse, since the Huzoor was quite comfortable in Meerut, and could *easily stay another day.* It was a nicer place than Delhi;

there were more sahibs in it, and the presence of the
" *ghora logue* " (*i. e.*, English soldiers) kept everyone
virtuous.

His hearer looked at him sharply. Here was some
other trick, no doubt, to cozen him out of another five
rupees; for something, maybe, as useless as the yellow
fakir. And there was really no reason for delay; it was
only a case of walking the mare quietly. For the matter
of that, the exercise would do her good, and help her to
work off the effects of the drug. So he would start
sooner, that was all. Nevertheless he gave an envious
look at the Major's little Arab in the next stall. It
would most likely be marching back to Delhi that night,
and he would have given something to ride it again. But
as he was returning from the stables, he learned by
chance that the Major's plans had been altered. An
orderly was coming from his room with letters and a
telegram, and knowing the man, Jim Douglas asked him
to take one for him also, and so save trouble. It did not
take long to write, for it only contained one word, " No."
It was in reply to one he had received a few hours before
from the military magnate, asking him to do some more
work. And as the orderly stowed away the accompanying rupee carefully, Jim Douglas—waiting to make over
the paper—saw quite involuntarily that the Major's telegram also consisted of one word, " Come." And he saw
the name also; big, black, bold, in the Major's handwrit-
ing. " Gissing, Delhi."

He gave a shrug of his shoulders as he turned away to
get ready for his start. So that was it; and even Kate
Erlton had not benefited by his sacrifice. No one had
benefited. There had been no chance for any of them.
" Come! " That ended Kate Erlton's hope of concealment, the Major's career. " No! " That ended his own
vague ambitions. Still, it was a strange chance in itself
that those two laconic renunciations should go the same
day by the same hand. No stranger telegrams, he
thought, could have left Meerut, or were likely to leave
it that night.

He was wrong, however. An hour or two later, the

strangest telegram that ever came as sole warning to an
Empire that its very foundation was attacked, left Meerut
for Agra; sent by the postmaster's niece.

"The Cavalry," it ran, "have risen, setting fire to their
own houses besides having killed and wounded all European officers and soldiers they could find near the lines.
If Aunt intends starting to-morrow, please detain her, as
the van has been prevented from leaving the station."

For, as Jim Douglas paced slowly down the Mall toward Delhi, and Soma, his buckles gleaming, his belts
pipe-clayed to dazzling whiteness, was swaggering
through the bazaar on his way to the rest-house with his
word of warning—the word which would have given Jim
Douglas the power for which he had longed—another
word was being spoken in that lane of lust, where the
time had come for which Nargeeza had waited all day.
But *she* did not say it.   It was only a big trollop of a girl
hung with jasmine garlands, painted, giggling.

"We of the bazaar kiss no cowards," she said derisively.   "Where are your comrades?"

The man to whom she said it, a young dissolute-faced
trooper, dressed in the loose rakish muslins beloved of
his class—the very man, perchance, who had gone cityward that morning, and dropped an alms into the yellow
fakir's bowl—stood for a second in the stifling, madden-
ing atmosphere of musk and rose and orange-blossom;
stood before all those insolent allurements, balked in his
passion, checked in his desires.   Then, with an oath, he
dashed from her insulting charms; dashed into the street
with a cry:

"To horse!   To horse, brothers!   To the jail! to our
comrades!"

The word had been spoken.   The speech which brings
more than speech, had come from the painted lips of a
harlot.

The first clang of the church bell—which the chaplain
had forgotten to postpone—came faintly audible across
the dusty plain, making other men pause and look at
each other.   Why not?   It was the hour of prayer—the
appointed time.   Their comrades could be easily rescued—there was but a native guard at the jail.   And

hark! from another pair of painted derisive lips came the same retort, flung from a balcony.

"*Trra! We of the bazaar kiss no cowards!*"

"To horse! To horse! Let the comrades be rescued first; and then——"

The word had been spoken. Nothing so very soul-stirring after all. No consideration of caste or religion, patriotism or ambition. Only a taunt from a pair of painted lips.

BOOK III.

FROM DUSK TO DAWN.

CHAPTER I.

NIGHT.

" To the rescue! To the rescue! "

The cry was no more than that at first. To the rescue of the eighty-five martyrs, the blows upon whose shackles still seemed to echo in their comrades' ears. Even so, the cry heard by Soma as he passed through the bazaar meant insubordination—the greatest crime he knew—and sent him flying to his own lines to give the alarm. Sent him thence by instinct, oblivious of that promise for the 31st—or perhaps mindful of it and seeing in this outburst a mere riot—to his Colonel's house with twenty or thirty comrades clamoring for their arms, protesting that with them they would soon settle matters for the Huzoors. But suspicion was in the air, and even the Colonel of the 11th could not trust all his regiment. Ready for church, he flung himself on his horse and raced back with the clamoring men to the lines.

And by this time there was another race going on. Captain Craigie's faithful troop of the 3d Cavalry were racing after his shout of " *Dau-ro! bhai-yan, Dau-ro!* " (Ride, brothers, ride!) toward the jail in the hopes of averting the rescue of their comrades. For, as the records are careful to say, he and his troop " were dressed as for parade "—not a buckle or a belt awry—ready to combat the danger before others had grasped it, and swiftly, without a thought, went for the first offenders. Too late! the doors were open, the birds flown.

What next was to be done? What but to bring the troop back without a defaulter—despite the taunts of escaping convicts, the temptations of comrades flushed by success—to the parade ground for orders. But there was no one to give them, for when the 3d Cavalry led the van of mutiny at Meerut their Colonel was in the European cantonment as field officer of the week, and there he " conceived it his duty to remain." Perhaps rightly. And it is also conceivable that his absence made no difference, since it is, palpably, an easier task to make a regiment mutiny than to bring it back to its allegiance.

Meanwhile the officers of the other regiments, the 11th and the 20th, were facing their men boldly; facing the problem how to keep them steady till that squadron of the Carabineers should sweep down, followed by a company or two of the Rifles at the double, and turn the balance in favor of loyalty. It could not be long now. Nearly an hour had passed since the first wild stampede to the jail. The refuse and rabble of the town were by this time swarming out of it, armed with sticks and staves; the two thousand and odd felons released from the jails were swarming in, seeking weapons. The danger grew every second, and the officers of the 11th, though their men stood steady as rocks behind them, counted the moments as they sped. For on the other side of the road, on the parade ground of the 20th regiment, the sepoys, ordered, as the 11th had been, to turn out unarmed, were barely restrained from rushing the bells by the entreaties of their native officers; the European ones being powerless.

" Keep the men steady for me," said Colonel Finnis to his second in command; " I'll go over and see what I can do."

He thought the voice of a man loved and trusted by one regiment, a man who could speak to his sepoys without an interpreter, might have power to steady another.

Jai bahâduri! (Victory to courage!) muttered Soma under his breath as he watched his Colonel canter quietly into danger. And his finger hungered on that hot May evening for the cool of the trigger which was denied him.

Jai bahâduri! A murmur seemed to run through the

ranks, they dressed themselves firmer, squarer. Colonel Finnis, glancing back, saw a sight to gladden any commandant's heart. A regiment steady as a rock, drawn up as for parade, absolutely in hand despite that strange new sound in the air. The sound which above all others gets into men's brains like new wine. The sound of a file upon fetters—the sound of escape, of freedom, of license! It had been rising unchecked for half an hour from the lines of the 3d, whither the martyrs had been brought in triumph. It was rising now from the bazaar, the city, from every quiet corner where a prisoner might pause to hack and hammer at his leg-irons with the first tool he could find.

What was one man's voice against this sound, strengthened as it was by the cry of a trooper galloping madly from the north shouting that the English were in sight? What more likely? Had not ample time passed for the whole British garrison to be coming with fixed bayonets and a whoop, to make short work of unarmed men who had not made up their minds?

That must be no longer!

"Quick! brothers. Quick! Kill! Kill! Down with the officers! Shoot ere the white faces come!"

It was a sudden wild yell of terror, of courage, of sheer cruelty. It drowned the scream of the Colonel's horse as it staggered under him. It drowned his steady appealing voice, his faint sob, as he threw up his hands at the next shot, and fell, the first victim to the Great Revolt.

It drowned something else also. It drowned Soma's groan of wild, half-stupefied, helpless rage as he saw his Colonel fall,—the sahib who had led him to victory,—the sahib whom he loved, whom he was pledged to save. And his groan was echoed by many another brave man in those ranks, thus brought face to face suddenly with the necessity for decision.

" Steady, men, steady!"

That call, in the alien voice, echoed above the whistling of the bullets as they found a billet here and there among the ranks; for the men of the 20th, maddened by that fresh murder, now shot wildly at their officers.

"Steady, men! Steady, for God's sake!"

The entreaty was not in vain; they were steady still. Ay, steady, but unarmed! Steady as a rock still, but helpless!

Helpless, unarmed! By all the gods all men worshiped, men could not suffer that for long, when bullets were whistling into their ranks.

So there was a waver at last in the long line. A faint tremble, like the tremble of a curving wave ere it falls. Then, with a confused roar, an aimless sweeping away of all things in its path, it broke as a wave breaks upon a pebbly shore.

"To arms, brothers! Quick! fire! fire!"

Upon whom?* God knows! Not on their officers, for these were already being hustled to the rear, hustled into safety.

"Quick, brothers, quick! Kill! Kill!"

The cry rose on all sides now, as the wave of revolt surged on. But there was none left to kill; for the work was done in the 20th lines, and no new white faces came to stem the tide. Two thousand and odd Englishmen who might have stemmed it being still on the parade-ground by the church, waiting for orders, for ammunition, for a General, for everything save—thank Heaven!—for courage.

So the wave surged on, to what end it scarcely knew, leaving behind it groups of sullen, startled faces.

"Whose fault but their own?" muttered an old man fiercely; an old man whose son served beside him in the regiment, whose grandson was on the roster for future enlistment. "Why were we left helpless as new-born babes?"

"Why?" echoed a scornful voice from the gathering clusters of undecided men, waiting, with growing fear, hope, despair, or triumph, for what was to come next:

---

* This question is one which must be asked as we look back through the years on this pitiful spectacle of the loyal regiment, unarmed, facing the disloyal one shooting down its officers. Briefly, on whom would the seventy men of the 11th, who never left the colors, the hundred and twenty men who returned to them after the short night of tumult was over, have fired if a company of English troops had come up to turn the balance in favor of loyalty ?

waiting, briefly, for the master to come, or not to come.
" Why? because they were afraid of us; because their'
time is past, baba jee. Let them go! "

Let them go. Incomprehensible suggestion to that
brave worn stiff in the master's service; so, with a great
numb ache in an old heart, an old body strode away,
elbowing younger ones from its path savagely.

" Old Dhurma hath grown milksop," jeered one
spectator; " that is with doing dry-nurse to his Captain's
babies."

The words caught the old man's ear and sent a quick
decision to his dazed face. The baba logue! Yes; they
must be safeguarded; for ominous smoke began to rise
from neighboring roof-trees, and a strange note of sheer
wild-beast ferocity grew to the confused roar of the
drifting, shifting, still aimless crowd.

" Quick, brothers, quick! Kill, root and branch!
Why dost linger? Art afraid? Afraid of cowards?
Quick—kill everyone! "

The cry, boastful, jeering, came from a sepoy in the
uniform of the 20th, who, with a face ablaze with mad exultation, forced his way forward. There was something
in his tone which seemed to send a shiver of fresh excitement through his comrades, for they paused in their
strange, aimless tumult, paused and listened to the jeers,
the reproaches.

" What! art cowards too? " he went on. " Then follow me. For I began it—I fired the first shot—I killed
the first infidel. I——"

The boast never ended, for above it came a quicker cry:

" Kill, kill, kill the traitor! Kill the man who
betrayed us."

There was a rush onward toward the boastful, arrogant
voice, the report of half a dozen muskets, and the crowd
surged on to revolt over the body of the man who had
fired the first shot of the mutiny.

For it was a strange crowd indeed; most of it powerless for good or ill, sheep without a shepherd, wandering
after the rabble of escaped convicts and the refuse of the
bazaars as they plundered and fired the houses. Joining
in the license helplessly, drifting inevitably to violence,

so that some looked on curiously, unconcernedly, while others, maddened by the smell of blood, the sounds of murder, dragged helpless Englishmen and Englishwomen from their carriages and did them to death savagely.

But there were more like Soma, who, as the darkness deepened and the glare and the dire confusion and dismay grew, stood aloof from it voluntarily, waiting, with a certain callousness, to see if the master would come, or if folk said true when they declared his time was past, his day done.

Where was he? He should have come hours ago, irresistible, overwhelming. But there was no sign. Not a hint of resistance, save every now and again a clatter of hoofs through the darkness, an alien voice calling " Mâro! Mâro! " to those behind him, and a fierce howl of an echo, " Mâro! Mâro! Mâ-roh! " from the faithful troop. For Captain Craigie, finding none to help him, had changed his cry. It was " kill, kill, kill " now. And the faithful troop obeyed orders.

Soma when he heard it gave a great sigh. If there had been more of that sort of thing he would dearly have loved to be in it; but the other was butchery. So he wandered alone, irresolute, drifting northward from the dire confusion and dismay, and crossing the Mall to question a sentry of his own regiment as to what had happened to the masters. But the man replied by eager questions as to what had happened to the servants. And they both agreed that if the two thousand could not quell a riot it would be idle to help them, the Lord's hand being so palpably against them.

Nevertheless, half an hour afterward the sentry still waited at his post, and the guard over the Treasury saluted as if nothing unusual was afoot to a group of Englishmen galloping past.

" Those men know nothing," called Major Erlton to another man. " It can't be so bad. Surely something can be done! "

" Something should have been done two hours ago," came a sharp voice. " However, the troops have started at last. If anyone——"

The remainder was lost in the clatter. But more than

one man's voice had been lost in those two hours at Meerut on the 10th of May, 1857; indeed, everything seems to have been lost save—thank Heaven once more! —personal courage.

It was now near eight o'clock, and Soma, skulking by the Mall, midway between the masters and the men, still irresolute, still uncertain, heard the first cry of " To Delhi! to Delhi! " which, as the night wore on, was to echo so often along that road.   The cry which came un- bidden as the astounding success of the revolt brought thoughts of greater success in the future.

The moon was now rising to silver the dense clouds of smoke which hung above the pillars of flame, and give an additional horror of light to the orgies going on unchecked.   It showed him a group of 3d Cavalry troop- ers galloping madly down the Mall.   It showed them the glitter of his buckles, making them shout again:

" To Delhi, brother, to Delhi! "

Not yet.   He had not seen the upshot yet.   He must go and see what was going on in the lines first.   So he struck rapidly across the open as the quickest way.   And then behind him, close upon him, came another clatter of hoofs, a very different cry.

" *Shâh bâsh! bhaiyân.   Mâro!   Mâro!* "

Remembering the glitter of his buckles, he turned and ran for the nearest cover.   None too soon, for a Mo- hammedan trooper was after him, shouting " *Deen! Deen!* Death to the Hindoo pig! "   For any cry comes handy when the blood is up and there is a saber in the hand.   Soma had to double like a hare, and even so, when he paused to get his breath in a tangle of lime- bushes there was a graze on his cheek.   He had judged his distance in one of those doubles a hair's breadth too little.   The faint trickle of blood sent a spasm of old inherited race hatred through him.   The outcaste should know that the Hindoo pig shot straight.   The means of showing this were not far to find in the track of the faith- ful troop.   Five minutes after, Soma, with a musket dragged from beneath something which lay huddled up face down upon Mother Earth, was crouching in a belt of cover, waiting for the troop to come flashing through the glare seeking more work. For there had been yells and screams enough round that bungalow to stop looting there. And as it came number seven bent lower to his saddle bow suddenly, then toppled over with a clang.

" Left wheel! clear those bushes!" came the order sharply. But Soma was too quick for that.

" Close up. Forward!" came the order again, as Captain Craigie's faithful troop went on, minus a man, and Soma, stumbling breathlessly in safety, knew that the die was cast. There was an answering quiver in his veins which comes when like blood has been spilled. He knew his foe now; he could go to Delhi now. And hark! There was a regular rattle of musketry, at last—not the dropping fire of mere butchery, but a regular volley. He gripped his musket tighter and listened: if the battle had begun he must be in it. The air was full of cracklings and hissings—an inarticulate background to murderous yells, terrified screams, horrors without end; but no more volleys came to tell of retribution.

What did it mean? Soma held his breath hard. Hark! what was that? A louder burst of that recurring cry, " To Delhi! to Delhi!" as the last stragglers of the 3d Cavalry, escaping from the lines at the long-delayed appearance there of law and order, followed their comrades' example.

So that the two thousand coming down in force found nothing but the women and children; poor, frightened, terror-struck hostages, left behind, inevitably, in the unforeseen success.

But Soma, knowing nothing of this, waited—that grip on his musket slackening—for the next volley. But none came. Only, suddenly, a bugle call.

The retreat!

Incredible! Impossible! Yes! Once, twice, thrice— the retreat! The masters were not going to fight at Meerut then, and he must try Delhi. So, turning swiftly, he cut into the road behind the cry.

" My God, Craigie! what's that? Not the retreat, surely!" came a boyish voice from the clatter and rattle of the faithful troop.

" Don't know! Hurry up all you can, Clark! There's

more of the devils needing cold steel yonder, and I'd like
to see to my wife's safety as soon as I can. *Shâh bâsh
bhaiyân Dân-ro. Mâro.*"

" Mâro—Mâ—ro—Mâ——roh!" echoed the howl.
What was the retreat to them when their Captain's voice
called to them as brothers? It is idle to ask the question,
but one cannot help wondering if the Captain's pocket
still held the official wigging. For the sake of picturesque effect it is to be hoped it did.

Nevertheless it *was* the retreat. A council of officers
had suggested that since the mutineers were not in their
lines, they might be looting the European cantonments.
So the two thousand returned thither, after firing that one
volley into a wood, and then finding all quiet to the north
proceeded to bivouac on the parade ground for the night.
Not a very peaceful spot, since it was within sight and
sound of blazing roof-trees and plundering ruffians.
The worst horrors of that night, we are told, can never
be known. Perhaps some people beg to differ, holding
that no horror can exceed the thought of women and
children hiding like hares on that southern side, creeping
for dear life from one friendly shadow to another, and
finding help in dark hands where white ones failed them,
within reach of that bivouac. But the faithful troop
did good service, and many another band of independent
braves also. Captain Craigie, finding leisure at last,
found also—it is a relief to know—that some of his own
men had sneaked away from duty to secure his wife's
safety when they saw their Captain would not. And if
anything can relieve the deadly depression which sinks
upon the soul at the thought of that horrible lack·of
emotion in the north, it is to picture that very different
scene on the south, when Captain Craigie, seeing his only
hope of getting the ladies safely escorted to the European barracks lay in his troopers, brought the two Englishwomen out to them and said, simply, " Here are the
mems! Save them."

And then the two score or so of rough men, swash-
bucklers by birth and training, flung themselves from
their horses, cast themselves at those alien women's feet
with tears and oaths. Oaths that were kept.

But, on the other side, people were more placid. One reads of Englishmen watching " their own sleeping children with gratitude in their hearts to God," with wonderings as " to the fate of their friends in the south," with anticipations of " what would befall their Christian brethren in Delhi on the coming morn, who, less happy than ourselves, had no faithful and friendly European battalions to shield them from the bloodthirsty rage of the sepoys."

What, indeed? considering that for two hours bands of armed men had clattered and marched down that dividing road crying " To Delhi, to Delhi! " But no warning of the coming danger had been sent thither; the confusion had been too great. And now, about midnight, the telegraph wires had been cut. Yet Delhi lay but thirty miles off along a broad white road, and there were horses galore and men ready to ride them. Men ready for more than that, like Captain Rosser of the Carabineers, who pleaded for a squadron, a field battery, a troop, a gun—anything with which to dash down the road and cut off that retreat to Delhi. But everything was refused. Lieutenant Mohler of the 11th offered to ride, and at least give warning; but that offer was also set aside. And many another brave man, no doubt, bound to obey orders, ate his heart out in inaction that night, possessing himself in some measure of patience with the thought that the dawn must see them on that Delhi road.

But there was one man who owed obedience to none; who was free to go if he chose. And he did choose. Ten minutes after it dawned upon Herbert Erlton that no warning had been given, that no succor would be sent, he had changed horses for the game little Arab which had once belonged to Jim Douglas, and was off, to reach Delhi as best he could; for a woman slept in the very city itself exposed to the first assault of ruffianism, whom he must save, if he could. So he set his teeth and rode straight. At first down the road, for the last of the fugitives had had a good hour's start of him, and he could count on four or five miles plain sailing. Then, since his object was to head the procession, and he did not dare to strike across country from his utter ignor-

ance both of the way or how to ask it, he must give the
road a half-mile berth or so, and, keeping it as a guide,
make his way somehow. There were bridges he knew
where he must hark back to the only path, but he must
trust to luck for a quiet interval.

The plan proved more difficult than he expected.
More than once he found himself in danger from being
too close to the disciplined tramp which he began to overtake about six miles out, and twice he lost himself from
being too far away, by mistaking one belt of trees for
another. Still there was plenty of time if the Arab held
out with his weight. The night was hot and stifling,
but if he took it coolly till the road was pretty clear again
he could forge ahead in no time; for the Arab had the
heels of every horse in Upper India. Major Erlton knew
this, and bent over to pat its neck with the pride of certainty with which he had patted it before many a race
which it had won for him since it had lost one for Jim
Douglas.

So he saved it all he knew; but he rode fourteen stone,
and that, over jumps, must tell. There was no other way,
however, that he knew of, by which an Englishman
could head that procession of shouting black devils.

One headed already, as it happened; though he was
unaware of the supreme importance of the fact, ignorant
of what lay behind him. Jim Douglas, who had left
Meerut all unwitting of that rescue party on its way to
the jail, was still about a mile from the halfway house
where he expected to find his relay. He had had the
greatest difficulty in getting the drugged mare to go
at all at first, and more than once had regretted having
refused old Tiddu's advice. She had pulled herself together a bit, but she was in a drip of sweat and still shaky
on her feet. Not that it mattered, he being close now to
Begum-a-bad, with plenty of time to reach Delhi by
dawn.

He rather preferred to pace slowly, his feet out of the
stirrups, his slight, easy figure dressed, as it always was
when in English costume, with the utmost daintiness,
sitting well back in the saddle. For the glamour of the
moonlight, the stillness of the night, possessed him.

Everything so soundless save when the jackals began; there were a number of them about. A good hunting country; the memory of many a run in his youthful days, with a bobbery pack, came to him. After all he had had the cream of life in a way. Few men had enjoyed theirs more, for even this idle pacing through the stillness was a pleasure. Pleasure? How many he had had! His mind, reverting from one to another, thought even of the owner of the golden curl without regret. She had taught him the religion of Love, the adoration of a spotless woman. And Zora, dear little Zora, had taught him the purity of passion. And then his mind went back suddenly to a scene of his boyhood. A boy of eighteen carrying a girl of sixteen who held a string of sea-trout midway in a wide, deep ford. And he heard, as if it had been yesterday, the faint splash of the fish as they slipped one by one into the water, and felt the fierce fighting of the girl to be set down, his own stolid resistance, their mutual abuse of each other's obstinacy and carelessness. Yes! he would like to see his sisters again, to know that pleasure again. Then his mind took another leap. Alice Gissing had not struggled in his hold, because she had been in unison with his ideal of conduct; but if she had not been, she would have fought as viciously, as unconsciously as any sister. Alice Gissing, who—— He settled his feet into the stirrups sternly, thinking of that telegram with its one word " Come," which ended so many chances.

Hark! What was that? A clatter of hoofs behind. And something more, surely. A jingle, a jangle, familiar to a soldier's ears. Cavalry at the gallop. He drew aside hastily into the shadow of the arcaded trees and waited.

Cavalry, no doubt. And the moon shone on their drawn sabers. By Heaven! Troopers of the 3d! Half a dozen or more!

" *Shâh bâsh*, brothers," cried one as they swept past, " we can breathe our beasts a bit at Begum-a-bad and let the others come up; no need to reach Delhi ere dawn. The Palace would be closed."

Delhi! The Palace! And who were the others?

That, if they were coming behind, could soon be settled. He turned the Belooch and trotted her back in the shadow, straining eyes and ears down the tree-fringed road which lay so still, so white, so silent.

Something was on it now, but something silent, almost ghost-like,—an old man, muttering texts, on a lame camel which bumped along as even no earthly camel ought to bump. That could not be the " others."

No! Surely that was a thud, a jingle, a clatter once more. And once more the glitter of cold steel in the moonlight. Forty or fifty of the 3d this time, with stragglers calling to others still further behind, " To Delhi! To Delhi! To Victory or Death! "

As he stood waiting for them all to pass ere he moved, his first thought was, that with all these armed men at Begum-a-bad there would be no chance of a remount. Then came a swift wonder as to what had happened. A row of some sort, of course, and these men had fled. Ere long, no doubt, a squadron of Carabineers would come rattling after them. No! That was not cavalry. That was infantry in the distance. Quite a number of men shouting the same cry. Men of the 20th, to judge by what he could see. Then the row had been a big one. Still the men were evidently fugitives. There was that in their recurring cry which told of almost hopeless, reckless enthusiasm.

And how the devil was he to get his remount? It was to be at the serai on the roadside, the very place where these men would rest. Yet he must get to Delhi, he must get there sharp! The possibility that Delhi was unwarned did not occur to him; he only thought how he might best get there in time for the row which must come. Should he wait for the English troops to come up, and chance his remount being coolly taken by the first rebel who wanted one? Or, Delhi being not more than fifteen miles off across country, should he take the mare as far as she would go, leave her in some field, and do the rest on foot? He looked at his watch. Half-past one! Say five miles in half an hour. The mare was good for that. Then ten miles, at five miles an hour. The very first glimmer of light should see him at the boat-bridge if—if the mare could gallop five miles.

He must try her a bit slowly at first. So, slipping across the broad, white streak of road to the Delhi side, he took her slanting through the tall tiger grass, for they were close on a nullah which must be forded by a rather deep ford lower down, since the bridge was denied to him. About half a mile from the road he came upon the track suddenly, in the midst of high tamarisk jungle growing in heavy sand, and the next moment was on the shining levels of the ford. The mare strained on his hand, and he paused to let her have a mouthful of water. As she stood there, head down, a horseman at the canter showed suddenly, silently, behind him, not five yards away, his horse's hoofs deadened by the sand.

There was a nasty movement, an ominous click on both sides. But the moon was too bright for mistakes; the recognition was mutual.

" My God, Erlton! " he cried, as the other, without a pause, went on into the ford. " What's up? "

" Is it fordable? " came the quick question, and as Jim Douglas for an answer gave a dig with his spurs, the Major slackened visibly; his eye telling him that the depth could not be taken, save at a walk.

" What's up? " he echoed fiercely. " Mutiny! murder! I say, how far am I from Delhi? "

" Delhi! " cried Jim Douglas, his voice keen as a knife. " By Heaven! you don't mean they don't know—that they didn't wire—but the troops—— "

" Hadn't started when I left," said the Major with a curse. " I came on alone. I say, Douglas," he gave a sharp glance at the other's mount and there was a pause.

" My mare's beat—been drugged," said Jim Douglas in the swish-swish of the water rising higher and higher on the horses' breasts, and there was a curious tone in his voice as if he was arguing out something to himself. " I've a remount at the serai, but the odds are a hundred to one on my getting it. I'd given up the chance of it. I meant to take the mare as many miles across country as she'd go—more, perhaps—for she

feels like falling at a fence, and walk the rest. I didn't
know then——" He paused and looked ahead. The
water, up to the girths, made a curious rushing sound,
like many wings. The long, shiny levels stretched away
softly, mysteriously. The tamarisk jungle reflected in
the water seemed almost as real as that which edged the
shining sky. A white egret stood in the shallows; tall,
ghostly.

"I thought it was only—a row."

The voice ceased again, the breathings of the tired
horses had slackened; there was no sound but that rushing, as of wings, as those two enemies rode side by side,
looking ahead. Suddenly Jim Douglas turned.

"You ride nigh four stone heavier than I do, Major
Erlton."

The heavy, handsome face came round swiftly, all
broken up with sheer passion.

"Do you suppose I haven't been thinking that ever
since I saw your cursed face. And you know the country, and I don't. You know the lingo, and I don't.
And—and—you're a deuce sight better rider than I am,
d——n you! But for all that, it's my chance, I tell you.
My chance, not yours."

A great surge of sympathy swept through the other
man's veins. But the water was shallowing rapidly.
A step or two and this must be decided.

"It's yours more than mine," he said slowly, "but it
isn't ours, is it? It's the others', in Delhi."

Herbert Erlton gave an odd sound between a sob and
an oath, a savage jag at the bridle as the little Arab, over-
weighted, slipped a bit coming up the bank. Then, without a word, he flung himself from the saddle and set to
work on the stirrup nearest him.

"How many holes?" he asked gruffly, as Jim Douglas, with a great ache in his heart, left the Belooch standing, and began on the other.

"Three; you're a good bit longer in the leg than I am."

"I suppose I am," said the Major sullenly; but he held
the stirrup for the other to mount.

Jim Douglas gathered the reins in his hand and
paused.

"You had better walk her back. Keep more to the left; it's easier."

"Oh! I'll do," came the sullen voice. "Stop a bit, the curb's too tight."

"Take it off, will you? he knows me."

Major Erlton gave an odd, quick, bitter laugh. "I suppose he does. Right you are."

He stood, putting the curb chain into his pocket, mechanically, but Jim Douglas paused again.

"Good-by! Shake hands on it, Erlton."

The Major looked at him resentfully, the big, coarse hand came reluctantly; but the touch of that other like iron in its grip, its determination, seemed to rouse something deeper than anger.

"The odds are on you," he said, with a quiver in his voice. "You'll look after her—not my wife, she's in cantonments—but in the city, you know."

The voice broke suddenly. He threw out one hand in a sort of passionate despair, and walked over to the Belooch.

"I'll do everything you could possibly do in my place, Erlton."

The words came clear and stern, and the next instant the thud of the Arab's galloping hoofs filled the still night air. The sound sent a spasm of angry pain through Major Erlton. The chance had been his, and he had had to give it up because he rode three stone heavier; and, curse it! knew only too well what a difference a pound or two might make in a race.

Nevertheless Jim Douglas had been right when he said the chance was neither his nor the Major's. For, less than an hour afterward, riding all he knew, doing his level best, the Arab put his foot in a rat hole just as his rider was congratulating himself on having headed the rebels, just as, across the level plain stretching from Ghazeabad to the only bridge over the Jumna, he fancied he could see a big shadowy bubble on the western sky, the dome of the Delhi mosque. Put its foot in a rat hole and came down heavily! The last thing Jim Douglas saw was—on the road which he had hoped to rejoin in a minute or two—a strange ghostlike figure. An old man on a lame camel, which bumped along as even no earthly camel ought to bump.

As he fell, the rushing roar in his ears which heralds unconsciousness seemed by a freak of memory to take a familiar rhythm:

"La! il-lah-il-Ullaho! La! il-lah-il-Ul-la-ho!"

CHAPTER II.

DAWN.

THE chill wind which comes with dawn swayed the tall grass beyond the river, and ruffling the calm stretches below the Palace wall died away again as an oldish man stepped out of a reed hut, built on a sandbank beside the boat-bridge, and looked eastward. He was a poojari, or master of ceremonial at the bathing-place where, with the first streak of light, the Hindoos came to perform their religious ablutions. So he had to be up betimes, in order to prepare the little saucers of vermilion and sandal and sacred gypsum needed in his profession; for he earned his livelihood by inherited right of hall-marking his fellow-creatures with their caste-signs when they came up out of the water. Thus he looked out over those eastern plains for the dawn, day after day. He looks for it still; this account is from his lips. And this dawn there was a cloud of dust no bigger than a man's hand upon the Meerut road. Someone was coming to Delhi.

But someone was already on the bridge, for it creaked and swayed, sending little shivers of ripples down the calm stretches. The poojari turned and looked to see the cause; then turned eastward again. It was only a man on a camel with a strange gait, bumping noiselessly even on the resounding wood. That was all.

The city was still asleep; though here and there a widow was stealing out in her white shroud for that touch of the sacred river without which she would indeed be accursed. And in a little mosque hard by the road from the boat-bridge a muezzin was about to give the very first call to prayer with pious self-complacency. But someone was ahead of him in devotion, for, upon the still air, came a continuous rolling of chanted texts. The muezzin leaned over the parapet, disappointed, to see who had thus forestalled him at heaven's gate; stared, then muttered a hasty charm. Were there visions about? The suggestion softened the disappointment, and he looked after the strange, wild figure, half-seen in the shimmering, shadowy dawn-light, with growing and awed satisfaction. This was no mere mortal, this green-clad figure on a camel, chanting texts and waving a scimitar. A vision has been vouchsafed to him for his diligence; a vision that would not lose in the telling. So he stood up and gave the cry from full lungs.

" Prayer is more than sleep! than sleep! than sleep! "

The echo from the rose-red fortifications took it up first; then one chanting voice after another, monotonously insistent.

" Prayer is more than sleep! than sleep! than sleep! "

And the city woke to another day of fasting. Woke hurriedly, so as to find time for food ere the sun rose, for it was Rumzàn, and one-half of the inhabitants would have no drop of water till the sun set, to assuage the terrible drought of every living, growing thing beneath the fierce May sun. The backwaters lay like a steel mirror reflecting the gray shadowy pile of the Palace, the poojari—waist-deep in them—was a solitary figure flinging water to the sacred airts, absorbed in a thorough purification from sin.

Then from the serrated line of the Ridge came a bugle followed by the roll of a time gun. All the world was waking now. Waking to give orders, to receive them; waking to mark itself apart with signs of salvation; waking to bow westward and pray for the discomfiture of the infidel; waking to stand on parade and salute the royal standard of a ruler, hell-doomed inevitably, according to both creeds.

A flock of purple pigeons, startled by the sound, rose like cloud flakes on the light gray sky above the glimmering dome of the big mosque, then flew westward toward the green fields and groves on the further side of the

town.   For the roll of the gun was followed by a reverberating roll, and groan, and creak, from the boat-bridge.
The little cloud on the Meerut road had grown into five
troopers dashing over the bridge at a gallop recklessly.
The poojari, busy now with his pigments, followed them
with his eyes as they clattered straight for the city gate.
They were waking in the Palace now, for a slender hand
set a lattice wide.   Perhaps from curiosity, perhaps
simply to let in the cool air of dawn.   It was a lattice in
the women's apartments.

The poojari went on rubbing up the colors that were to
bring such spiritual pride to the wearers, then turned to
look again.   The troopers, finding the city gate closed,
were back again; clamoring for admittance through the
low arched doorway leading from Selimgarh to the
Palace.   And as the yawning custodian fumbled for his
keys, the men cursed and swore at the delay; for in truth
they knew not what lay behind them.   The two thousand from Meerut, or some of them, of course.   But at
what distance?

As a matter of fact only one Englishman was close
enough to be considered a pursuer, and he was but a
poor creature on foot, still dazed by a fall, striking
across country to reach the Raj-ghât ferry below the
city.   For when Jim Douglas had recovered consciousness it had been to recognize that he was too late to be
the first in Delhi, and that he could only hope to help in
the struggle.   And that tardily, for the Arab was dead
lame.

So, removing its saddle and bridle to give it a better
chance of escaping notice, he had left it grazing peacefully in a field and stumbled on riverward, intending to
cross it as best he could; and so make for his own house
in Duryagunj for a fresh horse and a more suitable kit.
And as he plodded along doggedly he cursed the sheer
ill-luck which had made him late.

For he was late.

The five troopers were already galloping through the
grape-garden toward the women's apartments and the
King's sleeping rooms.

Their shouts of " The King!   The King!   Help for

the martyrs! Help for the Holy War!" dumfoundered the court muezzin, who was going late to his prayers in the Pearl Mosque; the reckless hoofs sent a squatting bronze image of a gardener, threading jasmine chaplets for his gods peacefully in the pathway, flying into a rose bush.

"The King! The King! Help! Help!"

The women woke with the cry, confused, alarmed, surprised; save one or two who, creeping to the Queen's room, found her awake, excited, calling to her maids.

"Too soon!" she echoed contemptuously. "Can a good thing come too soon? Quick, woman—I must see the King at once—nay, I will go as I am if it comes to that."

"The physician Ahsan-Oolah hath arrived as usual for the dawn pulse-feeling," protested the shocked tirewoman.

"All the more need for hurry," retorted Zeenut Maihl. "Quick! Slippers and a veil! Thine will do, Fâtma; sure what makes thee decent——" She gave a spiteful laugh as she snatched it from the woman's head and passed to the door; but there she paused a second. "See if Hafzân be below. I bid her come early, so she should be. Tell her to write word to Hussan Askuri to dream as he never dreamed before! And see," her voice grew shriller, keener, "the rest of you have leave. Go! cozen every man you know, every man you meet. I care not how. Make their blood flow! I care not wherefore, so that it leaps and bounds, and would spill other blood that checked it." She clenched her hands as she passed on muttering to herself. "Ah! if *hc* were a man—if *his* blood were not chilled with age—if I had someone——"

She broke off into smiles; for in the anteroom she entered was, man or no man, the representative of the Great Moghul.

"Ah, Zeenut!" he cried in tones of relief. "I would have sought thee." The trembling, shrunken figure in its wadded silk dressing gown paused and gave a backward glance at Ahsan-Oolah, whose shrewd face was full of alarm.

"Believe nothing, my liege!" he protested eagerly.

"These rioters are boasters. Are there not two thousand British soldiers in Meerut? Their tale is not possible. They are cowards fled from defeat; liars, hoping to be saved at your expense. The thing is impossible."

The Queen turned on him passionately. "Are not all things possible with God, and is not His Majesty the defender of the faith!"

"But not defender of five runaway rioters," sneered the physician. "My liege! Remember your pension."

Zeenut Maihl glared at his cunning; it was an argument needing all her art to combat.

"Five!" she echoed, passing to the lattice quickly. "Then miracles are about—the five have grown to fifty. Look, my lord, look! Hark! How they call on the defender of the faith."

With reckless hand she set the lattice wide, so becoming visible for an instant, and a shout of "The Queen! The Queen!" mingled with that other of "The Faith! The Faith! Lead us, Oh! Ghazee-o-din-Bahâdur-shâh, to die for the faith."

Pale as he was with age, the cry stirred the blood in the King's veins and sent it to his face.

"Stand back," he cried in sudden dignity, waving both counselors aside with trembling, outstretched hands. "I will speak mine own words."

But the sight of him, rousing a fresh burst of enthusiasm, left him no possibility of speech for a time. The Lord had been on their side, they cried. They had killed every hell-doomed infidel in Meerut! They would do so in Delhi if he would help! They were but an advance guard of an army coming from every cantonment in India to swear allegiance to the Pâdishah. Long live the King! and the Queen!

In the dim room behind, Zeenut Maihl and the physician listened to the wild, almost incredible, tale which drifted in with the scented air from the garden, and watched each other silently. Each found in it fresh cause for obstinacy. If this were true, what need to be foolhardy? time would show, the thing come of itself without risk. If this were true, decisive action should be taken at once; and would be taken.

But the King, assailed, molested by that rude interrupting loyalty, above all by that cry of the Queen, felt
the Turk stir in him also. Who were these intruders in
the sacred precincts, infringing the seclusion of the Great
Moghul's women? Trembling with impotent passion,
inherited from passions that had not been impotent, he
turned to Ahsan-Oolah, ignoring the Queen, who, he
felt, was mostly to blame for this outrage on her modesty.
Why had she come there? Why had she dared to be
seen?

" Your Majesty should send for the Captain of the
Palace Guards and bid him disperse the rioters, and force
them into respect for your royal person," suggested the
physician, carefully avoiding all but the immediate
present, " and your Majesty should pass to the Hall of
Audience. The King can scarce receive the Captain-
sahib here in presence of the Consort." He did not
add—" in her present costume "—but his tone implied
it, and the King, with an angry mortified glance toward
his favorite, took the physician's arm. If looks could
kill, Ahsan-Oolah would not, he knew, have supported
those tottering steps far; but it was no time to stick at
trifles.

When they had passed from the anteroom Zeenut
Maihl still stood as if half stupefied by the insult. Then
she dashed to the open lattice again, scornful and defiant;
dignified into positive beauty for the moment by her
recklessness.

" For the Faith! " she cried in her shrill woman's
voice, " if ye are men, as I would be, to be loved of
woman, as I am, strike for the Faith! "

A sort of shiver ran through the clustering crowd of
men below; the shiver of anticipation, of the marvelous,
the unexpected. The Queen had spoken to them as
men; of herself as woman. Inconceivable!—improper
of course—yet exciting. Their blood thrilled, the instinct of the man to fight for the woman rose at once.

" Quick, brothers! Rouse the guard! Close the
gates! Close the gates! "

It was a cry to heal all strife within those rose-red
walls, for the dearest wish of every faction was to close

them against civilization; against those prying Western eyes and sniffing Western noses, detecting drains and sinks of iniquity. So the clamor grew, and faces which had frowned at each other yesterday sought support in each other's ferocity to-day, and wild tales began to pass from mouth to mouth. Men, crowding recklessly over the flower-beds, trampling down the roses, talked of visions, of signs and warnings, while the troopers, dismounting for a pull at a pipe, became the center of eager circles listening not to dreams, but deeds.

"Dost feel the rope about thy neck, Sir Martyr?" said a bitter jeering voice behind one of the speakers. And something gripped him round the throat from behind, then as suddenly loosed its hold, as a shrouded woman's figure hobbled on through the crowd. The trooper started up with an oath, his own hand seeking his throat involuntarily.

"Heed her not!" said a bystander hastily, "'tis the Queen's scribe, Hafzân. She hath a craze against men. One made her what she is. Go on! Havildar-jee. So thou didst cut the *mem* down, and fling the babe——"

But the doer of the deed stood silent. He did in truth seem to feel the rope about his neck. And he seemed to feel it till he died; when it *was* there.

But Hafzân had passed on, and there were no more with words of warning. So the clamor grew and grew, till the garden swarmed with men ready for any deed.

Ahsan-Oolah saw this, and laid a detaining hand on the Captain of the Guard's arm, who, summoned in hot haste from his quarters over the Lahore gate, came in by the private way, and proposed to go down and harangue the crowd.

"It is not safe, Huzoor," he cried. "My liege, detain him. These men by their own confession are murderers——"

The King looked from one to the other doubtfully. Someone must get rid of the rioters; yet the physician said truth.

"And if aught befall," added the latter craftily, "your Majesty will be held responsible."

The old man's hand fell instantly on the Englishman's

arm. "Nay, nay, sahib! go not. Go not, my friend! Speak to them from the balcony. They will not dare to violate it."

So, backed by the sanctity of the Audience Hall of a dead dynasty, the Englishman stood and ordered the crowd to desist from profaning privacy in the name of the old man behind him; whose power he, in common with all his race, hoped and believed to be dead.

It was sufficient, however, to leave some respect for the royal person, and make the crowd disperse. To little purpose so far as peace and quiet went, since the only effect was to send a leaven of revolt to every corner of the Palace. And the Palace was so full of malcontents, docked of power, privilege, pensions; of all that makes life in a Palace worth living.

So the cry " Close the gates " grew wider. The dazed old King clung to the Englishman's arm imploring him to stay; but now a messenger came running to say that the Commissioner-sahib had called and left word that the Captain was to follow without delay to the Calcutta gate of the city. The courtiers, who had begun to assemble, looked at each other curiously; the disturbance, then, had spread beyond the Palace. Could, then, this amazing tale be true? The very thought sent them cringing round the old man, who might ere long be King indeed.

Yet as the Captain dashed at a gallop past the sentries standing calmly at the Lahore gate, there was no sign of trouble beyond, and he gave a quick glance of relief back at those cool quarters of his over the arched tunnel where the chaplain, his daughter, and her friend were staying as his guests. He felt less fear of leaving them when he saw that the city was waking to life as always, buckling down quietly to the burden and heat of a new day. It was now past seven o'clock, and the sunlight, still cool, was bright enough to cleave all things into dark or light, shade or shine. Up on the Ridge, the brigade, after listening to the sentence on the Barrackpore mutineers, was dispersing quietly; many of the men with that fiat of patience till the 31st in their minds, for the carriage-load of native officers returning from the Meerut court-martial had come into cantonments late the night before. On the roofs of the houses in the learned quarter women were giving the boys their breakfasts ere sending them off to school. The milkwomen were trooping in cityward from the country, the fruitsellers and hawkers trooping out Ridge-way as usual. The postman going his rounds had left letters, written in Meerut the day before, at two houses. And Kate Erlton returning from early church had found hers and was reading it with a scared face. Alice Gissing, however, having had that laconic telegram, had taken hers coolly. The decision had had to be made, since nothing had happened; and Herbert had the right to make it. For her part, she could make him happy; she had the knack of making most men happy, and she herself was always content when the people about her were jolly. So she was packing boxes in the back veranda of the little house on the city wall.

Thus she did not see the man who, between six and seven o'clock, ran breathlessly past her house, as a shortcut to the Court House from the bridge, taking a message from the toll-keeper to the nearest Huzoor, the Collector, who was holding early office, that a party of armed troopers had come down the Meerut road, that more could be seen coming, and would the Huzoor kindly issue orders. That first and final suggestion of the average native subordinate in any difficulty.

Armed men? That might mean much or nothing. Yet scarcely anything really serious, or warning would have been sent. The Commissioner, anyhow, must be told. So the Collector flung himself on his horse, which, in Indian fashion, was waiting under a tree outside the Court House, and galloped toward Ludlow Castle. No need for *that* warning, however, for just by the Cashmere gate he met the man he sought driving furiously down with a mounted escort to close the city gates. He had already heard the news.*

* (How? His house lay a mile at least further off, and the Collector's office was on the only route a messenger could take. No record explains this. But the best ones mention casually that a telegram of warning came to Delhi in the early morning of the 11th. Whence? the wires to Meerut were cut. Lahore, Umballa, Agra, did not know the news

Gathering graver apprehensions from this hasty meeting, the Collector was off again to warn the Resident,
then still further to beg help from cantonments. No
delay here, no hesitation. Simply a man on a horse
doing his best for the future, leaving the present for
those on the spot.

Nor was there delay anywhere. The Commissioner,
calling by the way for the Captain of the Guard, the
nearest man with men under him, was at the gate, giving
on the bridge of boats, by half-past seven. The Resident, calling on *his* way at the magazine for two guns to
sweep the bridge, joined him there soon after. Too late.
The enemy had crossed, and were in possession of the
only ground commanding the bridge. Nothing remained but to close the gate and keep the city quiet till
the columns of pursuit from Meerut should arrive; for
that there was one upon the road no one doubted. The
very rebels clamoring at the gate were listening for the
sound of those following footsteps. The very fanatics,
longing for another blow or two at an infidel to gain
Paradise withal ere martyrdom was theirs, listened too;
for during that moonlit night the certainty of failure had
been as myrrh and hyssop deadening them to the sacrifice of life.

So the little knot of Englishmen, looking hopefully
down the road, looked anxiously at each other; and
closed the river gate; kept it closed, too, even when the
20th claimed admittance from their friends the guard
within. For the 38th regiment, whose turn it was for
city work, was also rotten to the core.

But they could not close that way through Selimgarh,
though it, in truth, brought no trouble to the town. The

themselves. Can the story—improbable in any other history, but in this
record of fatal mistakes gaining a pathetic probability—which the old
folk in Delhi tell be true? The story of a telegram sent *unofficially* from
Meerut the night before, received while the Commissioner was at dinner,
put unopened into his pocket, and *forgotten*.

Not susceptible of proof or disproof, it certainly explains three things :
1. Whence the warning telegram came.
2. Why the Commissioner received information before a man a good
mile nearer the source.
3. Why the Collector *at once* sought for military aid.)

men who chose it being intriguers, fanatics, the better
class of patriots more anxious to intrench themselves for
the struggle within walls, than to swarm into a town they
could not hope to hold.   But there were others of different mettle, longing for loot and license.   The 3d Cavalry
had many friends in Delhi, especially in the Thunbi
Bazaar; so they made for it by braving the shallow
streams and shifting sandbanks below the eastern wall,
and so gaining the Raj-ghât gate.   Here, after compact
with vile friends in that vile quarter, they found admittance and help.   For what?

Between the bazaar and the Palace lay Duryagunj,
full of helpless Christian women and children; and so,
"*Deen! Deen! Futteh Mohammed,*" the convenient Cry
of Faith, was ready as, followed by the rabble and refuse
once more, the troopers raced through the peaceful gardens, pausing only to kill the infidels they met.   But
like a furious wind gathering up all vile things in the
street and carrying them along for a space, then dropping them again, the band left a legacy of license and
sheer murder behind it, while it sped on to loot.

But now the cry of " Close the gates " rose once more,
this time from the shopkeepers, the respectable quarters,
the secluded alleys, and courtyards.   And many a door
was closed on the confusion and never opened again,
except to pass in bare bread, for four long months.

" Close the gates! Close the gates! Close the gates! "
The cry rose from the Palace, the city, the little knot of
Englishmen looking down the Meerut road.   Yet no one
could compass that closing.   Recruits swarmed in
through Selimgarh to the Palace.   Robbers swarmed
in through the Raj-ghât gate to harry the bazaars.   Only
through the Cashmere gate, held by English officers and
a guard of the 38th, no help came.   The Collector arriving therein, hot from his gallop to cantonments, found
more wonder than alarm; for death was dealt in Delhi
by noiseless cold steel; and the main-guard having to
be kept, in order to secure retreat and safety to the European houses around it, no one had been able to leave it.
And all around was still peaceful utterly; even the roar
of growing tumult in the city had not reached it.   Sonny

Seymour was playing with his parrot in the veranda, Alice Gissing packing boxes methodically. The Collector galloping past—as, scorning the suggestion that it was needless risk to go further, he replied briefly, that he was the magistrate of the town, and struck spurs to his horse—made some folk look up—that was all.

But he could scarcely make his way through the growing crowd, which, led by troopers, was beginning to close in behind the knot of waiting Englishmen. And once more they looked down the Meerut road as they heard that some time must elapse ere they could hope for reinforcement. The guns could not be got ready at a moment's notice; nor could the Cashmere gate guard leave the post. But the 54th regiment should be down in about—— In about what? No one asked; but those waiting faces listened as for a verdict of life and death.

In about an hour.

An hour! And not a cloud of dust upon the Meerut road.

"They can't be long, though, now," said the eldest there hopefully. "And Ripley will bring his men down at the double. If we go into the guard-house we can hold our own till then, surely."

"I can hold mine," replied a young fellow with a rough-hewn homely face. He gave a curt nod as he spoke to a companion, and together they turned back, skirting the wall, followed by an older, burlier man. They belonged to the magazine, and they were off to see the best way of holding their own. And they found it—found it for all time.

But fate had denied to those other brave men the nameless something which makes men succeed together, or die together. Within half an hour they were scattered helplessly. The Resident, after seeking support from the city police for one whose name had been a terror to Delhi for fifty years, and finding insult instead, was flying for dear life through the Ajmere gate to the open country. The Commissioner, who, after seizing a musket from a wavering guard beside him and—with the first shot fired in Delhi—shooting the foremost trooper dead, seems to have lost hope, with mutiny around and treason beside him, jumped into his buggy alone and drove off to those cool quarters above the Palace gate, as his nearest refuge. Their owner, the Captain sought like refuge by flinging himself into the cover of the dry moat, and creeping—despite injuries from the fall—along it till some of his men, faithful so far, seeing him unable for more, carried him to his own room.

The Collector! Strangely enough there is no record of what the Magistrate of the city did, thus left alone. He had been wounded by the crowd at first, and was no doubt weary after his wild gallopings. Still he, holding his own so far, managed to gain the same refuge, somehow. What else could he do alone? One thing we know he could not do. That is, mount the broad, curving flight of shallow stone stairs leading to the cool upper rooms. So the chaplain helped him; the chaplain who had "from an early hour been watching the advance of the Meerut mutineers through a telescope and feeling there was mischief in the wind."

Mischief indeed! and danger; most of all in those rose-red walls within which refuge had been sought. For the King was back in the women's apartments listening to the Queen's cozenings and Hussan Askuri's visions, when that urgent appeal to send dhoolies to convey the English ladies at the gate to the security of the harem reached him; reached him in Ahsan-Oolah's warning voice of wisdom. And he listened to both the wheedling ambition and the crafty policy with a half-hearing for something beyond it of pity, honor, good faith; while Hafzân, pen in hand, sat with her large profoundly sad eyes fixed on the old man's face, waiting—waiting.

"If they come here—outcaste! infidel! I go," said Zeenut Maihl.

"Thou shalt go with a bowstring about thy neck, woman, if I choose," said the old King fiercely. "Write! girl—the Queen's dhoolies to the Lahore gate at once."

So, through the swarms of pensioners quarreling

already over new titles and perquisites, through the groups of excited fanatics preparing for martyrdom about the Mosque, past Abool-Bukr, three parts drunk, boasting to ruffling blades of the European mistresses he meant to keep, the Queen's dhoolies went swaying out of the precincts; all yielding place to them. And beyond, in the denser, more dangerous crowd without, they passed easily; for those tinsel-decked, tawdry canopies, screened with sodden musk and dirt-scented curtains, were sacred.

Sacred even to the refuse and rabble of the city, the dissolute eunuchs, the mob of retainers, palace guards, and blood-drunk soldierly surging through that long arched tunnel by the Lahore gate, and hustling to get round that wide arch, and so, a few steps further, see the Commissioner standing at bay upon that wide curving red-stone stair that led upward. Standing and thinking of the women above; of one woman mostly. Standing, facing the wild sea of faces, waiting to see if that last appeal for help had been heard.

" Room! Room! for the Queen's dhoolies!"

The cry echoed above the roar of the crowd.

At last! He turned, to pass on the welcome news, perchance; but it was enough—that one waver of that stern face! There was a rush, a cry, a clang of steel on stone, a fall! And then up those wide curving stairs, like fiends incarnate, jostled a mad crew, elbowing each other, cursing each other, in their eagerness for that blow which would win Paradise.

Four crowns of glory in the first room, where the chaplain, the Captain, and the two English girls fell side by side. One in the next, where the Collector and Magistrate, weary and wounded, still lay alone.

" Way! Way! for the Queen's dhoolies!"

But they had come too late, as all things seemed to come too late on that fatal 11th of May.

Too late! Too late! The words dinned themselves into a horseman's brain, as he dashed out of the compound of a small house in Duryagunj and headed straight through the bazaar for the little house on the city wall by the Cashmere gate. And as he rode he shouted: *"Deen! Deen!"*

It was a convenient cry, and suited the trooper's dress he wore. He had had to shoot a man to get it, but he hoped to shoot many more when he had seen Alice Gissing in safety, and the Meerut column had come in. It could not be long now.

CHAPTER III.

DAYLIGHT.

THREE miles away Kate Erlton sat in her home-like, peaceful drawing room, feeling dazzled. The sunshine, streaming through the open doors, seemed to stream into the very recesses of her mind as she sat, still looking at the letter which she had found half an hour before waiting for her beside a bunch of late roses which the gardener had laid on the table ready for her to arrange in the vases. The flowers were fading fast; the dog-cart waiting outside to take her on to see a sick friend ere the sun grew hot, shifted to find another shadow; but she did not move.

She was trying to understand what it all meant; really—deprived of her conventional thoughts about such things. And one sentence in the letter had a strange fascination for her. " I am not such a fool as to think you will mind. I know you will get on much better without me."

Of course. She had, in a way, accepted the truth of this years ago. The fact must have been patent to him also all that time; and she had known that he accepted it.

But now, set down in black and white, it forced her into seeing—as she had never seen before—the deadly injury she had done to the man by not minding. And then the question came keenly—" Why had she not minded? " Because she had not been content with her bargain. She had wanted something else. What? The emotion, the refinement, the *fin-fleur* of sentiment. Briefly, what made *her* happy; what gave *her* satisfaction. It was only, then, a question between different forms of enjoyment; the one as purely selfish as the other. More so, in a way, for it claimed more and carried the grievance of denial into every detail of life. She moved restlessly in her chair, confused by this sudden daylight in her mind; laid down the letter, then took it up again and read another sentence.

" I believe you used to think that I'd get the regiment some day; but I shouldn't—after all, the finish is the win or the lose of a race."

The letter went down on the table again, but this time her head went down with it to rest upon it above her clasped hands. Oh! the pity of it! the pity of it! Yet how could she have avoided standing aloof from this man's life as she had done from the moment she had discovered she did not love him?

Suddenly she stood up, pressing those clasped hands tight to her forehead as if to hold in her thoughts. The sunlight, streaming in, shone right into her cool gray eyes, showing in a ray on the iris, as if it were passing into her very soul.

If she had been this man's sister, instead of his wife, could she not have lived with him contentedly enough, palliating what could be palliated, gaining what influence she could with him, giving him affection and sympathy? Why, briefly, had she failed to make him what Alice Gissing had made him—a better man? And yet Alice Gissing did not love him; she had no romantic sentiment about him. Did she really lay less stress—she, the woman at whom other women held up pious hands of horror—on that elemental difference between the tie of husband and wife, and brother and sister than she, Kate Erlton, did, who had affected to rise superior to it altogether? It seemed so. She had asked for a purely selfish gratification of the mind. And Alice Gissing? A strange jealousy came to her with the thought, not for herself, but for her husband; for the man who was content to give up everything for a woman whom he " loved very dearly." That was true. Kate had watched him for those three months, and she had watched Mrs. Gissing too, and knew for a certainty the latter gave him nothing any woman might not have given him if she had been content to put her own claims for happiness, her own gratification, her own mental passion aside. So a quick resolve came to her. He must not give up the finish, the win or the lose of the race, for so little. There was time yet for the chance. She had pleaded for one with a man a year ago; she would plead for it with a woman to-day.

She passed into the veranda hastily, pausing involuntarily ere getting into the dog-cart before the still, sunlit beauty of that panorama of the eastern plains, stretching away behind the gardens which fringed the shining curves of the river. There was scarcely a shadow anywhere, not a sign to tell that three miles down that river the man with whom she had pleaded a year ago was straining every nerve to give her and himself a chance, and that within the rose-lit, lilac-shaded city the chance of some had come and gone.

Nor, as she drove along the road intent on that coming interview in the hot little house upon the wall, was there any sign to warn her of danger. The Cashmere gate stood open, and the guard saluted as usual. Perhaps, had the English officers seen her, they might have advised her return, even though there was as yet no anticipation of danger; had there been one, the first thought would have been to clear the neighboring bungalows. But they were in the main-guard, and she set down the stare of the natives to the fact that nine o'clock was unusually late for an English lady to be braving the May sun. The road beyond was also unusually deserted, but she was too busy searching for the winged words, barbed well, yet not too swift or sharp to wound beyond possibility of compromise, which she meant to use ere long, to pay any attention to her surroundings. She did not even catch the glimpse of Sonny, still playing with the cockatoo, as she sped past the Seymours' house, and she scarcely noticed the groom's "*Hut! teri, hut!*" (Out of the way! you there!) to a figure in a green turban, over which she nearly ran, as it came sneaking round a corner as if looking for something or someone; a figure which paused to look after her half doubtfully.

Yet these same words, which came so readily to her

imaginings, failed her, as set words will, before the commonplace matter-of-fact reality. If she could have
jumped from the dog-cart and dashed into them without
preamble, she would have been eloquent enough; but
the necessary inquiry if Mrs. Gissing could see her, the
ushering in as for an ordinary visit, the brief waiting,
the perfunctory hand-shake with the little figure in
familiar white-and-blue were so far from the high-strung
appeal in her thoughts that they left her silent, almost
shy.

" Find a comfy chair, do," came the high, hard voice.
" Isn't it dreadfully hot? My old Mai will have it something is going to happen. She has been dikking me
about it all the morning. An earthquake, I suppose; it
feels like it, rather. Don't you think so?"

Kate felt as if one had come already, as, quite auto-
matically, she satisfied Alice Gissing's choice of " a
really—really comfy chair."

How dizzily unreal it seemed! And yet not more so,
in fact, than the life they had been leading for months
past; knowing the truth about each other absolutely;
pretending to know nothing. Well! the sooner that
sort of thing came to an end, the better!

" I have had a letter from my husband," she began,
but had to pause to steady her voice.

" So I supposed when I saw you," replied Alice Gissing, without a quiver in hers. But she rose, crossed over
to Kate, and stood before her, like a naughty child, her
hands behind her back. She looked strangely young,
strangely innocent in the dim light of the sunshaded
room. So young, so small, so slight among the endless
frills and laces of a loose morning wrapper. And she
spoke like a child also, querulously, petulantly.

" I like you the better for coming, too, though I don't
see what possible good it can do. He said in his letter
to me he would tell you all about it, and if he has, I
don't see what else there is to say, do you?"

Kate rose also, as if to come nearer to her adversary,
and so the two women stood looking boldly enough into
each other's eyes. But the keenness, the passion, the
pity of the scene had somehow gone out of it for Kate

Erlton. Her tongue seemed tied by the tameness; she felt that they might have been discussing a trivial detail in some trivial future. Yet she fought against the feeling.

"I think there is a great deal to say; that is why I have come to say it," she replied, after a pause. "But I can say it quickly. You don't love my husband, Alice Gissing, let him go. Don't ruin his life."

Bald and crude as this was in comparison with her imagined appeal, it gave the gist of it, and Kate watched her hearer's face anxiously to see the effect. Was that by chance a faint smile? or was it only the barred light from the jalousies hitting the wide blue eyes?

"Love!" echoed Alice Gissing. "I don't know anything about love. I never pretended to. But I can make him happy; you never did."

There was not a trace of malice in the high voice. It simply stated a fact; but a fact so true that Kate's lip quivered.

"I know that as well as you do. But I think I could—now. I want you to give me the chance."

She had not meant to put it so humbly; but, being once more the gist of what she had intended to say, it must pass. There was no doubt about the smile now. It was almost a laugh, that hateful, inconsequent laugh; but, as if to soften its effect, a little jeweled hand hovered out as if it sought a resting-place on Kate's arm.

"You can't, my dear. It *is* so funny that you can't see that, when I, who know nothing about—about all that—can see it quite plainly. You are the sort of woman, Mrs. Erlton, who falls in love—who must fall in love—who—don't be angry!—likes being in love, and is unhappy if she isn't. Now I don't care a rap for people to be thinking, and thinking, and thinking of me, nothing but me! I like them to be pleasant and pleased. And I make them so, somehow——" She shrugged her shoulders whimsically as if to dismiss the puzzle, and went on gravely, "And you can't make people happy if you aren't happy yourself, you know, so there is no use in thinking you could."

It was bitter truth, but Kate was too honest to deny it.

There had always been the sense of grievance in the past, and the sense of self-sacrifice, at least, would remain in the future.

"But there are other considerations," she began slowly. "A man does not set such store by—by love and marriage as a woman. It is only a bit——"

"A very small bit," put in Mrs. Gissing, with a whimsical face.

"A very small bit of his life," continued Kate stolidly, "and if my husband gives up his profession——"

Mrs. Gissing interrupted her again; this time petulantly. "I told him it was a pity—I offered to go away anywhere. I did, indeed! And I couldn't do more, could I? But when a man gets a notion of honor into his head——"

"Honor!" interrupted Kate in her turn, "the less said about honor the better, surely, between you and me!"

The wide blue eyes looked at her doubtfully.

• "I never can understand women like you," said their owner. "You pretend not to care, and then you make so much fuss over so little."

"So little!" retorted Kate, her temper rising. "Is it little that my boy should have to know this about his father—about me? You have no children, Mrs. Gissing! If you had you would understand the shame better. Oh! I know about the baby and the flowers—who doesn't? But that is nothing. It was so long ago, it died so young, you have forgotten——"

She broke off before the expression on the face before her—that face with the shadowless eyes, but with deep shadows beneath the eyes and a nameless look of physical strain and stress upon it—and a sudden pallor came to her own cheek.

"So he hasn't told you," came the high voice half-fretfully, half-pitifully. "That was very mean of him; but I thought, somehow, he couldn't by your coming here. Well! I suppose I must. Mrs. Erlton——"

Kate stepped back from her defiantly, angrily. "He has told me all I need, all I care to know about this miserable business. Yes! he has! You can see the

letter if you like—there it is! I am not ashamed of it.
It is a good letter, better than I thought he could write—
better than you deserve. For he says he will marry you
if I will let him! And he says he is sorry it can't be
helped. But I deny that. It can, it must, it shall be
helped! And then he says it's a pity for the boy's sake;
but that it does not matter so much as if it was a
girl——"

It was the queerest sound which broke in on those
passionate reproaches. The queerest sound. Neither a
laugh nor a sob, nor a cry; but something compounded
of all three, infinitely soft, infinitely tender.

"*And the other may be,*" said Alice Gissing in a voice
of smiles and tears, as she pointed to the end of the sentence in the letter Kate had thrust upon her. "Poor
dear! What a way to put it! How like a man to
think you could understand; and I wonder what the old
Mai *would* say to its being——"

What did she say? What were the frantic words
which broke from the frantic figure, its sparse gray hair
showing, its shriveled bosom heaving unveiled, which
burst into the room and flung its arms round that little
be-frilled white one as if to protect and shield it?

Kate Erlton gave a half-choked, half-sobbing cry.
Even this seemed a relief from the incredible horror of
what had dawned upon her, frightening her by the wild
insensate jealousy it roused—the jealousy of motherhood.

"What is it? What does she say?" she cried passionately, "I have a right to know!"

Alice Gissing looked at her with a faint wonder. "It
is nothing about *that,*" she said, and her face, though it
had whitened, showed no fear. "It's something more
important. There has been a row in the city—the Commissioner and some other Englishmen have been killed
and she says we are not safe. I don't quite understand.
Oh! don't be a fool, Mai!" she went on in Hindustani, "I
won't excite myself. I never do. Don't be a fool, I
say!" Her foot came down almost savagely and she
turned to Kate. "If you will wait here for a second,
Mrs. Erlton, I'll go outside with the Mai and have a look

round, and bring my husband's pistol from the other
room. You had better stay, really. I shall be back in
a moment. And I dare say it's all the old Mai's nonsense—she is such a fool about me—nowadays." Her
white face, smiling over its own certainty of coming
trouble, was gone, and the door closed, almost before
Kate could say a word. Not that she had any to say.
She was too dazed to think of danger to the little
figure, which passed out into the shady back veranda
perched on the city wall, looking out into the peaceful
country beyond. She was too absorbed in what she had
just realized to think of anything else. So this was what
he had meant!—and this woman with her facile nature,
ready to please and be pleased with anyone—this woman
content to take the lowest place—had the highest of all
claims upon him. This woman who had no right to
motherhood, who did not know——

God in Heaven! What was that through the stillness
and the peace? A child's pitiful scream.

She was at the closed windows in an instant, peering
through the slits of the jalousies; but there was nothing
to be seen save a blare and blaze of sunlight on sun-
scorched grass and sun-withered beds of flowers. Nothing!—stay!—Christ help us! What was that? A vision
of white, and gold, and blue. White garments and
white wings, golden curls and flaming golden crest, fierce
gray-blue beak and claws among the fluttering blue
ribbons. Sonny! His little feet flying and failing fast
among the flower-beds. Sonny! still holding his
favorite's chain in the unconscious grip of terror, while
half-dragged, half-flying, the wide white wings fluttered
over the child's head.

"*Deen! Deen! Futtch Mohammed!*"

That was from the bird, terrified, yet still gentle.

"*Deen! Deen! Futtch Mohammed!*"

That was from the old man who followed fast on the
child with long lance in rest like a pig-sticker's. An old
man in a faded green turban with a spiritual, relentless
face.

Kate's fingers were at the bolts of the high French window—her only chance of speedy exit from that closed

room. Ah! would they never yield?—and the lance
was gaining on those poor little flying feet. Every atom
of motherhood in her—fierce, instinctive, animal, fought
with those unyielding bolts. . . .

What was that? Another vision of white, and gold,
and blue, dashing into the sunlight with something in a
little clenched right hand. Childish itself in frills, and
laces, and ribbons, but with a face as relentless as the
old man's, as spiritual. And a clear confident voice rang
above those discordant cries.

"All right, Sonny! All right, dear!"

On, swift and straight in the sunlight; and then a
pause to level the clenched right hand over the left arm
coolly, and fire. The lance wavered. It was two feet
further from that soft flesh and blood when Alice Gissing
caught the child up, turned and ran; ran for dear life
to shelter.

"*Deen! Deen! Futteh Mohammed!*"

The cry came after the woman and child, and over
them, released by Sonny's wild clutch at sheltering arms,
the bird fluttered, echoing the cry.

But one bolt was down at last, the next yielding—Ah!
who was that dressed like a native, riding like an Englishman, who leaped the high garden fence and was over
among the flower-beds where Sonny was being chased.
Was he friend or foe? No matter! Since under her
vehement hands the bolt had fallen, and Kate was out
in the veranda. Too late! The flying sunlit vision of
white, and gold, and blue had tripped and fallen. No!
not too late. The report of a revolver rang out, and the
Cry of Faith came only from the bird, for the fierce
relentless face was hidden among the laces, and frills, and
ribbons that hid the withered flowers.

But the lance? The lance whose perilous nearness
had made that shot Jim Douglas' only chance of keeping
his promise? He was on his knees on the scorched
grass choking down the curse as he saw a broken shaft
among the frills and ribbons, a slow stream oozing in
gushes to dye them crimson. There was another crimson spot, too, on the shoulder, showing where a bullet,
after crashing through a man's temples, had found its

spent resting place. But as the Englishman kicked away one body, and raised the other tenderly from the unhurt child, so as not to stir that broken shaft, he wished that if death had had to come, he might have dealt it. To his wild rage, his insane hatred, there seemed a desecration even in that cold touch of steel from a dark hand.

But Alice Gissing resented nothing. She lay propped by his arms with those wide blue eyes still wide, yet sightless, heedless of Kate's horrified whispers, or the poor old Mai's frantic whimper. Until suddenly a piteous little wail rose from the half-stunned child to mingle with that ceaseless iteration of grief. "*Oh! meri buchchi murgyia!*" (Oh, my girlie is dead!—dead!)

It seemed to bring her back, and a smile showed on the fast-paling face.

"Don't be a fool, Mai. It isn't a girl; it's a boy. Take care of him, do, and don't be stupid. I'm all right."

Her voice was strong enough, and Kate looked at Jim Douglas hopefully. She had recognized him at once, despite his dress, with a faint, dead wonder as to why things were so strange to-day. But he could feel something oozing wet and warm over his supporting arm, he knew the meaning of that whitening face; so he shook his head hopelessly, his eyes on those wide unseeing ones. She was as still, he thought, as she had been when he held her before. Then suddenly the eyes narrowed into sight, and looked him in the face curiously, clearly.

"It's you, is it?" came the old inconsequent laugh. "Why don't you say 'Bravo!—Bravo!—Bra——'"

The crimson rush of blood from her still-smiling lips dyed his hands also, as he caught her up recklessly with a swift order to the others to follow, and ran for the house. But as he ran, clasping her close, close, to him, his whispered bravos assailed her dead ears passionately, and when he laid her on her bed, he paused even in the mad tumult of his rage, his anxiety, his hope for others to kiss the palms of those brave hands ere he folded them decently on her breast, and was out to fetch his horse, and return to where Kate waited for him in the veranda,

the child in her arms.   Brave also; but the certainty that
he had left the flood-level of sympathy and admiration
behind him at the feet of a dead woman he had never
known, was with him even in his hurry.

" I can't see anyone else about as yet," he said, as he
reloaded hastily, " and but for that fiend—that devil of
a bird hounding him on—what did it mean?—not that
it matters now "—he threw his hand out in a gesture of
impotent regret and turned to mount.

Kate shivered.   What, indeed, did it mean?   A vague
recollection was adding to her horror.   Had she driven
away once from an uncomprehensible appeal in that
relentless face? when the bird——

" Don't think, please," said Jim Douglas, pausing to
give her a sharp glance.   " You will need all your nerve.
The troops mutinied at Meerut last night, and killed a
lot of people.   They have come on here, and I don't trust
the native regiments.   Go inside, and shut the door.   I
must reconnoiter a bit before we start."

" But my husband?" she cried, and her tone made
him remember the strangeness of finding her in that
house.   She looked unreliable, to his keen eye; the bitter truth might make her rigid, callous, and in such
callousness lay their only chance.

" All right.   He asked me to look after—her."

He saw her waver, then pull herself together; but he
saw also that her clasp on Sonny tightened convulsively,
and he held out his arms.

" Hand the child to me for a moment," he said briefly,
" and call that poor lady's ayah from her wailing."

The piteous whimperings from the darkened rooms
within ceased reluctantly.   The old woman came with
lagging step into the veranda, but Jim Douglas called to
her in the most matter-of-fact voice.

" Here, Mai!   Take your mem's charge.   She told
you to take care of the boy, remember."   The tear-dim
doubtful eyes looked at him half-resentfully, but he went
on coolly.   " Now, Sonny, go to your ayah, and be a
good boy.   Hold out your arms to old ayah, who has
had ever so many Sonnys—haven't you, ayah?"

The child, glad to escape from the prancing horse, the

purposely rough arms, held out its little dimpled hands. They seemed to draw the hesitating old feet, step by step, till with a sudden fierce snatch, a wild embrace, the old arms closed round the child with a croon of content.

Jim Douglas breathed more freely. " Now, Mrs. Erlton," he said, " I can't make you promise to leave Sonny there; but he is safer with her than he could be with you. She must have friends in the city. You haven't *one.*"

He was off as he spoke, leaving her to that knowledge. Not a friend! No! not one. Still, he need not have told her so, she thought proudly, as she passed in and closed the doors as she had been bidden to do. But he had succeeded. A certain fierce, dull resistance had replaced her emotion. So while the ayah, still carrying Sonny, returned to her dead mistress, Kate remained in the drawing room, feeling stunned. Too stunned to think of anything save those last words. Not a friend! Not one, saving a few cringing shop-keepers, in all that wide city to whom she had ever spoken a word! Whose fault was that? Whose fault was it that she had not understood that appeal?

A rattle of musketry quite close at hand roused her from apathy into fear for the child, and she passed rapidly into the next room. It was empty, save for that figure on the bed. The ayah with her charge had gone, closing the doors behind her; to her friends, no doubt. But she, Kate Erlton, had none. The renewed rattle of musketry sent her to peer through the jalousies; but she could see nothing. The sound seemed to come from the open space by the church, but gardens lay between her and that, blocking the view. Still it was quite close; seemed closer than it had been. No doubt it would come closer and closer till it found her waiting there, without a friend. Well! Since she was not even capable of saving Sonny, she could at least do what she was told—she could at least die alone.

No! not quite alone! She turned back to the bed and looked down on the slender figure lying there as if asleep. For the ayah's vain hopes of lingering life had left the face unstained, and the folded hands hid the crimson below them. Asleep, not dead; for the face had no look of rest. It was the face of one who dreams still of the stress and strain of coming life.

So this was to be her companion in death; this woman who had done her the greatest wrong. What wrong? the question came dully. What wrong had she done to one who refused to admit the claims or rights of passion? What had she stolen, this woman who had not cared at all? Whose mind had been unsullied utterly. Only motherhood; and that was given to saint and sinner alike.

Given rightly here, for those little hands were brave mother-hands. Kate put out hers softly and touched them. Still warm, still life-like, their companionship thrilled her through and through. With a faint sob, she sank on her knees beside the bed and laid her cheek on them. Let death come and find her there! Let the finish of the race, which was the win and the lose——

" Mrs. Erlton! quick, please! "

Jim Douglas' voice, calling to her from outside, roused her from a sort of apathy into sudden desire for life; she was out in the veranda in a second.

" The game's up," he said, scarcely able to speak from breathlessness; and his horse was in a white lather. " I had to see to the Seymours first, and now there's only one chance I can think of—desperate at that. Quick, your foot on mine—so—from the step—— Now your hand. One! two! three! That's right." He had her on the saddle before him and was off through the gardens cityward at a gallop. " The 54th came down from the cantonments all right," he went on rapidly, " but shot their officers at the church—the city scoundrels are killing and looting all about, but the main-guard is closed and safe as yet. I got Mrs. Seymour there. I'll get you if I can. I'm going to ride through the thick of the devils now with you as my prisoner. Do you see—there at the turn. I'll hark back down the road—it's the only chance of getting through. Slip down a bit across the saddle bow. Don't be afraid. I'll hold as long as I can. Now scream—scream like the devil. No! let your arms slack as if you'd fainted—people won't look so much— that's better—that's capital—now—ready! "

He swerved his horse with a dig of the spur and made for the crowd which lay between him and safety. The words describing the rape of the Sabine women, over the construing of which he remembered being birched at school, recurred to him, as such idle thoughts will at such times, as he hitched his hand tighter on Kate's dress and scattered the first group with a coarse jest or two. Thank Heaven! She would not understand these, his only weapons; since cold steel could not be used, till it had to be used to *prevent* her understanding. Thank Heaven, too! he could use both weapons fairly. So he dug in the spurs again and answered the crowd in its own kind, recklessly. A laugh, an oath, once or twice a blow with the flat of his sword. And Kate, with slack arms and closed eyes, lay and listened—listened to a sharper, angrier voice, a quick clash of steel, a shout of half-doubtful, half-pleased derision from those near, a jest provoking a roar of merriment for one who meant to hold his own in love and war. Then a sudden bound of the horse; a faint slackening of that iron grip on her waist-belt. The worst of the stream was past; another moment and they were in a quiet street, another, and they had turned at right-angles down a secluded alley where Jim Douglas paused to pass his right hand, still holding his sword, under Kate's head and bid her lean against him more comfortably. The rest was easy. He would take her out by the Moree gate—the alleys to it would be almost deserted—so, outside the walls, to the rear of the Cashmere gate. They were already twisting and turning through the narrow lanes as he told her this. Then, with a rush and a whoop, he made for the gate, and the next moment they had the open country, the world, before them. How still and peaceful it lay in the sunshine! But the main-guard was the nearest, safest shelter, so the galloping hoofs sped down the tree-set road along which Kate generally took her evening drive.

" And you? " she asked hurriedly as he set her down at the moat and bade her run for the wicket and knock, while he kept the drawbridge.

He shook his head. " The reliefs from Meerut must be in soon. If they started at dawn, in an hour. Besides, I'm off to the Palace to see what has really happened; information's everything."

She saw him turn with a wave of his sword for farewell as the wicket was opened cautiously, and make for the Moree gate once more. As he rode he told himself there should be no further cause for anxiety on her account. De Tessier's guns were in the main-guard now, and reinforcements of the loyal 74th. They could hold their own easily till the Meerut people smashed up the Palace. They could not be long now, and the city had not risen as yet. The bigger bazaars through which he cantered were almost deserted; everyone had gone home. But at the entrance to an alley a group of boys clustered, and one ran out to him crying, " Khân-sahib! What's the matter? Folk say people are being killed, but we want to go to school."

" Don't," said Jim Douglas as he passed on. He had seen the schoolmaster, stripped naked, lying on his back in the broad daylight as he galloped along the College road with Kate over his saddle-bow.

" *Ari*, brothers," reported the spokesman. " He said ' *don't*,' but he can know naught. He comes from the outside. And we shall lose places in class if we stop, and others go."

So in the cheerful daylight the schoolboys discussed the problem, school or no school; the Great Revolt had got no further than that, as yet.

But there was no cloud of dust upon the Meerut road, though straining eyes thought they saw one more than once.

CHAPTER IV.

NOON.

But if the schoolmaster of one school lay dead in the sunlight there was another, well able to teach a useful lesson, left alive; and his school remains for all time as a place where men may learn what men can do.

For about three hundred yards from the deserted

College, about six hundred from the main-guard of the Cashmere gate, stood the magazine, to which the two young Englishmen, followed by a burlier one, had walked back quietly after one of them had remarked that he could hold his own. For there were gates to be barred, four walls to be seen to, and various other preparations to be made before the nine men who formed the garrison could be certain of holding their own. And their own meant much to others; for with the stores and the munitions of war safe the city might rise, but it would be unarmed; but with them at the mercy of the rabble every pitiful pillager could become a recruit to the disloyal regiments.

" The mine's about finished now, sir," said Conductor Buckley, saluting gravely as he looked critically down a line ending in the powder magazine. " And, askin' your pardon, sir, mightn't it be as well to settle a signal beforehand, sir; in case it's wanted? And, if you have no objection, sir, here's Sergeant Scully here, sir, saying he would look on it as a kind favor——"

A man with a spade glanced up a trifle anxiously for the answer as he went on with his work.

" All right! Scully shall fire it. If you finish it there in the middle by that little lemon tree, we shan't forget the exact spot. Scully must see to having the portfire ready for himself. I'll give the word to you, as your gun will be near mine, and you can pass it on by raising your cap. That will do, I think."

" Nicely, sir," said Conductor Buckley, saluting again.

" I wish we had one more man," remarked the Head-of-the-nine, as he paused in passing a gun to look to something in its gear with swift professional eye. " I don't quite see how the nine of us are to work the ten guns."

" Oh! we'll manage somehow," said his second in command, " the native establishment—perhaps——"

George Willoughby, the Head-of-the-nine, looked at the sullen group of dark faces lounging distrustfully within those barred doors, and his own face grew stern. Well, if they would not work, they should at least stay and look on—stay till the end. Then he took out his watch.

"Twelve! The Meerut troops will be in soon—if they started at dawn." There was the finest inflection of scorn in his voice.

"They must have started," began his companion. But the tall figure with the grave young face was straining its eyes from the bastion they were passing; it gave upon the bridge of boats and the lessening white streak of road. He was looking for a cloud of dust upon it; but there was none.

"I hope so," he remarked as he went on. He gave a half-involuntary glance back, however, to the stunted lemon-bush. There was a black streak by it, which might be relied upon to give aid at dawn, or dusk, or noon; high noon as it was now.

The chime of it echoed methodically as ever from the main-guard, making a cheerful young voice in the officer's room say, "Well! the enemy is passing, anyhow. The reliefs can't be long—if they started at dawn."

"If they had started when they ought to have started, they would have been here hours ago," said an older man, almost petulantly, as he rose and wandered to the door, to stand looking out on the baking court where his men—the two companies of the 54th, who had come down under his charge after those under Colonel Riply had shot down their officers by the church—were lounging about sullenly. These men might have shot him also but for the timely arrival of the two guns; might have shot at him, even now, but for those loyal 74th over-awing them. He turned and looked at some of the latter with a sort of envy. These men had come forward in a body when the regiment was called upon by its commandant to give honest volunteers to keep order in the city. What had they had, which his men had lacked? Nothing that he knew of. And then, inevitably, he thought of his six murdered friends and comrades, officers apparently as popular as he, whose bodies were lying in the next room waiting for a cart to remove them to the Ridge. For even Major Paterson, saddened, depressed, looked forward to decent sepulture for his comrades by and by—by and by when the Meerut troops should arrive. And the half dozen or more of women upstairs were comforting each other with the same hope, and crushing down the cry that it seemed an eternity, already, since they had waited for that little cloud of dust upon the Meerut road. But for that hope they might have gone Meerutward themselves; for the country was peaceful.

Even in Duryagunj, though by noon it was a charnel-house, the score or so of men who kept cowards at bay in a miserable storehouse comforted themselves with the same hope; and women with the long languid eyes of one race, looked out of them with the temper and fire of the other, saying in soft staccato voices—" It will not be long now. They will be here soon, for they would start at dawn."

" They will come soon," said a young telegraph clerk coolly, as he stood by his instrument hoping for a welcome *kling;* sending, finally, that bulletin northward which ended with the reluctant admission, " we must shut up." Must indeed; seeing that some ruffians rushed in and sabered him with his hands still on the levers.

" They will be here soon," agreed the compositors of the *Delhi Gazette* as they worked at the strangest piece of printing the world is ever likely to see. That famous extra, wedged in between English election news, which told in bald journalese of a crisis, which became the crisis of their own lives before the whole edition was sent out.

But down in the Palace Zeenut Maihl had been watching that white streak of road also, and as the hours passed, her wild impatience would let her watch it no longer. She paced up and down the Queen's bastion like a caged tigress, leaving Hâfzan to take her place at the lattice. No sign of an avenging army yet! Then the troopers' tale must be true! The hour of decisive action had come, it was slipping past, the King was in the hands of Ahsan-Oolah, and Elahi Buksh, whose face was set both ways, like the physician's. And she, helpless, half in disgrace, caged, veiled, screened, unable to lay hands on anyone! Oh! why was she not a man! Why had she not a man to deal with! Her henna-stained nails bit into her palms as she clenched her hands, then in sheer childish passion tore off her hampering veil and, rolling it into a ball, flung it at the head of a drowsy eunuch in the outside arcade—the nearest thing to a man within her reach.

" No sign yet, Hâfzan? " she asked fiercely.

" No sign, my Queen," replied Hâfzan, with an odd derisive smile. If they did not come now, thought this woman with her warped nature, they would come later on; come and put a rope round the necks of men who had laid violent hands on women.

" Then I stop here no longer! " cried Zeenut Maihl recklessly; " I must see somewhat of it or die. Quick, girls, my dhooli, I will go back to my own rooms. 'Twill at least bear me through the crowd, and the jogging will keep the blood from tingling from very stillness."

So through the tawdry, dirty, musky curtains a woman's fierce eye watched the crowd hungrily, as the dhooli swung through it. A fierce crowd too in its way, but lacking cohesion. Like the world without those four rose-red walls, it was waiting for a master. And the man who should have been master was taking cooling draughts, and composing couplets, so her spies brought word. No hope from him till she could lure him back from his vexation and put some of her own energy into him. Who next was there likely to do her bidding? Her eye, taking in all the strangeness of the scene, troopers stabling their horses in the colonnades, sepoys bivouacking under the trees, courtiers hurrying up and down the private steps, found none in all that crowd of place-hunters, boasters, enthusiasts, whom she could trust. The King's eldest son Mirza Moghul was the fiercest tempered of them all, the only one whom she feared in any way; perhaps if she could get hold of him——

As her dhooli swayed up the steps he was standing on them talking to Mirza Khair Sultan. She could have put out her hand and touched him; but even she did not dare convention enough for that. Nevertheless, the sight of him determined her. If the King did not come back to her by noon, she must lure the Mirza to her side.

"Thou art a fool, Pir-jee," she said petulantly to Hussan Askuri who, as father confessor, had entrance to the womens' rooms and was awaiting her. "Thou hast no grip on the King when I am absent. Canst not even drive that slithering physician from his side?"

"Cooling draughts, seest thou, Pir-jee," put in Hâfzan maliciously, "have tangible effects. Thy dreams——"

"Peace, woman!" interrupted the Queen sternly, "'tis no time for jesting. Where sits the King now?"

"In the river balcony, Ornament-of-palaces," replied Fâtma glibly, "where he is not to be disturbed these two hours, so the physician says, lest the cooling draught——"

The Queen stamped her foot in sheer impotent rage.

"I must see someone. And Jewan Bukht, my son? why hath he not answered my summons?"

"His Highness," put in Hâfzan gravely, "was, as I came by just now, quarreling in his cups with his nephew, the princely 'Abool-Bukr, regarding the Inspectorship-of-Cavalry; which office both desire—a weighty matter——"

"Peace! she-devil!" almost screamed the Queen. "Can I not see, can I not hear for myself, that thy sharp wits must forever drag the rotten heart to light—thou wilt go too far, some day, Hâfzan, and then——"

"The Queen will have to find another scribe," replied Hâfzan meekly.

Zeenut Maihl glared at her, then rolled round into her cushions as if she were in actual physical pain. And hark! From the Lahore gate, as if nothing had happened, came the chime of noon. Noon! and nothing done. She sat up suddenly and signed to Hâfzan for pen and ink. She would wait no longer for the King; she would at least try the Mirza.

"'This, to the most illustrious the Mirza Moghul, Heir-Apparent by right to the throne of Timoor,'" she dictated firmly, and Hâfzan looked up startled. "Write on, fool," she continued; "hast never written lies before? 'After salutation the Begum Zeenut Maihl,'"—the humbler title came from her lips in a tone which boded ill for the recipient of the letter if he fell into the toils,—

"'seeing that in this hour of importance the King is sick, and by order of physicians not to be disturbed, would know if the Mirza, being by natural right the King's vice-regent, desires the private seal to any orders necessary for peace and protection. Such signet being in the hands of the Queen'—nay, not that, I was forgetting—'the Begum.'"

She gave an angry laugh as she lay back among her cushions and bid them send the letter forthwith. That should make him nibble. Not that she had the signet—the King kept that on his own finger—but if the Mirza came on pretense or rather in hopes of getting it? Why! then; if the proper order was given and if she could insure the aid of men to carry out her schemes, the signet should be got at somehow. The King was old and frail; the storm and stress might well kill him.

So her thoughts ranged from one plot to another as she waited for an answer. If this lure succeeded, she would but use the Heir-Apparent for a time. What use was there in plotting for him? He could die, as other heirs had died; and then the only person likely to put a spoke in her wheel was Abool-Bukr. He was teaching his young uncle the first pleasures of manhood, and might find it convenient to influence the boy against her. It would be well therefore to get hold of him also. That was not a hard task, and she sat up again without a moment's hesitation and signed once more to Hâfzan.

"Thy best flourishes," she said with an evil sneer, "for it goes to a rare scholar; to a fool for all that, who would have folk think nephews visit their aunts from duty! 'This to Newâsi loving and beloved, greeting. Consequent on the disturbances, the princely nephew Abool-Bukr lieth senseless here in the Palace.' Stare not, fool! senseless drunk he is by this time, I warrant. 'Those who have seen him think ill of him.'" Here she broke off into malicious enjoyment of her own wit. "Ay! and those who have but heard of him also! 'The course of events, however, being in the hands of Heaven, will be duly reported.'"

She coiled herself up again on the cushions, an insig-

nificant square homely figure draped in worn brocade
and laden with tarnished jewelry; ill-matched strings of
pearls, flawed emeralds, diamonds without sparkle.
Yet not without a certain dignity, a certain symmetry of
purpose, harmonizing with the arched and frescoed room
in which she lay; a room beautiful in design and decora-
tion, yet dirty, comfortless, almost squalid.

"Nay! not my signature," she yawned. "I am too
old a foe of the scholars; but a smudge o' the thumb will
do. If I know aught of aunts and nephews, she will be
too much flustered by the news to look at seals. And
have word sent to the Delhi gate that the Princess Farkhoonda be admitted, but goes not forth again."

Her hard voice ceased; there was no sound in the
room save that strange hum from the gardens outside,
which at this hour of the day were generally wrapped in
sun-drugged slumbers.

But the world beyond, toward which the old King's
lusterless eyes looked as he lay on the river balcony,
was sleepy, sun-drugged as ever. Through the tracery-
set arches showed yellow stretches of sand and curving
river, with tussocks of tall tiger-grass hiding the slender
stems of the palm-trees which shot up here and there
into the blue sky; blue with the yellow glaze upon it
which comes from sheer sunlight. A row of *saringhi*
players squatted in the room behind the balcony, thrumming softly, so as to hide that strange hum of life which
reached even here. For the King was writing a couplet
and was in difficulties with a rhyme for *cartouche* (cartridge); since he was a stickler for form, holding that the
keynote of the lines should jingle. And this couplet was
to epitomize the situation on the other side of the
saringhics. Cartouche? Cartouche? Suddenly he sat
up. "Quick! send for Hussan Askuri; or stay!" he
hesitated for an instant. Hussan Askuri would be with
the Queen, and no one ever admired his couplets as she
did. How many hours was it since he had seen her?
And what was the use of making couplets, if you were
denied their just meed of praise? "Stay," he repeated,
"I will go myself." It was a relief to feel himself on the

way back to be led by the nose, and as they helped him across the intervening courtyard he kept repeating his treasure, imagining her face when she heard it.

" Kuchch Chil-i-Room nahin kya, ya Shah-i-Roos, nahin
  Jo Kuchch kya na sara se, so cartouche ne."

A couplet, which, lingering still in the mouths of the people, warrants the old poetaster's conceit of it, and— dog-anglicized—runs thus:

" Nor Czar nor Sultan made the conquest easy,
  The only weapon was a cartridge greasy."

" The Queen? Where is the Queen?" fumed the old man, when he found an empty room instead of instant flattery; for he was, after all, the Great Moghul.

"She prays for the King's recovery," said Fâtma readily. " I will inform her that her prayer is granted." But as she passed on her errand, she winked at a companion, who hid her giggle in her veil; for Grand Turk or not, the women hold all the trump cards in seclusion. So how was the old man to know that the one who came in radiant with exaggerated delight at his return, had been interviewing his eldest son behind decorous screens, and that she was thanking Heaven piously for having sent him back to her apron-string in the very nick of time. Sent him, and Hussan Askuri, and pen and ink within reach of her quick wit.

" That is the best couplet my lord has done," she said superbly. " That must be signed and sealed."

So must a paper be, which lay concealed in her bosom. And as she spoke she drew the signet ring lovingly, playfully from the King's finger and walked over to where the scribe sat crouched on the floor.

" Ink it well, Pir-jee," she said, keeping her back to the King; " the impression must be as immortal as the verse."

Despite the warning, a very keen ear might have detected a double sound, as if the seal had needed a second pressure. That was all.

So it came about that, half an hour or so afterward, the Head-of-the-nine at the magazine was looking contemptuously at a paper brought by the Palace Guards, and passed under the door, ordering its instant opening. George Willoughby laughed; but some of the eight dashed people's impudence and cursed their cheek! Yet, after the laugh, the Head-of-the-nine walked over, yet another time, to that river bastion to look down at that white streak of road. How many times he had looked already, Heaven knows; but his grave face had grown graver, though it brightened again after a glance at the lemon bush. The black streak there would not fail them.

"In the King's name open!" The demand came from Mirza Moghul himself this time, for the Palace was without arms, without ammunition; and if they were to defend it, according to the Queen's idea, against all comers, till there was time for other regiments to rebel, this matter of the magazine was important. Abool-Bukr was with him, half-drunk, wholly incapable, but full of valor; for a scout sent by the Queen had returned with the news that no English soldier was within ten miles of Delhi, and within the last half hour an ominous word had begun to pass from lip to lip in the city.

Helpless!

The masters were helpless. Past two o'clock and not a blow in revenge. Helpless! The word made cowards brave, and brave folk cowards. And many who had spent the long hours in peeping from their closed doors at each fresh clatter in the street, hoping it was the master, looked at each other with startled eyes.

Helpless! Helpless!

The echo of the thought reached the main-guard, still in touch with the outside world, whence, as the day dragged by, fresh tidings of danger drifted down from the Ridge, where men, women, and children lay huddled helplessly in the Flagstaff Tower, watching the white streak of road. It seems like a bad dream, that hopeless, paralyzing strain of the eyes for a cloud of dust.

But the echo won no way into the magazine, for the simple reason that it knew it was not hopeless. It could hold its own.

"Shoot that man Kureem Buksh, please, Forrest, if he

comes bothering round the gate again. He is really very annoying. I have told him several times to keep back; so it is no use his trying to give information to the people outside."

For the Head-of-the-nine was very courteous. " Scaling ladders?" he echoed, when a native superintendent told him that the princes, finding him obdurate, had gone to send some down from the Palace. " Oh! by all means let them scale if they like."

Some of the Eight, hearing the reply, smiled grimly. By all means let the flies walk into the parlor; for if that straight streak of road was really going to remain empty, the fuller the four square walls round the lemon bush could be, the better.

" That's them, sir," said one of the Eight cheerfully, as a grating noise rose above the hum outside. " That's the grapnels." And as he turned to his particular gun of the ten, he told himself that he would nick the first head or two with his rifle and keep the grape for the bunches. So he smiled at his own little joke and waited. All the Nine waited, each to a gun, and of course there was one gun over, but, as the head of them had said, that could not be helped. And so the rifle-triggers clicked, and the stocks came up to the shoulders; and then?— then there was a sort of laugh, and someone said under his breath, " Well, I'm blowed!" And his mind went back to the streets of London, and he wondered how many years it was since he had seen a lamplighter. For up ropes and poles, on roofs and outhouses, somehow, clinging like limpets, running like squirrels along the top of the wall, upsetting the besiegers, monopolizing the ladders, was a rush, not of attack but of escape! Let what fool who liked scale the wall and come into the parlor of the Nine, those who knew the secret of the lemon-bush were off. No safety there beside the Nine! No life-insurance possible while that lay ready to their hand!

Would he ever see a lamplighter again? The trivial thought was with the bearded man who stood by his gun, the real self in him, hidden behind the reserve of courage, asking other questions too, as he waited for the upward

rush of fugitives to change into a downward rush of
foes worthy of good powder and shot.

It came at last—and the grape came too, mowing the
intruders down in bunches. And these were no mere
rabble of the city. They were the pick of the trained
mutineers swarming over the wall to stand on the out-
house roofs and fire at the Nine; and so, pressed in
gradually from behind, coming nearer and nearer, dropping to the ground in solid ranks, firing in platoons; so
by degrees hemming in the Nine, hemming in the lemon-
bush.

But the Nine were busy with the guns. They had to
be served quickly, and that left no time for thought.
Then the smoke, and the flashes, and the yells, and the
curses, filled up the rest of the world for the present.

" This is the last round, I'm afraid, sir; we shan't have
time for another," said a warning voice from the Nine,
and the Head of them looked round quietly. Not more
than forty yards now from the guns; barely time, certainly, unless they had had that other man! So he
nodded. And the last round pealed out as recklessly, as
defiantly, as if there had been a hundred to follow—
and a hundred thousand—a hundred million. But one
of the gunners threw down his fuse ere his gun recoiled,
and ran in lightly toward the lemon-tree, so as to be
ready for the favor he had begged.

" We're about full up, sir," came the warning voice
again, as the rest of the Nine fell back amid a desultory
rattle of small arms. The tinkle of the last church bell,
as it were, warning folk to hurry up—a last invitation to
walk into the parlor of the Nine.

" We're about full up, sir," came that one voice.

" Wait half a second," came another, and the Head-
of-the-nine ran lightly to that river bastion for a last
look down the white streak for that cloud of dust.

How sunny it was! How clear! How still! that world
beyond the smoke, beyond the flashes, beyond the deafen-
ing yells and curses. He gave one look at it, one short
look—only one—then turned to face his own world, the
world he had to keep. Full up indeed! No pyrotech-
nist could hope for better audience in so small a place.

" Now, if you please ! "

Someone in the thick of the smoke and the flashes heard the yells and curses and raised his cap—a last salute, as it were, to the school and schoolmaster. A final dismissal to the scholars—a thousand of them or so —about to finish their lesson of what men can do to hold their own. And someone else, standing beside the lemon-bush, bent over that faithful black streak, then ran for dear life from the hissing of that snake of fire flashing to the powder magazine.

A faint sob, a whispering gasp of horror, came from the thousand and odd; but above it came a roar, a rush, a rending. A little puff of white smoke went skyward first, and then slowly, majestically, a great cloud of rose-red dust grew above the ruins, to hang—a corona glittering in the slant sunbeams—over the school, the schoolmasters, and the scholars.

It hung there for hours. To those who know the story, it seems to hang there still—a bloody pall for the many; for the Nine, a crown indeed.

CHAPTER V.

SUNSET.

" What's that? "

The question sprung to every lip; yet all knew the answer. The magazine had saved itself.

But in the main-guard, not six hundred yards off, where the very ground rocked and the walls shook, the men and women, pent up since noon, looked at each other when the first shock was over, feeling that here was the end of inaction. Here was a distinct, definite challenge to Fate, and what would come of it? It was now close on to four o'clock; the day was over, the darkness at hand. What would it bring them? If Meerut, with its two thousand, was so sore bested that it could not spare one man to Delhi, what could they, a mere handful, hope for save annihilation?

Yet even Mrs. Seymour only clasped her baby closer, and said nothing. For there was no lack of courage anywhere. And Kate, with another child in her arms, paused as she laid it down, asleep at last, upon an officer's coat, to feel a certain relief. If they were to fare thus, that bitter self-reproach and agonizing doubt for vanished Sonny was unavailing. His chance might well be better than theirs.

Well indeed, pent up as they were cheek-by-jowl with four hundred unstable sepoys, and with the ominously rising hum of the unstable city on their unprotected rear. Up on the Flagstaff Tower crowning the extreme northern end of the Ridge, away from this hum, where Brigadier Graves had gathered together the remaining women and children, so as to guard them as best he could with such troops as he had remaining—many of them too unstable to be trusted cityward—they were in better plight. For they had the open country round them—a country where folk could still go and come with a fair chance of safety, since even the predatory tribes, always ready to take advantage of disorder, were still waiting to see what master the day would bring forth. And they had also the knowledge that something was being done, that they were not absolutely passive in the hands of Fate, after Dr. Batson started in disguise to summon that aid from Meerut which would not come of itself. Above all, they had the decision, they had the power to act; while down in the main-guard they could but obey orders. Not that the Flagstaff Tower did much with this advantage; for it was paralyzed by that straining of the eyes for a cloud of dust upon the Meerut road which was the damnation of Delhi. Yet even here that decisive roar, that corona of red dust brightening every instant as the sun dipped to the horizon, brought the conviction that something must be done at last. But what? Hampered by women and children, what could they do? If, earlier in the day, they had sent all the non-combatants off toward Kurnal or Meerut, with as many faithful sepoys as they could spare, arming everybody from the arsenal down by the river, they would have been free to make some forlorn hope— free, for instance, to go down *en-masse* to the main-guard and hold it, if they could.   That was what one man thought, who, seven miles out from Delhi—returning from a reconnoissance of his own to see if help were on the way—saw that little puff of smoke, heard the roar, and watched the red corona grow to brightness.

But on the Ridge, men thought differently.   The claims of those patient women and children seemed paramount, and so it was decided to get back the guns from the main-guard as a first step toward intrenching themselves for the night at the tower.   But the men in the main-guard looked at each other in doubt when the order reached them.   Was the garrison going to be withdrawn altogether, leaving merely a forlorn hope to keep the gate closed as long as possible against the outburst of rabble, to whom it would be the natural and shortest route to cantonments?   If so, surely it would have been better to send the women away first?   Still the orders were clear, and so the gate was set wide and the guns rumbled over the drawbridge under escort of a guard of the 38th.   That, at any rate, was good riddance of bad rubbish; though the wisdom of sending the guns in such charge was doubtful.   Yet how could the little garrison have afforded to give up a single man even of the still loyal 74th?—a company of whom had actually followed their captain to the ruins of the magazine to see if they could do anything, and returned, without a defaulter, to say that all was confusion—the dead lying about in hundreds, the enemy nowhere.

"How did the men behave, Gordon?" asked their commandant anxiously, getting his Captain into a quiet corner.   And the two men, both beloved of their regiment, both believing in it, both with a fierce, wild hope in their hearts that such belief would be justified, looked into each other's faces for a moment in silence.   There was a shadowing branch of neem overhead as they stood in the sunlight.   A squirrel upon it was chippering at the glitter of their buckles; a kite overhead was watching the squirrel.

"I think they hesitated, sir," said Captain Gordon quietly.

Major Abbott turned hastily, and looked through the

open gate, past the lumbering guns, to the open country lying peaceful, absolutely peaceful, beyond. If he could only have got his men there—away from the disloyalty of the 38th guard, the sullen silence of the 54th—if he could only have given them something to do! If he could only have said "Follow me!" they would have followed.

And Kate Erlton, who, weary of the deadly inaction in the room above, had drifted down to the courtyard, stood close to the archway looking through it also, thinking, not for the first time that weary day, of Alice Gissing's swift, heroic death with envy. It was something to die so that brave men turned away without a word when they heard of it. But as she thought this, the look on young Mainwaring's face as he stood with others listening to her story, came back to her. It had haunted her all day, and more than once she had sought him out, not for condolence—he was beyond that—but for a trivial word or two; just a human word or two to show him remembered by the living. And now the impulse came to her again, and she drifted back—for there was no hurry in that deadly, deadly inaction—to find him leaning listlessly against a wall digging holes in the dry dust idly with the point of his drawn sword for want of something better whereupon to use it. Such a young face, she thought, to be so old in its chill anger and despair! She went over to him swiftly, her reserve gone, and laid her hand upon his holding the sword.

" Don't fret so, dear boy," she said, and the fine curves of her mouth quivered. " She is at peace."

He looked at her in a blaze of fierce reproach. " At peace! How dare you say so? How dare you think so—when she lies—there."

He paused, impotent for speech before his unbridled hatred, then strode away indignantly from her pity, her consolation. And as she looked after him her own gentler nature was conscious of a pride, almost a pleasure in the thought of the revenge which would surely be taken sooner or later, by such as he, for every woman, every child killed, wounded—even touched. She was conscious of it, even though she stood aghast before a vision of the years stretching away into an eternity of division and mutual hate.

A fresh stir at the gate roused her, a quick stir among a group of senior officers, recruited now by two juniors who had earned their right to have their say in any council of war. These were two artillery subalterns, begrimed from head to foot, deafened, disfigured, hardly believing in their own safety as yet. Looking at each other queerly, wondering if indeed they could be the Head-of-the-nine and his second in command, escaped by a miracle through the sally port in the outer wall of the magazine, and so come back by the drawbridge, as Kate Erlton had come, to join the refugees in the main-guard. Was it possible? And—and—what would the world say? That thought must have been in their minds. And, no doubt, a vain regret that they were under orders now, as they listened while Major Abbott read out those just received from cantonments. Briefly, to take back the whole of the loyal 74th and leave the post to the 38th and the 54th—about a hundred and fifty openly disloyal men.

A sort of stunned silence fell on the little group, till Major Paterson of the 54th said quietly, officially to Major Abbott. "If you leave, sir, I shall have to abandon the post; I could not possibly hold it. Some of my men who have returned to the colors here might possibly fight were we to stick together. But with retreat, and the example of the 38th before them, they would not. I have, or I should have, lives in my charge when you are gone, and I warn you that I must use my own discretion in doing the best I can to protect them."

"Paterson is right, Abbott," put in the civil officer, who had stuck to his charge of the Treasury all day, and repelled the only attack made by the enemy during all those long hours. "If I am to do any good, I must have men who will fight. I don't trust the 54th; and the 38th are clearly just biding their time. This retreat might have done six hours ago—might do now if it were general; but I doubt it."

"Anyhow," put in another voice, "if the 74th are to go, they should take the women with them—they couldn't fare worse than they are sure to do here. I don't think the Brigadier can realize——"

"Couldn't you refer it?" asked someone; but the Major shook his head. The orders were clear; no doubt there was good cause for them. Anyhow they must be obeyed.

"Then as civil officer in charge of the Government Treasury, I ask for quarter-of-an-hour's law. If by then——"

The eager voice paused. Whether the owner thought once more of that expected cloud of dust, or whether he meant to gallop to cantonments in hope of getting the order rescinded is doubtful. Whether he went or stayed doubtful also. But the fifteen minutes of respite were given, during which the preparations for departure went on, the men of the 38th aiding in them with a new alacrity. Their time had come. Only a few minutes now before the last fear of a hand-to-hand fight would be over, the last chance of the master turning and rending them gone. It lingered a bit, though, for rumbling wheels came over the drawbridge once more, and voices clamored to be let in. The guns had returned. The gunners had deserted, said the escort insolently, and guns being in such case useless, they had preferred to rejoin their brethren; as for their officer, he had preferred to go on.

Kate Erlton, drawn from the inner room once again by the creaking of the gates, saw a look pass between one or two of the officers. And there stood the 74th, smart and steady, waiting for marching orders. No need to close the gates again, since time was up; the fifteen minutes had slipped by, bringing no help, just as the long hours had dragged by uselessly. So the gate stood open to the familiar, friendly landscape, all aglow with the rays of the setting sun. Close at hand, within a stone's throw, lay the tall trees and dense flowering thickets of the Koodsia gardens, where fugitives might have found cover. To the left were the ravines and rocks of the Ridge, fatal to mounted pursuit, and in the center lay the road northward, leading straight to the Punjâb, straight from that increasing roar of the city. There had been no attack as yet; but every soul within the main-guard knew for a certainty that the first hint of retreat would bring it.

How could it do otherwise?   The decisive answer of
the magazine, with its thousand-and-odd good reasons
against the belief that the master was helpless, had died
away.   The refuse and rabble of the city had ceased to
wander awestruck among the ruins, murmuring, " What
tyranny is here? "—that passive, resigned comment of
the weaker brother in India.   In the Palace, too, they had
recovered the shock of the mean trick of the Nine, who,
however, must, thank Heaven, be all dead too.

So as the gate stood open, and the sun streamed
through it into the wide courtyard, glinting on the
buckles and bayonets, Major Abbott's voice rose quietly.
" Are you ready, Gordon? "   The drawbridge was clear
of the guns now, clear of everything save the slant
shadows.

" All ready, sir," came the quiet reply.

" Number! " called the Commandant, but a voice at
his right hand pleaded swiftly.   " Don't wait for sections, Huzoor!   Let us go! "   And another at his left
whispered, " For God's sake, Huzoor! quick; get them
out quick! "

Major Abbott hesitated a second, only a second.   The
voices were the voices of good men and true, whom he
could trust.   " Fours about!   Quick march! " he corrected, and a sort of sigh of relief ran down the regiment
as it swung into position and the feet started rhythmically.   Action at last!—at long last!

" Good-by, old chap," said someone cheerfully, but
Major Abbott did not turn.   " Good-by!   Good-by! "
came voices all round; steady, quiet voices, as the disciplined tramp echoed on the drawbridge, and a bar of
scarlet coats grew on the rise of the white road outside.

" Good-by, Gordon!   Good-by! "

The tall figure in its red and gold was under the very
arch, shining, glittering in the sunlight streaming
through it.   Another step or two and he would have been
beyond it.   But the time for good-by had come.   The
time for which the 38th had been waiting all day.   He
threw up his arms and fell dead from his horse without
a cry, shot through the heart.   The next instant the
gate was closed, its creaking smothered in the wild,

senseless cry " To kill, to kill, to kill," in a wild, senseless
rattle of musketry. For there was really no hurry; the
handful of Englishmen were helpless. Major Abbott
and his men might clamor for re-entry at the gate if they
chose. They could not get in. Nor could the remnant
of the 74th, deprived of its loyal companions, of the only
two men who seemed to have controlled it, do anything.
And the 54th were helpless also by their own act; for they
had pushed Major Paterson through the gate before it
closed.

So there was no one left even to try and stem the tide.
No one to check that beast-like cry.

"*Mâro! Mâro! Mâro!*"

But, in truth, it would have been a hopeless task. The
game was up; the only chance was flight. And two,
foreseeing this for the last hour, had already made good
theirs by jumping from an embrasure in the rampart
into the ditch, while one, uninjured by the fall, had
scrambled up the counter-scarp, and was running like a
hare for those same thickets of the Koodsia.

" Come on! Come on! " cried others, seeing their success. And then? And then the cries and piteous
screams of women reminded them of something dearer
than life, and they ran back under a hail of bullets to that
upper room which they had forgotten for the moment.
And somehow, despite the cry of kill, despite the whistling bullets, they managed to drag its inmates to the
embrasure. But—oh! pathos and bathos of poor
humanity! making smiles and tears come together—the
women who had stared death in the face all day without
a wink, stood terrified before a twenty-feet scramble
with a rope of belts and handkerchiefs to help them. It
needed a round shot to come whizzing a message of certain death over their heads to give them back a courage
which never failed again in the long days of wandering
and desperate need which was theirs ere some of them
reached safety.

But Kate neither hesitated nor jumped. She had not
the chance of doing either. For that longing look of
hers through the open gates had tempted her to creep
along the wall nearer to them; so that the rush to close

them jammed her into a corner against a door, which yielded slightly to her weight. Quick enough to grasp her imminent danger, she stooped instantly to see if the door could be made to yield further. And that stoop saved her life, by hiding her from view behind the crowd. The next moment she had pushed aside a log which had evidently rolled from some pile within, and slipped sideways into a dark outhouse. She was safe so far. But was it worth it? The impulse to go out again and brave merciful death rose keen, until with a flash, the memory of that escape through the crowd came back to her; she seemed to hear the changing ready voice of the man who held her, to feel his quick instinctive grip on every chance of life.

Chance! There was a spell in the very word. A minute after logs jammed the door again, and even had it been set wide, none would have guessed that a woman, full of courage, ay! and hope, crouched behind the piles of brushwood. So she lay hidden, her strongest emotion, strange to say, being a raging curiosity to know what had become of the others, what was passing outside. But she could hear nothing save confused yells, with every now and again a dominant cry of "*Deen! Deen!*" or "*Jai Kali ma!*" For faith is one of the two great passions which make men militant. The other, sex. But as a rule it has no cry; it fights silently, giving and asking no words—only works.

So fought young Mainwaring, who, with his back to that same wall against which Kate had found him leaning, was using his sword to a better purpose than digging holes in the dust; or rather had adopted a new method of doing the task. He had not tried to escape as the others had done; not from superior courage, but because he never even thought of it. When he was free to choose, how could he think of leaving those devils unpunished, leaving them unchecked to touch her dead body, while he lived? He gave a little faint sob of sheer satisfaction as he felt the first soft resistance, which meant that his sword had cut into flesh and blood; for all his vigorous young life made for death, nothing but death. Was not she dead yonder?

So, after a bit, it seemed to him there was too little of
it there—that it came slowly, with his back to the wall
and only those who cared to go for him within reach—
for the crowd was dense, too dense for loading and firing. Dense with a hustling, horrified wonder, a confused prodding of bayonets. So, without a sound, he
charged ahead, hacking, hewing, never pausing, not even
making for freedom, but going for the thickest silently.

"*Amuk! Sayia! A-muk!*" The yell that he was mad,
possessed, rang hideously as men tumbled over each
other in their hurry to escape, their hurry to have at this
wild beast, this devil, this horror. And they were right.
He was possessed. He was life instinct with death;
filled with but one desire—to kill, or to be killed
quickly.

"*Saiya! Amuk! Saiya!*—out of his way—out of his
way! *Amuk! Saiya!* Fate is with him! The gods are
with him. *Saiya! Amuk!*"

So, by chance, not method; so by sheer terror as well
as hacking and hewing, the tall figure found itself, with
but a stagger or two, outside the wooden gates, out on
the city road, out among the gardens and the green trees.
And then, "Hip, hip, hurray!" His ringing cheer rose
with a sort of laugh in it. For yonder was her house!—
her house!

"Hip, hip, hurray!" As he ran, as he had run in races
at school, his young face glad, the fingers on the triggers
behind him wavered in sheer superstitious funk, and two
troopers coming down the road wheeled back as from a
mad dog. The scarlet coat with its gold epaulettes went
crashing into a group red-handed with their spoil, out of
it impartially into a knot of terrified bystanders, while
down the lane left behind it by the hacking and hewing
came bullet after bullet; the fingers on the triggers
wavered, but some found a billet. One badly. He
stumbled in the dust and his left arm fell oddly. But
the right still hacked and hewed as he ran, though the
crowd lessened; though it grew thin, too thin for his purpose; or else his sight was failing. But there, to the
right, the devils seemed thicker again. "Hip, hip, hooray!" No! trees. Only trees to hew—a garden—

perhaps the garden about her house—then, " Hip, hip——"

He fell headlong on his face, biting the soft earth in sheer despite as he fell.

" Don't touch him, brothers! " said one of the two or three who had followed at a distance, as they might have followed a mad dog, which they hoped others would meet and kill. " Provoke him not, or the demon possessing him may possess us. 'Tis never safe to touch till they have been dead a watch. Then the poison leaves them. Krishnjee, save us! Saw you how he turned our lead? "

" He has eaten mine, I'll swear," put in another sepoy boastfully, pointing gingerly with his booted foot to a round scorched hole in the red coat. " The muzzle was against him as I fired."

" And mine shall be his portion too," broke in a new arrival breathlessly, preparing to fire at the prostrate foe; but the first speaker knocked aside the barrel with an oath.

" Not while I stand by, since devils choose the best men. As 'tis, having women in our houses 'twere best to take precautions." He stooped down as he spoke, and muttering spells the while, raised a little heap of dust at the lad's head and feet and outstretched arms—a little cross of dust, as it were, on which the young body lay impaled.

" What is't? " asked a haughty-looking native officer, pausing as he rode by.

" 'Tis a hell-doomed who went possessed, and Dittu makes spells to keep him dead," said one.

" Fool! " muttered the man. " He was drunk, likely. They get like that, the cursed ones, when they take wine." And he spat piously on the red coat as he passed on. So they left the lad there lying face down in the growing gloom, hedged round by spells to keep him from harming women. Left him for dead.

But the scoffer had been right. He was drunk, but with the Elixir of Life and Love which holds a soul captive from the clasp of Death for a space. So, after a time, the cross of dust gave up its victim; he staggered to his feet again; and so, tumbling, falling, rising to fall again, he made his way to the haven where he would be, to the side of a dead woman.

And the birds, startled from their roosting-places by the stumbling, falling figure, waited, fluttering over the topmost branches for it to pass, or paused among them to fill up the time with a last twittering song of good-night to the day; for the sun still lingered in the heat-haze on the horizon as if loath to take its glow from that corona of red dust above the northern wall of Delhi, mute sign of the only protest made as yet by the master against mutiny.

And now he had left the city to its own devices. The rebels were free to do as they liked. The three thousand disciplined soldiers, more or less, might have marched out, had they chose, and annihilated the handful of loyal men about the Flagstaff Tower. But it was sunset—sunset in Rumzân. And the eyes of thousands, deprived even of a drop of water since dawn, were watching the red globe sink in the West, hungrily, thirstily; their ears were attuned but to one sound—the firework signal from the big mosque that the day's fast was over. The very children on the roofs were watching, listening, so as to send the joyful news that day was done, in shrill voices to their elders below, waiting with their water-pots ready in their hands.

Then, in good truth, there was no set purpose from one end of the city to another. From the Palace to the meanest brothel which had belched forth its vilest to swell the tide of sheer rascality which had ebbed and flowed all day, the one thought was still, "What does it mean? How long will it last? Where is the master?"

So men ate and drank their fill first, then looked at each other almost suspiciously, and drifted away to do what pleased them best. Some to the Palace to swell the turmoil of bellicose loyalty to the King—loyalty which sounded unreal, almost ridiculous, even as it was spoken. Others to plunder while they could. The bungalows had long since been rifled, the very church bells thrown down and broken; for the time had been ample even for wanton destruction. But the city remained. And while shops were being looted inside, the dispossessed Goojurs were busy over Metcalfe House, tearing up the very books in their revenge. The Flagstaff Tower lay not a mile away, almost helpless against attack. But there was no stomach for cold steel in Delhi on the 11th of May, 1857. No stomach for anything except safe murder, safe pillaging. Least of all was it to be found in the Palace, where men had given the rein to everything they possessed—to their emotions, their horses, their passions, their aspirations. Stabling some in the King's gardens, some in dream-palaces, some in pigstyes of sheer brutality. Weeping maudlin tears over heaven-sent success, and boasting of their own prowess in the same breath; squabbling insanely over the partition of coming honors and emoluments.

Abool-Bukr, drunk as a lord, lurched about asserting his intention of being Inspector-General of the King's cavalry, and not leaving man, woman, or child of the hell-doomed alive in India. For he had been right when he had warned Newâsi to leave him to his own life, his own death; when he had shrunk from the inherited blood-stains on his hands, the inherited tinder in his breast. It had caught fire with the first spark, and there was fresh blood on his hands: the blood of a Eurasian boy who had tried to defend his sister from drunken kisses. Someone in the melée had killed the girl and finished the boy: the Prince himself being saved from greater crime by tumbling into the gutter and setting his nose a-bleeding, a catastrophe which had sent him back to the Palace partially sobered.

But Princess Farkhoonda Zamâni, safe housed in the rooms kept for honored visitors, knew nothing of this, knew little even of the disturbances; for she had been a close prisoner since noon—a prisoner with servants who would answer no questions, with trays of jewels and dresses as if she had been a bride. She sat in a flutter, trying to piece out the reason for this kidnaping. Was she to be married by force to some royal nominee? But why to-day? Why in all this turmoil, unless she was required as a bribe. The arch-plotter was capable of that. But who? One thing was certain, Abool-Bukr could know nothing of this—he would not dare—and suddenly the hot blood tingled through every vein as she lay all unconsciously enjoying the return to the easeful idleness and luxury she had renounced. But if he did dare? If it was not mere anger which brought bewilderment to heart and brain, as she hid her face from the dim light which filtered in through the lattice—the dim, scented, voluptuous light from which she had fled once to purer air?

And not a hundred yards away from where she was trying to steady her bounding pulse, Abool-Bukr himself was bawling away at his favorite love-song to a circle of intimates, all of whom he had already provided with places on the civil list. His head was full of promises, his skin as full of wine as it could be, and he not be a mere wastrel unable to enjoy life. For Abool-Bukr gave care to this; since to be dead drunk was sheer loss of time.

> " Ah mistress rare, divine,
> Thy lover like a vine
> With tendril arms entwine."

Here his effort to combine gesture with song nearly caused him to fall off the steps, and roused a roar of laughter from some sepoys bivouacking under the trees hard by. But Mirza Moghul, passing hastily to an audience with the King, frowned. To-day, when none knew what might come, the Queen might have her way so far; but this idle drunkard must be got rid of soon. He would offend the pious to begin with, and then he could not be trusted. Who could trust a man who had been known to lure back his hawk because a bird's gay feathers shone in the sunshine?

But Ahsan-Oolah, dismissed from feeling the royal pulse once more, by the Mirza's audience, paused as he passed to recommend a cooling draught if the Inspector-General of Cavalry wanted to keep his head clear. It was the physician's panacea for excitement of all kinds. But an exhibition of steel would have done better on the 11th of May.

There was no one, however, to administer it to Delhi,

and even the refugees in the Flagstaff Tower were beginning to give up hope of its arriving from Meerut.
Those in the storehouse at Duryagunj still clung to the
belief that succor must come somehow; but Kate Erlton,
behind the wood-pile, knew that her hope lay only in
herself.

For how could Jim Douglas, as he more than once
passed through the now open and almost deserted Cashmere gate, in the hope, or rather the fear, of finding some
trace of her, know that she was hidden within a few yards
of him? or, how could she distinguish the sound of
his horse's hoofs from the hundreds which passed?

She must have escaped with the others, he concluded,
as he galloped toward the cantonments to see if she were
there. But she was not. He had failed again, he told
himself; failed through no fault of his own; for who could
have foretold that madness of retreat from the gate?

So now, there was nothing to be done in Delhi save
gather what information he could, give decent burial—
if he could—to Alice Gissing's body, and, if no troops
arrived before dawn, leave the city.

CHAPTER VI.

DUSK.

" 1 ENTREAT you to leave, sir. Believe me, there is
nothing else to be done now. It will be dark in half an
hour, and we shall need every minute of the night to
reach Kurnal."

It was said openly now by many voices. It had been
hinted first when, the corona of red dust having just
sprung to hide the swelling white dome of the distant
mosque, a dismal procession had come slowly up the
steep road to the tower with a ghastly addition to the
little knot of white faces there—slowly, slowly, the drivers
of the oxen whacking and jibing at them as if the cart
held logs or refuse, as if the driving of it were quite commonplace. Yet in a way the six bodies of English gen-

tlemen it held were welcome additions; since it was
something to see a dear face even when it is dead. But
they were fateful additions, making the disloyal 38th regiment, posted furthest from the Tower—partly commanded by it and the guns, in case of accident—shift
restlessly. If others had done such work, ought not
they to be up and doing? And now another procession
came filing up from the city—the two guns returning
from the Cashmere gate. They came on sullenly, slowly,
yet still they came on; another few minutes and the refugees would have been the stronger, the chances of
mutiny weaker. The 38th saw this. Their advanced
picket rushed out, drove off the gunners and the officers, and, fixing bayonets, forced the drivers to wheel
and set off down the road again at a trot. And down the
road, commanded by other guns, they went unchecked;
for the refugees did not dare to give the order to fire, lest
it should be disobeyed. The effect, we read, would
probably have been " that the guns would have been
swung round and fired on the orderers; and so not an
European would have escaped to tell the tale; this catastrophe, however, was mercifully averted and the crisis
passed over." It reads strangely, but once more, there
were women and children to think of. And few men are
strong enough to say, much less set it down in black and
white as John Nicholson did, that the protection " of
women and children in some crises is such a very minor
consideration that it ceases to be a consideration at all."

Still, it began to be patent to all that there was little
good in remaining in a place where they did not dare
to defend themselves. There were carriages and horses
ready; the road to Karnal was still fairly safe. Would
it not be better to retreat? But the Brigadier held out.
He had, in deference partly to others, wholly for the sake
of his helpless charges, weakened the city post. Why
should he have done that if he meant to abandon his
own? Then he was an old sepoy officer who had served
boy and man in one regiment, rising to its command at
last, and he was loath to believe that the 38th regiment,
which had been specially commended to him by his own,
would turn against him, if only he were free to handle it.

And this hope gained color from the fact, that to him personally and to his direct orders, the regiment was still cheerfully obedient.

So the waiting went on, and there were no signs of the 74th returning. What had happened? Fresh disaster? The voices urging retreat grew louder.

"Have it your own way, gentlemen," said the Brigadier at last. "The women and children had better go, at any rate, and they will need protection; so let all retire who will, and in what way seems best to them. I stay here."

So on foot, on horseback, in carriages, the exodus began forthwith; hastening more rapidly when the first man to jump from the embrasure at the Cashmere gate arrived with that tale of hopeless calamity.

But still the Brigadier refused to join the rout. He had been hanging on the skirts of Hope all day, trying, wisely or unwisely, to shield women and children behind that frail shelter. So he had been tied hand and foot. Now he would be free. True! the mystery of oncoming dusk made that red city in the distance loom larger, but a handful of desperate men unhampered, with plenty of ammunition, might hold such a post as the Flagstaff Tower till help arrived. He meant to try it, at any rate. Then nearly half of the 74th had got away safely—they were long in turning up certainly—but when they came they would form a nucleus. The 54th were not all bad, or they would not have saved their Major. Even the 38th, if they could once be got away from the sight of weakness, from that ghastly cart with its mute witness to successful murder, might respond to a familiar commonplace order. They were creatures of habit, with drill born in the blood, bred in the bone.

"I stay here," he said shortly. Said it again, even when neither the escaped officers nor men turned up. Said it again, when the guns rolled off toward Meerut, leaving him face to face with a sprinkling of the 74th and 54th, and the mass of the 38th, sullen, but still obedient.

The sun, now some time set, had left a flaming pennant in the sky, barring it low down on the horizon with a blood-red glow marking the top of the dust-haze, and the quick chill of color which in India comes with the lack of sunlight, even while its heat lingers to the touch, had fallen upon all things—upon the red Ridge, upon the distant line of trees marking the canal, upon the level plain between them where all the familiar landmarks of cantonment life still showed clearly, despite the darkening sky. Guard-rooms, lines, bells-of-arms, wide parade-grounds—all the familiar surroundings of a sepoy's life, and behind them that red flare of a day that was done.

"There is no use, sir, in stopping longer," said the Brigade-major, almost compassionately, to the figure which sat its horse steadfastly, but with a despondent droop of the shoulders.

"No possible use, sir," echoed the Staff Doctor kindly. The three were facing westward, for that vain hope of help from the east had been given up at last; and behind them, barely audible, was the faint hum of the distant city. A shaft of cormorants flying jheel-ward with barbed arrow head, trailed across the purpling sky; below them the red pennant was fading steadily. The day was done. But to one pair of eyes there seemed still a hope, still a last appeal to something beyond east or west.

"Bugler! sound the assembly!"   ·

The Brigadier's voice rang sharp over the plain, and was followed, quick as an echo, quick from that habit of obedience on which so much depended, by the cheerful notes.

"Come—to the co-lors! Come quick, come all—come quick, come all—come quick! Quick! Come to the colors!"

Last appeal to honor and good faith, to memory and confidence. But they had passed with the day. Yet not quite, for as the rocks and stones, the distant lines, the familiar landmarks gave back the call, a solitary figure, trim and smart in the uniform of the loyal 74th, fell in and saluted.

In all that wide plain one man true to his salt, heroic utterly, standing alone in the dusk. A nameless figure, like many another hero. Yet better so, when we remember that but a few hours before his regiment had *volun-*

teered to a man against their comrades and their country!
So sepoy ——, of company ——, can stand there, out-
lined against the dying day upon the parade-ground at
Delhi, as a type of others who might have stood there
also, but for the lack of that cloud of dust upon the
Meerut road.

Brigadier Graves wheeled his horse slowly northward;
but at the sight the sepoys of the 38th, still friendly to
him personally, crowded round him urging speed. It
was no place for him, they said. No place for the
master.

Palpably not. It was time, indeed, for the thud of
retreating hoofs to end the incident, so far as the master was concerned; the actual finale of the tragic mistake
being a disciplined tramp, as the sepoy who had fallen in
at the last Assembly fell out again, at his own word of
command, and followed the master doggedly. He was
killed fighting for us soon afterward.

"God be praised!" said the 38th, as with curious deliberation they took possession of the cantonments.
"That is over! He has gone in safety, and we have
kept the promise given to our brothers of the 56th not
to harm him." So, joined by their comrades from the
city, they set guards and gave out rations, with double
and treble doses of rum. Played the master, in fact,
perfectly; until, in the darkness, a rumble arose upon the
road, and one-half of the actors fled cityward incontinently and the other half went to bed in their huts like
good boys. But it was not the troops from Meerut at
last. It was only their old friends the guns, once more
brought back from the fugitives by comrades who had
finally decided to stand by the winning side.

So the question has once more to be asked, "What
would have happened, if, even at that eleventh hour, there
really *had* been a cloud of dust on the Meerut road?

As it was, confidence and peace were restored. In
the city they had never been disturbed. It seemed
weary, bewildered by the topsy-turvydom of the day,
desirous chiefly of sleep and dreams. So that Kate Erlton, peering out through a chink in the wood-store, felt
that if she were ever to escape from the slow starvation

which stared her in the face, she could choose no better time than this, when traffic had ceased, and the moon had not yet risen. She had settled that her best chance lay in creeping along the wall at first, then, taking advantage of the gardens, cutting across to that same sally-port through which the heroes of the magazine had told her they had made their escape. She did not know the exact situation, but she could surely find it. Besides, the ruins would most likely be deserted, and the other gates of the city, even if they were not closed for the night, as the gate here was, would be guarded. Once out of the city, she meant to make for the Flagstaff Tower; for, of course, she knew nothing of its desertion.

So she set the door ajar softly, and crept out. And as she did so, the whiteness of her own dress, even in the dense blackness, startled her, and roused the trivial wish that she had put on her navy-blue cotton instead, as she had meant to do that day. Strange! how a mere chance—the word was like a spur always, and she crept along the wall, hoping that the smoking, flaring fire of refuse in the opposite corner, round which the guard were sitting, so as to be free of mosquitoes, might dazzle their eyes. It was her only chance, however, so she must risk it. Then suddenly, under her foot, she felt something long, curved, snakelike. It was all she could do not to scream; but she set her teeth, and trod down hard with all her strength, her heart beating wildly in the awful suspense. But nothing struck her, there was no movement. Had she killed it? Her hand went down in the dark with a terror in it lest her touch should light on the head—perhaps within reach of the fangs. But she forced herself to the touch, telling herself she was a coward, a fool.

Thank Heaven! no snake after all, only a rope. A rope that must have been used for tethering a horse, for here under her foot was straw, rustling horribly. No! not now—that was something soft. A blanket; a horse's double blanket, dark as the darkness itself. Here was a chance, indeed. She caught it up and paused deliberately in the darkest corner of the square, to slip off shoes and stockings, petticoats and bodice; so, in the scantiest

of costumes, winding the long blanket round her, as a
skirt and veil in ayah's fashion.   Her face could be hidden by a modest down-drop over it, her white hands
hidden away by the modest drawing of a fold across her
mouth.   Her feet, then, were the only danger, and the
dust would darken them.   She must risk that anyhow.
So, boldly, she slipped out of the corner, and made for
the gate, remembering to her comfort that it was not
England where a lonely woman might be challenged all
the more for her loneliness.   In this heathen land, that
down-dropped veil hedged even a poor grass-cutter's
wife about with respect.   What is more, even if she
were challenged, her proper course would be to be silent
and hurry on.   But no one challenged her, and she
passed on into the denser shadows of the church garden
to regain her breath; for it had gone somehow.   Why,
she knew not; she had not felt frightened.   Then the
question came, what next?   Get to the magazine, somehow; but the strain of looking forward seemed far worse
than the actual doing, so she went on without settling
anything, save that she would avoid roads, and give the
still smoking roofless bungalows as wide a birth as possible, lest, in the dark, she should come on some dead
thing—a friend perhaps.   And with the thought came
that of Alice Gissing.   The house lay right on her path
to the magazine.   Surely she must be near it now.   Was
that the long sweep of its roof against the sky?   If she
could see so much, the moon must be rising, and she
could have no time to lose.   As she crept along through
the garden, she wondered why the bungalow had not
been burned like the others.   Perhaps the ayah's friends
had saved it, or, perhaps, there had not been much to
attract them in the little hired house.   Or, perhaps——

Hark!   She crouched back, from voices close beside
her, and doubled a bit; but they seemed to follow her.
And straight ahead the trees ended, and she must brave
the open space by the house itself; unless, indeed, she
slipped by the row of servant's houses to the veranda,
and so—through the rooms—gain the further side.   Or
she might hide in the house till these voices passed,
There they were again!   She made a breathless dash for

the shadow, ran on till she found the veranda, and deciding to hide for a time, passed in at the first door—the
door of the room where she had left Alice Gissing lying
dead a few hours before. But it was too dark, as yet,
to see if she lay there still, too dark to see even if the
house had been plundered. It must have been, however, for the very floor-cloths were gone; the concrete
struck cold to her feet. And a sudden terror at the darkness, the emptiness, coming over her, she passed on
rapidly to the faintly glimmering square of the further
door, seen through the intervening rooms. There were
three of them; bedroom, drawing room, dining room, set
in a row in Indian fashion, all leading into each other, all
opening on to the veranda; the two end ones opening also
into the side veranda. She could get out again, therefore,
by this further door. But it was bolted. She undid the
bolts, only to find it hasped on the outside. A feeling of
being trapped seized upon her. She ran to the other
door. Hasped also. The drawing-room door? Firmer
even than the others. But what a fool she was to feel
so frightened, when she could always go out as she had
come in when the voices had passed. She stole back
softly, knowing they must be just outside, and almost
fancying, in her alarm, that she heard a step in the
veranda. But there was the glimmering square of
escape, open. No! shut too! shut from the outside.

Had they seen her and shut the door? And there,
indeed, were footsteps! Loud footsteps and voices coming up the long flight of steps which led to the veranda
from the road. Coming straight, and she locked in,
helpless.

She threw up her hands involuntarily at a bright flash
in the veranda. Was it lightning? No! a pistol shot, a
quick curse, a fall. A yell of rage, a rush of those feet
upon the steps, and then another flash, another, and
another! More curses and a confused clashing! She
stood as if turned to stone, listening. Hark! down the
steps, surely, this time, another rush, a cry, a scuffle, a
fall. Then, loud and unmistakable, a laugh! Then
silence.

Merciful Heavens! what was it? What had happened?

She shook at the door gently, but still there was silence. Then, gripping the woodwork, she tried to peer out. But she could only see the bit of veranda in front of her which, being latticed in and hung with creepers, was very dark. The rest was invisible from within. She leaned her ear on the glass and listened. Was that a faint breathing? " Who's there? " she cried softly; but there was no answer. She sank down on the floor in sheer bewilderment and tried to think what to do, and after a time, a faint glimmer of the rising moon' aiding her, she went round to every door and tried it again. All locked inside and out. And now she could see that the house had been pillaged to the uttermost. There was literally nothing left in it. Nothing to aid her fingers if she tried to open the doors. By breaking the upper panes of glass, of course, she could undo the top bolt, but how was she to reach the bottom ones behind the lower panels? And why? why had they been locked? Who had locked the one by which she had come in? What was there that needed protection in that empty house. Was there by chance someone else? Then, suddenly, the remembrance of what she had left lying in the end room hours before came back to her. She had forgotten it utterly in her alarm and she crept back to see if Alice Gissing still kept her company. The bed was gone, but by the steadily growing glimmer of the moon she could see something lying on the floor in the very center of the room. Something strangely orderly, with a look of care and tidiness about it; but not white—and her dress had been white. Kate knelt down beside it and touched the still figure gently. What had it been covered with? Some sort of network, fine— silken—crimson. An officer's sash surely! And now her eyes becoming accustomed to what lay before them, and the light growing, she saw that the curly head rested on an officer's scarlet coat. The gold epaulettes were arranged neatly on either side the delicate ears so as not to touch them. Who had done this? Then that step she had thought she heard in the veranda must have been a real one. Someone must have been watching the dead woman.

She was at the door in an instant rapping at a pane, " Herbert! Herbert! are you there? Herbert! Herbert!" He might have done this thing. He might have come over from Meerut, for he had loved the dead woman, he had loved her dearly.

But there was no answer. Then wrapping the blanket round her hand she dashed it through the pane, and removing the glass, managed to crane out a little. She could see better so. Was that someone, or only a heap of clothes in the shadow of the corner by the inner wall? By this time the moonlight was shining white on the orange-trees on the further side of the road. She could see beyond them to the garden, but nothing of the road itself, nothing of the steep flight of steps leading down to it; a balustrade set with pots filling up all but the center arch prevented that.

" Herbert!" she cried again louder, " is that you?" But there was not a sound.

God in heaven! who lay there? dying or dead? helplessness broke down her self-control at last, and she crept back into the room, back to the old companionship, crying miserably. Ah! she was so tired, so weary of it all. So glad to rest! A sense of real physical relief came to her body as, for the first time for long, long hours, she let her muscles slacken, and to her mind as she let herself cry on, like a child, forgetting the cause of grief in the grief itself. Forgetting even that after a time in sheer rest; so that the moon, when it had climbed high enough to peep in through the closed doors, found her asleep, her arms spread out over the crimson network, her head resting on what lay beneath it. But she slept dreamfully and once her voice rose in the quick anxious tones of those who talk in their sleep.

" Freddy! Freddy!" she called. " Save Freddy, someone! Never mind, ayah! He is only a boy, and the other, the other may——" Then her words merged into each other uncertainly, after the manner of dreamers, and she slept sounder.

Soundest of all, however, in the cool before the dawn; so that she did not wake with a stealthy foot in the side veranda, a stealthy hand on the hasp outside; did not wake even when Jim Douglas stood beside her, looking down vexedly on the blanket-shrouded figure pillowed on the body he came to seek. For he had been delayed by a thousand difficulties, and though the shallow grave was ready dug in the garden, the presence of this native—even though a woman, apparently—must make his task longer. Was it a woman? One hand on his revolver, he laid the other on the sleeper's shoulder. His touch brought Kate to her feet blindly, without a cry, to meet Fate.

"My God! Mrs. Erlton!" he cried, and she recognized his voice at once. Fate indeed! His chance and hers. His chance and hers!

She stood half stupefied by her dreams, her waking; but he, after his nature, was ready in a second for action, and broke in on his own wondering questions impatiently. "But we are losing time. Quick! you must get to some safer place before dawn. Twist that blanket right—let me, please. That will do. Now, if you will follow close, I must get you hidden somewhere for to-day. It is too near dawn for anything else. Come!"

She put out her hand vaguely, as if to stave his swift decision away, and, looking in her face, he recognized that she must have time, that he must curb his own energy.

"Then it was you who fired," she said in a dull voice. "You who shut me in here? You who killed those voices. Why didn't you answer when I called, when I thought it was Herbert? It was very unkind—very unkind."

He stared at her for a second, and then his hand went out and closed on hers firmly. "Mrs. Erlton! I'm going to save you if I can. Come. I don't know what you're talking about, and there is no time for talk. Come."

So, hand in hand, they passed into the side veranda, through which he had entered, and so, since the nearest way to the city lay down that flight of steps, to the front one.

"Take care," he cried, half-stumbling himself, and forcing her to avoid something that lay huddled up against the wall. It was a dead man. And there, upon the steps which showed white as marble in the moonlight, were two others in a heap. A third lower down, ghastlier still, lying amid dark stains marring the whiteness, and with a gaping cut clearly visible on the shoulder.

But that still further down! Jim Douglas gave a quick cry, dropped Kate's hand, and was on his knees beside the tall young figure—coatless, its white shirt stiff with blood, which lay head downward on the last steps as if it had pitched forward in some mad pursuit. As he turned it over on its back gently, the young face showed in the moonlight stern, yet still exultant, and the sword, still clenched in the stiff right hand, rattled on the steps.

"Mainwaring! I don't understand," he said, looking up bewildered into Kate's face. The puzzle had gone from it; she semed roused to life again.

"I understand now," she said softly, and as she spoke she stooped and raised the boy's head tenderly in her hands. "Don't let us leave him here," she went on eagerly, hastily. "Leave him there, beside—beside—*her.*"

Jim Douglas made no reply. He understood also dimly, and he only signed to her to take the feet instead. So together they managed to place that dead weight within the threshold and close the door.

Then Jim Douglas held out his hand again, but there was a new friendliness in its grip. "Come!" he said, and there was a new ring in his voice, "the night is far spent, the day is at hand."

It was true. As they stepped from the now waning moonlight into the shadow of the trees, the birds, beginning to dream of dawn, shifted and twittered faintly among the branches. And once, startling them both, there was a louder rustling from a taller tree, a flutter of broad white wings to a perch nearer the city, a half-sleepy cry of:

"Deen! Deen! Futteh Mohammed!"

"If I had time," muttered Jim Douglas fiercely, "I would go and wring that cursed bird's neck! But for it——" Kate's tighter clasp on his hand seemed like an appeal, and he went on in silence.

So, as they slipped from the gardens into the silent streets, the muezzin's monotonous chant began from the shadowy minaret of the big mosque.

"Prayer is more than sleep!—than sleep!—than sleep!"

The night was far spent; the day was indeed at hand—and what would it bring forth? Jim Douglas, with a sinking at his heart, told himself he could at least be thankful that one day was done.

BOOK IV.

"SUCH STUFF AS DREAMS ARE MADE OF."

CHAPTER I.

THE DEATH PLEDGE.

THE outer court of the Palace lay steeped in the sun-shine of noon. Its hot rose-red walls and arcades seemed to shimmer in the glare, and the dazzle and glitter gave a strange air of unreality, of instability to all things. To the crowds of loungers taking their siesta in every arcade and every scrap of shadow, to the horses stabled in rows in the glare and the blaze, to the eager groups of new arrivals which, from time to time, came in from the outer world by the cool, dark tunnel of the Lahore gate to stand for a second, as if blinded by the shimmer and glitter, before becoming a part of that silent, drowsy stir of life.

From an arch close to the inner entry to the precincts rose a monotonous voice reading aloud. The reader was evidently the author also, for his frown of annoy-ance was unmistakable at a sudden diversion caused by the entry of a dozen or more armed men, shouting at the top of their voices: " *Pâdishâh, Pâdishâh, Pâdishâh!* We be fighters for The Faith. *Pâdishâh!* a blessing, a blessing! "

A malicious laugh came from one of the listeners in the arcade—a woman shrouded in a Pathan veil.

" 'Tis as well his Majesty hath taken another cooling draught," came her voice shrilly. " What with writing letters for help to the Huzoors to please Ahsan-Oolah and Elahi-Buksh, and blessing faith to please the Queen, he hath enough to do in keeping his brain from getting

275

dizzy with whirling this way and that. Mayhap faith will fail first, since it is not satisfied with blessings. They are windy diet, and I heard Mahboob say an hour agone that there was too much faith for the Treasury. Lo! moonshee-jee, put that fact down among thy heroics— they need balance!"

"Sure, niece Hâfzan," reproved the old editor of the Court Journal, "I see naught that needs it. Syyed Abdulla's periods fit the case as peas fit a pod; they hang together."

"As we shall when the Huzoors return," assented the voice from the veil.

"They will return no more, woman!" said another. It belonged to a man who leaned against a pilaster, looking dreamily out into the glare where, after a brief struggle, the band of fighters for the faith had pushed aside the timid door-keepers and forced their way to the inner garden. Through the open door they showed picturesquely, surging down the path, backed by green foliage and the white dome of the Pearl Mosque rising against the blue sky.

"The Faith! The Faith! We come to fight for the Faith!"

Their cry echoed over the drowsy, dreaming crowds, making men turn over in their sleep; that was all.

But the dreaminess grew in the face looking at the vista through the open door till its eyes became like those Botticelli gives to his Moses—the eyes of one who sees a promised land—and the dreamy voice went on:

"How can they return; seeing that He is Lord and Master? Changing the Day to Darkness, the Darkness into Day. Holding the unsupported skies, proving His existence by His existence, Omnipotent. High in Dignity, the Avenger of His Faithful people."

The old editor waggled his head with delighted approval; the author fidgeted over an eloquence not his own; but Hâfzan's high laugh rang cynically:

"That may be so, most learned divine; yet I, Hâfzan, the harem scribe, write no orders nowadays for King or Queen without the proviso of 'writ by a slave in pursuance of lawful order and under fear of death' in some quiet corner. For I have no fancy, see you, for hanging, even if it be in good company. But, go on with thy leading article, moonshee-jee, I will interrupt no more."

" Thus by a single revolution of time the state of affairs is completely reversed,* and the great and memorable event which took place four days ago must be looked upon as a practical warning to the uninformed and careless, namely the British officers and those who never dreamed of the decline and fall of their government, but who have now convincing proof of what has been written in the Indelible Tablets by God. The following brief account, therefore, of the horrible and memorable events is given here solely for the sake of those still inclined to treat them as a dream. On Monday, the 16th of Rumzân, that holy month in which the Word of God came down to earth, and in which, for all time, lies the Great Night of Power, the courts being open early on account of the hot weather, the magistrate discharging his wonted duties, suddenly the bridge toll-keeper appeared, informing him that a few Toork troopers had first crossed the bridge——"

The dreamy-faced divine turned in sharp reproach. " Not so, Syyed-jee. The vision came first—the vision of the blessed Lord Ali seen by the muezzin. Wouldst make this time as other times, and deny the miracles by which it is attested as of God?"

" Miracles!" echoed Hâfzan. " I see no miracle in an old man on a camel."

The divine frowned. " Nor in a strange white bird with a golden crown, which hovered over the city giving the sacred cry? Nor in the fulfillment of Hussan Askuri's dream?"

Hâfzan burst into shrill laughter. " Hussan Askuri! Lo! Moulvie Mohammed Ismail, didst thou know the arch dreamer as I, thou wouldst not credit his miracles. He dreams to the Queen's orders as a bear dances to the whip. And as thou knowest, my mistress hath the knack of jerking the puppet strings. She hath been busy these days, and even the Princess Farkhoonda——"

" What of the Princess?" asked the newswriter, eagerly, nibbling his pen in anticipation.

---

* From the account in the native papers,

" Nay, not so! " retorted Hâfzan. " I give no news nowadays, since I cannot set 'spoken under fear of death ' upon the words."

She rose as she spoke, yet lingered, to stand a second beside the divine and say in a softer tone, " Dreams are not safe, even to the pious, as thou, Moulvie-sahib. A bird is none the less a bird because it is strange to Delhi and hath been taught to speak. That it was seen all know; yet for all that, it may be one of Hussan Askuri's tricks."

" Let it be so, woman," retorted Mohammed Ismail almost fiercely, "is there not miracle enough and to spare without it? Did not the sun rise four days ago upon infidels in power? Where are they now? Were there not two thousand of them in Meerut? Did they strike a blow? Did they strike one here? Where is their strength? Gone! I tell thee—gone! "

Hâfzan laid a veiled clutch on his arm suddenly and her other hand, widening the folds of her shapeless form mysteriously, pointed into the blaze and shimmer of sunlight. " It lies there, Moulvie-sahib, it lies there," she said in a passionate whisper, " for God is on their side."

It was a pitiful little group to which she pointed. A woman, her mixed blood showing in her face, her Christianity in her dress, being driven along like a sheep to the shambles across the courtyard. She clasped a year-old baby to her breast and a handsome little fellow of three toddled at her skirts. She paused in a scrap of shade thrown by a tree which grew beside a small cistern or reservoir near the middle of the court, and shifted the heavy child in her arms, looking round, as she did so, with a sort of wild, fierce fear, like that of a hunted animal. The cluster of sepoys who had made their prisoner over to the Palace guard turned hastily from the sight; but the guard drove her on with coarse jibes.

" The rope dangles close, Moulvie-jee," came Hâfzan's voice again. " Ropes, said I? Gentle ropes? Nay! only as the wherewithal to tie writhing limbs as they roast. If thou hast a taste for visions, pious one, tell me what thou seest ahead for the murderers of such poor souls? "

" Murderers," echoed Mohammed Ismail swiftly;

"there is no talk of murder. 'Tis against our religion. Have I not signed the edict against it? Have we not protested against the past iniquity of criminals, and ignorant beasts, and vile libertines like Prince Abool-Bukr, who take advantage——"

"He was too drunk for much evil, learned one!" sneered Hâfzan. "Godly men do worse than he in their own homes, as I know to my cost. As for thine edict! Take it to the Princess Farkhoonda. She is a simple soul, though she holds the vilest liver of Delhi in a leash. But the Queen—the Queen is of different mettle, as you edict-signers will find. There are nigh fifty such prisoners in the old cook-room now. Wherefore?"

"For safety. There are nigh forty in the city police station also."

Hâfzan gathered her folds closer, "Truly thou art a simple soul, pious divine. Dost not think there is a difference, still, between the Palace and the city? But God save all women, black or white, say I! Save them from men, and since we be all bound to hell together by virtue of our sex, then will it be a better place than Paradise by having fewer men in it."

She flung her final taunts over her shoulder at her hearers as she went limping off.

"Heed her not, most pious!" said her uncle apologetically. "She hath been mad against men ever since hers, being old and near his end, took her, a child, and——"

But Moulvie Mohammed Ismail was striding across the courtyard to the long, low, half-ruinous shed in which the prisoners were kept.

"Have they proper food and water?" he asked sharply of the guard. "The King gave orders for it."

"It comes but now!" replied the sergeant glibly, pointing to a file of servants bearing dishes which were crossing the courtyard from the royal kitchens. The Moulvie gave a sigh of relief, for Hâfzan's hints had alarmed him. These same helpless prisoners lay on his conscience, since he and his like were mainly responsible for the diligent search for Christians which had been going on during the last few days; for it was not to be tolerated that the faithful should risk salvation by con-

cealing them.   The proper course was plain, unmistakable.   They should be given up to the authorities and
be made into good Mohammedans; by persuasion if
possible, if not, by force.   In truth the Moulvie dreamed
already of ninety and odd willing converts, as a further
manifestation of divine favor.   Perhaps more; though
most of these ill-advised attempts at concealment must
have come to an end by now.

They had indeed; those four days of peace, of hourly
increasing religious enthusiasm for a cause so evidently
favored by High Heaven, had made it well nigh impossible to carry on a task attempted by so many, when it
seemed likely to last for a few hours only.

Even Jim Douglas told himself he must fail unless he
could get help.   He had succeeded so far, simply because
—by a mere chance—he had, not one but several, places
of concealment ready to his hand without the necessity
for taking anyone into his confidence.   For he had found
it convenient in his work to have cities of refuge, as it
were, where he could escape from curiosity or change
a disguise at leisure.   The shilling or so a month required for the rent of a room in some tenement house
being more than repaid by the sense of security the possession gave him.   It was to one of these, therefore, that
he took Kate on the dawn of the 12th, leaving her locked
up in it alone; till night enabled him to take her on to
another; so by constant change managing to escape suspicion.   But as the days passed in miraculous peace, he
recognized the hopelessness of continuing this life for
long.   To begin with, Kate's nerves could not stand it.
She was brave enough, but she had an imagination, and
what woman with that could stand being left alone in the
dark for twelve hours at a time, never knowing if the slow
starvation, which would be her fate if anything untoward
happened to him, had not already begun?   He could not
expect her to stand it, when three days of something far
less difficult had left him haggard, his nerves unstrung;
left him with the possibility looming in the future of his
losing his self-control some day, and going madly for the
whole world as young Mainwaring had done.   Not that
he cared for Kate's safety so much, as that the mere

thought of failure roused a beast-like ferocity in him.
So, as he wandered restlessly about the city, waiting in a
fever of impatience for some sign of the world without
those rose-red walls—waiting day by day, with a growing
tempest of rage, for the night to return and let him creep
up some dark stairs and assure himself of a woman's
safety, he was piecing together a plan in case—— Of
what? In case the stories he heard in the bazaars were
true? No! that was impossible. How could the English have been wiped out of India? Yet as he saw the
deserted shops being reopened in solemn procession by
an old pantaloon on an elephant calling himself the
Emperor, when he saw Abool-Bukr letting off squibs
in general rejoicing over the re-establishment of Mohammedan empire; above all when he saw the tide of life
returning to the streets, his mad desire to strike a blow
and smash the sham was tempered by an almost unbear-
able curiosity as to what had really happened. But he
dared not try and find out. Useless though he knew it
was, he hung round the quarter where Kate lay concealed
for the day, feeling a certain consolation in knowing that
he was as close to her as he dared to be. Such a life was
manifestly impossible, and so, bit by bit, his plan grew.
Yet, when it had grown, he almost shrank from it, so
strange did it seem, in its linking of the past with the
present. For Kate must pass as his wife—his sick wife,
hidden, as Zora had been, on some terraced roof, with
Tara as her servant; he, meanwhile, passing as an Afghan
horse-dealer, kept from returning North, like others of
his trade, by this illness in his house. The plan was perfectly feasible if Tara would consent. And Jim Douglas,
though he ignored his own certainty, never really doubted
that she would. He had not been born in the mist-
covered mountains of the North for nothing. Their
mysticism was part of his nature, and he felt that he had
saved her for this; that for this, and this only, he had
played that childish but successful cantrip with her hair.
In a way, was not the pathetic idyl on the roof with little
Zora but a rehearsal of a tragedy—a rehearsal without
which he could not have played his part? Strange thread
of fate, indeed, linking these women together! and though

he shrank from admitting its very existence, it gave him confidence that the whole would hang together securely. So that when he sought Tara out, his only real doubt was whether it would be wiser to tell her the truth about Kate, or assert that she was his wife. He chose the latter as less risky, since, even if Tara refused aid, she would not overtly betray anyone belonging to him.

But Tara did not refuse. To begin with, she could have refused nothing in the first joy of finding him safe when she had believed him dead like all the other Huzoors. And then a vast confusion of love, and pride, and remorse, and fierce passionate denial of all three, led her into consent. If the Huzoor wanted her to help to save his wife why should she object? Though it was nothing to her if the mem was *his* mem or not. Jim Douglas, listening to the eager protest, wondered if he might not safely have saved himself an unnecessary complication; but then he wondered at many things Tara said and did. At her quick frown when he promised her both hair and locket as her reward. At the faint quiver amid the scorn with which she had replied that he would still want the latter for the mem's hair. At her slow smile when he opened the gold oval to show the black lock still in sole possession. She had turned aside to look at the hearth-cakes she had been toasting when he came in, and then gone into the necessary details of arrangement in the most matter-of-fact way. Naturally the Huzoor had sought help from his servant. From whom else could he seek it? As for her saintship, there was nothing new in that. She had been suttee always as the master very well knew. So nothing she did for him, or he for her, could make that suffer. Therefore she would arrange as she had arranged for Zora. The Huzoor must rent a roof—roofs were safest—and she would engage a half-blind, half-deaf old sweeper-woman she knew of. Perhaps another if need be. But the Huzoor need have no fear of such details if he gave her money. And this Jim Douglas had hidden in the garden of his deserted bungalow in Duryagunj; so that in truth it seemed as if the whole plan had been evolved for them by a kindly fate.

And yet Jim Douglas felt a keen pang of regret when, for the first time, he gave the familiar knock of those old Lucknow days at the door of a Delhi roof and Tara opened it to him, dressed in the old crimson drapery, the gold bangles restored to her beautiful brown arms. He had brought Kate round during the previous night to the lodging he had managed to secure in the Mufti's quarter, and, leaving her there alone, had taken the key to Tara; this being the safest plan, since everything could then be arranged in discreet woman's fashion before he put in an appearance.

And the task had been done well. The outside square or yard of parapeted roof which he entered lay conventional to the uttermost. A spinning-wheel here, a row of water-pots there, a mat, a reed stool or two, a cooking place in one corner, a ragged canvas screen at the inner doors. Nothing there to prepare him for finding an Englishwoman within; an Englishwoman with a faint color in her wan cheeks; a new peace in her gray eyes, busy—Heaven save the mark!—in sticking some disjointed jasmine buds into the shallow saucer of a water-pot.

" Tara brought them strung on a string," said Kate half apologetically after her first welcome, as she noted his look. " I suppose she meant me to wear them— with the other things," she paused to glance down with a smile at her dress, " but it seemed a pity. They were like a new world to me—like a promise—somehow."

He sat down on the edge of the string bed feeling a little dazed and looked at her and her surroundings critically. It was a pleasant sunshiny bit of roof, vaulted by the still cool morning sky. There was a little arcaded room at one end, the topmost branches of a neem tree showed over one side; on the other, the swelling dome of the big mosque looked like a great white cloud, and in one corner was a sort of square turret, from the roof of which, gained by a narrow brick ladder, the whole city was visible. For it was the highest house in the quarter, higher even than the roof beside it, over which the same neem tree cast a shadow.

And as he looked, he thought idly that no dress in the

world was more graceful than the Delhi dress with its
billowy train and loose, soft, filmy veil. And Kate
looked well in white—all in white. He pulled himself
up sharply; but indeed memory was playing him tricks,
and the stress and strain of reality seemed far from that
slip of sun-saturated roof where a graceful woman in
white was sticking jasmine buds into water. And suddenly the thought came that Zora would have worn the
chaplets heedlessly; there would have been no sentimentality over withered flowers on her part.

" A promise," he echoed half-bitterly. " Well! one
must hope so. And even if the worst comes, it will come
easier here."

She looked up at him reproachfully. " Don't remind
me of that, please," she said hurriedly; " I seem to have
forgotten—here under the blue sky. I dare say it's very
trivial of me, but I can't help it. Everything amuses me,
interests me. It is so quaint, so new. Even this dress;
it is hardly credible, but I wished so much for a looking-
glass just now, to see how I looked in it."

Her eyes met his almost gayly, and he felt an odd
resentment in recognizing that Zora would have said the
words as frankly.

" I have one here—in a ring," he replied somewhat
stiffly, with a vague feeling he had done all this before,
as he untied the knot of a small bundle he had brought
with him. " It is not much use—for that sort of thing—
I'm afraid," he went on, " but I think you had better
have these: it is a great point—even for your own sake—
to dress as well as play the part."

Kate, with a sudden gravity, looked at the pile of
native ornaments he emptied out on to the bed. Bracelets in gold and silver, anklets, odd little jeweled tassels
for the hair, quaint silk-strung necklets and talismans.

" Here is the looking-glass," he said, choosing out a
tiny round one set in filigree gold; " you must wear it on
your thumb—but it will barely go on my little finger,"
he spoke half to himself, and Kate, fitting on the ring,
looked at him and set her lips.

" It is too small for me also," she said, laying it down
with a faint air of distaste. " They are very pretty, Mr.

Greyman," she added quickly, " but I would rather not—unless it is really necessary—unless you think——"

He rose half-wearily, half-impatiently. " I should prefer it; but you can do as you like. The jewels belonged to a woman I loved very dearly, Mrs. Erlton. She was not my wife—but she was a good woman for all that. You need not be afraid."

Kate felt the blood tingle to her face as she laid violent hands on the first ornament she touched. It happened to be a solid gold bangle. " It is too small too," she said petulantly, trying to squeeze her hand through it. " Really it would be better——"

" Excuse me," he replied coolly, " if you will let me." He drew the great carved knobs apart deftly, slipped her wrist sideways through the opening, and had them closed again in a second.

" You can't take it off at night, that is all," he went on, " but I will tell Tara to show you how to wear the rest. I must be off now and settle a thousand things."

As he passed into the outer roof once more, Kate felt that flush, half of resentment, half of shame, still on her face. In such surroundings how trivial it was, and yet he had guessed her thought truly. Had he guessed also the odd thrill which the touch of that gold fetter gave her? Half-mechanically she tried to loosen it, to remove it, and then with an impatient frown desisted and began to put on the other bracelets. What did it matter, one way or the other? And then, becoming interested despite herself, she set to work to puzzle out uses and places for the pile.

Meanwhile Jim Douglas was dinning instructions into Tara's ear; but she also, he told himself angrily, was trivial to the last degree. And when finally he urged an immediate darkening of Kate's hair and a faint staining of the face to suit the only part possible with her gray eyes—that of a fair Afghan—he flung away in despair from the irrelevant remark:

" But the mem will never be so pretty as Zora; and besides she has such big feet."

Big feet! He swore under his breath that all women were alike in this, that they saw the whole world through the medium of their sex; and *that* was at the bottom of all the mischief. Delhi had been lost to save women; the trouble had begun to please them. Even now, as far as he could see, resistance would collapse but for one woman's ambition; though despite the Queen and her plots, a hundred brave men or so might still be masters of Delhi if they chose. Since it was still each for himself, and the devil take the hindmost with the mutineers. The certainty of this had made these long days of inaction almost beyond bearing to him; and as Jim Douglas passed out into the street he thought bitterly that here again a woman stood in the way; since but for Kate he could surely have forced Meerut into making reprisals by reporting the true state of affairs.

Yet every hour made these reprisals more difficult. Indeed, as he left the Mufti's quarters on that morning of the 16th of May, something was going on in the Palace which ended indecision for many a man and left no chance of retreat. For Zeenut Maihl saw facts as clearly as Jim Douglas, and knew that the first tramp of disciplined feet would be the signal for scuttle; if a chance of escape remained.

And so this something was going on. By someone's orders of course; by whose is one of the unanswered questions of the Indian Mutiny.

The Queen herself was sitting with the King, amicably, innocently, applauding his latest couplet; which was in sober truth, one of his best:

> "God takes this dice-box world, shakes upside down,
> Throws one defeat, and one a kingly crown."

He was beginning to feel the latter on the old head, which was so diligently stuffed with dreams; but the Queen knew in her heart of hearts that the fight for sovereignty had only just begun. So her mind was chiefly occupied in a spiteful exultation at the thought of some folk's useless terror when—this thing being done—they would find their hands irrevocably on the plow. Ahsan-Oolah and Elahi-Buksh, for instance; their elaborate bridges would be useless; and Abool-Bukr with his squibs and processions, Farkhoonda with her patter of virtue and religion. If only for the sake of immeshing this last victim Zeenut Maihl would not have shrunk; since those three or four days of cozening had left the Queen with a still more vigorous hate for the Princess Farkhoonda, who had fallen into the trap so easily, and who already began to give herself airs and discuss the future on a plane of equality. Pretty, conceited fool! who even now, so the spies said, was waiting to receive the Prince, her nephew, for the first time since she came to the Palace. The very fact that it was the first time seemed an aggravation in the Queen's angry eyes, proving as it did a certain reality in Farkhoonda's pretensions to decorum.

In truth they were very real to the Princess herself; had been gaining reality ever since that first deft suggestion of a possibility had set her heart beating. The possibility, briefly, of the King choosing to set aside that early marriage so tragically interrupted; choosing to declare it no marriage and give his consent to another. Newâsi had indignantly scouted the suggestion, had stopped her ears, her heart; but the remembrance of it lingered, enervating her mind, and as she waited for the interview with the Prince she felt vaguely that it was a very different matter receiving him in these bride-like garments, in these dim, heavily scented rooms, to what it had been under the clear sky in her scholar's dress. Yet as she stooped from mere habit, aroused by the finery itself, to arrange her long brocaded train into better folds, she gave something between a sigh and a laugh at the certainty of his admiration. And after all, why should she not have it if the King——

The sound of a distant shot made her start and pause, listening for another. So she stood a slim figure ablaze with color and jewels, a figure with studied seductiveness in every detail of its dress; and she knew that it was so. Why not? If—if he liked it so, and if the King——

Newâsi clasped her hands nervously and walked up and down the dim room. Abool was late, and he had no right to be late on this his first visit of ceremony to his aunt. The Mirza-sahib was no doubt late, admitted her attendants, but the door-keeper had reported a disturbance of some kind in the outer court which might be the cause of delay.

A disturbance! Newâsi, a born coward, shrank from the very thought, though she felt that it could be nothing—nothing but one of the many brawls, the constant quarrels.

God and his prophet! who—what was that? She recoiled with a scream of terror from the wild figure which burst in on her unceremoniously, which followed her retreat into the far corner, flung itself at her knees, clasping them, burying its face among her scented draperies. But by that time her terror was gone, and she stooped, trying to free herself from those clinging arms, from the disgrace, from the outrage; from the drunken——

"Abool!" she cried fiercely, then turning to the curious tittering women, stamped her foot at them and bade them begone. And when they had obeyed, she beat her little hands against those clinging ones again with wild upbraidings, till suddenly they fell as if paralyzed before the awful horror and dread in the face which rose from her fineries.

"Come, Newâsi!" stammered the white trembling lips, "come from this hangman's den. Did I not warn thee? But thou hast put the rope round my neck—I who only wanted to live my own life, die my own death. Come! Come!"

He stumbled to his feet, but seemed unable to stir. So he stood looking at his hands stupidly.

Farkhoonda looked too, her face growing gray.

"What is't, Abool?" she faltered; "what is't, dear?"

But she knew; it was blood, new shed, still wet.

He stood silent, gazing at the stains stupidly. "I did not strike," he muttered to himself, "but I called; or did I strike? I—I——" He threw up his head and his words rushed recklessly in a high shrill voice, "I warned thee! I told thee it was not safe! They were herded like sheep in the sunshine by the cistern, and the smell of blood rose up. It was in my very nostrils, for, look you, that first shot missed them and killed one of my men. I saw it. A round red spot oozing over the white—and they herded like sheep——"

" Who?" she asked faintly.

" I told thee; the prisoners, with the cry to kill above the cries of the children, the flash of blood-dulled swords above women's heads—and I—— Nay! I warned thee, Newâsi, there was butcher *here* "—his blood-stained hands left their mark on his gay clothes.

" Abool! " she cried, " thou didst not——"

" Did I?" he almost screamed. " God! will it ever leave my sight? I gave the call, I ran in, I drew my sword. It spurted over my hands from a child's throat as I would have struck—or—or—did I strike? Ne-wâsi!" his voice had sunk again almost to a whisper, " it was in its mother's arms,—she did not cry,—she looked and I—I——" he buried his face in his hands— " I came to thee."

She stood looking at him for a moment, her hands clenched, her beautiful soft eyes ablaze; then recklessly she tore the jewels from her arms, her neck, her hair.

" So she has dared! Yea! Come! thou art right, Abool! " The words mixed themselves with the tinkle of bracelets as, flung from her in wild passion, they rolled into the corners of the room, with the chink of necklaces as they fell, with the rustle of brocade and tinsel as she tore them from her. " She has killed them—the helpless fugitives, guests who have eaten the King's salt! She thinks to beguile us all—to beguile thee. But she shall not. It is not too late. Come! Come! Abool—thou shalt have all from me—yea! all, sooner than she should beguile thee thus—Come! "

She had snatched an old white veil from its peg and wrapped it round her, as she passed rapidly to the door; but he did not move. So she passed back again as swiftly to take his hand, stained as it was, and lay her cheek to it caressingly.

" Thou didst not strike, dear, thou didst not! Come, dear, that she-devil shall not have thee—I will hold thee fast."

Five minutes after a plain curtained dhoolie left the precincts and swayed past the Great Hall of Audience with its toothed red arches, looking as if they yawned for victims. The courtyard beyond lay strangely silent, despite the shifting crowd, which gathered and melted and gathered again round the little tree-shaded cistern where but the day before Hâfzan and the Moulvie had watched a mother pause to clasp her baby to softer, securer rest.

The woman and the child were at the cistern now, and the Rest had come. Softer, securer than all other rest, and the mother shared it; shared it with other women, other children.

But as the Princess Farkhoonda, fearful of what she might see, peeped through the dhoolie curtains, there was nothing to be seen save the shifting, curious crowd, while the impartial sunshine streamed down on it, and those on whom it gazed.

So let the shifting, crowding years with their relentless questioning eyes shut out all thought of what lay by the cistern, save that of rest and the impartial sunshine streaming upon it.

For as the beautiful soft eyes drew back relieved, a bugle rang through the arcades, echoed from the wall, floated out into the city. The bugle to set watch and ward, to close the gates; since the irrevocable step had been taken, the death-pledge made.

So the dream of sovereignty began in earnest behind closed gates. But if women had lost Delhi, those who lay murdered about the little cistern had regained it. For Hâfzan had spoken truth; the strength of the Huzoors lay there.

The strength of the real Master.

CHAPTER II.

PEACE! PEACE!

THREE weeks had passed, and still the dream of sovereignty went on behind the closed gates, while all things shimmered and simmered in the fierce blaze of summer sunlight. The city lay—a rose-red glare dazzling to look at—beside the glittering curves of the river, and the deserted Ridge, more like a lizard than ever, sweltered and slept lazily, its tail in the cool blue water, its head upon the cool green groves of the Subz-mundi. And over all lay a liquid yellow heat-haze blurring every out-line, till the whole seemed some vast mirage.

And still there were no tidings of the master, no cloud of dust upon the Meerut road. None.

Amazing, incredible fact! Men whispered of it on the steps of the Great Mosque when, the last Friday of the fast coming round, its commination service brought many from behind closed doors to realize that by such signs of kingship as beatings of drums, firing of salutes, and levying of loans, Bahâdur Shâh really had filched the throne of his ancestors from the finest fighters in the world. Filched it without a blow, without a struggle, without even a threat, a defiance.

So here they were in a new world without posts or telegraphs, laws or order. Time itself turned back hun-dreds of years and all power of progress vested abso-lutely in one old man, the Light of Religion, the Defender of the Faith, the Great Moghul. If that were not a miracle it came too perilously near to one for some folk's loyalty; and so they drifted palaceward when prayers were over to swell the growing crowd of cour-tiers about the Dream King. And even the learned and most loyal lingered on the steps to whisper, and call obscure prophecies and ingenious commentaries to mind, and admit that it was strange, wondrous strange, that the numerical values of the year should yield the anagram "*Ungrez tubbah shood ba hur soorut*," briefly "The British shall be annihilated." For the Oriental mind loves such trivialities.

And, to all intents and purposes, the English were annihilated, during that short month of peace between the 11th of May and the 8th of June, 1857; for Delhi knew nothing of the vain striving, the ceaseless efforts of the master to find tents and carriages, horses, ammu-nition, medicine, everything once more, save, thank Heaven! courage, and the determination to be master still.

Even Soma admitted the miracle grudgingly; for he

had so far bolstered up his disloyalty by thoughts of a fair fight. He had not, after all, gone to Delhi direct, but had cut across country to his own village near Hansi, and had waited there, hoping to hear of a regular outbreak of hostilities before definitely choosing his side; and he was still waiting when, after a fortnight, his greatest chum in the regiment had turned up from Meerut. For Davee Singh had been one of the many sepoys of the 11th who had gone back to the colors after that one brief night of temptation was over. Soma had known this, and more than once as he waited, the knowledge had been as a magnet drawing him back to the old pole of thought; for that his chum should be led to victory and he be among the defeated was probable enough to make Soma hate himself in anticipation.

But here was Davee Singh, a deserter like he was, sulkily uncommunicative to the village gossips, but to his fellow admitting fiercely that the latter had been right. The Huzoors had forgotten how to fight. Meerut was quiet as the grave; but there was no word of Delhi, and folk said—what did they not say?

So these two, with a strange mixture of regret and relief in their hearts, set out for Delhi to see what was happening there; not knowing that many of their fellows were drifting from it, weary like themselves of inaction.

They had arrived there, two swaggering Rajpoots, in the midst of the thanksgivings and jollity of the Mohammedan Easter which followed on the last Friday of Fast; and they had fallen foul of it frankly. As frankly as the Mohammedans would have fallen foul of a Hindoo Saturnalia, or both Mohammedans and Hindoos would have fallen foul of the festivities in honor of the Queen's Birthday which, on this 25th of May, 1857, were going on in every cantonment in India as if there was no such thing as mutiny in the world. So, annoyed with what they saw and heard, they joined themselves to other Rajpoot malcontents promptly. They sneered at the old pantaloon's procession, which was in truth a poor one, though half the tailors in Delhi had been impressed to hurry up trappings and robes. Perhaps if Abool-Bukr had still been in charge of squibs and such like, it would have been better; but he was not. The order he had given to let the Princess Farkhoonda's dhoolie pass out, before the gates were closed on that day of the death-pledge, had been his last exercise of authority; for the next Court Journal contained the announcement that he was dismissed from his appointment. So he, hovering between the Thunbi Bazaar and the Mufti's quarter, had nothing to do with the procession at which the Rajpoots sneered, criticising Mirza Moghul, the Commander-in-Chief's seat on a horse, and talking boastfully of Vicra-maditya and Pertap as warlike Hindoos will. Until, about dusk, words came to blows amid a tinkling of anklets and a terrible smell of musk; for valor drifted as a matter of course to the wooden balconies of the Thunbi Bazaar during the month of miracle. So that the inmates, coining money, called down blessings on the new régime.

Soma, however, with a cut over one eye sorely in need of a stitch, swore loudly when he could find none to patch him up save a doddering old Hakeem, who proposed dosing him with paper pills inscribed with the name of Providence; an incredible remedy to one accustomed to all the appliances of hospitals and skilled surgery.

" Yea! no doubt he is a fool," assented the other sepoys in frank commiseration, " yet he is the best you will get. For see you, brother, the doctors belong to the Huzoors; so many a brave man must expect to die needlessly, since those cursed dressers are not safe. There was one took the bottles and things and swore he could use them as well as any. And luck went with him until he gave five heroes who had been drunk the night before somewhat to clear their heads. By all the gods in Indra's heaven they were clear even of life in half an hour. So we fell on the dresser and cleared him too. Yea! fool or no fool, paper pills are safer! "

Jim Douglas, who, profiting by the dusk and confusion, had lingered by the group after recognizing Soma's voice, turned away with a savage chuckle; not that the tale amused him, but that he was glad to think six of the devils had gone to their account. For those long days of peace and enforced inaction had sunk him lower and

lower into sheer animal hatred of those he dare not rebuke.   He knew it himself, he felt that his very courage
was becoming ferocity, and the thought that others,
biding their time as he was, must be sinking into
it also, filled him with fierce joy at the thought of
future revenge.   And yet, so far as he personally
was concerned, those long days had passed quietly,
securely,   peacefully,   and   he   could   at   any   time
climb out of all sight and sound of turmoil to a slip of
sunlit roof where a woman waited for him with confidence
and welcome in her eyes.   With something obtrusively
English also for his refreshment, since tragedy, even the
fear of death, cannot claim a whole life, and Kate took to
amusing herself once more by making her corner of the
East as much like the West as she dare.   That was not
much, but Jim Douglas' eye noted the indescribable
difference which the position of a reed stool, the presence
of a poor bunch of flowers, the little row of books in a
niche, made in the familiar surroundings.   For there
were books and to spare in Delhi; for the price of a few
pennies Jim Douglas might have brought her a cartload
of such loot had he deemed it safe; but he did not, and so
the library consisted of grammars and vocabularies from
which Kate learned with a rapidity which surprised and
interested her teacher.   In truth she had nothing else to
do.   Yet when he came, as he often did, to find her absorbed in her work, her eyes dreamy with the puzzle of
tense, he resented it inwardly, telling himself once more
that women were trivial creatures, and life seemed
trivial too, for in truth his nerves were all jangled and
out of tune with the desire to get away from this strange
shadow of a past idyll; to leave all womanhood behind
and fall to fighting manfully.   So that often as he sat
beside her, patient outwardly, inwardly fretting to be
gone even in the nightmare of the city, his eye would
fall on the circlet of gold he had slipped, out of sheer
arrogance and imperious temper, round that slender
wrist, and feel that somehow he had fettered himself
hopelessly when, more than a year past, he had given
that promise.   His chance and hers!   Was this all?
One woman's safety.   And she, following his eyes to the

bangle, would feel the thrill of its first touch once more, and think how strange it was that his chance and hers were so linked together.   But, being a woman, her heart would soften instinctively to the man who sat beside her, and whose face grew sterner and more haggard day by day; while hers?—she could see enough of it in the little looking-glass on her thumb to recognize that she was positively getting fat!   She tried to amuse him by telling him so, by telling him many of the little humorous touches which come even into tragic life, and he was quite ready to smile at them.   But only to please her.   So day by day a silence grew between them as they sat on the inner roof, while Tara spun outside, or watched them furtively from some corner.   And the flare of the sunset, unseen behind the parapeted wall, would lie on the swelling dome and spiked minarets of the mosque and make the paper kites, flown in this month of May by half the town, look like drifting jewels; fit canopy for the City of Dreams and for this strangest of dreams upon the housetop.

" Has—has anything gone wrong? " she asked in desperation one day, when he had sat moodily silent for a longer time than usual.   " I would rather you told me, Mr. Greyman."

He looked at her, vaguely surprised at the name; for he had almost forgotten it.   Forgotten utterly that she could not know any other.   And why should she?   He had made the promise under that name; let them stick to it so long as Fate had linked their chances together.

" Nothing; not for us at least," he said, and then a sudden remorse at his own unfriendliness came over him. " There was another poor chap discovered to-day," he added in a softer tone.   " I believe that you and I, Mrs. Erlton, must be the only two left now."

" I dare say," she echoed a little wearily, " they—they killed him I suppose."

He nodded.   " I saw his body in the bazaar afterward.   I used to know him a bit—a clever sort——"

" Yes——"

" Mixed blood, of course, or he could not have passed muster so long as a greengrocer's assistant."

" Well—I would rather hear if you don't mind."

His dark eyes met hers with a sudden eagerness, a sudden passion in them.

" What a little thing life is after all!   He only said one word—only one.   He was selling watermelons, and some brute tried to cheat him first, and then cheeked him. And he forgot a moment and said: ' *Chup-raho*,' (be silent)—only that!—' *chup-raho* ' !   They were bragging of it—the devils.   ' We knew he couldn't be a coolie, they said, ' that is a master's word.'   My God!   What wouldn't I give to say it sometimes!   I could have shouted to them then, ' *Chup-raho*, you fools! you cowards!'   and some of them would have been silent enough——"

He broke off hurriedly, clenching his hands like a vise on each other, as if to curb the tempest of words.

" I beg your pardon," he said after a pause, rising to walk away; " I—I lose control——"   He paused again and shook his head silently.   Kate followed him and laid her hand on his arm; the loose gold fetter slipped to her wrist and touched him too.

" You think I don't understand," she said with a sudden sob in her voice, " but I do—you must go away—it isn't worth it—no woman is worth it."

He turned on her sharply.   " Go?   You know I can't. What is the use of suggesting it?   Mrs. Erlton!   Tara is faithful; but she is faithful to me—only to me—you must see that surely——"

" If you mean that she loves you—worships the very ground you tread on," interrupted Kate sharply, " that is evident enough."

" Is that my fault?" he began angrily; " I happened——"

" Thank you, I have no wish to hear the story."

The commonplace, second-rate, mock-dignified phrase came to her lips unsought, and she felt she could have cried in sheer vexation at having used it there; in the very face of Death as it were.   But Jim Douglas laughed; laughed good-naturedly.

" I wonder how many years it is since I heard a woman say that?   In another world surely," he said with quite a confidential tone. "But the fact remains that Tara protects you as my wife, and if I were to go——"

Kate looked at him with a quick resentment flaming up in her face beneath the stain.

"I think you are mistaken," she said slowly. "I believe Tara would be better pleased if—if she knew the truth."

"You mean if I were to tell her you are not my wife?" he replied quickly. "Why?"

"Because I should be less of a tie to you—because——" She paused, then added sharply, "Mr. Greyman, I must ask you to tell her the truth, please. I have a right to so much, surely. I have my reasons for it, and if you do not, I shall."

Jim Douglas shrugged his shoulders. "In that case I had better tell her myself; not that I think it matters much one way or another, so long as I am here. And the whole thing from beginning to end is chance, nothing but chance."

"Your chance and mine," she murmured half to herself. It was the first time she had alluded openly to the strange linking of their fates, and he looked at her almost impatiently.

"Yes! your chance and mine; and we must make the best of it. I'll tell her as I go out."

But Tara interrupted him at the beginning.

"If the Huzoor means that he does not love the mem as he loved Zora, that requires no telling, and for the rest what does it matter to this slave?"

"And it matters nothing to me either," he retorted roughly, "but of this be sure. Who kills the mem kills me, unless I kill first; and by Krishnu, and Vishnu, and the lot, I'd as lief kill you, Tara, as anyone else, if you get in my way."

A great broad flash of white teeth lit up her face as she salaamed, remarking that the Huzoor's mother must have been as Kunti. And Jim Douglas understanding the complimentary allusion to the God-visited mother of the Lunar race, wished as he went downstairs, that he was like the Five Heroes in one respect, at least, and that was in having only a fifth part of a woman to look after,

instead of two whole ones who talked of love! So he
passed out to listen, and watch, and wait, while the fire-
balloons went up into the velvety sky, replacing the kites.
For May is the month of marriages also, and night after
night these false stars floated out from the Dream-City
to form new constellations on the horizon for a few minutes and then disappear with a flare into the darkness.
Into the darkness whence the master did not come. Yet,
as the month ended, villagers passing in with grain from
Meerut averred that the masters were not all dead, or
else God gave their ghosts a like power in cursing and
smiting—which was all poor folk had to look for; since
some had appeared and burned a village.

Not all dead? The news drifted from market to market, but if it penetrated through the Palace gates it did
not filter through the new curtains and hangings of the
private apartments where the King took perpetual cooling draughts and wrote perpetual appeals for more etiquette and decorum. For nothing likely to disturb the
unities of dreams was allowed within the precincts, where
every day the old King sat on a mock peacock throne
with a new cushion to it, and listened for hours to the
high-flown letters of congratulation which poured in,
each with its own little covering bag of brocade, from
the neighboring chiefs. And if any day there happened
to be a paucity of real ones, Hussan Askuri could supply
them, like other dreams, at so much a dozen; since
nothing more costly than the brocade bag came with
them. So that the Mahboob's face, as Treasurer, grew
longer and longer over the dressmaker's and upholster-
er's bills, and the Court Journal was driven into record-
ing the fact that someone actually presented a bottle
of *Pandanus odoratissimus*, whatever that may be. Some
subtle essence, mayhap, favorable to dreaminess; since,
in the month of peace, drugs were necessary to prevent
awakening.

Especially when, on the 30th of May, a sound came
over the distant horizon; the sound of artillery.

At last! At last! Jim Douglas, who, in sheer dread
of his own growing despair, had taken to spending all
the time he dared in moody silence on that peaceful roof,

started as if he had been shot, and was down the stairs
seeking news. The streets were full of a silent, restless
crowd, almost empty of soldiers. They had gone out
during the night, he learned, Meerutward; tidings of
an army on the banks of the Hindu river, seven or eight
miles out, having been brought in by scouts.

At last! At last! He wandered through the bazaars
scarcely able to think, wondering only when the army
could possibly arrive, feeling a mad joy in the anxious
faces around him, lingering by the groups of men collected in every open space simply for the satisfaction of
hearing the wonder and alarm in the words: "So the
master lives."

He lived indeed! Listen! That was his voice over
the eastern horizon! Kate, when he came back to the
roof about noon, had never seen him in this mood before,
and wondered at his fire, his gayety, his youth. But the
recognition brought a dull pain with it, in the thought
that this was natural to the man; that gloomy moodiness
the result of her presence.

" You are not afraid, surely? " he said suddenly, breaking off in the recital of some future event which seemed
to him certain.

" No. I am only glad," she replied slowly. " It could
not have lasted much longer. It is a great relief."

" Relief," he echoed, " I wonder if you know the relief
it is to me? " And then he looked at her remorsefully.
" I have been an awful brute, Mrs. Erlton, but women
can scarcely understand what inaction means to a man."

Could they not? she wondered bitterly as he hastened
off again, leaving her to long weary hours of waiting;
till the red flush of sunset on the bubble dome of the
mosque brought him back with a new look on his face;
a look of angry doubt.

" The sepoys are coming in again," he said; " they
claim a victory—but that, of course, is impossible. Still
I don't understand, and it is so difficult to get any reliable
information."

" You should go out yourself—I believe it would be
best for us both," replied Kate, " Tara——"

He shook his head impatiently. " Not now. What

is the use of risking all at the last. We can only have
to wait till to-morrow. But I don't understand it, all the
same. The sepoys say they surprised the camp—that
the buglers were still calling to arms when their artillery
opened fire. But so far as I can make out they have lost
five guns, and from the amount of bhang they are drinking, I believe it was a rout. However, if you don't mind,
I'll be off again—and—and don't be alarmed if I stay
out."

"I'm not in the least alarmed," she replied. "As I
have told you before, I don't think it is necessary you
should come here at all."

He paused at the door to glance back at her half-
resentfully. To be sure she did not know that he had
slept on its threshold as a rule; but anyhow, after eating
your heart out over one woman's safety for three weeks,
it was hard to be told that you were not wanted. But,
thank Heaven! the end was at hand. And yet as he
lingered round the watch-fires he heard nothing but
boasting, and in more than one of the mosques thanksgivings were being offered up; while outside the walls
volunteers to complete the task so well begun were
assembling to go forth with the dawn and kill the few
remaining infidels. Some drunk with bhang, more in-
toxicated by the lust of blood which comes to fighting
races like the Rajpoot with the first blow. It had come
to Soma, as, with fierce face seamed with tears, he told
the tale again and again of his chum's gallant death.
How Davee Singh, brother in arms, his boyhood's play-
mate, seeing some cowards of artillerymen abandoning
a tumbril full of ammunition to the cursed Mlechchas,
had leaped to it like a black-buck, and with a cry to
Kali, Mother of Death, had fired his musket into it;
so sending a dozen or more of the hell-doomed to their
place, and one more brave Rajpoot to Swarga.

" *Jai! Jai! Kâli mâ ki jai!* "

An echo of the dead man's last cry came from many
a living one, as muskets were gripped tighter in the resolve to be no whit behind. A few more such heroes and
the Golden Age would come again; the age of the blessed
Pandâva, who forgot the cause in the quarrel.

And so for one day more Jim Douglas strained his
ears for that distant thunder on the horizon, while the
people of the town, becoming more accustomed to it,
went about their business, vaguely relieved at anything
which should keep the sepoys' hands from mischief.

The red sunset glow was on the mosque again when
he returned to the little slip of roof to find Kate working
away at her grammars calmly. The best thing she could
do, since every word she learned was an additional safeguard; and yet the man could not help a scornful smile.

"It is a rout this time, I am sure," he said; "and yet
there is no sign of pursuit. I cannot understand it;
there seems a Fate about it!"

"Is that anything new?" she asked wearily, as she
laid down her book, and with the certain precision which
marked all her actions, saw that the water was really
boiling before she made the tea. It was made in a *lota*,
and drunk out of handleless basins, yet for all that it was
Western-made tea, strong and unspiced, with cream to
put to it also, which she skimmed from a dish set in cold
water in the coolest, darkest place she could find.
Dreamlike indeed, and Jim Douglas, drinking his tea,
felt, that with his eyes shut, he might have dreamed himself in an English drawing room.

"Nothing new," he retorted, "but it seems incomprehensible. Hark! That is a salute; for the victory, I
suppose. Upon my soul I feel as if—as if I were a dream
myself—as if I should go mad! Don't look startled—
I shan't. The whole thing is a sham—I can see that.
But why has no one the pluck to give the House-of-
Cards a push and bring it about their ears? And what
has become of the army at the Hindun? It took three
days to march there from Meerut, I hear—not more than
twenty-four miles. No! I cannot understand it. No
wonder the people say we are all dead. I begin to believe it myself."

He heard the saying often enough certainly to bring
relief during the 1st and 2d of June, when there was no
more distant thunder on the horizon, and the whole town,
steeped and saturated with sunshine, lay half-asleep, the
soldiers drowsing off the effect of their drugs.

Dead? Yea! the masters were dead, and those who
had escaped were in full retreat up the river; so at least
said villagers coming in with supplies. But someone
else who had come in with supplies also, sat crouched
up like a grasshopper on a great pile of wool-betasseled
sacks in the corn market and laughed creakily. "Dead!
not they. As the *tanda* passed Karnal four days agone
the camping ground was white as a poppy field with
tents, and the soldiers like the flies buzzing round them.
And if folk want to hear more, I, Tiddu Baharupa-Bun-
jârah, can tell tales beyond the Cashmere gate on the
river island where the bullocks graze."

The creaking voice rose unnecessarily loud, and a man
in the dress of an Afghan who had been listening, his
back to the speaker, moved off with a surprised smile.
Tiddu had proved his vaunted superiority in that instance; though by what arts he had penetrated the back
of a disguise, Jim Douglas could not imagine. Still
here was news indeed—news which explained some of
the mystery, since the seeming retreat up the river had
been, no doubt, for the purpose of joining forces. But
it was something almost better than news—it was a
chance of giving them. He had not dared, for Kate's
sake, to risk any confederate as yet; but here was one
ready to hand—a confederate, too, who would do anything for money.

So that night he sat in tamarisk shadow on the river
island talking in whispers, while the monotonous clank
of the bells hung on the wandering bullocks sounded fit-
fully, the flicker of the watchfires gleamed here and there
on the half-dried pools of water, the fireflies flashed
among the bushes, and every now and again a rough,
rude chant rose on the still air.

"They have been there these ten days, Huzoor," came
Tiddu's indifferent voice. "They are waiting for the
siege train. Nigh on three thousand of them, and some
black faces besides."

Jim Douglas gave an exclamation of sheer despair.
To him, living in the House-of-Cards, the Palace-of-
Dreams, such caution seemed unnecessary. Still, the
past being irretrievable, the present remained in which

by hook or by crook to get the letter he had with him, ready written, conveyed to the army at Kurnal. And Tiddu, with fifty rupees stowed away in his waistband, being lavish of promise and confidence, there was no more to be done save creep back to the city, feeling as if the luck had turned at last.

But the next morning he found the Thunbi Bazaar in a turmoil of talk. There were spies in the city. A letter had been found, written in the Persian character, it is true but with the devilish knowledge of the West in its details of likely spots for attack, the indecision of certain quarters in the city, its general unpreparedness for anything like resistance. Who had written it? As the day went on the camps were in uproar, the Palace invaded, the dream disturbed by denouncings of Ahsan-Oolah, the giver of composing draughts—Mahboob Ali, the checker of the purse strings; even of Mirza Moghul, commander-in-chief himself, who might well be eager to buy his recognition as heir by treachery.

The net result of the letter being that, as Jim Douglas, with wrath in his heart, crept out at dusk to the low levels by the Water Bastion, intent on having it out with Tiddu, he could see gangs of sepoys still at work by torchlight strengthening the bridge defense, and had to dodge a measuring party of artillerymen busy range-finding. His suggestions had been of use!

But the old Bunjârah took his fierce reproaches philosophically. " 'Tis the miscreant Bhungi," he assented mournfully. " He is not to be trusted, but Jhungi having a tertian ague, I deemed a surer foot advisable. Yet the Huzoor need not be afraid. Even the miscreant would not betray his person; and for the rest, the Presence writes Persian like any court moonshee."

The calm assumption that personal fear was at the bottom of his reproaches, made Jim Douglas desire to throttle the old man, and only the certainty that he dare not risk a row prevented him from going for the ill-gotten rupees at any rate. His thought, however, seemed read by the old rascal, for a lean protesting hand, holding a bag, flourished out of the darkness, and the creaking voice said magnificently:

" Before Murri-âm and the sacred neem, Huzoor, I
have kept my bargain. As for Jhungi or Bhungi, did
I make them that I should know the evil in them? But
if the Huzoor suspects one who holds his tongue, let the
bargain between us end."

His hearer could not repress a smile at the consummate cunning of the speech. " You can keep the money
for the next job," he said briefly; " I haven't done with
you yet, you scoundrel."

A grim chuckle came out of the shadows as the hand
went back into them.

" The Huzoor need not fret himself, whatever happens.
The end is nigh."

It seemed as if it must be with three thousand British
soldiers within sixty miles of Delhi; or less, since they
might have marched during those five days. They
might be at Delhi any moment. Three thousand men!
Enough and to spare even though in the last few days a
detachment or two of fresh mutineers had arrived. Ah!
if the blow had been struck sooner. If—if——

Kate listened during those first days of June to many
such wishes, despairs, hopes, from one whose only solace
lay in words; since with relief staring him in the face,
Jim Douglas crushed down his craving for action.
There was no real need for it, he told her; it must involve
risk, so they must wait—sleep and dream like the city!

For, lulled by the delay, stimulated to fresh fancy by
the newcomers, the townspeople went on their daily
round monotonously; the sepoys boasted and drank
bhang. And in the Palace, the King, in new robes of
state sat on his new cushion and put the sign-manual
to such trifles as a concession to a home-born slave that
he might " continue, as heretofore, a-tinning the royal
sauce-pans!" though Mahboob Ali's face lengthened as
he doled out something on account for faith and finery,
and suggested that the army might at least be employed
in collecting revenue somewhere. But the army grinned
in the commander-in-chief's face, scorned laborious
days, and between the seductions of the Thunbi Bazaar
gave peaceful citizens what one petitioner against plunder calls " a foretaste of the Day of Judgment."

But one soul in Delhi felt in every fiber of him that the Judgment had come—that atonement must be made. " Thou wilt kill thyself with prayers and fastings and seekings of other folks' salvations, Moulvie-sahib," said Hâfzan almost petulantly as, passing on her rounds, she saw Mohammed Ismail's anxious face, seeking audience with everyone in authority, " Thou hast done thy best. The rest is with God; and if these find death also, the blame will lie elsewhere."

" But the blame of those, woman?" he asked fiercely, pointing with trembling finger to the little cistern shaded by the peepul tree.

Hâfzan gave a shrill laugh as she passed on.

" Fear not that either, learned one! This world's atonement for that will be sufficient for future pardon."

It might be so, Mohammed Ismail told himself as he hurried off feverishly to another appeal. He had erred in ignorance there; but what of the forty prisoners still at the Kotwâli—forty stubborn Christians despite their dark skins? They were safe so far, but if the city were assaulted?—if some of the fresh, fiery-faithed newcomers—— The doubt left him no peace.

" If thou wilt swear, Moulvie-jee, on thine own eternal salvation that they are Mohammedans, or stake thy soul on their conversion," jeered those who held the keys. A heavy stake, that! A solemn oath with forty stubborn Christians to deal with. No wonder Mohammed Ismail felt judgment upon him already.

But the stake was staked, the oath spoken on the 6th of June. The record of it is brief, but it stands as history in the evidence of one of the forty. " We were released in consequence of a Moulvie of the name of Mohammed Ismail giving evidence that we were all Mohammedan; or that if any were Christian they would become Mohammedan."

And it was given none too soon. For on the 6th of June as the sun set, a silhouette of a man on a horse stood clear against the red-gold in the west, looking down from the Ridge on Delhi. Looking down on the city bathed in the dreamy glamour of the slanting sunbeams; rose-red and violet-shadowed, with the great white dome hovering above the smoke wreaths, and a glitter of gold on the eastern wall, where, backed by that arcaded view of the darkening Eastern plains, an old man sat listening to sentiments of fidelity from a pile of little brocaded bags.

It was Hodson of Hodson's Horse, reconnoitering ahead. So there was an Englishman on the Ridge once more as the paper kites came down on the 6th of June. But the fire balloons did not go up; for the night set in gusty and wet, giving no chance to new constellations.

Jim Douglas did not sleep at all that night, for Tiddu had brought word that the English were at Alipore, ten miles out; and nothing but the dread of needless risk kept him in Delhi. For any risk was needless when to a certainty the English flag would be flying over the city in a few hours.

And Hodson of Hodson's Horse back at Alipore slept late, for he lingered, weary and wet after his long ride, to write to his wife ere turning in, that " if he had had a hundred of the Guides he could have gone right up to the city wall."

But Mohammed Ismail slept peacefully, his work being over, and dreamed of Paradise.

CHAPTER III.

THE CHALLENGE.

" For Gawd's sake, sir! don't say I'm unfit for dooty, sir," pleaded a lad, who, as he stood to attention, tried hard to keep the sharp shivers of coming ague from the doctor's keen eyes. " I'm all right, aint I, mates? It aint a bad sort o' fever at worst, as I oughter know, havin' it constant. It's go ter hell, an' lick the blood up fust as I'm fit for with Jack Pandy. That's all the matter—you see if it aint, sir! "

He threw his fair curly head back, his blue eyes blazed with the coming fever light, but the bearded man next to him murmured, " 'Ee's all right, sir. 'Ee'll 'old 'is musket straight, never fear," and the Doctor walked on with a nod.

" They killed his girl at Meerut," said his company officer in a whisper, and Herbert Erlton, standing by, set his teeth and glanced back, blue eye meeting blue eye with a sort of triumph.

For it was the 7th of June, and the blow was to be struck, the challenge given at last.

Nearly a month, thought Herbert Erlton, since *it* had happened. He had spent much of the time in bed, struck down with fever; for he had regained Meerut with difficulty, wounded and exhausted. And then it had been too late—too late for anything save to hang round hungrily in the hopes of that challenge to come, with many another such as he.

But it had come at last. The camp was ringing with cheers for the final reinforcement, every soul who could stand was coming out of hospital, and the air, new washed with rain, and cool, seemed to put fresh life, and with it a desire to kill, into the veins of every son of the cold North.

And now the dusk was at hand. The men, half-mad with impatience, laughed and joked over each trivial preparation. Yet, when the order came with midnight, weapons were never gripped more firmly, more sternly, than by those three thousand Englishmen marching to their long-deferred chance of revenge. And some, not able to march, toiled behind in hopes of one fair blow; and not a few, unable even for so much, slipped desperately from hospital beds to see at least one murderer meet with his reward.

For, to the three thousand marching upon Delhi that cool dewy night, sent—so they told themselves—for special solace and succor of the Right, there were but two things to be reckoned with in the wide world: Themselves—Men. Those others—Murderers.

The fireflies, myriad-born from the rain, glimmered giddily in the low marshy land, the steady stars shone overhead, and Major Erlton looked at both indifferently as he rode, long-limbed and heavy, through the night whose soft silence was broken only by the jingle of spurs and the squelching of light gun-wheels in water-logged ruts; save when—from a distance—the familiar tramp, tramp, of disciplined feet along a road came wafted on the cool wind; for the column in which he was doing duty moved along the canal bank so as to take the enemy, who held an intrenched position five miles from Alipore, in flank. But Herbert Erlton was not thinking of stars or fireflies; was not thinking of anything. He was watching for other lights, the twinkling cresset lights which would tell where the Murderers waited for that first blow. He did not even think of the cause of his desire; he was absorbed in the revenge itself, and a bitter curse rose to his lips, when just before dawn the roll of a gun and the startled flocks of birds flying westward told him that others were before him.

"Hurry up, men! For God's sake hurry up!" The entreaty passed along the line where the troopers of the 9th Lancers were setting shoulders to the gun-wheels, and everyone, men and officers alike, was listening with fierce regret to the continuous roll of cannon, the casual rattle of musketry, telling that the heavy guns were bearing the brunt of it so far.

"Hurry up, men! Hurry up. That's the bridge ahead! Then we can go for them!"

Hark! A silence; if silence it could be called, now that the shouts, and yells, and confused murmur of battle could be heard. But the guns were silent; and hark again. A ringing cheer! Bayonet work that, at last, at last! And yonder, behind the fireflies in the bushes? Surely men in flight! Hurrah! Hurrah!

When Major Erlton returned from that wild charge it was to find that one splendid rush from the 75th Regiment had cleared the road to Delhi. The Murderers had been swept from their shelter, their guns—some fighting desperately, others standing stupidly to meet death, and many with clasped hands and vain protestations of loyalty on their lips paying the debt of their race. But one man had paid some other debt, Heaven knows what; and the Rifle Brigade cleared the road to Delhi of an English deserter fighting against his old regiment.

It had not taken an hour; and now, as the yellow sun

peered over the eastern horizon, a little knot of staff officers consulted what to do next.

What to do? Herbert Erlton and many another wondered stupidly what the deuce fellows could mean by asking the question when the jagged line of the Ridge lay not three miles off, and Delhi lay behind that? Could any sane person think that England had done its duty at sunrise, even though forty good men and true of the three thousand had dealt their first and last blow?

But if some did, there were not many; so, after a pause, the march began again. Westward, by a forking road, to the flat head of the Lizard lying above the Subz-mundi, eastward toward the tail and the old cantonment. And this time the bayonets went with the jingling spurs, and together they cleared the green groves merrily. Still, even so, it was barely nine o'clock when they met the eastward column again at Hindoo Rao's house and shook hands over their bloodless victory. For the eastward force had lost one man, the westward seven, despite the fact that the retreating Murderers had attempted a rally in their old lines.

Nine o'clock! In seven hours the ten miles had been marched, the battle of Budli-ke-serai won, and below them lay Delhi. Within twelve hundred yards rose the Moree Bastion, the extreme western point of that city face which, with the Cashmere gate jutting about its middle and the Water Bastion guarding its eastern end, must be the natural target of their valor—a target three-quarters of a mile long by twenty-four feet high.

Seven hours! And the Murderers had been driven into the city, while the men had gained "twenty-six guns and the finest possible base for the conduct of future operations." For the Ridge, the old cantonments were once more echoing to the master's step, and the city folk, as they looked eagerly from the walls, had the first notice of defeat in the smoke and flames of the sepoy lines which the English soldiers fired in reckless revenge; reckless because the tents were not up, and they might at least have been a shelter from the sun.

But the Delhi force, taken as a whole, was in no mood to think; and so perhaps those at the head of it felt bound to think the more.   There was Delhi, undoubtedly, but the rose-red walls with their violet shadows looked formidable.   And who could tell how many Murderers it harbored?   A thousand of them or thereabouts would return to Delhi no more; but, even so, if all the regiments known to have mutinied and come to Delhi were at their full strength, the odds must still be close on four to one.   And then there was the rabble, armed no doubt from the larger magazine below the Flagstaff Tower, which, alas, had found no Willoughby for its destruction on the 11th of May.   And then there was the May sun. And then—and then——

   "What's up?   When are we going on?" asked Major Erlton, sitting fair and square on his horse, in the shadow the big trees by Hindoo Rao's house, as an orderly officer rode past him.

   "Aren't going on to-day.   Chief thinks it safer not—these native cities——"

   He was gone, and Herbert Erlton without a word threw himself heavily from his horse with a clatter and jingle of swords and scabbards and Heaven knows what of all the panoply of war; so with the bridle over his arm stood looking out over the bloody city which lay quiet as the grave.   Only, every now and again, a white puff of smoke followed by a dull roar came from a bastion like a salute of welcome to the living, or a parting honor to the dead.

   Was it possible?   His eyes followed the familiar outline mechanically till they rested half-unconsciously on some ruins beside the city wall.   Then with a rush memory came back to him, and as he turned hurriedly to loosen his horse's girths, the tears seemed to scald his tired angry eyes.   Yet it was not the memory of Alice Gissing only, which sent these unwonted visitors to Herbert Erlton's eyes; it was a wild desperate pity and despair for all women.

   And as he stood there ignoring his own emotion, or at least hiding it, one of the women whom he pitied was looking up with a certain resentful eagerness at a man, who, from the corner turret of that roof in the Mufti's quarter, was straining his eyes Ridgeways.

" They must rest, surely," she said sharply; " you cannot expect them to be made of iron——"; as you are,
she was about to add, but withheld even that suspicion
of praise.

" Well! There goes the bugle to pitch tents, anyhow," retorted Jim Douglas recklessly. " So I suppose
we had better have our breakfast too—coffee and a rasher
of bacon and a boiled egg or so. By God! its incredible—it's——" He flung himself on a reed stool and
covered his face with his hands for a second; but he was
up facing her the next. " I've no right to say these
things—no one knows better than I how worse than idle
it is to press others to one's own tether—I learned that
lesson early, Mrs. Erlton. But "—he gave a quick
gesture of impotent impatience—" when the news first
came in, the men who brought it ran in at the Cashmere
and Moree gates in hundreds, and out at the Ajmere
and Turkoman, calling that the masters had come
back; and people were keeking round the doors hopefully. I tell you the very boys as I came in here were
talking of school again—of holiday tasks, perhaps—
Heaven knows! People were running in the streets—
they will be walking now—in another hour they will be
standing; and then! Well! I suppose the General
funks the sun. So I'll be off. I only came because I
thought I had better be here in case; you see the men
would have had their blood up rushing the city——"

" And your breakfast?" she asked coldly, almost
sarcastically; for he seemed to her so hard, so grudging,
while her sympathies, her enthusiasms were red-hot for
the newcomers.

He laughed bitterly. " I've learned to live on parched
grain like a native, if need be, and I take opium too; so
I shall manage." He was back again to the turret, however, before two o'clock, curtly apologetic, calmer, yet
still eager. The people, to be sure, he said, had given
up keeking round their doors at every clatter, and the
gates had been closed on deserters by the Palace folk;
but no one had thought of bricking them up, and after
going round everywhere he doubted if there were more
than seven or eight thousand real soldiers in Delhi. The

74th and the 11th regiments had been slipping away for
days, and numbers of men who had remained did not
really mean to fight.   Tiddu, who seemed to know everything, said that the mutineers had been very strongly intrenched at Budli-serai, so the resistance could not have
been very dogged, or our troops could not have fought
their way in before nine o'clock.   Yes! since she
pressed for an answer, the General might have been wise
in waiting for the cool.   Only he personally wished he
had thought it possible, for then he would at any rate
have tried to get a letter sent to the Ridge.   Now it was
too late.

And then suddenly, as he spoke, a fierce elation
flashed to his face again at the sound of bugles, the roll
of a gun from the Moree Bastion; and he was up the
stairs of the turret in a second, casting a half-humorous,
wholly deprecating glance back at her.

" A hare and a tortoise once—I learned that at school
—put it into Latin! " he said lightly, as the walls round
them quivered to the reverberating rolls, thundering
from the city wall.

Kate walked up and down the roof restlessly, passing
into the outer one so as to be further from that eager
sentinel and his criticisms.   Tara was spinning calmly,
and Kate wondered if the woman could be alive.   Did
she not know that brave men on both sides were going
to their deaths?   And Tara, from under her heavy eye-
lashes, watched Kate, and wondered how any woman
who had brought Life into the world could fear Death.
Did not the Great Wheel spin unceasingly?   Let brave
men, then, die bravely—even Soma.   For she knew by
this time that her brother was in Delhi, and by the master's orders had dodged his detection more than once.
So the two women waited, each after their nature; while
like the pulse of time itself, the beat of artillery shook
the walls.   It came so regularly that Kate, crouching in
a corner weary of restless pacing to and fro, grew almost
drowsy and started at a step beside her.

" A false alarm," said Jim Douglas quietly; " a sortie,
as far as I could judge, from the Moree; easily driven
back."

His tone roused her antagonism instantly. " Perhaps they are waiting for night."

" There is a full moon—almost," he replied; " besides, there is fair cover up to within four hundred yards of the Cabul gate. They could rush that, and a bag or two of gunpowder would finish the business."

" They could do that as well to-morrow," she remarked hotly.

" I hope to God they won't be such fools as to try it! " he replied as hotly. " If they don't come in to-night they will have to batter down the walls, and then the city will go against them. What city wouldn't? It will rouse memories we can't afford to rouse. Who could? And every wounded man who creeps in to-day will be a center of resistance by to-morrow. The women will hound others on to protect him. It is their way. You have always to allow for humanity in war. Well! we must wait and see." He paused and rubbed his forehead vexedly. " If I had known, I might have got out with the sortie; but I suppose I couldn't really——" He paused, shrugged his shoulders, and went out.

And Kate, as she sat watching the red flush of sunset grow to the dome, remembered his look at her with a half-angry pang. Why should she be in this man's way always? So the day died away in soft silence, and there on the housetop it seemed incredible that so much hung in the balance, and that down in the streets the crowds must be drifting to and fro restlessly. At least she supposed so. Yet, monotonous as ever, there was the evening cry of the muezzin and the persistent thrumming of toms-toms and saringis which evening brings to a native city. It rose louder than usual from a roof hard by, where, so Tara told her, a princess of the blood royal lived; a great friend of Abool-Bukr's. The remembrance of little Sonny's hands all red with blood, and the cruel face smiling over an apology, made her shiver, and wonder as she often did with a desperate craving what the child's fate had been. Why had she let the old ayah take him? Why was he not here, safe; making life bearable? As she sat, the tears falling quietly over her cheeks, Tara came and looked at her

curiously. "The mem should not cry," she said consolingly. "The Huzoor will save her somehow."

For an instant Kate felt as if she would rather he did
not. Then on the distance and the darkening air came
a familiar sound: the evening bugle from the Ridge
with its cheerful invitation:

"Come - and - set-a-picket-boys! come - and - keep -
a - watch."

So someone else was within hail, ready to help! The
knowledge brought her a vast consolation, and for
the first time in that environment she slept through
the night without wakening in deadly dreamy fear at the
least sound.

Even the uproarious devilry of Prince Abool in the
alley below did not rouse her, when about midnight he
broke loose from the feverish detaining hold which
Newâsi had kept on him by every art of her power during
the day, lest the master returning should find the Prince
in mischief. But now he lurched away with a party of
young bloods who had come to fetch him, swearing that
he must celebrate the victory properly. But for a moment's weakness, fostered by a foolish, fearful woman,
he might have led the cavalry. He wept maudlin tears
over the thought, swearing he would yet show his mettle.
He would not leave one hell-doomed alive; and, suiting the action to the word, he began incontinently to
search for fugitives in some open cowyards close by, till
the strapping dairymaids, roused from slumber, declared
in revenge that they had seen a man slip down the culvert
of the big drain. Five minutes afterward Prince Abool,
half-choked, half-drowned, was dragged from the sewer
by his comrades, protesting feebly that he must have
killed an infidel; else why did the blood smell so horribly?

But after that the city sank into the soundlessness, the
stillness, of the hour before dawn, save for a recurring
call of the watch bugles on wall and Ridge and the
twinkling lights which burned all night in camp and
court. For those two had challenged each other, and
the fight was to the bitter end. What else could it be

with a death-pledge between them? The townspeople
might sleep uncertain which side they would espouse, but
between the Men and the Murderers the issue was clear.

And it remained so, even though the month-of-miracle
lingered, and no assault came on the morrow, or the day
after, or the day after that. So that the old King himself
set his back to the wall and for once spoke as a King
should. " If the army will not fight without pay, punish
it," he said to the Commander-in-chief. But it was only
a flash in the pan, and he retired once more to the latticed marble balcony and set the sign-manual to a
general fiat that " those who would be satisfied with a
trifle might be paid something." Whereat Mahboob Ali
shook his head, for there was not even a trifle in the
privy purse.

As for the city people, their ears and tongues grew
longer during those three days, when the sepoys, returning from the sorties and skirmishes, brought back tales
of glorious victory, stupendous slaughter. Her man
had killed fifteen Huzoors himself, and there were not
five hundred left on the Ridge, said Futteh-deen's wife
to Pera-Khân's as they gossiped at the wall; and a good
job too. When they were gone there would be an end
of these sword cuts and bullet wounds. Not a wink of
sleep had she had for nights, yawned Zainub, what with
thirsts and poultices! And on the steps of the mosque,
too, the learned lingered to discuss the newspapers. So
Bukht Khân with fifty thousand men was on his way
to swear allegiance, and the Shah of Persia had sacked
Lahore, where Jan Larnce himself had been caught trying to escape on an elephant and identified by wounds
on his back. And the London correspondent of the
Authentic News was no doubt right in saying the Queen
was dumfoundered, while the St. Petersburg one was
clearly correct in asserting that the Czar was about to
put on his crown at last. Why not, since his vow
was at an end with the passing of India from British
supremacy?

So the dream went on; the little brocaded bags kept
coming in; the stupendous slaughter continued. Yet

every night the Widow's Cruse of a Ridge echoed to the picket bugles, and the court and the camp twinkled at each other till dawn.

A sort of vexed despairing patience came to Jim Douglas, and more than once he apologized to Kate for his moodiness, like a patient who apologizes to his nurse when unfavorable symptoms set in. He gave her what news he could glean, which was not much, for Tiddu had gone south for another consignment of grain. But on the morning of the 12th he turned up with a face clearer than it had been, and a friendlier look in his eyes.

" The guides came in to camp yesterday. Splendid fellows. They were at it hammer and tongs immediately, though that man Rujjub Ali I told you of—it was he who said Hodson was with the force—declares they marched from Murdân in twenty-one days. Over thirty miles a day! Well! they looked like it. I saw them ride slap up to the Cabul gate. And—and I saw someone else with them, Mrs. Erlton. I wasn't sure at first if I had better tell you; but I think I had. I saw your husband."

" My husband," she echoed faintly. In truth the past seemed to have slipped from her. She seemed to have forgotten so much; and then suddenly she remembered that the letter he had written must still be in the pocket of the dress Tara had hidden away. How strange! She must find it, and look at it again.

Jim Douglas watched her curiously with a quick recognition of his own rough touch. Yet it could not be helped.

" Yes. He was looking splendid, doing splendidly. I couldn't help wishing—— Well! I wish you could have seen him; you would have been proud."

She interrupted him with swift, appealing hand. " Oh!—don't—please don't—what have I to do with it? Can't you see—can't you understand he was thinking of—of her—and doesn't she deserve it? while I—I——"

It was the first breakdown he had seen during those long weeks of strain, and he stood absolutely, wholly compassionate before it.

" My dear lady," he said gently, as he walked away to

give her time, "if you good women would only recognize the fact which worse ones do, that most men think
of many women in their lives, you would be happier.
But I doubt if Major Erlton was thinking of anyone in
particular. He was thinking of the dead, and you are
among them, for *him;* remember that. Come," he
continued, crossing over to her again and holding out
his hand. "Cheer up! Aren't you always telling me it
is bad for a man to have one woman on the brain, and
think, think how many there may be to avenge by this
time!"

His voice, sounding a whole gamut of emotion, a
whole cadence of consolation, seemed to find an echo in
her heart, and she looked up at him gratefully.

It would have found one also in most hearts upon the
Ridge, where men were beginning to think with a sort
of mad fury of women and children in a hundred places
to which this unchecked conflagration of mutiny was
spreading swiftly. What would become of Lucknow,
Cawnpore, Agra, if something were not done at Delhi?
if the challenge so well given were not followed up?
And men elsewhere telegraphed the same question, until,
half-heartedly, the General listened, and finally gave a
grudging assent to a plan of assault urged by four subalterns.

What the details were matters little. A bag of gunpowder somewhere, with fixed bayonets to follow. A
gamester's throw for sixes or deuce-ace, so said even its
supporters. But anything seemed better than being a
target for artillery practice five times better than their
own, while the mutiny spread around them.

The secret was well kept as such secrets must be.
Still the afternoon of the 12th saw a vague stir on the
Ridge, and though even the fighting men turned in to
sleep, each man knew what the midnight order meant
which sent him fumbling hurriedly with belts and buckles.

"The city at last, mates! No more playin' ball," they
said to each other as they fell in, and stood waiting the
next order under the stars; waiting with growing impatience as the minutes slipped by.

"My God! where is Graves?" fumed Hodson. "We

can't go on without him and his three hundred. Ride, someone, and see. The explosion party is ready, the Rifles safe within three hundred yards of the wall. The dawn will be on us in no time—ride sharp!"

"Something has gone wrong," whispered a comrade. "There were lights in the General's tent and two mounted officers—there! I thought so! It's all up!"

All up indeed! For the bugle which rang out was the retreat. Some of those who heard it remembered a moonlight night just a month before when it had echoed over the Meerut parade ground; and if muttered curses could have silenced it the bugle would have sounded in vain. But they could not, and so the men went back sulkily, despondently to bed. Back to inaction, back to target practice.

"Graves says he misunderstood the verbal orders, so I understand," palliated a staff-officer in a mess tent whither others drifted to find solace from the chill of disappointment, the heat of anger. A tall man with hawk's eyes and sparse red hair paused for a moment ere passing out into the night again. "I dislike euphemisms," he said curtly. "In these days I prefer to call a spade a spade. Then you can tell what you have to trust to."

"Hodson's in a towering temper," said an artilleryman as he watched a native servant thirstily; "I don't wonder. Well! here's to better luck next time."

"I don't believe there will be a next time," echoed a lad gloomily. And there was not, for him, the target practice settling that point definitely next day.

"But why the devil couldn't——" began another vexed voice, then paused. "Ah! here comes Erlton from the General. He'll know. I say, Major——" he broke off aghast.

"Have a glass of something, Erlton?" put in a senior hastily, "you look as if you had seen a ghost, man!"

The Major gave an odd hollow laugh. "The other way on—I mean—I—I can't believe it—but my wife—she—she's alive—she's in Delhi." The startled faces around seemed too much for him; he sat down hurriedly and hid his face in his hands, only to look up in a second more collectedly. "It has brought the whole d——d business home, somehow, to have her there."

" But how? " the eager voices got so far—no further.

" I nearly shot him—should have if he had not ducked, for the get up was perfect. Some of you may know the man—Douglas—Greyman—a trainer chap, but my God! a well plucked one. He sneaked into my tent to tell. But I don't understand it yet, and he said he would come back and arrange. It was all so hurried, you see; I was due at the muster, and he was off when he heard what was up to see Graves—whom he knows. Oh, curse the whole lot of them! Here, khânsaman! brandy—anything! "

He gulped it down fiercely, for he had heard of more than life from Jim Douglas.

The latter, meanwhile, was racing down a ravine as his shortest way back to the city. His getting out had been the merest chance, depending on his finding Soma as sentry at the sally port of the ruined magazine. He had instantly risked the danger of another confederate for the opportunity, and he was just telling himself with a triumph of gladness that he had been right, when a curious sound like the rustling of dry leaves at his very feet, made him spring into the air and cross the flat shelf of rock he was passing at a bound; for he knew what the noise meant. A true lover's knot of deadly viper, angry at intrusion, lay there; the dry Ridge swarms with them. But, as he came down lightly on his feet again, something slipped from under one, and though he did not fall, he knew in a second that he was crippled. Break or sprain, he knew instantly that he could not hope to reach the sally-port before Soma's watch was up. Yet get back he must to the city; for this—he had tried a step by this time with the aid of a projecting rock—might make it impossible for him to return for days if he did the easiest thing and crawled upward again hands and knees. That, then, was not to be thought of. The Ajmere gate, however, *might* be open for traffic; the Delhi one certainly was, morning and evening. The latter meant a round of nearly four miles, and endless danger of discovery; but it must be done. So he set his face westward.

It was just twenty-four hours after this, that Tara, unable for longer patience, told Kate that she must lock herself in, while she went out to seek news of the master. Something must have happened. It was thirty-six hours since they had seen him, and if he was gone, that was an end.

Her face as she spoke was fierce, but Kate did not seem to care; she had, in truth, almost ceased to care for her own safety except for the sake of the man who had taken so much trouble about it. So she sat down quietly, resolved to open the locked door no more. They might break it in if they chose, or she could starve. What did it matter?

Tara meanwhile went, naturally, to seek Soma's aid, all other considerations fading before the master's safety; and so of course came instantly on the clew she sought. He had left the city, let out by Soma's own hands; hands which had never meant to let him in again, that being a different affair. And though he had said he would return, why should he? asked Soma. Whereupon Tara, to prove her ground for fear, told of the hidden mem. She would have told anything for the sake of the master. And Soma looked at her fierce face apprehensively.

"That is for after!" she said curtly, impatiently. "Now we must make sure he is not wounded. There was fighting to-day. Come, thou canst give the password and we can search before dawn if we take a light. That is the first thing."

But as, cresset in hand, Tara stooped over many a huddled heap or long, still stretch of limb, Kate, with a beating heart, was listening to the sound of someone on the stairs. The next moment she had flung the door wide at the first hint of the first familiar knock.

"Where is Tara?" asked Jim Douglas peremptorily, still holding to the door jamb for support.

"She went—to look for you—we thought—what has happened?—what is the matter?" she faltered.

"Fool! as if that would do any good! Nothing's the matter, Mrs. Erlton. I hurt my ankle, that's all." He tried to step over the threshold as he spoke, but even that short pause, from sheer dogged effort, had made its renewal an agony, and he put out his hand to her blindly.

" I shall have to ask you to help me," he began, then paused. Her arm was round him in a second, but he stood still, looking up at her curiously, " To—to help," he repeated. Then she had to drag him forward by main force so that he might fall clear of the door and enable her to close it swiftly. For who could tell what lay behind?

One thing was certain. That hand on her arm had almost scorched her—the ankle he had spoken of must have been agony to move. Yet there was nothing to be done save lay cold water to it, and to his burning head, settle him as best she could on a pillow and quilt as he lay, and then sit beside him waiting for Tara to return; for Tara could bring what was wanted. But if Tara was never to return? Kate sat, listening to the heavy breathing, broken by half-delirious moans, and changing the cool cloths, while the stars dipped and the gray of dawn grew to that dominant bubble of the mosque; and, as she sat, a thousand wild schemes to help this man, who had helped her for so long, passed through her brain, filling her with a certain gladness.

Until in the early dawn Tara's voice, calling on her, stole through the door.

It was still so dark that Kate, opening it with the quick cry—" He is here, Tara, he is here safe," did not see the tall figure standing behind the woman's, did not see the menace of either face, did not see Tara's quick thrust of a hand backward as if to check someone behind.

So she never knew that Jim Douglas, helpless, unconscious, had yet stepped once more between her and death; for Tara was on her knees beside the prostrate figure in a second, and Soma, closing the door carefully, salaamed to Kate with a look of relief in his handsome face. This settled the doubtful duty of denouncing the hidden Mlechchas. How could that be done in a house where the master lay sick?

And he lay sick for days and weeks, fighting against sun-fever and inflammation, against the general strain of that month of inaction, which, as Kate found with a pulse of soft pity, had sprinkled the hair about his temples with gray.

"He would die for her," said Tara gloomily, grudgingly, "so she must live, Soma——"

"Nay! 'twas not I——" began her brother, then held his peace, doubtful if the disavowal was to his praise or blame; for duty was a puzzle to most folk in those hot, lingering days of June, when the Ridge and the City skirmished with each other and wondered mutually if anything were gained by it. Yet both Men and Murderers were cheerful, and Major Erlton going to see the hospital after that fifteen hours' fight of the 23d of June, when the centenary of Plassey, a Hindoo fast and a Mohammedan festival, made the sepoys come out to certain victory in full parade uniform, with all their medals on, heard the lad whose girl had been killed at Meerut say in an aggrieved tone, "And the nigger as stuck me 'ad 'er Majesty's scarlet coatee on 'is d——d carcass, and a 'eap of medals she give him a-blazin' on his breast—dash 'is impudence."

So blue eye met blue eye again sympathetically, for that was no time to see the pathos of the story.

CHAPTER IV.

BUGLES AND FIFES.

THERE was a blessed coolness in the air, for the rains had broken, the molten heats of June had passed. And still that handful of obstinate aliens clung like barnacles to the bare red rocks of the Ridge. Clung all the closer because in one corner of it, beside the canal, they had become part of the soil itself in rows on rows of new-made graves. A strong rear-guard this, what with disease and exposure superadded to skirmishes and target-practice. Yet, though not a gun in the city had been silenced, not a battery advanced a yard, the living garrison day after day dug these earthworks for the dead one, firm as it, in silent resolve to yield no inch of foothold on those rocks till the Judgment Day, when Men and Murderers should pass together to the great settlement of this world's quarrels.

And yet those in command began to look at each other, and ask what the end was to be, for though, despite the daily drain, the Widow's Cruse grew in numbers as time went on, the city grew also, portentously.

Still the men were cheerful, the Ridge strangely unlike a war-camp in some ways; for the country to the rear was peaceful, posts came every day, and there was no lack even of luxuries. Grain merchants deserting their city shops set up amid the surer payments of the cantonment bazaar, and the greed for gain brought hawkers of fruit, milk, and vegetables to run the gauntlet of the guns, while some poor folk living on their wits, when there was not a rag or a patch or a bit of wood left to be looted in the deserted bungalows, took to earning pennies by tracking the big shot as they trundled in the ravines, and bringing them to the masters, who needed them.

Between the rain-showers too, men, after the manner of Englishmen, began to talk of football matches, sky races, and bewail the fact of the racket court being within range of the walls. But some, like Major Reid, who never left his post at Hindoo Rao's house for three months, preferred to face the city always. To watch it as a cat watches a mouse to which she means to deal death by and by. Herbert Erlton was one of these, and so his old khânsaman, with whom Kate used to quarrel over his terribly Oriental ideas of Irish stew and such like—would bring him his lunch, sometimes his dinner, to the pickets. It was quite a dignified procession, with a cook-boy carrying a brazier, so that the Huzoor's food should be hot, and the bhisti carrying a porous pot of water holding bottles, so that the Huzoor's drink might be cool. The khânsaman, a wizened figure with many yards of waistband swathed round his middle, leading the way with the mint sauce for the lamb, or the mustard for the beefsteak. He used at first to mumble charms and vows for safe passage as he crossed the valley of the shadow; as a dip where round shot loved to dance was nicknamed by the men. But so many others of his trade were bringing food to the master that he soon grew callous to the danger, and grinned like the rest when a wild caper to dodge a trundling, thundering

ball made a fair-haired laddie remark sardonically to the
caperer, " It's well for you, my boy, that you haven't
spilled my dinner."

Perhaps it was, considering the temper of the times.
Herbert Erlton, eating his lunch, sheltered from the pelt-
ing rain behind the low scarp which by this time scored
the summit of the Ridge, smiled also.   He was all grimed
and smirched with helping young Light—the gayest
dancer in Upper India—with his guns.   He helped wherever he could in his spare time, for a great restlessness
came over him when out of sight of those rose-red walls.
They had a fascination for him since Jim Douglas' failure to return had left him uncertain what they held.   So,
when the day's work slackened, as it always did toward
sunset, and the rain clearing, he had drifted back to his
tent for a bath and a change, he drifted out again along
the central road, where those off duty were lounging,
and the sick had their beds set out for the sake of company and cooler air.   It was a quieter company than
usual, for some two days before the General himself had
joined the rear-guard by the canal; struck down by
cholera, and dying with the half-conscious, wholly
pathetic words on his lips, " strengthen the right."

And that very day the auctions of his and other dead
comrades' effects had been held; so that more than one
usually thoughtless youngster looked down, maybe, on
a pair of shoes into which he had stepped over a grave.

Still it was an eager company, as it discussed Lieutenant Hills' exploit of the morning, and asked for the
latest bulletin of that reckless young fighter with fists
against the swords.

" How was it? " asked the Major, " I only heard the
row.   The beggars must have got clean into camp."

" Right up to the artillery lines.   You see it was so
beastly misty and rainy, and they were dressed like the
native vidette.   So Hills, thinking them friends, let them
pass his two guns, until they began charging the Carabineers; and then it was too late to stop 'em."

" Why? "

" Carabineers—didn't stand, somehow, except their
officer.   So Hills charged instead.   By George! I'd

have given a fiver to see him do it. You know what a little chap he is—a boy to look at. And then——"

"And then," interrupted the Doctor, who had been giving a glance at a ticklish bandage as he passed the bed round which the speakers were gathered, " I think I can tell you in his own words; for he was quite cool and collected when they brought him in—said it was from bleeding so much about the head——"

A ripple of mirth ran through the listeners, but Major Erlton did not smile this time; the laugh was too tender.

"He said he thought if he charged it would be a diversion, and give time to load up. So he rode—Yes! I should like to have seen it too!—slap at the front rank, cut down the first fellow, slashed the next over the face. Then the two following crashed into him, and down he went at such a pace that he only got a slice to his jacket and lay snug till the troop—a hundred and fifty or so— rode over him. Then—ha—ha! he got up and looked for his sword! Had just found it ten yards off, when three of them turned back for him. He dropped one from his horse, dodged the other, who had a lance, and finally gashed him over the head. Number three was on foot— the man he'd dropped, he thinks, at first—and they had a regular set to. Then Hill's cloak, soaked with rain, got round his throat and half choked him, and the brute managed to disarm him. So he had to go for him with his fists, and by punching merrily at his head managed all right till he tripped over his cloak and fell——"

"And then," put in another voice eagerly, " Tombs, his Major, who had been running from his tent through the thick of those charging devils on foot to see what was up that the Carabineers should be retiring, saw him lying on the ground, took a pot shot at thirty paces—and dropped his man! "

"By George, what luck! " commented someone; " he must have been blown! "

"Accustomed to turnips, I should say," remarked another, with a curiously even voice; the voice of one with a lump in his throat, and a slight difficulty in keeping steady.

"Did they kill the lot? " asked Major Erlton quickly.

" Bungled it rather, but it was all right in the end.
They were a plucky set, though; charged to the very middle 'of the camp, shouting to the black artillery to join
them, to come back with them to Delhi."

" But they met with a pluckier lot! " interrupted the
man who had suggested turnips.   " The black company
wasn't ready for action.   The white one behind it was;
unlimbered, loaded.   And the blackies knew it.   So they
called out to fire—fire at once—fire sharp—fire through
them—Well! d——n it all, black or white, I don't care,
it's as plucky a thing as has been done yet."   He moved
away, his hands in his pockets, attempting a whistle; perhaps to hide his trembling lips.

" I agree," said the Doctor gravely, " though it wasn't
necessary to take them at their word.   But somehow it
makes that mistake afterward all the worse."

" How many of the poor beggars were killed, Doctor,"
asked an uneasy voice in the pause which followed.

" Twenty or so.   Grass-cutters and such like.   They
were hiding in the cemetery from the troopers, who were
slashing at everyone, and our men pursuing the party
which escaped over the canal bridge—made—made
a mistake.   And—I'm sorry to say there was a
woman——"

" There have been too many mistakes of that sort,"
said an older voice, breaking the silence.   " I wish to God
some of us would think a bit.   What would our lives be
without our servants, who, let us remember, outnumber
us by ten to one?   If they weren't faithful——"

" Not quite so many, Colonel," remarked the Doctor
with a nod of approval.   " Twenty families came to the
Brigade-major to-day with their bundles, and told him
they preferred the quiet of home to the distraction of
camp.   I don't wonder."

" It is all their own fault," broke in an angry young
voice, " why did they——"

And so began one of the arguments, so common in
camp, as to the right of revenge pure and simple.   Arguments fostered by the newspapers, where, every day, letters appeared from " Spartacus," or " Fiat Justitia," or
some such *nom de plume*.   Letters all alike in one thing,

that they quoted texts of Scripture. Notably one about a daughter of Babylon and the blessedness of throwing children on stones.

But Major Erlton did not stop to listen to it. The ethics of the question did not interest him, and in truth mere revenge was lost in him in the desire, not so much to kill, as to fight. To go on hacking and hewing for ever and ever. As he drifted on smoking his cigar he thought quite kindly of the poor devils of grass-cutters who really worked uncommonly well; just, in fact, as if nothing had happened. So did the old khânsaman, and the sweeper who had come back to him on his return to the Ridge, saying that the Huzoor would find the tale of chickens complete. And the garden of the ruined house near the Flagstaff Tower whither his feet led him unconsciously, as they often did of an evening, was kept tidy; the gardener—when he saw the tall figure approaching—going over to a rose-bush, which, now that the rain had fallen, was new budding with white buds, and picking him a buttonhole. He sat down on the plinth of the veranda twiddling it idly in his fingers as he looked out over the panorama of the eastern plains, the curving river, and the city with the white dome of the mosque hanging unsupported above the smoke and mist wreaths. For now, at sunsetting, the sky was a mass of rose-red and violet cloud and a white steam rose from the dripping trees and the moist ground. It was a perfect picture. But he only saw the city. That, to him, was India. That filled his eye. The wide plains east and west, north and south, where the recent rain had driven every thought save one of a harvest to come, from the minds of millions, where the master meant simply the claimer of revenue, might have been non-existent so far as he, and his like, were concerned.

Yet even for the city he had no definite conception. He merely looked at it idly, then at the rosebud he held. And that reminding him of a certain white marble cross with " Thy will be done " on it, he rose suddenly, almost impatiently. But there was no resignation in *his* face, as he wandered toward the batteries again with the white flower of a blameless life stuck in his old flannel coat and a strange conglomerate of pity and passion in his heart, while the city—as the light faded—grew more and more like the clouds above it, rose-red and purple; until, in the distance, it seemed a city of dreams.

In truth it was so still, despite the clangor of bugles and fifes which Bukht Khân brought with him when, on the 1st of July, he crossed the swollen river in boats with five thousand mutineers. A square-shouldered man was Bukht Khân, with a broad face and massive beard; a massive sonorous voice to match. A man of the Cromwell type, of the church militant, disciplinarian to the back-bone, believing in drill, yet with an eye to a Providence above platoon exercise. And there was no lack of soldiers to drill in Delhi by this time. They came in squads and battalions, to jostle each other in the streets and overflow into the camp on the southern side of the city; that furthest from the obstinate colony on the Ridge. But first they flung themselves against it in all the ardor of new brooms, and failing to sweep the barnacles away, subsided into the general state of dreaminess and drugs. For the bugles and fifes could always be disobeyed on the plea that they were not sounded by the right Commander-in-Chief. There were three of them now. Bukht Khân the Queen's nominee, Mirza Moghul, and another son of the King's, Khair Sultân. So that Abool-Bukr's maudlin regrets for possible office became acute, and Newâsi's despairing hold on his hand had to gain strength from every influence she could bring to bear upon it. Even drunkenness and debauchery were safer than intrigue, to that vision of retribution which seemed to have left him, and taken to haunting her day and night. So she held him fast, and when he was not there wept and prayed, and listened hollow-eyed to a Moulvie who preached at the neighboring mosque; a man who preached a judgment.

" Thou art losing thy looks, mine Aunt," said the Prince to her one day. Not unkindly; on the contrary, almost tenderly. " Dost know, Newâsi, thou art more woman than most, for thou dost brave all things, even loss of good name—for I swear even these Mufti folk complain of thee—for nothing. None other I know would

do it, so I would not have it—for something. Yet some
day we shall quarrel over it; some day thy patience will
go; some day thou wilt be as others, thinking of thyself;
and then——"

"And then, nephew?" she asked coldly.

He laughed, mimicking her tone. "And then I shall
grow tired and go mine own way to mine own end."

In the meantime, however, the thrummings and drummings went on until Kate Erlton, watching a sick bed
hard by, felt as if she must send round and beg for
quiet. It seemed quite natural she should do so, for
she was completely absorbed over that patient of hers,
who, without being seriously ill, would not get better.
Who passed from one relapse of fever to another with a
listless impatience, and now, nearly a month after he had
stumbled over the threshold, lay barely convalescent. It
had been a strange month. Stranger even than the previous one, when she had dragged through the lonely days
as best she could, and he had wandered in and out restlessly, full of strain and stress. If even that had been a
curious linking of their fates, what was this when she
tended him day and night, when the weeks slipped by
securely, almost ignorantly? For though Soma came
every day to inquire after the master, standing at the
door to salute to her, spick and span in full uniform, he
brought no disturbing news.

It seemed to her, now, that she had known Jim Douglas all his life. And in truth she had learned something
of the real man during the few days of delirium consequent on the violent inflammation which set in on the injured ankle. But for the most part he had muttered and
moaned in liquid Persian. He had always spoken it with
Zora, who had been taught it as part of her attractions,
and no doubt it was the jingle of the jewels as Kate
tended him, which reminded him of that particular part
of his life.

By the time he came to himself, however, she had removed all the fineries, finding them in the way; save the
heavy gold bangle which would not come off—at least
not without help. He used to watch it half confusedly
at first as it slipped up and down her arm, and wondered

why she had not asked Tara to take it off for her; but he grew rather to like the look of it; to fancy that she had kept it on on purpose, to be glad that she had; though it was distinctly hard when she raised him up on his pillows! For, after all, fate linked them strangely, and he was grateful to her—very grateful.

"You are laughing at me," she said one morning as she came up to his bed, with a tray improvised out of a brass platter, and found him smiling.

"I have been laughing at you all the morning, when I haven't been grumbling," he replied, "at you and the chicken tea, and that little fringed business, to do duty as a napkin, I suppose, and the fly-paper—which isn't the least use, by the way, and I'm sure I could make a better one—and the mosquito net to give additional protection to my beauty when I fall asleep. Who could help laughing at it?"

She looked at him reproachfully. "But it makes you more comfortable, surely?"

"Comfortable," he echoed, "my dear lady! It is a perfect convalescent home!"

But in the silence which followed his right hand clenched itself over a fold in the quilt unmistakably.

"If you will take your chicken tea," she replied cheerfully, despite a faint tremble in her voice, "you will soon get out of it. And really, Mr. Greyman, you don't seem to have lost any chance. Soma is not very communicative, but everything seems as it was. I never keep back anything from you. But, indeed, the chief thing in the city seems that there is no money to pay the soldiers. Do you know, I'm afraid Soma must loot the shops like the others. He seems to get things for nothing; though of course they are extraordinarily cheap. When I was a mem I used to pay twice as much for eggs."

He interrupted her with a laugh that had a tinge of bitterness in it. "Do you happen to know the story of the Jew who was eating ham during a thunderstorm, Mrs. Erlton?"

She shook her head, smiling, being accustomed by this time to his unsparing, rather reckless ridicule.

" He looked up and said, ' All this fuss about a little bit of pork.' So all this fuss has taught you the price of eggs. Upon my word! it is worse than the convalescent home! " He lay back upon his pillows with a half-irritated weariness.

" I have learned more than that, surely——" she began.

" Learned! " he echoed sharply. " You've learned everything, my dear lady, necessary to salvation. That's the worst of it! Your chatter to Tara—I hear when you think I am asleep. You draw your veil over your face when the water-carrier comes to fill the pots as if you had been born on a housetop. You—Mrs. Erlton! If I were not a helpless idiot I could pass you out of the city to-morrow, I believe. It isn't your fault any longer. It's mine, and Heaven only knows how long. Oh! confound that thrumming and drumming. It gets on my nerves— my nerves!—pshaw! "

It was then that Kate declared that she would really send Tara——

" Mrs. Erlton presents her compliments to the Princess Farkhoonda Zamâni, and will be obliged," jested Jim Douglas; then paused, in truth more irritated than amused, despite the humor on his face. And suddenly he appealed to her almost pitifully, " Mrs. Erlton! if any-one had told you it would be like this—your chance and mine—when the world outside us was alive—was struggling for life—would you—would you have believed it? "

She bent to push the chicken tea to a securer position. " No," she said softly; then to change the subject, added, " How white your hands are getting again! I must put some more stain on them, I suppose." She spoke regretfully, though she did not mind putting it on her own. But he looked at the whiteness with distinct distaste.

" It is with doing nothing and lying like a log. Well! I suppose I shall wake from the dream some day, and then the moment I can walk——"

" There will be an end of peace," she interrupted, quite resolutely. " I know it is very hard for you to lie still, but really you must see how much safer and smoother life has been since you were forced to give in to Fate."

" And Kate," he muttered crossly under his breath,

But she heard it, and bit her lip to prevent a tender smile as she went off to give an order to Tara. For the vein of almost boyish mischief and lighthearted recklessness which showed in him at times always made her think how charming he must have been before the cloud shadowed his life.

"The master is much better to-day, Tara," she said cheerfully. "I really think the fever has gone for good."

"Then he will soon be able to take the mem away," replied the woman quickly.

"Are you in such a hurry to get rid of me?" asked Kate with a smile, for she had grown fond of the tall, stately creature, with her solemn airs of duty, and absolute disregard of anything which came in its way. The intensity of the emotion which swept over the face, which was usually calm as a bronze statue, startled Kate.

"Of a truth I shall be glad to go back. The Huzoors' life is not my life, their death not my death."

It was as if the woman's whole nature had recoiled, as one might recoil from a snake in the path, and a chill struck Kate Erlton's heart, as she realized on how frail a foundation peace and security rested. A look, a word, might bring death. It seemed to her incredible that she should have forgotten this, but she had. She had almost forgotten that they were living in a beleagured city, though the reverberating roll of artillery, the rush and roar of shells, and the crackle of musketry never ceased for more than a few hours at a time.

She was not alone, however, in her forgetfulness. Half Delhi had become accustomed to cannon, to bugles and fifes, and went on its daily round indifferently. But in the Palace the dream grew ominously thin once or twice. For not a fraction remained in the Treasury, no effort to collect revenue had been made anywhere, and fat Mahboob, the only man who knew how to screw money out of a stone, lay dying of dropsy. And as he lay, the mists of personal interest in the future dispersing, he told his old master, the King, some home truths privately, while Ahsan-Oolah, the physician, administering cooling draughts as usual, added his wisdom to the eunuch's. There was no hope where there was no money. Life

was not worth living without a regular pension. Let the
King secure his and secure pardon while there was
yet time, by sending a letter to the General on the Ridge,
and offering to let the English in by Selimgarh and betray the city. When all was said and done, others had
betrayed *him*, had forced *his* hand; so let him save himself if he could, quietly, without a word to any but
Ahsan-Oolah. Above all, not one word to Zeenut
Maihl, Hussan Askuri, and Bukht Khân—that Trinity of
Dreams!

With which words of wisdom mayhap lightening his
load of sins, the fat eunuch left the court once and for
all. So the old King, as he sat listening to the quarrels
of his Commander-in-Chief, had other consolation besides couplets; and when he wrote

> " No peace, no rest, since armies round me riot,
> Life lingers yet, but ere long I shall die o't,"

he knew—though his yellow, wax-like mask hid the
knowledge from all—that a chance of escape remained.

The old King's letter reached the Ridge easily. There
was no difficulty in communication now. Spies were
plentiful, and if Jim Douglas had been able to get about,
he could have set Major Erlton's mind at rest without
delay. But Soma positively refused to be a go-between;
to do anything, in short, save secure the master's safety.
And the offer of betrayal arrived when the man who held
command of the Ridge felt uncertain of the future; all the
more so because of the telegrams, the letters—almost the
orders—which came pouring in to take Delhi—to take it
at once! Early in the month, the gamester's throw of
assault had been revived with the arrival of reinforcements, only to be abandoned once more, within an hour
of the appointed time, in favor of the grip-of-death. But
now, though the whisper had gone no further than the
General's tent, a third possibility was allowed—retreat.
The six thousand were dwindling day by day, the men
were half dead with picket duty, wearied out with needless skirmishes, crushed by the tyranny of bugles and
fifes.

If this then could be? There was no lack of desire to

believe it possible; but Greathed of the politicals, and Sir Theophilus Metcalfe shook their heads doubtfully. Hodson, they said, had better be consulted.   So the tall man with the blue hawk's eyes, who had lost his temper many times since that dawn of the 12th of June, when the first assault had hung fire, was asked for his opinion.

" We had a chance at the beginning," he said.   " We could have a chance now, if there was someone—but that is beside the question.   As for this, it is not worth the paper it is written on.   The King has no power to fulfill his promise.   He is virtually a prisoner himself.   That is the truth.   But don't send an answer.   Refer it, and keep him quiet."

" And retreat? "

" Retreat is impossible, sir.   It would lose us India."

" Any news, Hodson? " asked Major Erlton, meeting the free-lance as he rode back to his tent after his fashion, with loose rein and loose seat, unkempt, undeviating, with an eye for any and every advantage.

" None."

" Any chance of—of anything? "

" None with our present chiefs.   If we had Sir Henry Lawrence here it would be different."

But Sir Henry Lawrence, having done his duty to the uttermost, already lay dead in the residency at Lucknow, though the tidings had not reached the Ridge.   And yet more direful tidings were on their way to bring July, that month of clouds and cholera, of flies and funerals, of endless buglings and fifings, to a close.

It came to the city first.   Came one afternoon when the King sat in the private Hall of Audience, his back toward the arcaded view of the eastern plains, ablaze with sunlight, his face toward the garden, which, through the marble-mosaic traced arches, showed like an embroidered curtain of green set with jeweled flowers. Above him, on the roof, circled the boastful legend:

> " If earth holds a haven of bliss
> It is this—it is this—it is this ! "

And all around him, in due order of precedence, according to the latest army lists procurable in Delhi, were

ranged the mutinous native officers; for half the King's
sovereignty showed itself in punctilious etiquette. At his
feet, below the peacock throne, stood a gilded cage containing a cockatoo. For Hâfzan had been so far right
in her estimate of Hussan Askuri's wonders that poor little Sonny's pet, duly caught, and with its crest dyed an
orthodox green, had been used—like the stuffed lizard—
to play on the old man's love of the marvelous. So, for
the time being, the bird followed him in his brief journey-
ings from Audience Hall to balcony, from balcony to bed.

The usual pile of brocaded bags lay below that again,
upon the marble floor, where a reader crouched,
sampling the most loyal to be used as a sedative. One
would be needed ere long, for the Commanders-in-Chief
were at war; Bukht Khân, backed by Hussan Askuri,
with his long black robe, his white beard, and the wild
eyes beneath his bushy brows, and by all the puritans and
fanatics of the city; Mirza Moghul by his brother, Khair
Sultân, and most of the Northern Indian rebels who refused a mere ex-soubadar's right to be better than they.

"Let the Light-of-the-World choose between us,"
came the sonorous voice almost indifferently; in truth
those secret counsels of Bukht Khân with the Queen, of
which the Palace was big with gossip, held small place,
allowed small consideration for the puppet King.

"Yea! let the Pillar-of-State choose," bawled the shrill
voice of the Moghul, whose yellow, small-featured face
was ablaze with passion. "Choose between his son and
heir and this low-born upstart, this soubadar of artillery,
this puritan by profession, this debaucher of King's——"

He paused, for Bukht Khân's hand was on his sword,
and there was an ominous stir behind Hussan Askuri.
Ahsan-Oolah, a discreet figure in black standing by the
side of the throne, craned his long neck forward, and his
crafty face wore an amused smile.

Bukht Khân laughed disdainfully at the Mirza's full
stop. "What I am, sire, matters little if I can lead
armies to victory. The Mirza hath not led his, *as yet.*"

"Not led them?" interrupted an officious peace-
bringer. "Lo! the hell-doomed are reduced to five hundred; the colonels are eating their horses' grain, the

captains are starving, and our shells cause terror as they
cry, ' Coffin! Coffin! (*boccus! boccus!*)——' "

" The Mirza could do as well as thou," put in a partisan, heedless of the tales to which the King, however,
had been nodding his head, " if, as thou hast, he had
money to pay his troops. The Begum Zeenut Maihl's
hoards——"

The sword and the hand kept company again significantly. " I pay my men by the hoard I took from the
infidel, Meean-jee," retorted the loud, indifferent voice.
" And when it is done I can get more. The Palace is
not sucked dry yet, nor Delhi either."

The Meean, well known to have feathered his nest
bravely, muttered something inaudible, but a stout,
white-robed gentleman bleated hastily:

" There is no more money to be loaned in Delhi, be
the interest ever so high."

The broad face broadened with a sardonic smile. " I
borrow, banker-jee, according to the tenets of the faith,
without interest! For the rest, five minutes in thy house
with a spade and a string bed to hang thee on head down,
and I pay every fighter for the faith in Delhi his arrears."

" *Wâh! Wâh!* " A fierce murmur of approval ran
round the audience, for all liked that way of dealing with
folk who kept their money to themselves.

" But, Khân-jee! there is no such hurry," protested
the keeper of peace, the promoter of dreams. " The
hell-doomed are at the last gasp. Have not two
Commanders-in-Chief had to commit suicide before their
troops? And was not the third allowed by special favor
of the Queen to go away and do it privately? This one
will have to do it also, and then——"

" And a letter has but this day come in," said a grave,
clever-looking man, interrupting the tale once more,
" offering ten lakhs; but as the writer makes stipulations, we are asking what treasury he means to loot, or
if it is hidden hoards."

Bukht Khân shrugged his shoulders. " The Meean's
or the banker's hoards are nearer," he said brutally,
" and money we must have, if we are to fight as soldiers.
Otherwise——" He paused. There was a stir at the

entrance, where a news-runner had unceremoniously pushed his way in to flourish a letter in a long envelope, and pant with vehement show of breathlessness. " In haste! In haste! and buksheesh for the bringer."

The King, who had been listening wearily to the dispute, thinking possibly that the paucity of commanders on the Ridge was preferable to the plethora of them at court, looked up indifferently. They came so often, these bearers of wonderful news. Not so often as the little brocaded bags; but they had no more effect.

" Reward him, Keeper-of-the-Purse," he said punctiliously, " and read, slave. It is some victory to our troops, no doubt."

There was a pause, during which people waited indifferently, wondering, some of them, if it was bogus news that was to come or not.

Then the court moonshee stood up with a doubtful face. " 'Tis from Cawnpore," he murmured, forgetting decorum and etiquette; forgetting everything save the news that the Nâna of Bithoor had killed the two hundred women and children he had pledged himself to save.

Bukht Khân's hand went to his sword once more, as he listened, and he turned hastily to Hussan Askuri. " That settles it as *thou* wouldst have it," he whispered. " It is Holy War indeed, or defeat."

But Mirza Moghul shrank as a man shrinks from the scaffold.

The old King stood up quickly; stood up between the lights looking out on the curtain of flowers. " Whatever happens," he said tremulously, " happens by the will of God."

His sanctimoniousness never failed him.

So on the night of the 23d of August there was an unwonted stillness in the city, and the coming of day did not break it. The rain, it is true, fell in torrents, but many an attack had been made in rain before. There was none now. The bugles and fifes had ended, and folk were waiting for the drum ecclesiastic to begin. What they thought meanwhile, who knows? Delhi held a hundred and fifty thousand souls, swelled to nigh two hundred thousand by soldiers. Only this, therefore, is certain, the thoughts must have been diverse.

But on the Ridge, when, after a few days, the tidings reached it with certainty, there was but one. It found expression in a letter which the General wrote on the last day of July. " It is my firm intention to hold my present position and resist attack to the last. The enemy are very numerous, and may possibly break through our intrenchments and overwhelm us, but the force will die at its post."

No talk of retirement now! The millions of peasants plowing their land peaceably in firm faith of a just master who would take no more than his due, the thousands even in the bloody city itself waiting for this tyranny to pass, were not to be deserted. The fight would go on. The fight for law and order.

So the sanctimonious old King had said sooth, " Whatever happens, happens by the will of God."

Those two hundred had not died in vain.

CHAPTER V.

THE DRUM ECCLESIASTIC.

THE silence of the city had lasted for seven days. And now, on the 1st of August, the dawn was at hand, and the rain which had been falling all night had ceased, leaving pools of water about the city walls. Still, smooth pools like plates of steel, dimly reflecting the gray misty sky against which the minarets of the mosque showed as darker streaks, its dome like a faint cloud.

And suddenly the silence ended. The first shuddering beat of a royal salute vibrated through the heavy dewy air, the first chord of " God save the Queen," played by every band in Delhi, floated Ridgeward.

The cheek of it!

That phrase—no other less trenchant, more refined— expressed purely the feeling with which the roused six thousand listened from picket or tent, comfortable bed or damp sentry-go, to this topsy-turveydom of anthems! The cheek of it! The very walls ought to fall Jericho-wise before such sacrilegious music.

But in the city it sent a thrill through hearts and brains. For it roused many a dreamer who had never felt the chill of a sword-hilt on his palm to the knowl-edge that the time for gripping one had come.

Since this was Bukr-eed, the Great Day of Sacrifice. No common Bukr-eed either, when the blood of a goat or a bull would worthily commemorate Abraham's sacri-fice of his best and dearest, but something more akin to the old patriarch's devotion. Since on Bukr-eed, 1857, the infidel was to be sacrificed by the faithful, and the faithful by the infidel.

For the silence of seven days had been a silence only from bugles and fifes; the drum ecclesiastic had taken their place. The mosques had resounded day and night to the wild tirades of preachers, and even Mohammed Ismail, feeling that in religious war lay the only chance of forgiveness for past horrors, spent every hour in paint-ing its perfections, in deprecating any deviation from its rule. The sword or the faith for men; the faith without the sword for those who could not fight. But others were less scrupulous, their denunciations less guarded, and as the processions passed through the narrow streets flaunting the green banner, half the Mohammedan popu-lation felt that the time had come to strike their blow for the faith. And Hussan Askuri dreamed dreams; and the Bird-of-Heaven, with its crest new-dyed for the occa-sion, gave the Great Cry viciously as it was paraded through jostling crowds in the Thunbi Bazaar, where religion found recruits by the score even among the women. While Abool-Bukr, vaguely impressed by the stir, the color, the noise, took to the green and swore to live cleanly. So that Newâsi's soft eyes shone as she repeated Mohammed Ismail's theories. They were very true, the Prince said; besides this could be nothing but honest fighting since there were no women on the Ridge; whereupon she stitched away at his green banner fear-lessly.

But in the Palace it needed all Bukht Khân's determi-

nation and Hussan Askuri's wily dreams to reconcile the
old King to the breach of etiquette which the sacrifice
of a camel instead of a bull by the royal hands involved.
For the army—three-quarters Brahmin and Rajpoot—
had been promised, as a reward for helping to drive out
the infidel, that no sacred kine should be killed in
Hindustan.

And others besides the King objected to the restric-
tion. Old Fâtma, for instance, Shumsha-deen the seal-
cutter's wife, as she swathed her husband's white beard
with pounded henna leaves to give it the orthodox red
dye.

" What matters it, woman? " he replied sternly, but
with an odd quaver in his voice. " There is a greater
sacrifice than the blood of bulls and goats, and that I
may yet offer this blessed Eed."

" And mayhap, mother," suggested the widowed,
childless daughter-in-law, " a goat will serve our turn
better than a stirk this year: there will be enough for
offering, and belike there may be no feasting."

The old lady, high-featured, high-tempered, wept profusely between her railings at the ill-omened suggestion;
but the old Turk admitted the possibility with a strained
wondering look in the eyes which had lost their keenness
with graving texts. So, as the day passed the women
helped him faithfully in his bath of purification, and the
daughter-in-law, having the steadiest hand, put the antimony into the old man's eyes as he squatted on a clean
white cloth stretched in the center of the odd little courtyard. She used the stylus she had brought with her to
the house as a bride, and it woke past memories in the
old brain, making the black-edged old eyes look at the
wife of his youth with a wistful tenderness. For it was
years since a woman had performed the kindly office;
not since the finery and folly of life had passed into the
next generation's hands. But old Fâtma thought he
still looked as handsome as any as he finally stepped into
the streets in his baggy trousers with one green shawl
twisted into a voluminous waistband, another into a turban, his flaming red beard flowing over his white tunic,

and a curved scimitar—it was rather difficult to get out of its scabbard by reason of rust—at his side.

"Lo! here comes old Fâtma's Shumsha-deen," whispered other women, peeping through other chinks. "He looks well for sure; better by far than Murri-am's Faiz-Ahmud for all his new gold shoes!"

And those two, daughter and mother-in-law, huddled in unaccustomed embrace to see the last of their martyr through the only convenient crack, felt a glow of pitiful pride before they fell a-weeping and a-praying the old pitiful prayer of quarrelers that God would be good to His own.

There were thousands in Delhi about sunsetting on the 1st of August praying that prayer, though there were hundreds who held aloof, talking learnedly of the House of Protection as distinguished from the House of the Enemy, as they listened to the evening call to prayer. How could there be Holy War, when that had echoed freely during the British rule? And Mohammed Ismail, listening to their arguments feverishly, knew in his heart that they were right.

But the old Shumsha-deens did not split hairs. So as the sun set they went forth in thousands and the gates were closed behind them; for they were to conquer or die. They were to hurl themselves recklessly on the low breastworks which now furrowed the long line of hill. Above all, on that which had crept down its side to a ruined temple within seven hundred yards of the Moree Bastion.

' So, about the rising of the moon, two days from full, began such a cannonading and fusillading as was not surpassed even on that final day when the Ridge, taking similar heart of grace, was to fling itself against the city.

Major Erlton, off duty but on pleasure in the Saming-House breastwork, said to his neighbor that they must be mad, as a confused wild rush burst from the Moree gate. Six thousand or so of soldiers and Shumsha-deens with elephants, camels, field-pieces, distinct in the moonlight. And behind them came a hail of shell and shot, with them a rain of grape and musket-balls. But

above all the din and rattle could be heard two things:
The cries of the muezzins from the minarets, chanting
to the four corners of Earth and Sky that " Glory is for
all and Heaven for those who bleed," and an incessant
bugling.

" It's that man in front," remarked Major Erlton.
" Do you think we shall manage, Reid? There's an
awful lot of them."

Major Reid looked round on his little garrison of
dark faces; for there was not an Englishman in the post;
only a hundred quaint squat Ghoorkas, and fifty tall fair
Guides from the Western frontier.

" We'll do for just now, and I can send for the Rifles
by and by. There's to be no pursuit, you know. The
order's out. Ought to have been out long ago. Reserve your fire, men, till they come close up."

And come close they did, while Walidad Khân, fierce
fanatic from Peshawur, and Gorakh-nâth, fiercer Bhud-
dist from Nepâl, with fingers on trigger, called on them
jibingly to come closer still; though twenty yards from
a breastwork bristling with rifles was surely close
enough for anyone? But it was not for the bugler who
led the van, sounding assemblies, advances, doubles;
anything which might stir the hearts behind.

" He has got a magnificent pair of bellows," remarked
an officer, who, after a time, came down with a hundred
and fifty of the Rifles to aid that hundred and fifty natives
in holding the post against six thousand and more of
their countrymen.

" Splendid! he has been at it this hour or more," said
Major Erlton. " I really think they are mad. They
don't seem to aim or to care. There they are again!"

It was darker now, and Walidad Khân from Peshawur
and Gorakh-nâth from Nepâl, and Bill Atkins from
Lambeth had to listen for that tootling of assemblies and
advances to tell them when to fire blindly from the
embrazures into the smoke and the roar and the rattle.
So they fell to wondering among themselves if they had
nicked him that time. Once or twice the silence seemed
to say they had; but after a bit the tootling began again,
and a disappointed pair of eyes peeping curiously, reck-

lessly, would see a dim figure running madly to the assault again.

" Plucky devil! " muttered Major Erlton as with the loan of a rifle he had his try. There was a look of hope on dark faces and white alike as they cuddled down to the rifle stocks and came up to listen. It was like shooting into a herd of does for the one royal head; and some of the sportsmen had tempers.

" *Shaitân-ke-butcha!* " (Child of the devil), muttered Walidad Khân, whereat Gorakh-nâth grinned from ear to ear.

" Wot cher laughin' at? " asked Bill Atkins, who had been indulging in language of his own. " A feller can't 'it ghosts. An' 'e's the piper as played afore Moses; that's what 'ee is."

" Look sharp, men! " came the officer's warning. " There's a new lot coming on. Wait and let them have it."

They did. The din was terrific. The incessant flashes lighting up the city, showed its roofs crowded with the families of absent Shumsha-deens. So High Heaven must have been assailed, indeed, that night.

And even when dawn came it brought no Sabbath calm. Only a fresh batch of martyrs. But they had no bugler; for with the dawn some fierce frontiersman, jesting Cockney, or grinning Ghoorkha may have risked his life for a fair shot in daylight at the piper who played before Moses. Anyhow, he played no more. Perhaps the lack of him, perhaps the torrents of rain which began to fall as the sun rose, quenched the fires of faith. Anyhow, by nine o'clock the din was over, the drum ecclesiastic ceased to beat, and the English going out to count the dead found the bugler lying close to the breastwork, his bugle still in his hand; a nameless hero save for that passing jest.

But someone in the city no doubt mourned the piper who played before Moses, as they mourned other martyrs. More than a thousand of them.

Yet the Ridge, despite the faith, and fury, and fusillading, had only to dig one grave; for fourteen hours of what the records call " unusual intrepidity "—contemptuously cool equivalent for all that faith and fury—had only killed one infidel.

Shumsha-deen's Fâtma, however, was as proud as if he had killed a hundred; for he had bled profusely for the faith, having been at the very outset of it all kicked by a camel and sent flying on to a rock to dream confused dreams of valor till the bleeding from his nose relieved the slight concussion of his brain, and enabled him to go home, much shaken, but none the worse.

But many hundreds of women never saw their Shumsha-deens again, or if they saw them, only saw something to weep over and bind in white swaddling clothes and gold thread.

So by dark on the 2d of August the sound of wailing women rose from every alley, and the men, wandering restlessly about the bazaars, listened to the sound of tattoo from the Ridge and looked at each other almost startled.

" Go-to-bed-Tom! Go-to-bed-Tom! Drunk-or-sober-go-to-bed-Tom! "

The Day of Sacrifice was over, and Tom was going to bed quietly as if nothing had happened! They did not know that three-quarters of the Toms had been in bed the night before, undisturbed by the martyrs' supreme effort. If they had, they might have wondered still more persistently what Providence was about.

But in the big mosque, among the great white bars of moonlight slanting beneath the dome, one man knew. He stood, a tall white figure beneath a furled green banner, his arms outspread, his voice rising in fierce denunciation.

" Cursed * be they who did the deed, who killed jehad! Lo! I told you in my dream in the past and ye would not believe. I tell it again that ye may know. It was dawn. And the Lord Christ and the Lord Mohammed sat over the World striving each for His own according to the Will of the Most High who sets men's quarrels before the Saints in Heaven with a commander to each. And I saw the Lord Christ weep, knowing that justice

---

* From a contemporaneous account.

was on our side. So the fiat for victory went forth, and I slept. But I dreamed again and lo! it was eve with a blood-red sunsetting westward. And the Lord Christ wept still, but the Lord Mohammed's voice rang loud and stern. 'Reverse the fiat. Give the victory to the women and the children.' So I woke. And it is true! is true! Cursed be they who killed jehad!'"

The voice died away among the arches where, in delicate tracery, the attributes of the Great Creator were cut into changeless marble. Truth, Justice, Mercy, all the virtues from which all religions make their God.

"He is mad," said some; but for the most part men were silent as they drifted down the great Flights-of-Steps to the city, leaving Mohammed Ismail alone under the dome.

"Didst expect otherwise, my Queen?" said Bukht Khân hardily. "So did not I! But the end is gained. Delhi was not ours in heart and soul before. It is now. When the assault comes those who fought for faith will fight for their skins. And at the worst there is Lucknow for good Sheeahs like the Queen and her slave. We have no tie here among these Sunnies who think only of their hoards."

Zeenut Maihl shrank from him with her first touch of fear, for she had eight or nine lakhs of rupees hidden in that very house. This man whom she had summoned to her aid bid fair to make flight necessary even for a woman. Had she ventured too much? Was there yet time to throw him over, throw everyone over and make her peace? She turned instinctively in her thoughts to one who loved money also, who also had hoards to save. And so, within half an hour of Bukht Khân's departure, Ahsan-Oolah was closeted with the Queen, who after the excitement of the day needed a cooling draught.

Most people in the Palace needed one that night, for by this time almost all the possible permutations of confederacy had come about, with the result that—each combination's intrigue being known to the next—a general distrust had fallen upon all. In addition, there was now a fourth Commander-in-Chief; one Ghaus Khân, from Neemuch, who declared the rest were fools.

In truth the Dream was wearing thin indeed within the Palace.

But on that peaceful little housetop in the Mufti's quarter it seemed more profound than ever; it seemed as if Fate was determined to leave nothing wanting to the strange unreal life that was being lived in the very heart of the city. Jim Douglas was almost himself again. A little lame, a little uncertain still of his own strength; and so, remembering a piece of advice given him by the old Baharupa never to attempt using the Gift when he was not strong enough for it to be strong, he had been patient beyond Kate's hopes. But on this 2d of August, after lying awake all night listening to the roar and the din, he had insisted on going out when Soma did not turn up as usual to bring the news. He would not be long, he said, not more than an hour or two, and the attempt must be made some time. At no better one than now, perchance, since folk would be occupied in their own affairs.

" Besides," he added with a smile, " I'm ready to allow the convalescent home its due. While I've been kept quiet the very thought of concealed Europeans has died out."

" I don't know!" she interrupted quickly. " It isn't long since Prince Abool-Bukr chased that blue-eyed boy of the Mufti's over the roofs thinking he was one—don't you remember I was so afraid he might climb up here?"

" That's the advantage of being up-top," he replied lightly. " Now, if anything were to happen, *you* could scramble down. But the Prince was drunk, and I won't go near his haunts—there isn't any danger—really there isn't!"

" I shall have to get accustomed to it even if there is," she replied in the same tone.

Jim Douglas paused at the door irresolutely. " Shall I wait till Tara returns?"

" No, please don't. She is not coming back till late. She grows restless if she does not go—and I am all right."

In truth Tara had been growing restless of late. Kate, looking up from the game of chess—at which her convalescent gave her half the pieces on the board and then beat her easily—used to find those dark eyes watching them furtively. Zora Begum had never played shatrinj with the master, had never read with him from books, had never treated him as an equal. And, strangely enough, the familiar companionship—inevitable under the circumstances—roused her jealousy more than the love-making on that other terraced roof had done. *That* she understood. *That* she could crush with her cry of suttee. But *this*—this which to her real devotion seemed so utterly desirable; what did it mean? So she crept away, when she could, to take up the saintly rôle as the only certain solace she knew for the ache in her heart.

Therefore Kate sat alone, darning Jim Douglas' white socks—which as a better-class Afghan he was bound to wear—and thinking as she did so how incredibly domestic a task it was! Still socks had to be darned, and with Tara at hand to buy odds and ends, and Soma with his knowledge of the Huzoor's life ready to bring chessboards, and soap, and even a book or two, it seemed as if the roof would soon be a very fair imitation of home. So she sat peacefully till, about dusk, hearing a footfall on the stairs halting with long pauses between the steps, her vexation at her patient's evident fatigue overcame her usual caution; and without waiting for his signal knock she set the door wide and stepped out on to the stairs to give him a hand if need be. And then out of the shadow of the narrow brick ladder came a strange voice panting breathlessly:

" Salaam! mem-sahib." She started back, but not in time to prevent a bent figure with a bundle on its back from stumbling past her on to the roof; where, as if exhausted, it leaned against the wall before slipping the bundle to the floor. It was an ordinary brown blanket bundle full of uncarded cotton, and the old woman who carried it was ragged and feeble. Emaciated too beyond belief, as if cotton-spinning had not been able to keep soul and body comfortably together. Not a very formidable foe this—if foe it was. Why! surely she knew the face.

"I have brought Sonny back, Huzoor," came the breathless voice.

Sonny! Kate Erlton gave a little cry. She recollected now. "Oh, ayah!" she began recklessly, "what? where is he?"

The old woman stumbled to the door, closed the catch, and then leaned exhausted upon the lintel, sinking down slowly to a squatting position, her hand upon her heart. There was more in this than the fatigue of the stairs, Kate recognized.

"He is in the bundle, Huzoor. The mem did not know me. She will know the baba."

Know him! As her almost incredulous fingers fumbled at the knots, her mind was busy with an adorable vision of white embroideries, golden curls, and kissable, dimpled milk and roses. So it was no wonder that she recoiled from the ragged shift and dark skin, the black close-cropped hair shaved horribly into a wide gangway from nape to forehead.

"Oh, ayah!" she cried reproachfully, "what have you done to Sonny baba!" for Sonny it was unmistakably in the guise of a street urchin. A foolish remark to make, doubtless, but the old Mai, most of whose life had been passed in the curling of golden curls, the prinking of mother's darlings, did not think it strange. She looked wistfully at her charge, then at Kate apologetically.

"It was safer, Huzoor. And at least he is fat and fresh. I gave him milk and *chikken-brât.** And it was but a tiny morsel of opium just to make him quiet in the bundle."

Something in the quavering old voice made Kate cross quickly to the old woman and kneel beside her.

"You have done splendidly, ayah, no one could have done better!"

But the interest had died from the haggard face. "They said folk would be damned for it," she muttered half to herself, "but what could I do? The mem, my mem, said 'Take care of the boy.' So I gave him *chikken-brât* and milk." She paused, then looked up at

* Chicken broth.

Kate slowly. "But I can grind and spin no more, Huzoor. My life is done. So I have brought him here—and——" she paused again for breath.

"How did you find me out?" asked Kate, longing to give the old woman some restorative, yet not daring to offer it, for she was a Mussulmâni.

The old Mai reached out a skeleton of a hand, half-mechanically, to flick away a fluff of cotton wool from the still sleeping child's face. "It was the *chikken-brât*, Huzoor. The Huzoor will remember the old mess khânsaman? He did the *pagul khanas* [picnics] and nautches for the sahib logue. A big man with gold lace who made the cake at Christmas for the babas and set fire to plum-puddeens as no other khânsaman did. And made *estârît* turkeys and *sassets* [stuffed turkey and sausages]—and——" She seemed afloat on a Bagh-o-bahâr list of comestibles, a dream of days when, as ayah, she had watched many a big dinner go from the cook room.

"But about the *chikken-brât*, ayah?" asked Kate with a lump in her throat; for the wasted figure babbling of old days was evidently close on death.

"Huzoor! Mungul Khân keeps life in him, these hard times, with the selling of eggs and fowls. So he, knowing me, said there was more *chikken-brât* than mine being made in the quarter. The Huzoor need have no fear. Mungul weeps every day and prays the sahibs may return, because his last month's account was not paid. A sweeper woman, he said, bought 'halflings' for an Afghan's bibi. As if an Afghani would use three halflings in one day! No one but a mem making *chikken-brât* would do that. So I watched and made sure, against this day; for I was old, and I had not spun or ground for long."

"You should have come before," said Kate gently. "You have worn yourself out."

The old woman stumbled to her feet. "My life was worn before, Huzoor. I am very old. I have put many boy-babies into the mem's arms to make them forget their pain, and taken them from them to put the flowers round them when they were dead. He was safer with

me speaking our language; with you he may remember.
But I shall be dead, so I can do no more."

"Wait, do wait till the sahib returns," pleaded Kate.

The Mai paused, her hand on the latch. "What have
I to do with the sahibs, Huzoor? Mine were not much
count. They made my mems cry, or laugh; cry first,
then laugh. It is bad for mems. But my mem did
not care, she only cared for the babies and so there was
always a flower for the grave. Matadeen, the gardener,
made it and the big Huzoor—Erlton sahib——"

She ceased suddenly and went mumbling down the
stairs leaving Kate to close the door again and drop on
her knees beside the sleeping child. Was he sleeping
or had the opium——? She gave a sigh of relief as—her
hair tickling his cheek as she bent to listen—up came a
chubby unconscious hand to brush the tickle away.

Sonny! It seemed incredible. The house would be
a home indeed with his sweet "Mifis Erlton" echoing
through it. No! what the old Mai had said was true.
There would be danger in English prattle. She must
not tell him who she was. He must be kept as safe as
that other child over across the seas whose empty place
this one had partly filled; that other child who in all
these storms and stress was, thank Heaven! so safe.
She must deny herself that pleasure, and be content with
this terribly disguised Sonny. Then she wondered if
the dye came off as hers did; so with wet finger began
trying the experiment on the child's cheek. A little;
but perhaps soap and warm water might—— She gathered Sonny in her arms and went over to the cooking-
place. And there, to her unreasoning delight, after a
space, was a square inch or so of milk and roses. It was
trivial, of course; Mr. Greyman would say womanish,
but she should like to see the real Sonny just once! She
could dye him again. So, with the sleeping child on her
lap, she began soft dabbings and wipings on the forehead
and cheeks. It was a fascinating task and she forgot
everything else; till, as she began work on the nose, what
with the tickling and the tepid bathings dispelling the
opium drowsiness, Sonny woke, and finding himself in
strange arms began to scream horribly. And there she

was forgetful of caution among other things, kissing and cuddling the frightened child, asking him if he didn't know her and telling him he was a good little Sonnikins whom nobody in the world would hurt! At which juncture, with brain started in a new-old groove, he said amid lingering sobs:

" Oh, Mifis Erlton! What *has* a-come of my polly? "

She recognized her slip in a second; but it was too late. And hark! Steps on the stair, and Sonny prattling on in his high, clear lisp! Not one step, but two; and voices. A visitor no doubt. Sometimes, to avoid suspicion, it was necessary to bring them in. She knew the routine. The modest claim for seclusion to her supposed husband in Persian, the leaving of the door on the latch, the swift retreat into the inner roof during the interval decorously allowed for such escape. All this was easy without Sonny. The only chance now was to stop his prattle even by force, give the excuse that other women were within, and trust to a man's quickness outside.

Vain hope! Sonny wriggled like an eel, and, just as the expected knock came, evaded her silencing hand, so that the roof rang with outraged yells:

" Oh! 'oo's hurtin' me! Oo's hurtin' me! "

Without the words even, the sound was unmistakable. No native child was ever so ear-piercing, so wildly indignant. Kate, beside herself, tried soothings and force distractedly, in the midst of which an imperative voice called fiercely:

" Open the door quick, for God's sake! Anything's better than that."

For the moment, doubtless, Sonny's yells ending with victory; but another cry came sharp and short, as—the door giving under Kate's hasty fingers—two men tumbled over the threshold. Jim Douglas uppermost, his hands gripping the other's throat.

" Shut the door! " he gasped. " Lock it. Then my revolver—no—a knife—no noise—quick. I can't hold—— the brute long."

Kate turned and ran mechanically, and the steel in her hand gleamed as she flew back. Jim Douglas, digging his knees into the ribs below them, loosened one hand cautiously from the throat and held it out, trembling, eager.

But Kate saw his face. It might have been the Gorgon's, for she stood as if turned to stone.

"Don't be a fool!" he panted—"give it me! It's the only——" A sudden twist beneath him sent his hand back to the throat. "It's—it's death anyway——"

Death! What did that matter? she asked herself. Let it come, rather than murder!

"No!" she said suddenly, "you shall not. It is not worth it." The knife, flung backward, fell with a clang, but the eyes which—though that choking grip on the throat made all things dim—had been fixed on its gleam, turned swiftly to those above them and the writhing body lay still as a corpse. None too soon, for Jim Douglas was almost spent.

"A rope," he muttered briefly, "or stay, your veil will do."

But Kate, trembling with the great passion and pity of her decision, had scarce removed it ere Jim Douglas, changing his mind, rose to his feet, leaving his antagonist free to do so likewise.

"Get up, Tiddu," he said breathlessly, "and thank the mem for saving your life. But the door's locked, and if you don't swear——"

"The Huzoor need not threaten," retorted Tiddu, far more calmly as he retwisted his rag of a turban. "The Many-Faced know gratitude. They do not fall on those who find them helpless and protect them."

The thrust was keen, for in truth the old Baharupa had, not half an hour before, by sheer chance found his pupil in difficulties and insisted on seeing him safe home, and on his promising not to go out again till he was stronger; to both of which coercions Jim Douglas, in order to evade suspicion, had consented. Yet, but for Kate, he would have knifed the old man remorselessly. Even now he felt doubtful.

Tiddu, however, saved him further anxiety by stepping close to Kate and salaaming theatrically.

"By Murri-âm and the neem, the mem is as my mother, the child as my child."

So, for the first time, both he and Jim Douglas looked toward Sonny, who, with wide-planted legs and wondering eyes, had been watching Tiddu solemnly; the quaintest little figure with his red and white cheeks and black muzzle.

The old mime burst into a guffaw. "*Wâh!* what a monkeyling! *Wâh!* what a *tamâsha*" (spectacle), he cried, squatting down on his heels to look closer. In truth Sonny was like a hill baboon, especially when he smiled too; broadly, expectantly, at the familiar word.

"*Tamathâ-wallah!*" he said superbly, "*bunao ramâtha, juldi bunao!*" (Make an amusement; make it quick.)

Tiddu, a child himself like all his race in his delight in children, a child also in his capacity of sudden serenity, caught up Kate's fallen veil, and in an instant dashed into the hackneyed part of the daughter-in-law, while Kate and Jim Douglas stared; left behind, as it were, by this strange irresponsible pair—the mimic of life, and the child ignorant of what was mimicked. Tragedy a minute ago! Now Farce! They looked at each other, startled, for sympathy.

"Make a funny man now," came Sonny's confident voice, "a funny man behind a curtain—a funny man—wif a gween face an' a white face, an' a lot of fwowers an' a bit o' tring."

Tiddu looked round quickly at Jim Douglas. "*Wâh!*" he said, "the little Huzoor has a good memory. He remembers the Lord of Life and Death."

But Kate had remembered it too, and she also had turned to Jim Douglas passionately, almost accusingly. "It was you! You were Fate—you—— Ah! I understand now!"

"Do you?" he answered with a frown. "Then it's more than I do." He walked away moodily toward the knife Kate had flung away, and stooped to pick it up. "But you were right in what you did. It was an inspiration. Look there!"

He pointed to the old Baharupa, who was playing antics to amuse Sonny, who lisped, "*Thâ bâth!*" (bravo!) solemnly at each fresh effort. But Kate shivered. "I did nothing. I thought I did; but it was Fate."

"My dear lady," he retorted with a kindly smile, "it is all in the nature of dreams. The convalescent home is turned into a *crèche*. But we must transfigure the street urchin into the darling of his parents' hearts——" He paused and looked at Kate queerly. "I'll tell Tara to rig him out properly; and you must take off half the stain, you know, and leave some color on his cheeks; for he must play the part as well as——" He laughed suddenly. "It is really more dream-like than ever!" he added. And Kate thought so too.

CHAPTER VI.

VOX HUMANA.

THE five days following on the 2d of August were a time of festivity for the Camp, a time of funerals for the City. There was a break in the rains, and on the Ridge the sunshine fell in floods upon the fresh green grass, and the air, bright and cool, set men's minds toward making the best of Nature's kindness; for she had been kind, indeed, to the faithful little colony, and few even of the seniors could remember a season so favorable in every way. And so the messes talked of games, of races; and men, fresh from seeing their fellows killed by balls on one side of the Ridge, joined those who, on the other side, were crying "Well bowled!" as wickets went down before other balls.

But in the city the unswept alleys fermented and festered in the vapors and odors which rose from the great mass of humanity pent within the rose-red walls. For the gates had been closed strictly save for those with permits to come and go. This was Bukht Khân's policy. Delhi was to stand or fall as one man. There was to be no sneaking away while yet there was time. So hundreds of sepoys protesting illness, hunger, urgent private affairs—every possible excuse for getting leave—were told that if they would not fight they could sulk. Starve they might, stay they should. The other Commanders-in-Chief, it is true, spent money in bribing mercenaries for one week's more fighting; but Bukht Khân only smiled sardonically. He had tried bugles and fifes, he had tried the drum-ecclesiastic; he was now trying his last stop. The *vox humana* of self-preservation.

In the city itself, however, the preservation of life took for the present another form, and never within the memory of man had there been such a pounding of pestles and mortars over leaf-poultices. The sound of it rose up at dawn and eve like the sound of the querns, mingling with the *vox humana* of grief as the eastern and southern gates were set wide to let the dead pass out, and allow the stores for the living to pass in.

It formed a background to the gossip at the wells where the women met to draw water.

"Faiz-Ahmed found freedom at dawn," said one between her yawns. "He was long in the throes. The bibis made a great wailing, so I could not even sleep since then. There are no sons, see you, and no money now the old man's annuity is gone."

"Loh, sister!" retorted another, "thou speakest as if death were a morsel of news to let dissolve on the tongue. There be plenty such soppets in Delhi, and if I know aught of wounds there will be another at nightfall. My mistress wastes time in the pounding of simples, and I waste time in waiting for them till my turn comes at the shop; for if it be not gangrened, I have no eyes." The speaker jerked her pot to her shoulder deftly and passed down the alley.

"Juntu is wise in such matters," said a worn-looking woman with sad eyes; "I must get her to glance at my man's cut. 'Tis right to my mind—he will put naught but water to it, after some foreign fashion—but who can tell these times?"

"Save that none pass their day, sister. Death will come of the Great Sickness, or the wound, as it chooses," put in a half-starved soul who had to carry a baby besides her pot. "The cholera rages in our alley. 'Tis the smell. None sweep the streets or flush the gutters now."

"Ari, Fukra!" cried a fierce virago, "thou art a traitor at heart! She bewails the pig-eating infidels who gave her man five rupees a month to bring water to the drains. Ai teri! If they saved one life from good cholera, have they not reft a hundred in exchange from widows and orphans? Oo-ai-ie-ee!"

Her howling wail, like a jackal's, was caught up whimperingly by the others; and so they passed on with their water pots, to spread through the city the tale of Faiz-Ahmed's freedom, Juntu's suspicions of gangrene, and Karúna the butcher's big wife's retort. And, in the evening, folk gathered at the gates, and talked over it all again as the funerals passed out; old Faiz-Ahmed, in his new gold shoes, looking better as a corpse, tied up in tinsel, than as a martyr, so the spectators agreed. Whereat *his* family had their glow of pride also.

Then, when the show was over, the crowd dispersed to pay visits of condolence, and raise the wailing *vox humana* in every alley.

Greatly to Jim Douglas' relief, for there was another voice difficult to keep quiet when the cool evenings came, and all Kate's replies in Hindustani would not beguile Sonny's tongue from English. He was the quaintest mother's darling now, in a little tinsel cap fringed with brown silk tassels hiding that dreadful gangway, anklets, and bracelets on his bare corn-colored limbs, the ruddy color showing through the dye on his cheeks, his palms all henna-stained, his eyes blackened with kohl, and a variety of little tinsel and brocaded cootees ending far above his dimpled knees. There were little muslin and net ones too, cunningly streaked with silver and gold, for Tara was reckless over the boy. She insisted, too, on a great black smudge on his forehead to keep away the evil eye; and Soma, coming now with the greatest regularity, brought odd little coral and grass necklets such as Rajpoot bairns ought to wear; while Tiddu, the child's great favorite, had a new toy every day for the little Huzoor. Paper whirligigs, cotton-wool bears on a stick, mud parrots, and such like, whereat Sonny would lisp, " *Thâ bâth*, Tiddu." Though sometimes he would go over to Kate and ask appealingly, " Miffis Erlton! What has a-come of my polly?"

Then she, startled into realities by the words, would

catch him up in her arms, and look around as if for protection to Jim Douglas, who, having overdone himself
in the struggle with Tiddu, had felt it wiser to defer further action for a day or two. The more so because Tiddu
had promised to help him to the uttermost if he would
only be reasonable and leave times and seasons to one
who had ten times the choice that he had.

So he would smile back at Kate and say, " It's all
right, Mrs. Erlton. At least as right as it can be. The
lot of them are devoted to the child."

Yet in his heart he knew that there was danger in so
many confederates. He felt that this incredibly peaceful
home on the housetop could not last. Here he was looking at a woman who was not his wife, a child who was not
his child, and feeling vaguely that they were as much a
part of his life as if they were. As if, had they been
so, he would have been quite contented. More contented
than he had been on that other roof. He was, even now,
more contented than he had been there. As he sat, his
head on his hand, watching the pretty picture which Kate,
in Zora's jewels, made with the be-tinseled, be-scented,
bedecked child, he thought of his relief when years before
he had looked at a still little morsel lying in Zora's veil.
Had it been brutal of him? Would that dead baby have
grown into a Sonny? Or was it because Sonny's skin
was really white beneath the stain that he thought of him
as something to be proud of possessing; of a boy who
would go to school and be fagged and flogged and inherit
familiar virtues and vices instead of strange ones?

" What are you thinking of, Mr. Greyman? Do you
want anything? " came Kate's kind voice.

" Nothing," he replied in the half-bantering tone he so
often used toward her; " I have more than my fair share
of things already, surely! I was only meditating on the
word ' Om '—the final mystery of all things."

So, in a way, he was. On the mystery of fatherhood
and motherhood, which had nothing to do with that pure
idyl of romantic passion on the terraced roof at Lucknow,
yet which seemed to touch him here, where there was not
even love. Yet it was a better thing. The passion of
protection, of absolute self-forgetfulness, seeking no re-

ward, which the sight of those two raised in him, was a
better thing than that absorption in another self.   The
thought made him cross over to where Kate sat with the
child in her lap, and say gravely:

"The *crèche* is more interesting than the convalescent home, at least to me, Mrs. Erlton!   I shall be quite
sorry when it ends."

" When it ends? " she echoed quickly.   " There is nothing wrong, is there?   Sonny has been so good, and that
time when he was naughty the sweeper-woman seemed
quite satisfied when Tara said he was speaking Pushtoo."

" But it cannot last for all that," he replied.   " It is
dangerous.   I feel it is.   This is the 5th, and I am nearly
all right.   I must get Tiddu to arrange for Sonny first.
Then for you."

" And you? " she asked.

" I'll follow.   It will be safer, and there is no fear for
me.   I can't understand why I've had no answer from
your husband.   The letter went two days ago, and I am
convinced we ought."

The frown was back on his face, the restlessness in his
brain; and both grew when in private talk with Tiddu
the latter hinted at suspicions in the caravan which had
made it necessary for him to be very cautious.   The letter, therefore, had certainly been delayed, might never
have reached.   If no answer came by the morrow, he
himself would take the opportunity of a portion of the
caravan having a permit to pass out, and so insure the
news reaching the Ridge; trusting to get into the city
again without delay, though the gates were very strictly
kept.   Nevertheless, in his opinion, the Huzoor would
be wiser with patience.   There was no immediate danger
in continuing as they were, and the end could not be
long if it were true that the great Nikalseyn was with
the Punjâb reinforcements.   Since all the world knew
that Nikalseyn was the prince of sahibs, having the gift,
not only of being all things to all people, but of making
all people be all things to him, which was more than the
Baharupas could do.

In truth, the news that John Nicholson was coming to
Delhi made even Jim Douglas hesitate at risking any-

thing unnecessarily, so long as things went smoothly. As for the letter to Major Erlton, it was no doubt true that the number of spies sending information to the Ridge had made it difficult of late to send any, since the guards were on the alert.

It was, indeed, even for the Queen herself, who had a missive she was peculiarly anxious should not fall into strange hands.

" There is no fear, Ornament of Palaces,'' said Ahsan-Oolah urbanely; " I will stake my life on its reaching." He did not add that his chief reason for saying so was that a similar letter, written by the King, had been safely delivered by Rujjub Ali, the spy, whose house lay conveniently near the physician's own, and from whom both the latter and Elahi-Buksh heard authentic news from the Ridge. News which made them both pity the poor old pantaloon who, as they knew well, had been a mere puppet in stronger hands. And these two, laying their heads together, in one of those kaleidoscope combinations of intrigue which made Delhi politics a puzzle even at the time, advised the King to use the *vox celeste* as an antidote to the *vox humana* of the city, which was being so diligently fostered by the Queen and Bukht Khân. Let him say he was too old for this world, let him profess himself unable longer to cope with his coercers and claim to be allowed to resign and become a fakir! But the dream still lingered in the old man's brain. He loved the brocaded bags, he loved the new cushion of the Peacock throne; and though the cockatoo's crest was once more showing a yellow tinge through the green, the thought of jehâd lingered sanctimoniously. But other folk in the Palace were beginning to awake. Other people in Delhi besides Tiddu had heard that Nikalseyn was on his way from the Punjâb and not even the rose-red walls had been able to keep out his reputation. Folk talked of him in whispers. The soldiers, unable to retreat, unwilling to fight, swore loudly that they were betrayed; that there were too many spies in the city. Of that there could be no doubt. Were not letters found concealed in innocent looking cakes and such like? Had not one, vaguely suggesting that some cursed infidels were still concealed in the city, been brought in for reward by a Bunjârah who swore he had picked it up by chance? The tales grew by the telling in the Thunbi Bazaar, making Prince Abool-Bukr, who had returned to it incontinently after the disastrous failure of faith on the 2d, hiccough magnificently that, poor as he was, he would give ten golden mohurs to any-one who would set him on the track of a hell-doomed. Yea! folk might laugh, but he was good for ten still. Ay! and a rupee besides, to have the offer cried through the bazaar; so there would be an end to scoffers!

"What is't?" asked the languid loungers in the wooden balconies, as the drum came beating down the street.

"Only Abool offering ten mohurs for a Christian to kill," said one.

"And he swore he had not a rupee when I danced for him but yesterday," said another.

"He has to pay Newâsi, sister," yawned a third.

"Then let her dance for him—I do it no longer," re-torted the grumbler.

So the crier and his drums passed down the scoffing bazaar. "He will find many at that price," quoth some, winking at their neighbors; for the Prince was a butt when in his cups.

Thus at earliest dawn next morning, the 7th of August, Tiddu gave a signal knock at the door of the roof, rousing Jim Douglas who, since the child's arrival, had taken to sleeping across it once more.

"There is danger in the air, Huzoor," he said briefly; "they cried a reward for the infidels in the bazaar yester-day. There is talk of some letter."

"The child must go—go at once," replied his hearer, alert in an instant; but Tiddu shook his head.

"Not till dark, Huzoor. The bullocks are to pass out with the moon, and he must pass out with them. In a sack, Huzoor. Say nothing till the last. Then, the Huzoor knows the cloth merchant's by the Delhi gate?"

Jim Douglas nodded.

"There is a court at the back. The bullocks are there, for we are taking cloth the Lâla wants to smuggle out. A length or two in each empty sack; for he hath been looted beyond limits. So he will have no eyes, nor the caravan either, for secret work in dark corners. Bring the boy drugged as he came here, the Rajpootni will carry the bundle as a spinner, to the third door down the lane. " 'Tis an empty yard; I will have the bullock there with the half-load of raw cotton. We have two or three more as foils to the empty bags. Come as a Bunjârah, then the Huzoor can see the last of the child, and see old Tiddu's loyalty."

The familiar whine came back to his voice; he could scarcely resist a thrust forward of his open hand. But dignity or no dignity, Jim Douglas knew that itching palm well, and said significantly:

" It will be worth a thousand rupees to you, Tiddu, if the child gets safe."

A look of offended virtue came over the smooth face. " This slave is not thinking of money. The child is as his own child."

" And the mem as your mother, remember," put in the other quickly.

Tiddu hesitated. " If his servant saves the baba, cannot the master save the lady?" he said with the effrontery of a child trying how far he might go; but Jim Douglas' revolver was out in a second, and Tiddu, with an air of injured innocence, went on without a pause:

" The mem will be safe enough, Huzoor, when the child is gone, if the Huzoor will himself remain day and night to answer for the screened, sick woman within. His slave will be back by dawn; and if he smells trouble, the mem must be moved in a dhoolie to another house, the Rajpootni must go home, and I will be mother-in-law. I can play the part, Huzoor."

. He could indeed! If Kate were to be safe anywhere, it would be with this old scoundrel with his thousand-faces, his undoubted gift for influencing the eyes of men. Three days of passing from one place to another, with him in some new character, and their traces must be lost. A good plan certainly!

" And there is no danger to-day?" he asked finally.

Tiddu paused again, and his luminous eyes sought the sahib's. " Who can say that, Huzoor, for a mem, in this

city. But I think none. We can do no more, danger
or not. And I will watch. And see, here is the dream-
giver. The Rajpootni will know the dose for the child."

The dream-giver! All that day the little screw of
paper Tiddu had taken from his waistbelt lay in a fold
of Jim Douglas' high-twined pugri, and its contents
seemed to make him dull. Not that it mattered, since
there was literally nothing to be done before dusk; for
it would be cruel to tell Kate and keep her on tenter-
hooks all day to no purpose. But after a while she
noticed his dullness, and came over to where he sat, his
head on his hand, in his favorite attitude.

" I believe you are going to have fever and ague
again," she said solicitously; " do take some aconite; if
we could only get some quinine, that would end the tire-
some thing at once."

He took some to please her, and because her suggestion gave him a reasonable excuse for being slack; but as
he lounged about lazily, watching her playing with the
boy, seeing her put him to sleep as the heat of the day
came on, noting the cheerful content with which she
adapted herself to a simplicity of life unknown to her
three months before, the wonder of the circumstances
which had led to it faded in the regret that it should be
coming to an end. It had been three months of incredible peace and good-will; and to-day the peace and good-
will seemed to strike him all the more keenly because he
knew that in an hour or so at most he must disturb it.
It seemed hard.

But something else began the task for him. About
sunset a sudden flash dazzled his eyes, and ere he grasped
its vividness the walls were rocking silently, and a second
after a roar as of a thousand thunder-claps deafened his
ears. Kate had Sonny in her arms ere he could reach
her, thrusting her away from the high parapet wall,
which, in one already cracked corner, looked as if it must
come down; which did indeed crumble outward, leaving
a jagged gap halfway down its height, the débris falling
with a rattle on the roof of the next house.

But ere the noise ended the vibration had passed, leav-

ing him with relief on his face looking at a great mush-
room of smoke and steam which had shot up into the sky.

" It's the powder factory! " he exclaimed, using Hindustani for Tara's benefit as well, since she had rushed in
from the outer court at the first hint of danger to cling
round his feet. " It is all over now, but it's lucky we
were no nearer."

As he spoke he was wondering if this would make any
difference in Tiddu's plans for the night, since the powder
factory had stood equa-distant between them and the
Delhi gate. He wondered also what had caused the explosion. Not a shell certainly. The factory had purposely been placed at the furthest point from the Ridge.
However, there was a fine supply of powder gone, and,
he hoped, a few mutineers. But Kate's mind had reverted to that other explosion which had been the pro-
logue to the three months of peace and quiet. Was this
one to be the epilogue? A vague dread, a sudden pre-
monition made her ask quickly:

" Can it mean anything serious? Can anything be
the matter, Mr. Greyman? Is anything wrong? "

It was a trifle early, he thought. She might have had
another half hour or so. But this was a good beginning,
or rather a fitting end.

" And you have known this all day? " she said reproachfully when he told her the truth. " How unkind
of you not to tell me! "

" Unkind! " he echoed. " What possible good——"

" I should have known it was the last day—I—I should
have made the—the most of it."

He felt glad of his own impatience of the sentimentality
as he turned away, for in truth the look on her face hit
him hard. It sent him to pace up and down the outer
roof resting till the time for action came. Then he had a
whispered consultation with Tara regarding the dose of
raw opium safe for a child of Sonny's years.

" Are you sure that is not too much? " he asked
anxiously.

Tara looked at the little black pellet she was rolling
gravely. " It is large, Huzoor, but it is for life or death;

and if it was the Huzoor's own son I would give no less."

Once more the remembrance of the still little morsel in Zora's tinsel veil brought an odd compunction; the very possibility of this strange child's death roused greater pain than that certainty had done. He felt unnerved at the responsibility; but Kate, looking up as he rejoined her, held out her hand without a tremor.

"Give it me, please," she said, and her voice was steady also; "he will take it best from me. I have some sugar here."

The child, drowsy already with the near approach of bedtime, was in her lap, and rested its head on her breast, as with her arms still round him her hands disguised the drug.

"It is a very large dose," she said dully. "I knew it must be; that's why I wanted to give it—myself. Sonny! Open your mouth, darling—it's sweet—there—swallow it quick—that's a good Sonnikins."

"You are very brave," he said with a catch in his voice.

She glanced up at him for a second with a sort of scorn in her eyes. "I knew he would take it from me," she replied, and then, shifting the child to an easier position, began to sing in a half voice:

"There is a happy land——"

"Far—farze—away," echoed Sonny contentedly. It was his usual lullaby, chosen because it resembled a native air, beloved of ayahs.

And as she sang and Sonny's eyelids drooped the man watched them both with a tender awe in his heart; and the other woman, crouching in the corner, watched all three with hungry, passionate eyes. Here, in this group of man, woman, and child, without a personal claim on each other, was something new, half incomprehensible, wholly sweet.

"He is asleep now," said Kate after a time. "You had better take him."

He stooped to obey, and she stooped also to leave a long, lingering kiss on the boy's soft cheek. It sent a thrill through the man as he recognized that in giving him the child she had given him more than kisses.

The feeling that it was so made him linger a few minutes afterward at the door with a new sense of his responsibilities toward her to say:

" I wish I had not to leave you alone."

" You will be back directly, and I shall be all right," she said, pausing in her closing of the door, for Tara had already passed down the stair with her bundle.

" Shall I lock it outside? " he began. Tara and he had been used to do so in those first days when they left her.

She laid her hand lightly on his arm. " Don't," she said, " don't get anxious about me again. What can happen in half an hour? "

He heard her slip the catch on the staple, however, before he ran downstairs. He was to take a different road to the Delhi gate from the quiet, more devious alleys which Tara would choose in her character of poor spinner carrying her raw stuff home. She was to await his arrival, to deposit the bundle somewhere close to the third door in the back lane by the cloth merchant's shop, leaving it to him to take inside, as if he were one of the caravan; this plan insuring two things—immunity from notice in the streets, and also in the yard. But, as Tara would be longer than he by a few minutes in reaching the tryst, he purposely went through a bit of the Thunbi Bazaar to hear what he could of the explosion. He was surprised—a trifle alarmed—at the excitement. Crowds were gathered round many of the balconies, talking of spies, swearing that half the court was in league with the Ridge, and that, after all, Abool-Bukr might not have a wild-goose chase.

" There will be naught but slops and slaps for him in *my* information, I'll swear," said one with a laugh. " I'll back old Mother Sobrai to beat off a dozen princes."

" And blows and bludgeons in *mine*," chuckled another. " I chose the house of Bahadur, the single-stick player."

And as, having no more time to lose, he cut across gateward, he saw down an alley a mob surging round Ahsan-Oolah, the physician's, house, and heard a passer-by say, "They have the traitor safe." It made him vaguely uneasy, since he knew that when once the talk turns on hidden things, people, not to be behindhand in gossip, rake up every trivial doubt and wonder.

Still there was a file of bullocks waiting by the cloth merchant's as arranged. And as he passed into the lane a dim figure, scarce seen in the dark, slipped out of the further end. And there was the bundle. He caught it up as if it belonged to him, and after knocking gently at the third door, pushed it open, knowing that he must show no hesitation. He found himself in a sort of out-house or covered entrance, pitch dark save for a faintly lighter square showing an outlet, doubtless into the yard beyond. He moved toward it, and stumbled over some-thing unmistakably upon the floor. A man! He dropped the bundle promptly to be ready in case the sleeper should be a stranger. But there was no move-ment, and he kneeled down to feel if it was Tiddu. A Bunjârah!—that was unmistakable at the first touch—but the limpness was unmistakable too. The man was dead—still warm, but dead! By all that was unlucky!—not Tiddu surely! With the flint and steel in his waist-cloth, he lit a tuft of cotton from the bundle as a torch.

It was Jhungi!—Jhungi, with a knife in his heart!

"Huzoor!" came the familiar creak, as Tiddu, attracted by the sudden light, stole in from the yard be-yond. "Quick! there is no time to lose. Give me the bundle and go back."

"Go back!" echoed Jim Douglas amazed.

"Huzoor! take off the Bunjârah's dress. I have a green turban and shawl here. The Huzoor must go back to the mem at once. There is treachery."

Jim Douglas swore under his breath as he obeyed.

"I know not what, but the mem must not stay there. I heard him boasting before, and just now I caught him prying."

"Who, Jhungi?"

Even at such a moment Tiddu demurred.

"The Huzoor mistakes. It is the miscreant Bhungi—Jhungi is virtuous——"

"You killed him then?" interrupted the hearer, putting the last touch to his disguise.

"What else could I do, Huzoor? I had only my knife. And it is not as if it were—Jhupgi——"

But Jim Douglas was already out of the door, running through the dark, deserted lanes while he dared, since he must walk through the bazaar. And as he ran he told himself that he was a fool to be so anxious. What could go wrong in half an hour?

What indeed!

As he stood five minutes after, staring into the dark emptiness of the roof, he asked himself again and again what could have happened? There had been no answer to his knock; the door had been hasped on the outside, yet the first glance as he entered made him realize that the place was empty of life. And though he had lit the cresset, with a fierce fear at what it might reveal, he could find no trace, even of a struggle. Kate had disappeared! Had she gone out? Impossible. Had Tara heard of the danger, returned, and taken her elsewhere? Possible, but improbable. He passed rapidly down the stairs again. The story below the roof, being reserved for the owner's use on his occasional visits to Delhi, was empty; the occupants of the second floor, pious folk, had fled from the city a day or two before; and when he paused to inquire on the ground floor to know if there had been any disturbance he found the door padlocked outside— sure sign that everyone was out. Oh! why, he thought, had he not padlocked that other door upstairs? He passed out into the street, beginning to realize that his task was over just as he had ceased to gird at it. There was nothing unusual to be seen. The godly folk about were beginning to close their gates for the night, and some paused to listen with an outraged air to the thrummings and drummings from the Princess Farkhoonda's roof. And that was Abool Bukr's voice singing:

" Oh, mistress rare, divine ! "

Then it could scarcely be he, and Kate might have found friends in that quarter, where so many learned folk deemed the slaughter of women unlawful. But there was no use in speculating. He must find Tara first. He paused, however, to inquire from the cobbler at the corner. "Disturbance?" echoed the man. Not much more than usual; the Prince, who had passed in half an hour agone, being perhaps a bit wilder after his wild-goose-chase. Had not the Agha-sahib heard? The wags of the bazaar had taken up the offer made by the Prince, and his servants had sworn they were glad to get him to the Princess', since they had been whacked out of half a dozen houses. He was safe now, however, since when he was of that humor Newâsi Begum never let him go till he was too drunk for mischief.

Then, thought Jim Douglas, it was possible that Jhungi might have given real information; still but one thing was certain—the roof was empty; the dream had vanished into thin air.

He did not know as he passed through the dim streets that their dream was over also, and that John Nicholson stood looking down from the Ridge on the shadowy mass of the town. He had posted in a hundred and twenty miles that day, arriving in time to hear the explosion of the magazine. The city's salute of welcome, as it were, to the man who was to take it.

He had been dining at the Headquarters mess, taciturn and grave, a wet blanket on the jollity, and the Moselle cup, and the fresh cut of cheese from the new Europe shop; and now, when others were calling cheery good-nights as they passed to their tents, he was off to wander alone round the walls, measuring them with his keen, kindly eyes. A giant of a man, biting his lips beneath his heavy brown beard, making his way over the rocks, sheltering in the shadow, doggedly, moodily, lost in thought. He was parceling out his world for conquest, settling already where to prick the bubble.

But, in a way, it was pricked already. For, as he prowled about the Palace walls, a miserable old man, minus even the solace of pulse-feeling and cooling draughts, was dictating a letter to Hâfzan, the woman scribe. A miserable letter, to be sent duly the next day to the Commanders-in-Chief, and forwarded by them to the volunteers of Delhi. A disjointed rambling effusion worthy of the shrunken mind and body which held but a rambling disjointed memory even of the advice given it.

"Have I not done all in my power to please the soldiery?" it ran. "But it is to be deplored that you have, notwithstanding, shown no concern for my life, no consideration for my old age. The care of my health was in the hands of Ahsan-Oolah, who kept himself constantly informed of the changes it underwent. Now there is none to care for me but God, while the changes in my health are such as may not be imagined; therefore the soldiers and officers ought to gratify me and release the physician, so that he may come whenever he thinks it necessary to examine my pulse. Furthermore, the property plundered from his house belonged to the King, therefore it should be traced and collected and conveyed to our presence. If you are not disposed to comply, let me be conveyed to the Kutb shrine and employ myself as a sweeper of the Mosque. And if even this be not acceded I will still relinquish every concern and jump up from my seat. Not having been killed by the English I will be killed by you; for I shall swallow a diamond and go to sleep. Moreover, in the plunder of the physician's house, a small box containing our seal was carried away. No paper, therefore, of a date subsequent to the 7th of August, 1857, bearing our seal, will be valid."

A miserable letter indeed. The dream of sovereignty had come to an end with that salute of welcome to John Nicholson.

BOOK V.

"THERE AROSE A MAN."

CHAPTER I.

FORWARD.

" ARE you here on duty, sir? " asked a brief, imperious voice. Major Erlton, startled from a half dream as he sat listlessly watching the target practice from the Crow's Nest, rose and saluted. His height almost matched the speaker's, but he looked small in comparison with the indescribable air of dominant power and almost arrogant strength in the other figure. It seemed to impress him, for he pulled himself together smartly with a certain confidence, and looked, in truth, every inch a soldier.

" No, sir," he replied as briefly, " on pleasure."

A distinct twinkle showed for a second in General Nicholson's deep-set hazel eyes. " Then go to your bed, sir, and sleep. You look as if you wanted some." He spoke almost rudely; but as he turned on his heel he added in a louder voice than was necessary had he meant the remark for his companion's ear only, " I shall want good fighting men before long, I expect."

If he did, he might reckon on one. Herbert Erlton was not good at formulating his feelings into definite thoughts, but as he went back to the peaceful side of the Ridge he told himself vaguely that he was glad Nicholson had come. He was the sort of a man a fellow would be glad to follow, especially when he was dead-sick and weary of waiting and doing nothing save get killed! Yes! he was a real good sort, and as even the Chaplain had said at mess, they hadn't felt quite so besieged on the

Ridge these last two days since he came. And, by George! he had hit the right nail on the head. A man wasn't much good without sleep.

So, with a certain pride in following the advice, Major Erlton flung himself on his cot and promptly dozed off. In truth he needed rest. Sonny Seymour's safe arrival in camp two nights before, in charge of a Bunjârah, from whom even Hodson had been unable to extract anything—save that the Agha-sahib had forgotten a letter in his hurry, and that the mem was safe, or had been safe—had sent Major Erlton to watch those devilish walls more feverishly than ever. Not that it really mattered whether Kate was alive or dead, he told himself. No! he did not mean that, quite. He would be awfully glad—God! how glad! to know her safe. But it wouldn't alter other things, would not even alter them in regard to her. So, once more he waited for the further news promised him, with a strange indifference, save to the thought that, alive or dead, Kate was within the walls—like another woman—like many women.

And now he was dreaming that he was inside them also, sword in hand.

There seemed some chance of it indeed, men were saying to each other, as they looked after John Nicholson's tall figure as it wandered into every post and picket; asking brief questions, pleased with brief replies. Every now and again pausing, as it were, to come out of his absorption and take a sudden, keen interest in something beyond the great question. As when, passing the tents of the only lady in camp, he saw Sonny, who had been made over to her till he could be sent back to his mother, who had escaped to Meerut, during which brief time he was the plaything of a parcel of subalterns who delighted in him, tinsel cap, anklets, and all. Major Erlton had at first rather monopolized the child, trying to find out something definite from him; but as he insisted that " Miffis Erlton lived up in the 'ky wif a man wif a gween face, and a white face, and a lot of fwowers, and a bit of tring," and spoke familiarly of Tiddu, and Tara, and Soma, without being able to say who they were, the Major had given it up as a bad job, and gone back to the walls. So the subalterns had the child to themselves, and were playing pranks with him as the General passed by.

"Fine little fellow!" he said suddenly. "I like to see children's legs and arms. Up in Bunnoo the babies were just like that young monkey. Real corn-color. I got quite smitten with them and sent for a lot of toys from Lahore. Only I had to bar Lawrence from peg-tops, for I knew I should have got peg-topping with the boys, and that would have been fatal to my dignity as D. C. That is the worst of high estates. You daren't make friends, and you have to make enemies."

The smile which had made him look years younger faded, and he was back in the great problem of his life: how to keep pace with his yoke-fellows, how to scorn consequences and steer straight to independent action, without spoiling himself by setting his seniors and superiors in arms against him. He had never solved it yet. His career had been one long race with the curb on. A year before he had thrown up the game in disgust, and begged to be transferred from the Punjab while he could go with honor, and even his triumphant march Delhi-ward—in which he found disaffection, disobedience, and doubt, and left fear, trembling, and peace—had been marred by much rebuking. So that once, nothing but the inner sense that pin-points ought not to let out the heart's blood, kept him at his post; and but two days before, on the very eve of that hundred-and-twenty mile rush to Delhi, he had written claiming definitely the right of an officer in his position to quarrel with anybody's opinion, and asserting his duty of speaking out, no matter at what risk of giving offense.

And now, a man years younger than those in nominal command,—he was but six-and-thirty,—and holding views diametrically opposed to theirs, he had been sent here, virtually, to take Delhi because those others could not. No wonder, then, that the question how to avoid collision puzzled him. Not because he knew that his appointment was in itself an offense, that some people affected to speak of him still as Mr. Nicholson—that being his real rank; but because he knew in his heart of hearts that at any moment he might do something appalling. Move troops under someone else's command, without a reference, as he had done before, during his career! Then, naturally, there must be ructions. He had a smile for the thought himself. Still, for the present, concord was assured; since until his column arrived, the repose of the lion crouching for a spring was manifestly the only policy; though it might be necessary to wag the tail a bit—to do more than merely forbid sorties and buglings. The fools, for instance, who harrassed the Metcalfe House picket might be shown their mistake and made to understand that, if the Ridge called "time!" for a little decent rest before the final round, it meant to have it. So he passed on his errand to inculcate Headquarters with his decision, leaving Sonny playing with the boys.

Meanwhile one of the garrison, at least, had found the benefit of his keen judgment. Herbert Erlton had passed from dreams of conflict to the real rest of unconscious sleep, oblivious of everything, even those rose-red walls.

. But within them another man, haggard and anxious as he had been, was still allowing himself none in his search for Kate Erlton. Tara, as much at a loss as he, helping him; for though at first she had been relieved at the idea of the mem's disappearance, she had soon realized that the master ran more risk than ever in his reckless determination to find-some trace of the missing woman. And Tiddu, who had returned, helped also. The mem, he said, must have found friends; must be alive. Such a piece of gossip as the discovery and death of an English woman could not have been kept from the Thunbi Bazaar. Then those who had passed from the roof had been calm enough to hasp the door behind them; that did not look like violence. If the Huzoor would only be patient and wait, something would turn up. There were other kindly folk in the city besides himself! But, in the meantime, he would do well to allow Soma to slip into the sulky indifference he semed to prefer, and take no notice of it. It only meant that he, and half the good soldiers in Delhi, were mad with themselves for having chosen the losing side. For with Nikalseyn on the Ridge, what chance had Delhi?

This was rather an exaggerated picture; still it was a fairly faithful presentment of the inward thoughts of many, who, long before this, had begun to ask themselves what the devil they were doing in that galley? Yet there they were, and there they must fight. Soma, however, was doubtful even of that. His heart positively ached as he listened to the tales told in the very heart of Delhi of the man whom other men worshiped—the man who took forts single-handed, and said that, given the powers of a provost-marshal, he would control a disobedient army in two days! The man who yoked bribe-taking tahseeldars into the village well-wheel to draw water for the robbed ryots, and set women of loose virtue, who came into his camp, to cool in muddy tanks. The man who flung every law-book on his office table at his clerks' heads, and then—with a kindly apologetic smile—paused while they replaced them for future use. The man who gave toys to children, and remorselessly hung two abettors of a vile murder, when he could not lay hands on the principal. The man, finally, who flogged those who worshiped him into promising adoration for the future to a very ordinary mortal of his acquaintance! Briefly the hero, the demi-god, who perhaps was neither, but, as Tiddu declared, had simply the greatest gift of all—the gift of making men what he wished them to be. Either way it was gall and wormwood to Soma—hero-worshiper by birth—that his side should have no such colossal figure to follow. So, sulky and sore, he held aloof from both sides, doing his bounden duty to both, and no more. Keeping guards when his fellows took bribes to fight, and agreeing with Tiddu, that since some other besides themselves knew of the roof, it was safer for the master to lock it up, and live for a time elsewhere.

So, all unwittingly, the only chance of finding Kate was lost. For what had happened was briefly this: Five minutes after Jim Douglas had left her, Prince Abool-Bukr, who had kept this *renseignement*—given him by a Bunjârah, who had promised to be in waiting and was

not—to the last, because it was close to the haven where
he would be, had come roystering up the stairs followed
by his unwilling retainers, suggesting that the Most
Illustrious had really better desist from violating seclusion since they were all black and blue already. But,
from sheer devilry and desire to outrage the quarter,
which by its complaints had already brought him into
trouble, the Prince had begun battering at the door.
Kate, running to bar it more securely, saw that the hasp,
carelessly hitched over the staple, was slipping—had
slipped; and had barely time to dash into the inner roof
ere the Prince, unexpectant of the sudden giving way,
tumbled headlong into the outer one. The fall gave
her an instant more, but made him angry; and the end
would have been certain, if Kate, seeing the new-made
gap in the wall before her, had not availed herself of it.
There was a roof not far below she knew; the *débris*
would be on a slope perhaps—the blue-eyed boy had
escaped by the roofs. All this flashed through her, as
by the aid of a stool, which she kicked over in her
scramble, she gained the top of the gap and peered over.
The next instant she had dropped herself down some
four feet, finding a precarious foothold on a sliding
slope of rubble, and still clinging to the wall with her
hands. If no one looked over, she thought breathlessly,
she was safe! And no one did. The general air of
decent privacy alarmed the retainers into remembering
that two of their number had found death their reward
for their master's last escapade in that quarter; so, after
one glance round, they swore the place was empty, and
dragged him off, feebly protesting that it was his last
chance, and he had not bagged a single Christian.

Kate heard the door closed, heard the voices retreat
downstairs, and then set herself to get back over the gap.
It did not seem a difficult task. The slope on which she
hung gave fair foothold, and by getting a good grip on
the brickwork, and perhaps displacing a brick or two in
the crack lower down, as a step, she ought to get up
easily. It was lucky the crack was there, she thought.
In one way, not in another, for, as in her effort she necessarily threw all her weight on the wall, another bit of it

gave way, she fell backward, and so, half covered with
bricks and mud, rolled to the roof below, which was
luckily not more than eight or nine feet down. It was far
enough, however, for the fall to have killed her; but,
though she lay quite unconscious, she was not dead, only
stunned, shaken, confused, unable absolutely to think.
It was almost dawn, indeed, before she realized that her
only chance of getting up again was in calling for help,
and by that time the door of the roof above had been
locked, and there was no one to hear her. The few
square yards of roof on to which she had rolled belonged
to one of those box-like buildings, half-turrets, half-sum-
mer houses, which natives build here, there, and everywhere at all sorts of elevations, until the view of a town
from a topmost roof resembles nothing so much as the
piles of luggage awaiting the tidal train at Victoria.

This particular square of roof belonged to a tiny out-
house, which stood on a long narrow roof belonging in
its turn to an arcaded slip of summer-house standing on
a square, set round by high parapet walls. Quite a staircase of roofs. Her one had had a thatch set against
the wall, but it had fallen in with the weight of bricks and
mortar. Still she might be able to creep between it and
the wall for shelter. And on the slip of roof below,
Indian corn was drying, during this break in the rains.
Rains which had filled a row of water-pots quite full.
Since she could not make those above her hear, she
thought it might be as well to secure herself from absolute starvation, before broad daylight brought life to the
wilderness of roofs around her. So she scrambled down
a rough ladder of bamboo tied with string, and, after a
brief look into the square below, came back with some
parched grain she had found in a basket, and a pot of
water. She would not starve for that day. By this time
it was dawn, and she crept into her shelter, listening
all the while for a sound from above; every now and
again venturing on a call. But there was no answer,
and by degrees it came to her that she must rely on herself only for safety. She was not likely to be disturbed
that day where she was, unless people came to repair
the thatch. And under cover of night she might surely

creep from roof to roof down to some alley. What alley? True, her goal now lay behind her, but these roofs, set at every angle, might lead her far from it. And how was she to know her own stair, her own house, from the outside? She had passed into it in darkness and never left it again. Then what sort of people lived in these houses through which she must creep like a thief? Murderers, perhaps. Still it was her only chance; and all that burning, blistering day, as she crouched between the thatch and the wall, she was bolstering up her courage for the effort. She could see the Ridge clearly from her hiding place. Ah! if she had only the wings of the doves—those purple pigeons which, circling from the great dome of the mosque, came to feast unchecked on the Indian corn. The people below, then, must be pious folk.

It was past midnight and the silence of sleep had settled over the city before she nerved herself to the chance and crept down among the corn. No difficulty in that; but to her surprise, a cresset was still burning in the arcaded veranda below, sending three bars of light across the square through which she must pass. It would be better to wait a while; but an hour slipped by and still the light gleamed into the silence. Perhaps it had been forgotten. The possibility made her creep down the brick ladder, prepared to creep up again if the silence proved deceptive. But what she saw made her pause, hesitating. It was a woman reading from a large book held in a book-rest. The Koran, of course. Kate recognized it at once, for just such another had been part of the necessary furniture of her roof. And what a beautiful face! Tender, refined, charming. Not the face of a murderess, surely? Surely it might be trusted? Those three months behind the veil had made Kate realize the emotionality of the East; its instinctive sympathy with the dramatic element in life. She remembered her sudden impulse in regard to the knife and its effect on Tiddu; she felt a similar impulse toward confidence here. And then she knew that the doors might be locked below, and that her best chance might be to throw herself on the mercy of this woman.

The next moment she was standing full in the light
close to the student, who started to her feet with a faint
cry, gazing almost incredulously at the figure so like her
own, save for the jewels gleaming among the white
draperies.

" Bibi," she faltered.

" I am no bibi," interrupted Kate hurriedly in Hindustani. " I am a Christian—but a woman like yourself—a mother. For the sake of yours—or the sake of
your sons, if you are a mother too—for the sake of what
you love best—save me."

" A Christian! a mem! " In the pause of sheer astonishment the two women stood facing each other, looking
into each other's eyes. Prince Abool-Bukr had been
right when he said that Kate Erlton reminded him of
the Princess Farkhoonda da Zamâni. Standing so,
they showed strangely alike indeed, not in feature, but
in type; in the soul which looked out of the soft dark,
and the clear gray eyes.

" Save you! " The faint echo was lost in a new sound,
close at hand. A careless voice humming a song; a
step coming up the dark stair.

"O mistress rare, divine ! "

God and His Prophet! Abool himself! Newâsi
flung her hands up in sheer horror. Abool! and this
Christian here! The next instant with a fierce " Keep
still," she had thrust Kate into the deepest shadow and
was out to bar the brick ladder with her tall white grace.
She had no time for thought. One sentence beat on her
brain—" for the sake of what you love best, save me! "
Yea! for his sake this strange woman must not be seen—
he must not, should not guess she was there!

" Stand back, kind one, and let me pass," came the
gay voice carelessly. It made Kate shudder back into
further shadow, for she knew now where she was; and
but that she would have to pass those bars of light would
have essayed escape to the roofs again.

But Newâsi stood still as stone on the first step of the
stairs.

" Pass! " she repeated clearly, coldly. " Art mad,

Abool? that thou comest hither with no excuse of drunkenness and alone, at this hour of the night. For shame! "

Why, indeed, she asked herself wildly, had he come? He was not used to do so. Could he have heard? Had he come on purpose? There was a sound as if he retreated a step, and from the dark his voice came with a wonder in it.

" What ails thee, Newâsi? "

" What ails me! " she echoed, " what I have lacked too long. Just anger at thy thoughtless ways. Go——"

" But I have that to tell thee of serious import that none but thou must hear. That which will please thee. That which needs thy kind wise eyes upon it."

" Then let them see it by daylight, not now. I will not, Abool. Stand back, or I will call for help."

The sound of retreat was louder this time, and a muttered curse came with it; but the voice had a trace of anxiety in it now—anxiety and anger.

" Thou dost not mean it, kind one; thou canst not! When have I done that which would make thee need help? Newâsi! be not a fool. Remember it is I, Abool; Abool-Bukr, who has a devil in him at times! "

Did she not know it by this time? Was not that the reason why he must not find this Christian? Why she must refuse him hearing? Though it was true that he had a right to be trusted; in all those long years, when had he failed to treat her tenderly, respectfully? As she stood barring his way, where he had never before been denied entrance, she felt as if she herself could have killed that strange woman for being there, for coming between them.

" Listen, Abool! " she said, stretching out her hands to find his in the dark. " I mean naught, dear, that is unkind. How could it be so between me and thee? But 'tis not wise." She paused, catching her breath in a faint sob. He could not see her face, perhaps if he had, he would have been less relentless.

" Wherefore? Canst not trust thy nephew, fair aunt? "

The sarcasm bit deep.

"Nephew! A truce, Abool, to this foolish tale," she began hotly, when he interrupted her.

"Of a surety, if the Princess Farkhoonda desires it! Yet would Mirza Abool-Bukr still like to know wherefore he is not received?"

His tone sent a thrill of terror through her, his use of the name he hated warned her that his temper was rising—the devil awakening.

"Canst not see, dear," she pleaded, trying to keep the hands he would have drawn from hers—"folk have evil minds."

He gave an ugly laugh. "Since when hast thou begun to think of thy good name, like other women, Newâsi? But if it be so, if all my virtue—and God knows 'tis ill-got—is to go for naught, let it end."

She heard him, felt him turn, and a wild despair surged up in her. Which was worst? To let him go in anger beyond the reach of her controlling hand mayhap—go to unknown evils—or chance this one? Since—since at the worst death might be concealed. God and His Prophet! What a thought! No! she would plead again—she would stoop—she would keep him at any price.

"Listen!" she whispered passionately, leaning toward him in the dark, "dost ask since when I have feared for my good name? Canst not guess?—Abool! what—what does a woman, as I am, fear—save herself—save her own love——"

There was an instant's silence, and then his reckless jeering laugh jarred loud.

"So it has come at last! and there is another woman for kisses. That is an end indeed! Did I not tell thee we should quarrel over it some day? Well, be it so, Princess! I will take my virtue elsewhere."

She stood as if turned to stone, listening to his retreating steps, listening to his nonchalant humming of the old refrain as he passed through the courtyard into the alley. Then, without a word, but quivering with passion, she turned to where Kate cowered, and dragged her by main force to the stairs where, a minute before, she had sacrificed everything for her. No! not for her, for him!

" Go," she said bitterly. " Go! and my curse go with you."

Kate fled before the anger she saw but did not understand. Yet as she flew down the steep stairs she paused involuntarily to listen to the sound—a sound which needed no interpreter as the liquid Persian had done—of a woman sobbing as if her heart would break.

She had no time, however, even for wonder, and the next instant she was out in the alley, turning to the right. For the knowledge that it was the Princess Farkhoonda who had helped her, gave the clew to her position. But the house, the stair? How could she know it? She must try them one after another; since she would know the landing, the door she had so often opened and shut. Still it was perilously near dawn ere she found what she was sure was the right one; but it was padlocked.

They must have gone; gone and left her alone!

For the first time, ghastly, unreasoning fear seized on her; she could have beaten at the door and screamed her claim to be let in. And even when, the rush of terror passed, she sat stupidly on the step, not even wondering what to do next, till suddenly she remembered that she had keys in her pocket. That of the inner padlock, certainly; perhaps of the outer one, also, since Tara had given up using her duplicate altogether.

She had; and five minutes after, having satisfied herself that the roof remained as it was—that it was merely empty for a time—she tried to feel grateful. But the loneliness, the dimness, were too much for her fatigue, her excitement. So once more the sound which needs no interpreter rose on the warm soft night.

It was two days after this that Tiddu held a secret consultation with Soma and Tara. The Agha-sahib, he said, was getting desperate. He was losing his head, as the Huzoors did over women-folk, and he must be got out of the city. It was not as if he did any good by staying in it. The mem was either dead, or safely concealed. There was no alternative, unless, indeed, she had already been passed out to the Ridge. There was talk of that sort among Hodson's spies, and he was going to utilize the fact and persuade the Huzoor to creep out

to the camp and see. Soma could pass him out, and
would not pass him in again; which was fortunate.
Since folk in addition to protecting masters had to make
money, when every other corn-carrier in the place was
coining it by smuggling gold and silver out of the city
for the rich merchants. Tara, with a sudden fierce exultation in her somber eyes, agreed. Let the Huzoor go
back to his own life, she said; let him go to safety, and
leave her free. As for the mem, the master had done
enough for her. And Soma, sulky and lowering with
the dull glow of opium in his brain—for the drug was
his only solace now—swore that Tiddu was right. Delhi
was no place for the master. And once out of it, the
fighting would keep him: he knew him of old. As for
the mem, he would not harm her, as Tara had once suggested he should. That dream was over. The Huzoors
were the true masters; they had men who could lead
men. Not Princes in Cashmere shawls who couldn't
understand a word of what you said, and mere *soubadars*
cocked up, but real *Colonels* and *Generáls.*

The result of this being that on the night of the 11th,
between midnight and dawn, Jim Douglas, with that elation which came to him always at the prospect of action,
prepared to slip out of the sally-port by the Magazine,
disguised as a sepoy. This was to please Soma. To
please Tiddu, however, he wore underneath this disguise
the old staff uniform from the theatrical properties. It
reminded him of Alice Gissing, making him whisper
another " bravo " to the memory of the woman whom
he had buried under the orange-trees in the crimson-
netted shroud made of an officer's scarf.

But Tiddu's remark, that an English uniform would be
the safest, once he was beyond the city, sent sadness flying, in its frank admission that the tide had turned.

Turned, indeed! The certainty came with a great
throb of fierce joy as, half an hour afterward, slipping
past the gardens of Ludlow Castle, he found himself in
the thick of English bayonets, and felt grateful for the
foresight of the old staff uniform. They were on their
way to surprise and take the picket; not to defend but
to attack.

The opportunity was too good to be lost. There was no hurry. He had arranged to remain three days on the Ridge—he might not have another opportunity of a free fair fight.

He had forgotten every woman in the world, everything save the welcome silence before him as he turned and stole through the trees also, sword in hand.

By all that was lucky and well-planned! the picket must be asleep! Not a sound save the faint crackle of stealthy feet almost lost in the insistent quiver of the cicalas. No! there was a challenge at last within a foot or two.

" Who—kum—dar? "

And swift as an echo a young voice beside him came jibingly:

" It's me, Pandy! Take that."

It's me! Just so; me with a vengeance. For the right attack and the left were both well up. There was a short, sharp volley; then the welcome familiar order. A cheer, a clatter, a rush and clashing with the bayonets. It seemed but half a minute before Jim Douglas found himself among the guns slashing at a dazed artilleryman who had a port-fire in his hand. So the artillery on either side never had a chance, and Major Erlton, riding up with the 9th Lancers as the central attack, found that bit of the fighting over. The picket was taken, the mutineers had fled cityward leaving four guns behind them. And against one of these, as the Major rode close to gloat over it, leaned a man whom he recognized at once.

" My God! Douglas," he said, " where—where's Kate?—where's my wife? "

It was rather an abrupt transition of thought, and Jim Douglas, who was feeling rather queer from something, he scarcely knew what, looked up at the speaker doubtfully.

" Oh, it is you, Major Erlton," he said slowly. " I thought—I mean I hoped she was here—if she isn't— why, I suppose I'd better go back."

He took his arm off the gun and half-stumbled forward, when Major Erlton flung himself from his horse and laid hold of him.

" You're hit, man—the blood's pouring from your sleeve.   Here, off with your coat, sharp! "

" I can't think why it bleeds so? " said Jim Douglas feebly, looking down at a clean cut at the inside of the elbow from which the blood was literally spouting.   " It is nothing—nothing at all."

The Major gave a short laugh.   " Take the go out of you a bit, though.   I'll get a tourniquet on sharp, and send you up in a dhooli."

" What an unlucky devil I am! " muttered Jim Douglas to himself, and the Major did not deny it: he was in a hurry to be off again with the party told to clear the Koodsia Gardens.   Which they did successfully before sunrise, when the expedition returned to camp cheering like demons and dragging in the captured guns, on which some of the wounded men sat triumphantly.   It was their first real success since Budli-ke-serai, two months before; and they were in wild spirits.

Even the Doctor, fresh from shaking his head over many a form lifted helplessly from the dhoolis, was jubilant as he sorted Jim Douglas' arm.

" Keep you here ten days or so I should say.   There's always a chance of its breaking out again till the wound is quite healed.   Never mind!   You can go into Delhi with the rest of us, before then."

" Yoicks forward! " cried a wounded lad in the cot close by.   The Doctor turned sharply.

" If you don't keep quiet, Jones, I'll send you back to Meerut.   And you too, Maloney.   I've told you to lie still a dozen times."

" Sure, Docther dear, ye couldn't be so cruel," said a big Irishman sitting at the foot of his bed so as to get nearer to a new arrival who was telling the tale of the fight.   " And me able-bodied and spoiling to be at me wurrk this three days."

" It's a curious fact," remarked the Doctor to Jim Douglas as he finished bandaging him, " the hospital has been twice as insubordinate since Nicholson came in. The men seem to think we are to assault Delhi to-morrow.   But we can't till the siege train comes, of course.   So you may be in at the death! "

Jim Douglas felt glad and sorry in a breath. Finally he told himself he could let decision stand over for a day or two. He must see Hodson first, and find out if the letter he had had from his spies about an Englishwoman, concealed in Delhi, referred to Kate Erlton.

CHAPTER II.

BITS, BRIDLES, SPURS.

THE letter, however, did not refer to Kate; though, curiously enough, the Englishwoman it concerned had been, and still was concealed in an Afghan's house. Kate, then, had not been the only Englishwoman in Delhi. There was a certain consolation in the thought, since what was being done for one person by kindly natives might very well be done for another. Besides, removed as he was now from the fret and strain of actual search, Jim Douglas admitted frankly to Major Hodson that he was right in saying that Mrs. Erlton must either have come to an end of her troubles altogether, or have found friends better able, perhaps, than he to protect her.

Regarding the first possibility also Major Hodson was skeptical. He had hundreds of spies in the city. Such a piece of good luck as the discovery of a Christian must have been noised abroad. They had not mentioned it; he did not, therefore, believe it had occurred. He would, however, inquire, and till the answer came it would be foolish to go back to the city. Jim Douglas admitted this also; but as the days passed, the desire to return increased; especially when Major Erlton came to see him, which he did with dutiful regularity. Jim Douglas could not help admiring him when he stood, stiff and square, thanking him as Englishmen thank their fellows for what they know to be beyond thanks.

" I am sure no one could have done more, and I know I couldn't have done a quarter so much; and I'm grateful," he said awkwardly. Then with the best intentions, born from a real pity for the haggard man who sat on

the edge of his cot looking as men do after a struggle of
weeks with malarial fever, he added, "And the luck has
been a bit against you all the time, hasn't it?"

"As yet, perhaps," replied Jim Douglas, feeling inclined then and there to start cityward, "but the game
isn't over.   When I go back——"

"Hodson says you could do no good," continued the
big man, still with the best intentions.

"I don't agree with him," retorted the other sharply.

"Perhaps not—but—but I wouldn't, if I were you.
Or—rather—*I* should of course—only—you see it is
different for me.   She——"   Major Erlton paused, finding it difficult to explain himself.   The memory of that
last letter he had written to Kate was always with him,
making him feel she was not, in a way, his wife.   He had
never regretted it.   He had scarcely thought what would
happen if she came back from the dead, as it were, to
answer it; for he hated thought.   Even now the complexity of his emotions irritated him, and he broke
through them almost brutally.   "She was my wife, you
see.   But you had nothing to do with it; so you had
better leave it alone.   You've done enough already.
And as I said before, I'm grateful."

So he had stalked away, leaving his hearer frowning.
It was true.   The luck had been against him.   But what
right had it to be so?   Above all, what right had that big
brutal fellow to say so?   There he was going off to win
more distinction, no doubt.   He would end by getting
the Victoria Cross, and confound him! from what people
said of him, he would well deserve it.

While he?   Even these two days had brought his
failure home to him.   And yet he told himself, that if he
had failed to save one Englishwoman, others had failed
to save hundreds.   Fresh as he was to the facts, they
seemed to him almost incredible.   As he wandered round
the Ridge inspecting that rear-guard of graves, or sat
talking to some of the thousand-and-odd sick and
wounded in hospital, listening to endless tales of courage,
pluck, sheer dogged resistance, he realized at what a terrible cost that armed force, varying from three to six
thousand men, had simply clung to the rocks and looked

at the city. There seemed enough heroism in it to have removed mountains; and coming upon him, not in the monotonous sequence of day-to-day experience, but in a single impression, the futility of it left him appalled. So did the news of the world beyond Delhi, heard, reliably, for the first time. Briefly, England was everywhere on her defense. It seemed to him as if from that mad dream of conquest within the city he had passed to as strange a dream of defeat. And why? The fire, unchecked at first, had blazed up with fresh fuel in place after place and left?—Nothing. Not a single attempt to wrest the government of the country from us; not even an organized resistance, when once the order to advance had been given. Had there been some mysterious influence abroad making men blind to the truth?

It was about to pass away if there had been, he felt, when on the 14th, he watched John Nicholson re-enter the Ridge at the head of his column. And many others felt the same, without in any way disparaging those who for long months of defense had borne the burden and heat of the day. They simply saw that Fate had sent a new factor into the problem, that the old order was changing. The defense was to be attack.

And why not, with that reinforcement of fine fighting men? Played in by the band of the 8th, amid cheering and counter-cheering, which almost drowned the music, it seemed fit—as the joke ran—if not to face hell itself, at any rate to take *Pandymonium*. The 52d Regiment looked like the mastiff to which its leader had likened it. The 2d Sikhs were admittedly the biggest fellows ever seen. The wild Mooltânee Horse sat their lean Beloochees with the loose security of seat which tells of men born to the saddle.

Jim Douglas noted these things like his fellows; but what sent that thrill of confidence through him was the look on many a face, as at some pause or turn it caught a glimpse of the General's figure. It was that heroic figure itself, seen for the first time, riding ahead of all with no unconsciousness of the attention it attracted! but with a self-reliant acceptance of the fact—as far from modesty as it was from vanity—that here rode John

Nicholson ready to do what John Nicholson could do. But in the pale face, made paler by the darkness of the beard, there was more than this. There was an almost languid patience as if the owner knew that the men around him said of him, " If ever there is a desperate deed to do in India, John Nicholson is the man to do it," and was biding his time to fulfill their hopes.

The look haunted Jim Douglas all day, stimulating him strangely. Here was a man, he felt, who was in the grip of Fate, but who gave back the grip so firmly that his Fate could not escape him. Gave it back frankly, freely, as one man might grip another's hand in friendship. And then he smiled, thinking that John Nicholson's hand-clasp would go a long way in giving anyone a help over a hard stile. If he had had a lead-over like that after the smash came; if even now—— Idle thoughts, he told himself; and all because the picturesqueness of a man's outward appearance had taken his fancy, his imagination. For all he knew, or was ever likely to know——

He had been sitting idly on the edge of his cot in the tiny tent Major Erlton had lent him, having in truth nothing better to do, and now a voice from the blaze and blare of the heat and light outside startled him.

" May I come in—John Nicholson? "

He almost stammered in his surprise; but without waiting for more than a word the General walked in, alone. He was still in full uniform; and surely no man could become it more, thought Jim Douglas involuntarily.

" I have heard your story, Mr. Douglas," he began in a sonorous but very pleasant voice. " It is a curious one. And I was curious to see you. You must know so much." He paused, fixed his eyes in a perfectly unembarassed stare on his host's face, then said suddenly, with a sort of old-fashioned courtesy: " Sit you down again, please; there isn't a chair, I see; but the cot will stand two of us. If it doesn't it will be clearly my fault." He smiled kindly. " Wounded too—I didn't know that."

" A scratch, sir," put in his hearer hastily, fighting shy even of that commiseration. " I had a little fever in the city; that is all."

The bright hazel eyes, with a hint of sunlight in them, took rather an absent look. " I should like to have done it myself. I've tried that sort of thing; but they always find me out."

" I fancy you must be rather difficult to disguise," began Jim Douglas with a smile, when John Nicholson plunged straight into the heart of things.

" You must know a lot I want to know. Of course I've seen Hodson and his letters; but this is different. First: Will the city fight? "

" As well as it knows how, and it knows better than it did."

" So I fancied. Hodson said not. By the way, he told me that you declared his Intelligence Department was simply perfect. And his accounts—I mean his information—wonderfully accurate."

" I did, indeed, sir," replied Jim Douglas, smiling again.

Nicholson gave him a sharp look. " And he is a wonderfully fine soldier too, sir; one of the finest we have. Wilson is sending him out this afternoon to punish those Rânghars at Rohtuck. I don't know why I should present you with this information, Mr. Douglas? "

" Don't you, sir? " was the cool reply; " I think I do. Major Hodson may have his faults, sir, but the Ridge couldn't do without him. And I'm glad to hear he is going out. It is time we punished those chaps; time we got some grip on the country again."

The General's face cleared. " Hm," he said, " you don't mince matters; but I don't think we lost much grip in the Punjâb. And as for punishments! Do you know over two thousand have been executed already? "

" I don't, sir; though I knew Sir John's hand was out. But if you'll excuse me, we don't want the hangings now —they can come by-and-by. We want to lick them— show them we are not really in a blind funk."

" You use strong language too, sir—very strong language."

" I did not say we *were* in one——" began Jim Douglas eagerly, when a voice asking if General Nicholson were within interrupted him.

" He is," replied the sonorous voice calmly. " Come in, Hodson, and I hope you are prepared to fight." The bright hazel eyes met Jim Douglas' with a distinct twinkle in them; but Major Hodson entering—a perfect blaze of scarlet and fawn and gold, loose, lank, lavish—gave the speech a different turn.

" I hope you'll excuse the intrusion, sir," he said saluting, as it were, loudly, " but being certain I owed this piece of luck to your kind offices, I ventured to follow you. And as for the fighting, sir, trust Hodson's Horse to give a good account of itself."

" I do, Major, I do," replied Nicholson gravely, despite the twinkle, " but at present I want you to fight Mr. Douglas for me. He suggests we are all in a blind funk."

With anyone else Jim Douglas might have refused this cool demand, for it was little else, that he should defend his statement against a man who in himself was a refutation of it, who was a type of the most reckless, dare-devil courage and dash; but the thought of that umpire, ready to give an overwhelming thrust at any time, roused his temper and pugnacity.

" I'm not conscious of being in one myself," said the Major, turning with a swing and a brief " How do, Douglas." He was the most martial of figures in the last-developed uniform of the Flamingoes, or the Ring-tailed Roarers, or the *Aloo Bokhâra's*, as Hodson's levies were called indiscriminately during their lengthy process of dress evolution. " And what is more, I don't understand what you mean, sir! "

" General Nicholson does, I think," replied the other. " But I will go further than I did, sir;" he added, facing the General boldly: " I only said that the natives thought we were in a blind funk. I now assert that they had a right to say so. We never stirred hand or foot for a whole month."

" Oh! I give you in Meerut," interrupted Hodson hastily. " It was pitiable. Our leaders lost their heads."

" Not only our leaders. We all lost them. From that moment to this it seems to me we have never been calm."

" Calm! " echoed Hodson disdainfully. " Who wants
to be calm? Who would be calm with those massacred
women and children to avenge."

" Exactly so. The horrors of those ghastly murders
got on our nerves, and no wonder. We exaggerated the
position from the first; we exaggerate the dangers of it
now."

" Of taking Delhi, you mean? " interrupted Nicholson
dryly.

Jim Douglas smiled. " No, sir! Even you will find
that difficult. I meant the ultimate danger to our
rule——"

" There you mistake utterly," put in Hodson magnificently. " We mean to win—we admit no danger. There
isn't an Englishman, or, thank Heaven, an Englishwoman——"

" Is the crisis so desperate that we need levy the
ladies? " asked his adversary sarcastically. " Personally
I want to leave them out of the question as much as I
can. It is their intrusion into it which has done the mischief. I don't want to minimize these horrors; but if
we could forget those massacres——"

" Forget them! I hope to God every Englishman
will remember them when the time comes to avenge
them! Ay! and make the murderers remember them,
too."

" If I had them in my power to-day," put in the
sonorous voice, " and knew I was to die to-morrow, I
would inflict the most excruciating tortures I could think
of on them with an easy conscience."

" Bravo! sir," cried Hodson, " and I'd do executioner
gladly."

John Nicholson's face flinched slightly. " There is
generally a common hangman, I believe," he said; then
turned on Jim Douglas with bent brows: "And you, sir? "

" I would kill them, sir; as I would kill a mad dog in
the quickest way handy; as I'd kill every man found with
arms in his hands. Treason is a worse crime than murder to us now; and by God! if I tortured anyone it would
be the men who betrayed the garrison at Cawnpore. Yet
even there, in our only real collapse, what has happened?

It is reoccupied already—the road to it is hung with dead bodies. Havelock's march is one long procession of success. Yet we count ourselves beleaguered. Why? I can't understand it! Where has an order to charge, to advance boldly, met with a reverse? It seems to me that but for these massacres, this fear for women and children, we could hold our own gayly. Look at Lucknow——"

"Yes, Lucknow," assented Hodson savagely. "Sir Henry, the bravest, gentlest, dead! Women and children pent up—by Heaven! it's sickening to think what may have happened."

John Nicholson shot a quick glance at Jim Douglas. "It proves my contention," said the latter. "Think of it! Fifteen hundred, English and natives, in a weak position with not even a palisade in some places between them and five times their number of trained soldiers backed by the wildest, wickedest, wantonest town rabble in India! What does it mean? Make every one of the fifteen hundred a paladin, and, by Heaven! they are heroes. Still, what does it mean?"

He spoke to the General, but he was silent.

"Mean?" echoed Hodson. "Palpably that the foe is contemptible. So he is. Pandy can't fight——"

"He fought well enough for us in the past. I know my regiment——" Jim Douglas caught himself up hard. "I believe they will fight for us again. The truth is that half, even of the army, does not want to fight, and the country does not mean fight at all."

"Delhi?" came the dry voice again.

"Delhi is exceptional. Besides, it can do nothing else now. Remember we condemned it, unheard, on the 8th of June."

"I told you that before, sir; didn't I?" put in Hodson quickly. "If we had gone in on the 11th, as I suggested."

"You wouldn't have succeeded," replied Jim Douglas coolly. Nicholson rose with a smile.

"Well, we are going to succeed now. So, good-luck in the meantime, Hodson. Put bit and bridle on the Rånghars. Show them we can't have 'em disturbing the public peace, and kicking up futile rows. Eh—Mr. Douglas?"

"No fear, sir!" said Hodson effusively. "The Ring-tailed Roarers are not in a blind funk. I only wish that I was as sure that the politicals will keep order when we've made it. I had to do it twice over at Bhâgput. And it is hard, sir, when one has fagged horses and men to death, to be told one has exceeded orders——"

"If you served under me, Major Hodson," said the General with a sudden freeze of formality, "that would be impossible. My instructions are always to do everything that can be done."

Jim Douglas felt that he could well believe it, as with a regret that the interview was over, he held the flap of the tent aside for the imperial figure to pass out. But it lingered in the blaze of sunshine after Major Hodson had jingled off.

"You are right in some things, Mr. Douglas," said the sonorous voice suddenly: "I'd ask no finer soldiers than some of those against us. By and by, unless I'm wrong, men of their stock will be our best war weapons; for, mind you, war is a primitive art and needs a primitive people. And the country isn't against us. If it were, we shouldn't be standing here. It is too busy plowing, Mr. Douglas; this rain is points in our favor. As for the women and children—poor souls"—his voice softened infinitely—"they have been in our way terribly; but —we shall fight all the better for that, by and by. Meanwhile we have got to smash Delhi. The odds are bigger than they were first. But Baird Smith will sap us in somehow, and then——" He paused, looking kindly at Jim Douglas, and said, "You had better stop and go in with—with the rest of us."

"I think not, sir——"

"Why? Because of that poor lady? Woman again —eh?"

"In a way; besides, I really have nothing else to do."

John Nicholson looked at him for a moment from head to foot; then said sharply:

"I didn't know, sir. I give my personal staff plenty of work."

For an instant the offer took his hearer's breath away, and he stood silent.

" I'm afraid not, sir," he said at last, though from the first he had known what his answer would be. " I—I can't, that's the fact. I was cashiered from the army fifteen years ago."

General Nicholson stepped back, with sheer anger in his face. " Then what do you mean, sir, by wearing Her Majesty's uniform? "

Jim Douglas looked down hastily on old Tiddu's staff properties, which he had quite forgotten. They had passed muster in the darkness of the tent, but here, in the sunlight, looked inconceivably worn, and shabby, and unreal. He smiled rather bitterly; then held out his sleeve to show the braiding.

" It's a general's coat, sir," he said defiantly. " God knows what old duffer it belonged to; but I might have worn it first- instead of second-hand, if I hadn't been a d——d young fool."

The splendid figure drew itself together formally, but the other's pride was up too, and so for a minute the two men faced each other honestly, Nicholson's eyes narrowing under their bent brows.

" What was it? A woman, I expect."

" Perhaps. I don't see that it matters."

A faint smile of approval rather took from the sternness of the military salute. " Not at all. That ends it, of course."

" Of course."

Not quite; for ere Jim Douglas could drop the curtain between himself and that brilliant, successful figure, it had turned sharply and laid a hand on his shoulder. A curiously characteristic hand—large, thin, smooth, and white as a woman's, with a grip in it beyond most men's.

" You have a vile habit of telling the truth to superior officers, Mr. Douglas. So have I. Shake hands on it."

With that hand on his shoulder, that clasp on his, Jim Douglas felt as if he were in the grip of Fate itself, and following John Nicholson's example, gave it back frankly, freely. So, suddenly the whole face before him melted into perfect friendliness. " Stick to it, man—stick to it!

Save that poor lady—or—or kill somebody. It's what we are all doing. As for the rest "—the smile was almost boyish—" I may get the sack myself before the general's coat. I'm insubordinate enough, they tell me—but I shall have taken Delhi first. So—so good-luck to you! "

As he walked away, he seemed to the eyes watching him bigger, more king-like, more heroic than ever; perhaps because they were dim with tears. But as Jim Douglas went off with a new cheerfulness to see Hodson's Horse jingle out on their lesson of peace, he told himself that the old scoundrel, Tiddu, had once more been right. Nikalseyn had the Great Gift. He could take a man's heart out and look at it, and put it back sounder than it had been for years. He could put his own heart into a whole camp and make it believe it was its own.

Such a clattering of hoofs and clinking of bits and bridles had been heard often before, but never with such gay light-heartedness. Only two days before a lesson had been given to the city. There had been no more harrassing of pickets at night. Now the arm of the law was going coolly to reach out forty miles. It was a change indeed. And more than Jim Douglas watched the sun set red on the city wall that evening with a certain content in their hearts. As for him, he seemed still to feel that grip, and hear the voice saying, " Stick to it, man, stick to it! Save that poor lady or kill somebody. It's what we are all doing."

He sat dreaming over the whole strange dream with a curious sense of comradeship and sympathy through it all, until the glow faded and left the city dark and stern beneath the storm-clouds which had been gathering all day.

Then he rose and went back to his tent cheerfully. He would run no needless risks; he would not lose his head; but as soon as the doctors said it was safe, he would find and save Kate, or—*kill somebody.* That was the whole duty of man.

Kate, however, had already been found, or rather she had never been lost; and when Tara, a few hours after Jim Douglas slipped out of the city, had gone to the roof to fetch away her spinning wheel, and finding the door padlocked on the inside, had in sheer bewilderment tried the effect of a signal knock, Kate had let her in as if, so poor Tara told herself, it was all to begin over again.

All over again, even though she had spent those few hours of freedom in a perfect passion of purification, so that she might return to her saintship once more.

The gold circlets were gone already, her head was shaven, the coarse white shroud had replaced the crimson scarf. Yet here was the mem asking for the Huzoor, and setting her blood on fire with vague jealousies.

She squatted down almost helplessly on the floor, answering all Kate's eager questions, until suddenly in the midst of it all she started to her feet, and flung up her arms in the old wild cry for righteousness, " I am suttee! before God! I am suttee! "

Then she had said with a gloomy calm, " I will bring the mem more food and drink. But I must think. Tiddu is away; Soma will not help. I am alone; but I am suttee."

Kate, frightened at her wild eyes, felt relieved when she was left alone, and inclined not to open the door to her again. She could manage, she told herself, as she had managed, for a few days, and by that time Mr. Greyman would have come back. But as the long hours dragged by, giving her endless opportunity of thought, she began to ask herself why he should come back at all. She had not realized at first that he had escaped, that he was safe; that he was, as it were, quit of her. But he was, and he must remain so. A new decision, almost a content, came to her with the suggestion. She was busy in a moment over details. To begin with, no news must be sent. Then, in case he were to return, she must leave the roof. Tara might do so much for her, especially if it was made clear that it was for the master's benefit. But Tara might never return. There had been that in her manner which hinted at such a possibility, and the stores she had brought in had been unduly lavish. In that case, Kate told herself, she would creep out some night, go back to the Princess Farkhoonda, and see if she could not help. If not, there was always the alternative of ending everything by going into the streets boldly and declaring herself a Christian. But she would appeal to these two women first.

And as she sat resolving this, the two women were cursing her in their inmost hearts. For there had been no bangings of drums or thrumming of *sutâras* on Newâsi's roof these three days. Abool-Bukr had broken away from her kind, detaining hand, and gone back to the intrigues of the Palace. So the Mufti's quarter benefited in decent quiet, during which the poor Princess began that process of weeping her eyes out, which left her blind at last. But not blind yet. And so she sat swaying gracefully before the book-rest, on which lay the Word of her God, her voice quavering sometimes over the monotonous chant, as she tried to distill comfort to her own heart from the proposition that " He is Might and Right."

And far away in another quarter of the town Tara, crouched up before a mere block of stone, half hidden in flowers, was telling her beads feverishly. " *Râm-Râm-Sita-Râm!* " That was the form she used for a whole tragedy of appeal and aspiration, remorse, despair, and hope. And as she muttered on, looking dully at the little row of platters she had presented to the shrine that morning—going far beyond necessity in her determination to be heard—the groups of women coming in to lay a fresh chaplet among the withered ones and give a " jow " to the deep-toned bell hung in the archway in order to attract the god's attention to their offering, paused to whisper among themselves of her piety. While more than once a widow crept close to kiss the edge of her veil humbly.

It was balm indeed! It was peace. The mem might starve, she told herself fiercely, but she would be suttee. After all the strain, and the pain, and the wondering ache at her heart, she had come back to her own life. This she understood. Let the Huzoors keep to their own. This was hers.

The sun danced in motes through the branches of the peepul tree above the little shrine, the squirrels chirruped

among them, the parrots chattered, sending a rain of soft
little figs to fall with a faint sound on the hard stones, and
still Tara counted her beads feverishly.

"*Râm-Râm-Sita-Râm!   Râm-Râm-Sita-Râm!*"

"Ari! sisters! she is a saint indeed.   She was here at
dawn and she prays still," said the women, coming in the
lengthening shadows with odd little bits of feastings.   A
handful of cocoa-nut chips, a platter of flour, a dish of
curds, or a dab of butter.

"*Râm-Râm-Sita-Râm!*"

And all the while poor Tara was thinking of the
Huzoor's face, if he ever found out that she had left the
mem to starve.   It was almost dark when she stood up,
abandoning the useless struggle, so she waited to see the
sacred Circling of the Lights and get her little sip of holy
water before she went back to her perch among the pigeons, to put on the crimson scarf and the gold circlets
again.   Since it was hopeless trying to be a saint till she
had done what she had promised the Huzoor she would
do.   She must go back to the mem first.

But Kate, opening the door to her with eyes a-glitter
and a whole cut-and-dried plan for the future, almost
took her breath away, and reduced her into looking at
the Englishwoman with a sort of fear.

"The mem will be suttee too," she said stupidly, after
listening a while.   "The mem will shave her head and
put away her jewels!   The mem will wear a widow's
shroud and sweep the floor, saying she comes from Bengal to serve the saint?"

"I do not care, Tara, how it is done.   Perhaps you
may have a better plan.   But we must prevent the master from finding me again.   He has done too much for
me as it is; you know he has," replied Kate, her eyes
shining like stars with determination.   "I only want you
to save him; that is all.   You may take me away and kill
me if you like; and if you won't help me to hide, I'll go
out into the streets and let them kill me there.   I will not
have him risk his life for me again."

"*Râm-Râm-Sita-Râm!*" said Tara under her breath.
That settled it, and at dawn the next day Tara stood in
her odd little perch above the shrine among the pigeons,

looking down curiously at the mem who, wearied out by her long midnight walk through the city and all the excitement of the day, had dozed off on a bare mat in the corner, her head resting on her arm. Three months ago Kate could not have slept without a pillow; now, as she lay on the hard ground, her face looked soft and peaceful in sheer honest dreamless sleep. But Tara had not slept; that was to be told from the anxious strain of her eyes. She had sat out since she had returned home, on her two square yards of balcony in the waning moonlight, looking down on the unseen shrine, hidden by the tall peepul tree whose branches she could almost touch.

Would the mem really be suttee? she had asked herself again and again. Would she do so much for the master? Would she—would she really shave her head? A grim smile of incredulity came to Tara's face, then a quick, sharp frown of pain. If she did, she must care very much for the Huzoor. Besides, she had no right to do it! The mems were never suttee. They married again many times. And then this mem was married to someone else. No! she would never shave her head for a strange man. She might take off her jewels, she might even sweep the floor. But shave her head? Never!

But supposing she did?

The oddest jumble of jealousy and approbation filled Tara's heart. So, as the yellow dawn broke, she bent over Kate.

"Wake, mem sahib!" she said, "wake. It is time to prepare for the day. It is time to get ready."

Kate started up, rubbing her eyes, wondering where she was; as in truth she well might, for she had never been in such a place before. The long, low slip of a room was absolutely empty save for a reed mat or two; but every inch of it, floor, walls, ceiling, was freshly plastered with mud. That on the floor was still wet, for Tara had been at work on it already. Over each doorway hung a faded chaplet, on each lintel was printed the mark of a bloody hand, and round and about, in broad finger-marks of red and white, ran the eternal *Râm-Râm-Sita-Râm* in Sanskrit letterings. In truth, Tara's knowledge of secular and religious learning was strictly confined to this sentence. There was a faint smell of incense in the room, rising from a tiny brazier sending up a blue spiral flame of smoke before a two-inch high brass idol with an elephant's head which sat on a niche in the wall. It represented Eternal Wisdom. But Kate did not know this. Nor in a way did Tara. She only knew it was Guneshjee. And outside was the yellow dawn, the purple pigeons beginning to coo and sidle, the quivering hearts of the peepul leaves.

" I have everything ready for the mem," began Tara hurriedly, " if she will take off her jewels."

" You must pull this one open for me, Tara," said Kate, holding out her arm with the gold bangle on it. " The master put it on for me, and I have never had it off since."

Tara knew that as well as she. Knew that the master must have put it on, since *she* had not. Had, in fact, watched it with jealous eyes over and over again. And there was the mem without it, smiling over the scantiness and the intricacies of a coarse cotton shroud.

" There is the hair yet," said Tara with quite a catch in her voice; " if the mem will undo the plaits, I will go round to the old poojârnis and get the loan of her razor—she only lives up the next stair."

" We shall have to snip it off first," said Kate quite eagerly, for, in truth, she was becoming interested in her own adventures, now that she had, as it were, the control over them. " It is so long." She held up a tress as she spoke. It was beautiful hair; soft, wavy, even, and the dye—unrenewed for days—had almost gone, leaving the coppery sheen distinct.

" She would never cut it off! " said Tara to herself as she went for the razor. No woman would ever shave her head willingly. Why! when she had had it done for the first time, she had screamed and fought. Her mother-in-law had held her hands, and——

She paused at the door as she re-entered, paralyzed by what she saw. Kate had found the knife Tara used for her limited cooking, and, seated on the ground cheerfully, was already surrounded by rippling hair which she had cut off by clubbing it in her hand and sawing away as a groom does at a horse's tail.

Tara's cry made her pause. The next moment the Rajpootni had snatched the knife from her and flung it one way, the razor another, and stood before her with blazing eyes and heaving breast.

"It is foolishness!" she said fiercely. "The mems cannot be suttee. I will not have it."

Kate stared at her. "But I must——" she began.

"There is no must at all," interrupted Tara superbly; "I will find some other way." And then she bent over quickly, and Kate felt her hands upon her hair. "There is plenty left," she said with a sigh of relief. "I will plait it up so that no one will see the difference."

And she did. She put the gold bangle on again also, and by dawn the next day Kate found herself once more installed as a screened woman; but this time as a Hindoo lady under a vow of silence and solitude in the hopes of securing a son for her lord through the intercession of old Anunda, the Swâmi.

"I have told Sri Anunda," said Tara with a new respect in her manner. "I had to trust someone. And he is as God. He would not hurt a fly." She paused, then went on with a tone of satisfaction, "But he says the mem could not have been suttee, so that foolishness is well over."

"But what is to be done next, Tara?" asked Kate, looking in astonishment round the wide old garden, arched over by tall forest trees, and set round with high walls, in which she found herself. In the faint dawn she could just see glimmering straight paths parceling it out into squares; and she could hear the faint tinkle of the water runnels. "I can't surely stop here."

"The mem will only have to keep still all day in the darkest corner with her face to the wall," said Tara. "Sri Anunda will do the rest. And when Soma returns he must take the mem away before the thirty regiments come and the trouble begins."

"Thirty regiments!" echoed Kate, startled.

"He and others have gone out to see if it is true. They say so in the Palace; but it is full of lies," said Tara indifferently.

It was indeed. More than ever. But they began to

need confirmation, and so there was big talk of action, and jingling of bits and bridles and spurs in the city as well as in the camp.   They were to intercept the siege train from Firozpur; they were to get round to the rear of the Ridge and overwhelm it.   They were to do everything save attack it in face.

And, meanwhile, other people besides Soma and such-like Sadducean sepoys had gone out to find the thirty regiments, and secret scouts from the Palace were hunting about for someone to whom they might deliver a letter addressed

" To the Officers, Subadars, Chiefs, and others of the
    whole military force coming from the Bombay Presi-
    dency:
    " To the effect that the statement of the defeat of the
Royal troops at Delhi is a false and lying fabrication con-
trived by contemptible infidels—the English.   The true
story is that nearly eighty or ninety thousand organized
Military Troops, and nearly ten or fifteen thousand regular and other Cavalry, are now here in Delhi.   The
troops are constantly engaged, night and day, in attacks
on the infidels, and have driven back their batteries from
the Ridge.   In three or four days, please God, the whole
Ridge will be taken, when every one of the base unbe-
lievers will be sent to hell.   You are, therefore, on seeing
this order, to use all endeavors to reach the Royal Presence, so, joining the Faithful, give proofs of zeal, and
establish your renown.   Consider this imperative."

But though they hunted high and low, east, north, south, and west, the Royal scouts found no one to receive the order.   So it came back to Delhi, damp and pulpy; for the rains had begun again, turning great tracts of country into marsh and bog, and generally wetting the blankets in which the sepoys kept guard sulkily.

CHAPTER III.

THE BEGINNING OF THE END.

THEY drenched Kate Erlton also, despite the arcaded trees above her corner as she sat with her face to the wall in the wide old garden. At first her heart beat at each step on the walk behind her, but she soon realized that she was hidden by her vow, happed about from the possibility of intrusion by her penance. But not many steps came by her; they kept chiefly to the other end of the garden where Sri Anunda was to be found. It was a curious experience. There was a yard of two of thatch, screened by matting and suported by bamboos, leaning not far off against the wall; and into this she crept at night to find the indulgence of a dry blanket. At first she felt inclined to seek its shelter when the rain poured loudly on the leaves above her and fell thence in big blobs, making a noise like the little ripe figs when the squirrels shook them down; but the remembrance that such women as Tara performed like vows cheerfully kept her steady. And after a day or two she often started to find it was already noon or dusk, the day half gone or done. Time slipped by with incredible swiftness in watching the squirrels and the birds, in counting the raindrops fall from a peepul leaf. And what a strange peace and contentment the life brought! As she sat after dark in the thatch, eating the rice and milk and fruit which Tara brought her stealthily, she felt, at times, a terrified amaze at herself. If she ever came through the long struggle for life, this surely would be the strangest part of the dream. Tara, indeed, used to remark with a satisfied smile that though the mem could not of course be suttee, still she did very well as a devoted and repentant wife. Sri Anunda could never have had a better penitent. And then, in reply to Kate's curious questions, she would say that Sri Anunda was a Swâmi. If the mem once saw and spoke to him she would know what that meant. He had lived in the garden for fifteen years. Not as a penance. A Swâmi needed no penance as men and women did; for he was not a man. Oh, dear no! not a man at all.

So Kate, going on this hint of inhumanity, and guided by her conventional ideas of Hindoo ascetics, imagined a monstrosity, and felt rather glad than otherwise that Sri Anunda kept out of her way.

She was eager also to know how long she might have to stay in his garden. The vow, Tara said, lasted for fifteen days. Till then no one would question her right to sit and look at the wall; and by that time Soma would have returned, and a plan for getting the mem away to the Ridge settled. For the master was evidently not going to return to the city; perhaps he had forgotten the mem? Kate smiled at this, drearily, thinking that indeed he might; for he might be dead. But even this uncertainty about all things, save that she sat and watched the squirrels and the birds, had ceased to disturb her peace.

As a matter of fact, however, he was thinking of her more than ever, and with a sense of proprietorship that was new to him. Here, by God's grace, was the one woman for him to save; the somebody to kill, should he fail, needing no selection. There were enough enemies and to spare within the walls still, even though they had been melting away of late. But a new one had come to the Ridge itself, which, though it killed few, sapped steadily at the vigor of the garrison. This was the autumnal fever, bad at Delhi in all years, worse than usual in this wet season, counterbalancing the benefit of the coolness and sending half a regiment to hospital one day and letting them out of it the next, sensibly less fit for arduous work. It claimed Jim Douglas, already weakened by it, and made his wound slow of healing.

" You haven't good luck certainly," said Major Erlton, finding him with chattering teeth taking quinine dismally. " I don't know how it is, but though I'm a lot thinner, this life seems to suit me. I haven't felt so fit for ages."

He had not been so fit, in truth. It was a healthier, simpler life than he had led for many a long year; and ever since John Nicholson had bidden him go back to his tent and sleep, even the haggardness had left his face;

the restlessness having been replaced by an eager certainty of success. He was coming steadily to the front, too, so the Ridge said, since Nicholson had taken him up. And he had well deserved this, since there was not a better soldier; cool, stubborn, certain to carry out orders. The very man, in short, whom men like the General wanted; and if he stayed to the finish he would have a distinguished career before him.

But Herbert Erlton himself never thought of this; he hated thought instinctively, and of late had even given up thinking of the city. He never sat and watched the rose-red walls now. Perhaps because he was too busy. So he left that to Jim Douglas, who had nothing else to do, while he went about joyously preparing to accompany Nicholson in his next lesson of law and order.

For in the city it was becoming more and more difficult every day to make the lies pass muster, even in the Palace; and so, in despair, the four Commanders-in-Chief for once had laid their heads together and concocted a plan for intercepting the siege train from Ferozpur. So it was necessary that they should be taught the futility of such attempts. Not that even the Palace people really believed them possible. How could they? when almost every day, now, letters came to the Ridge from some member or another of the Royal family asking effusively how he could serve the English cause. Only the old King, revising his lists of precedence, listening still to brocaded bags, taking cooling draughts, making couplets, being cozened by the Queen, and breathed upon by Hussan Askuri, hovered between the policy of being the great Moghul and a poor prisoner in the hands of fate. But the delights of the former were too much for him as a rule, and he would sit and finger the single gold coin which had come as a present from Oude as if he were to have the chance of minting millions with a similar inscription.

" Bahâdur Shâh Ghâzee has struck upon gold the coin of Victory."

Even in its solitary grandeur it had, in truth, a surpassing dignity of its own in the phrase—" struck upon gold the coin of Victory." So, looking at it, he forgot that it was a mere sample, sent, as the accompanying brocaded bag said, with a promise to pay more when more victory brought more gold.   But Zeenut Maihl, as she looked at it, thought with a sort of fury of certain gold within reach, hidden in her house.   What was to become of these coins with John Company's mark on them?   For she still lingered in the Palace.   Other women had fled, but she was wiser than they.   She knew that, come what might, her life was safe with the English as victors; so there was nothing but the gold to think of.   The gold, and Jewun Bukht, her son.   The royal signet was in her possession altogether now, and sometimes the orders, especially when they were for payment of money, had to go without it, because "the Queen of the World was asleep."   But she did not dream.   That was over; though in a way she clung fiercely to hope.   So Ghaus Khân with the Neemuch Brigade, and Bukht Khân with the Bareilly Brigade, and Khair Sultân with the scrapings and leavings of the regiments, who, owning no leader of their own, did what was right in their own eyes, set out to intercept the big guns; and Nicholson set out on the dawn of the 25th to intercept them.

The rain poured down in torrents, the guns sank to their axles in mud, the infantry slipped and slithered, the cavalry were blinded by the mire from the floundering horses.   So from daybreak till sunset the little force, two thousand in all—more than one-half of whom were natives—labored eighteen miles through swamps.   At noon, it is true, they called a halt nine miles out at a village where the women clustered on the housetops in wild alarm, remembering a day—months back—when they had clustered round an unleavened cake, and the head-man's wife had bidden them listen to the master's gun over the far horizon.

They were to listen to it again that day.   For the enemy was ten miles further over the marshes; and it was but noon.   The force, no doubt, had been afoot since four; but General Nicholson was emphatically not an eight-hour man.   So the shovings and slitherings of guns and mortals began again cheerfully.

Still it was nigh on sundown when, across a deep

stream flowing from the big marshes to the west, these contract-workers came on the job they were eager to finish ere nightfall. Six thousand rebels of all arms, holding three villages, a bastioned old serai, and a town. It was a strong position, in the right angle formed by the stream and the flooded canal into which it flowed. Water, impassable save by an unknown ford in the stream, by a bridge held in force over the canal, on two sides of it. On the others dismal swamps. A desperately strong position to attack at sundown after eighteen miles slithering and shoving in the pouring rain; especially with unknown odds against you. Not less, anyhow, than three to one. But John Nicholson had a single eye; that is, an eye which sees one salient point. Here, it was that bridge to the left, leading back to safe shelter within the walls of Delhi. A cowardly foe must have no chance of using that bridge during silent night watches. So, without a pause, fifteen hundred of the two thousand waded breast-high across the stream to attack the six thousand, Nicholson himself riding ahead for a hasty reconnoissance, since the growing dusk left scant leisure for anything save action. Yet once more a glance was sufficient; and, ere the men, exposed to a heavy fire of grape in crossing the ford, were ready to advance, the orders were given.

There was a hint of cover in some rising ground before the old serai—the strongest point of the defense. He would utilize this, rush the position, change front, and sweep down on the bridge. That must not remain as a chance for cowards an instant longer than he could help; for Nicholson in everything he did seems never to have contemplated defeat.

So flanked by the guns, supported by squadrons of the 9th Lancers and the Guides cavalry, the three regiments * marched steadily toward the rising ground, following that colossal figure riding, as ever, ahead. Till suddenly, as his charger's feet touched the highest ground, Nicholson wheeled and held up his hand to those below him.

" Lie down, men! " came his clear strong voice as he

* 61st, 1st Fusiliers, 2d Punjabees.

rode slowly along the line; "lie down and listen to what I've got to say. It's only a few words."

So, sheltered from the fire, they lay and listened. "You of the 61st know what Sir Colin Campbell said to you at Chillianwallah. He said the same thing to others at the Alma. I say it to you all now. 'Hold your fire till within twenty or thirty yards of that battery, and then, my boys! we will make short work of it!'"

Men cannot cheer lying on their stomachs, but the unmelodious grunt—"We will, sir, by God, we will!"—was as good as one.

Nicholson faced round on the serai again, and gave the order to the artillery. So, in sharp thuds widening into a roar, the flanking guns began work. Half a dozen rounds or so, and then the rider—motionless as a statue in the center—looked back quickly, waved his sword, and went on. The men were up, after him, over the hillock, into the morass beyond, silently.

"Steady, men! steady with it. On with you! Steady!"

They listened to the clear sonorous voice once more, though there was no shelter now from the grape and canister, and musket balls; or rather only the shelter of that one tall figure ahead riding at a foot's-pace.

"Steady! Hold your fire! I'll give the word, never fear! Come on! Come on!"

So through a perfect bog they stumbled on doggedly. Here and there a man fell; but men will fall sometimes.

"Now then! Let them have it."

They were within the limit. Twenty yards off lay the guns. There was one furious volley; above it one word answered by a cheer.

So at the point of the bayonet the serai was carried. Then without a pause the troops changed front with a swiftness unforeseen and swept on to the left.

"To Delhi, brothers! To Delhi!" The old cry, begun at Meerut, rose now with a new meaning as the panic-stricken guns limbered up and made for the bridge. Too late! Captain Blunt's were after them, chasing them. The wheel of the foremost, driven wildly, jammed; those following couldn't pull up. So, helter skelter, they were in a jumble, out of which Englishmen helped the whole thirteen! The day, or rather the night, was won; for Nature's dark flag of truce hung even between the assailants and the few desperate defenders of the third village, who, with escape cut off, were selling their lives at a cost to the attackers of seventeen out of that total death-roll of twenty-five. But Nicholson knew his position sure, so he left night to finish the rout, and, with his men, bivouacked without food or cover among the marshes; for it was too dark to get the baggage over the ford. Yet the troops were ready to start at daybreak for an eighteen miles tramp back to the Ridge again. There was no talk of exhaustion now, as at Budli-ke-serai; so just thirty-six hours after they started, that is, just one hour for every mile of morass and none for the fight, they startled the Ridge by marching in again and clamoring for food! But Nicholson was in a towering temper. He had found that another brigade had been lurking behind the canal, and that if he had had decent information he might have smashed it also, on his way home.

"He hadn't even a guide that he didn't pick up himself," commented Major Erlton angrily. "By George! how those niggers cave in to him! And his political information was all rot. If the General had obeyed instructions he would have been kicking his heels at Bahâdagurh still."

"We heard you at it about two o'clock," said a new listener. "I suppose it was a night attack—risky business rather."

Herbert Erlton burst into a laugh; but the elation on his face had a pathetic tenderness in it. "That was the bridge, I expect. *He* blew it up before starting. *He* sat on it till then. Besides there were the wagons and tumbrils and things. *He* told Tombs to blow them up, too, for of course *he* had to bring the guns back, and *he* couldn't shove the lot."

As he passed on some of his listeners smiled.

"It's a case of possession," said one to his neighbor.

"Pardon me," said another, who had known the Major for years. "It's a case of casting out. I wonder——" The speaker paused and shrugged his shoulders.

" Did you hear his name had gone up for the V. C.?" began his companion.

" Gone up! My dear fellow! It might have gone up fifty times over. But it isn't his pluck that I wonder at; it is his steadiness. He never shirks the little things. It is almost as if he had found a conscience."

Perhaps he had. He was cheerful enough to have had the testimony of a good one, as, in passing, he looked in on Jim Douglas and met his congratulations.

" Bad shilling!" replied the Major, beautifully unconscious. " So you've heard—and—hello! what's up?" For Jim Douglas was busy getting into disguise.

" That old scoundrel Tiddu came into camp with the news an hour ago," said the latter, whose face was by no means cheerful. " He was out carrying grain—saw the fugitives, and came in here, hoping for backsheesh, I believe. But "—Jim Douglas looked round rapidly at the Major—" I'm awfully afraid, Erlton, that he has not been in Delhi, to speak of, since I left. And I was relying on him for news——"

" There isn't any—is there?" broke in Major Erlton with a queer hush in his voice.

" None. But there may be. So I'm off at once. I couldn't have a better chance. The villain says the sepoys are slipping in on the sly in hundreds; for the Palace folk, or at least the King, thinks the troops are still engaged, and is sending out reinforcements. So I shall have no trouble in getting through the gates."

Major Erlton, radiant, splashed from head to foot, covered at once with mud and glory, looked at the man opposite him with a curious deliberation.

" I don't see why you should go at all," he said slowly. " I wouldn't, if I—I mean I would rather you didn't."

" Why?" The question came sharply.

" Do you want the truth?" asked Herbert Erlton with a sudden frown.

" Certainly."

" Then I'll tell it, Mr. Greyman—I mean Douglas— I—I'm grateful, but—d——n me, sir, if—if I want to be more so! I—I gave you my chance once—like a fool; for I might have saved her——"

The hard handsome face was all broken up with passionate regret, and the pity of it kept Jim Douglas silent for a moment. For he understood it.

" You might," he said at last. " But I don't interfere with you here. You can't save her—your wife, I mean— and if I fail you can always——"

" There is no need to tell me what to do then," interrupted Major Erlton grimly. " I'll do it without your help."

He turned on his heel, then paused. " It isn't that I'm ungrateful," he repeated, almost with an appeal in his voice. " And I don't mean to be offensive; only you and I can't——"

His own mental position seemed beyond him, and he stood for a moment irresolute. Then he held out his hand.

" Well, good-by. I suppose you mean to stick to it? "

" I mean to stick to it. Good-by."

" And I must be off to my bed. Haven't slept a wink for two nights, and I shall be on duty to-morrow. Well! I believe I've as good a chance of seeing Kate here as you have of finding her there; but I can't prevent your going, of course."

So he went off to his bed, and Jim Douglas, following Tiddu, who was waiting for him in the Koodsia Gardens, carried out his intention of sticking to it; while John Nicholson in his tent, forgetful of his advice to both of them, was jotting down notes for his dispatch. One of them was: " The enemy was driven from the serai with scarcely any loss to us, and made little resistance as we advanced." The other was: " Query? How many men in buckram? Most say seven or eight thousand. I think between three and four."

He had, indeed, a vile habit of telling the truth, even in dispatches. So ended the day of Nujjufghar.

The next morning, the 27th, broke fine and clear. Kate Erlton waking with the birds, found the sky full of light already, clear as a pale topaz beyond the overarching trees.

She stood after leaving her thatch, looking into the garden, lost in a sort of still content. It seemed impossible she should be in the heart of a big city.   There was no sound but the faint rustling of the wet leaves drying themselves in the soft breeze, and the twitterings of squirrels and birds.   There was nothing to be seen but the trees, and the broad paths rising above the flooding water from the canal-cut which ran at the further side.

And Sri Anunda had lived here for fifteen years; while she?   How long had she been there?   She smiled to herself, for, in truth. she had lost count of days alto-gether, almost of Time itself.   She was losing hold of life.   She told herself this, with that vague amaze at finding it so.   Yes! she was losing her grip on this world without gaining, without even desiring, a hold on the next.   She was learning a strange new fellowship with the dream of which she was a part, because it would soon be past; because the trees, the flowers, the birds, the beasts, were mortal as herself.   A squirrel, its tail a-fluff, was coming down the trunk of the next tree in fitful half-defiant jerks, its bright eyes watching her. The corner of her veil was full of the leavings of her simple morning meal, which she always took with her to scatter under the trees; and now, in sudden impulse, she sank down to her knees and held a morsel of plantain out tenderly.

Dear little mortal, she thought, with a new tenderness, watching it as it paused uncertain; until the conscious-ness that she was being watched in her turn made her look up; then pause, as she was, astonished, yet not alarmed, at the figure before her.   It was neither tall nor short, dark nor fair, and it was wrapped from knee to shoulder in a dazzling white cloth draped like a Greek chiton, which showed the thin yet not emaciated curves of the limbs, and left the poise of the long throat bare. The head was clean shaven, smooth as the cheek, and the face, destitute even of eyebrows, was softly seamed with lines and wrinkles which seemed to leave it younger, and brighter, as if in an eternity of smile-provoking con-tent.   But the eyes!   Kate felt a strange shock, as they brought back to her the innocent dignity Raphael gave to his San-Sistine Bambino.   For this was Sri Anunda; could be no one else.   In his hand he held a bunch of henna-blossom, the camphire of Scripture, the cypress of the Greeks; yellowish green, insignificant, incomparably sweet. He held it out to her, smiling, then laid it on her outstretched hand.

"The lesson is learned, sister," he said softly. "Go in peace, and have no fear."

The voice, musical exceedingly, thrilled her through and through. She knelt looking after him regretfully as, without a pause, he passed on his way. So that was a Swâmi! She went back to her corner—for already early visitors were drifting in for Sri Anunda's blessing—and with the bunch of henna-blossom on the ground before her sat thinking.

What an extraordinary face it was! So young, so old. So wise, so strangely innocent. Tara was right. It was not a man's face. Yet it could not be called angelic, for it was the face of a mortal. Yes! that was it, a mortal face immortal through its mortality; through the circling wheel of life and death. The strong perfume of the flowers reaching her, set her a-thinking of them. Did he always give a bunch when the penance was over and say the lesson was learned? It was a significant choice, these flowers of life and death. For bridal hands had been stained with henna, and corpses embalmed with it for ages, and ages, and ages. Or was that " peace go with you," that " have no fear " meant as an encouragement in something new? Had they been making plans? had anything happened? She scarcely seemed to care. So, as the cloudless day passed on, she sat looking at the henna-blossom and thinking of Sri Anunda's face.

But something *had* happened. Jim Douglas had come back to the city and Tara knew it. She had barely escaped his seeing her, and she felt she could not escape it long. And then, it seemed to her, the old life would begin again; for she would never be able to keep the truth from him. The mem might talk of deceit glibly; but if it came to telling lies to the master she would fail.

There was only one chance. If she could get the mem safely out of the city at once; then she could tell the truth without fear. The necessity for immediate action came upon her by surprise. She had ceased to expect the master's return, she had not cared personally for Kate's safety, and so had been content to let the future take care of itself. But now everything was changed. If Kate were not got rid of, sent out of the city, one of two things must happen: The master must be left to get her out as best he could, at the risk of his life; or she, Tara, must return to the old allegiance; return and sit by, while the mem in a language she did not understand, told the Huzoor how she had been willing to be suttee for him!

So while Kate sat looking at the henna-blossom, Tara sat telling herself that at all costs, all risks, she must be got out of the city that night. She, and her jewels. They were at present tied up in a bundle in Tara's room, but the Huzoor might think her a thief if the mem went without them. And another thing she decided. She would not tell the mem the reason of this sudden action. True, Kate had professed herself determined that the master should not risk his life for her again; but women were not—not always—to be trusted. For the rest, Soma must help.

She waited till dusk, however, before appealing to him, knowing that her only chance lay in taking him by storm, in leaving him no time for reflection. So, just as the lights were beginning to twinkle in the bazaars, she made her way, full of purpose, to the half ruined sort of cell in the thickness of the wall not far from the sally-port, in which of late—since he had taken morosely to drugs—he was generally to be found at this time, waking drowsily to his evening meal before going out.

She found him thus, sure enough, and began at once on her task. He must help. He could easily pass out the mem. That was all she asked of him. But his handsome face settled into sheer obstinacy at once. He was not going to help anyone, he said, or harm anyone, till they struck the first blow, and then they had better defend themselves. That was the end. And so it seemed; for after ten minutes of entreaty, he stood up with something of a lurch ere he found his feet, and bid her go. She only wasted her time and his, since he must eat his food ere he went to relieve the sentry at the sally-port.

She caught him up reproachfully, almost indignantly.

" Then thou art there, on guard! and it needs but the opening of a door, a thrusting of a woman out—to—*die*, perchance, Soma. Remember that! "

She spoke with a feverish eagerness, as if the suggestion had its weight with her, but he treated it contemptuously.

" Loh! " he said in scorn. " What a woman's word! Thank the Gods I was not born one."

The taunt bit deep, and Tara drew herself up angrily. So the brother and sister stood face to face, strangely alike.

" Was't not? " she retorted bitterly. " The Gods know. Is there not woman in man, and man in woman, among those born at a birth? Soma! for the sake of that—do this for me——" It was her last appeal; she had kept it for the last, and now her somber eyes were ablaze with passionate entreaty. " See, brother! I claim it of you as a right. Thou didst take my sainthood from me once. Count this as giving it back again."

" Back again? " echoed Soma thickly. " What fool's talk is this? "

" Let it be fool's talk, brother," she interrupted, with a strange intensity in her voice. " I care not—thou dost not know; I cannot tell thee. But—but *this* will be counted to thee in restitution. Soma! think of it as my sainthood! Sure thou dost owe me it! Soma! for the sake of the hand which lay in thine."

In her excitement she moved a step forward, and he shrank back instinctively. True, she was a saint in another way if those scars were true; but—at the moment, being angry with her, he chose to doubt, to remember. " Stand back! " he cried roughly, unsteadily. " What do I owe thee? What claim hast thou? "

The question, the gesture outraged her utterly. The memory of a whole life of vain struggling after self-respect surged to her brain, bringing that almost insane

light to her eyes. "What?" she echoed fiercely—
"this!" Ere he could prevent it, her hand was in his,
gripping it like a vice.

"So in the beginning—so in the end!" she gasped, as
he struggled with her madly. "Tara and Soma hand in
hand. Nay! I am strong as thou."

She spoke truth, for his nerve and muscle were slack
with opium; yet he fought wildly, striking at her with
his left hand, until in a supreme effort she lost her foot-
ing, they both staggered, and he—as she loosed her
hold—fell backward, striking his head against a projecting brick in the ruined wall.

"Soma!" she whispered to his prostrate figure, "art
hurt, brother? Speak to me!"

But he lay still, and, with a cry, she flung herself on
her knees beside him, feeling his heart, listening to his
breathing, searching for the injury. It was a big cut on
the crown of the head; but it did not seem a bad one,
and she began to take his unconsciousness more calmly.
She had seen folk like that before from a sudden fall, and
they came to themselves, none the worse, after a while.
But scarcely, here, in time to relieve guard.

She stood up suddenly and looked round her. Soma's
uniform hung on a peg, his musket stood in a corner.

Half an hour after this, Kate, waiting in the thatch
for Tara to come as usual, gave a cry, more of surprise
than alarm, as a tall figure, in uniform, stepped into the
flickering light of the cresset.

"Soma!" she cried, "what is it?"

A gratified smile came to the curled mustachios.
"Soma or Tara, it matters not," replied a familiar voice.
"They were one in the beginning. Quick, mem-sahib.
On with the jewels. I have a dark veil too for the gate."

Kate stood up, her heart throbbing. "Am I to go,
then? Is that what Sri Anunda meant?"

"Sri Anunda! hath he been here?" Tara paused,
sniffed, and once more those dark eyes met the light
ones with a fierce jealousy. "He hath given thee henna-
blossom. I smell it: and he gives it to none but those
who—— So the Swâmi's lesson is learned—and the
disciple can go in peace——" She broke off with a

petulant laugh. "Well! so be it. It ends my part. The mem will sleep among her own to-night; Sri Anunda hath said it. Come——"

" But how? I must know how," protested Kate.

The laugh rose again. "Wherefore? The mem is Sri Anunda's disciple. For the rest, I will let the mem out through the little river-gate. There is a boat, and she can go in peace."

There was something so wild, so almost menacing in Tara's face, that Kate felt her only hope was to obey. And, in good sooth, the scent of the henna-blossom she carried with her, tucked into her bosom, gave her, some-how, an irrational hope that all would go well as she followed her guide swiftly through the alleys and bazaars.

" The mem must wait here," whispered Tara at last, pausing behind one of the ungainly mausoleums in what had been the old Christian cemetery. " When she hears me singing Sonny-baba's song, she must follow to the Water-gate. It is behind the ruins, there."

Kate crouched down, setting her back, native fashion, against the tomb. And as she waited she wondered idly what mortal lay there; so, being strangely calm, she let her fingers stray to the recess she felt behind her. There should be a marble tablet there; and even in the dark she might trace the lettering. But the recess was empty, the marble having evidently been picked out. So it was a nameless grave. And the next? She moved over to it stealthily, then to the next. But the tablets had been taken out of all and carried off—for curry-stones most likely. So the graves were nameless; those beneath them mortals—nothing more. As she waited under the stars, her mind reverted to Sri Anunda and the Wheel of Life and Death. The immortality of mortality! Was that the lesson which was to let her go in peace?

She started from the thought as that native version of the " Happy Land " came, nasally, from behind the ruins. As she passed them, a group of men were squatted gos-siping round a hookah, and more than one figure passed her. But a woman with her veil drawn, and a clank of anklets on her feet, did not even invite a curious eye;

for it was still early enough for such folk to be going home.

Then, as she passed down a flight of steps, a hand stole out from a niche and drew her back into a dark shadow. The next minute, with a low whisper, " There is no fear! Sri Anunda hath said it.   Go in peace!" she felt herself thrust through a door into darkness.   But a feeble glimmer showed below her, and creeping down another flight of steps, she found herself outside Delhi, looking over the strip of low-lying land where in the winter the buffaloes had grazed beneath Alice Gissing's house, but which was now flooded into a still backwater by the rising of the river.   And out of it the stunted kikar and tamarisks grew strangely, their feathery branches arching over it.   But to the left, beyond the Water Bastion, rose a mass of darker foliage—the Koodsia Gardens. Once there she would be beyond floods, and Tara had said there was a boat.   Kate found it, moored a little further toward the river—a flat-bottomed punt, with a pole.   It proved easier to manage than she had expected; for the water was shallow, and the trunks and branches of the trees helped her to get along, so that after a time she decided on keeping to that method of progress as long as she could.   It enabled her to skirt the river bank, where there were fewer lights telling of watch-fires.   Besides, she knew the path by the river leading to Metcalfe House.   It might be under water now; but if she crept into the park at the ravine—if she could take the boat so far—she might manage to reach Metcalfe House.   There was an English picket there, she knew.   So, as she mapped out her best way, a sudden recollection came to her of the last time she had seen that river path, when her husband and Alice Gissing were walking down it, and Captain Morecombe——

Ah! was it credible?   Was it not all a dream?   Could this be real—could it be the same world?

She asked herself the question with a dull indifference as she struggled on doggedly.

But not more than two hours afterward the conviction that the world had not changed came upon her with a strange pang as she stood once more on the terrace of Metcalfe House with English faces around her.

" By Heaven, it's Mrs. Erlton! " she heard a familiar voice say. It seemed to her hundreds of miles away in some far, far country to which she had been journeying for years. " Here! let me get hold of her—and fetch some water—wine—anything. How—how was it, Sergeant? "

" In a boat, sir, coming hand over hand down at the stables. She sang out quite calmly she was an Englishwoman, and——"

" Then—then they touched their caps to me," said Kate, making an effort, " and so I knew that I was safe. It was so strange; it—it rather upset me. But I am all right now, Captain Morecombe."

" We had better send up for Erlton," said another officer aside; but Kate caught the whisper.

" Please not. I can walk up to cantonments quite well. And—I would rather have no fuss—I—I couldn't stand it."

She had stood enough and to spare, agreed the little knot of men with a thrill at their hearts as they watched her set off in the moonlight with Captain Morecombe and an orderly. They were to go straight to the Major's tent; and if he was still at mess, which was more than likely, since it was only half-past nine, Captain Morecombe was to leave her there and go on with the news. There would be no fuss, of that she might be sure, said the latter, forbearing even to speak to her on the way, save to ask her if she felt all right.

" I feel as if I had just been born," she said slowly. In truth, she was wondering if that spinning of the Great Wheel toward Life again brought with it this forlornness, this familiarity.

CHAPTER IV.

AT LAST.

No fuss indeed! Kate, as she sat in her husband's little tent waiting for him to come to her, felt that so far she might have arrived from a very ordinary journey. The bearer, it is true, who had been the Major's valet for years, had salaamed more profoundly than usual, had even put up a pious prayer, and expressed himself pleased; but he had immediately gone off to fetch hot water, and returning with it and clean towels, had suggested mildly that the mem might like to wash her face and hands. Kate, with a faint smile, felt there was no reason why she should not. She need not look worse than necessary. But she paused almost with a gasp at the familiar half-forgotten luxuries. Scented soap! a sponge—and there on the camp table a looking-glass! She glanced down with a start at the little round one in the ring she wore; then went over to the other. A toilet cover, brushes, and combs, her husband's razors, gold studs in a box; and there, her own photograph in a frame, a Bible, and a prayer book, the latter things bringing her no surprise, no emotion of any kind. For they had always been fixtures on Major Erlton's dressing-table, mute evidences to no sentiment on his part, but simply to the bearer's knowledge of the proprieties and the ways of real sahibs. But the other things she saw made her heart grow soft. The little camp bed, the simplicity and hardness of all in comparison with what her husband had been wont to demand of life; for he had always been a real prince, feeling the rose-leaf beneath the feather bed, and never stinting himself in comfort. Then the swords, and belts, and Heaven knows what panoply of war—not spick-and-span decorations as they used to be in the old days, but worn and used—gave her a pang. Well! he had always been a good soldier, they said.

And then, interrupting her thoughts, the old khânsaman had come in, having taken time to array himself gorgeously in livery. The Father of the fatherless and orphan, he said, whimperingly, alluding to the fact that he had lost both parents—which, considering he was past sixty, was only to be expected—had heard his prayer. The mem was spared to Freddy-baba. And would she please to order dinner. As the Major-sahib dined at mess, her slave was unprepared with a roast. Fish also would partake of tyranny; but he could open a tin of Europe soup, and with a chicken cutlet—Kate cut him short with a request for tea; by and by, when— when the Major-sahib should have come. And when she was alone again, she shivered and rested her head on her crossed arms upon the table beside which she sat, with a sort of sob. This—Yes!—this of all she had come through was the hardest to bear. This surge of pity, of tenderness, of unavailing regret for the past, the present, the future. What?—What could she say to him, or he to her, that would make remembrance easier, anticipation happier?

Hark! there was his step! His voice saying good-night to Captain Morecombe.

" I hope she will be none the worse," came the reply. " Good-night, Erlton—I'm—I'm awfully glad, old fellow."

" Thanks! "

She stood up with a sickening throb at her heart. Oh! she was glad too! So glad to see him and tell him to——

How tall he was, she thought, with a swift recognition of his good looks, as he came in, stooping to pass under the low entrance. Very tall, and thin. Much thinner, and—and—different somehow.

" Kate! " He paused half a second, looking at her curiously—" Kate! I'm—I'm awfully glad." He was beside her now, his big hands holding hers; but she felt that she was further away from him than she had been in that brief pause when she had half-expected, half-wished him to take her in his arms and kiss her as if nothing had happened, as if life were to begin again. It would have been so much easier; they might have forgotten then, both of them. But now, what came, must come without that chrism of impulse; must come in remembrance and regret. *Awfully glad!* That was what Captain Morecombe had said. Was there no more between them than that? No more between her and this man, who was the father of her child. The sting of the thought made her draw him closer, and with a sob rest her head on his shoulder. Then he stooped and kissed her. "I—I didn't know. I wasn't sure if you'd like it," he said, "but I'm awfully glad, old girl, upon my life I am. You must have had a terrible time."

She looked up with a hopeless pain in her eyes. He was gone from her again; gone utterly. "It was not so bad as you might think," she answered, trying to smile. "Mr. Greyman did so much——"

"Greyman! You mean Douglas, I suppose?"

She stared for a second. "Douglas? I don't know. I mean——" Then she paused. How could she say, "The man you rode against at Lucknow," when she wanted to forget all that; forget everything? And then a sudden fear made her add hastily, "He is here, surely—he came long ago."

Major Erlton nodded. "I know; but his real name is Douglas; at least he says so. Do you mean to say you haven't seen him? That he didn't help you to get out?"

"You mean that—that he has gone back?" asked Kate faintly.

Her husband gave a low whistle. "What a queer start; a sort of Box and Cox. He went back to find you yesterday."

Kate's hand went up to her forehead almost wildly. Then Tara must have known. But why had she not mentioned it? Still, in a way, it was best as it was; since once he heard she, Kate, had gone, he would return. For Tara would tell him, of course.

These thoughts claimed her for the moment, and when she looked up, she found her husband watching her curiously.

"He must have done an awful lot for you, of course," he said shortly; "but I'd rather it had been anyone else, and that's a fact. However, it can't be helped. Hullo! here's the khânsaman with some tea. Thoughtful of the old scoundrel, isn't it?"

"I—I ordered it," put in Kate, feeling glad of the diversion.

Major Erlton laughed kindly. "What, begun already? The old sinner's had a precious easy time of it; but now——" He pulled himself up awkwardly, and, as if

to cover his hesitation, walked over to a box, and after
rummaging in it, brought out a packet of letters.
" Freddy's," he said cheerfully. " He's all right. Jolly
as a sandboy. I kept them—in—in case——"

A great gratitude made the past dim for a moment.
He seemed nearer to her again. " I can't look at them
to-night, Herbert," she said softly, laying her hand beside his upon them. " I'm—I'm too tired."

" No wonder. You must have your tea and go to
bed," he replied. Then he looked round the tent. " It
isn't a bad little place, you'll find—I'm on duty to-
night—so—so you'll manage, I dare say."

" On duty? " she echoed, pouring herself out a cup of
tea rather hastily. " Where? "

" Oh! at the front. There is never anything worth
going for now. We are both waiting for the assault;
that's the fact. But I shan't be back till dawn, so——"

He was standing looking at her, tall, handsome, full of
vitality; and suddenly he lifted a fold of her tinsel-set
veil and smiled.

" Jolly dress that for a fancy ball, and what a jolly
scent it's got. It is that flower, isn't it? You look
awfully well in it, Kate! In fact, you look wonderfully
fit all round."

" So do you! " she said hurriedly, her hand going up
to the henna blossom. There was a sudden quiver in her
voice, a sudden fierce pain in her heart. " You—you
look——"

" Oh! I," he replied carelessly, still with admiring
eyes, " I'm as fit as a fiddle. I say! where did you get
all those jewels? What a lot you have! They're awfully
becoming."

" They are Mr. Greyman's," she said; " they belonged
to his—to——" then she paused. But the contemptuously comprehending smile on her husband's face made
her add quietly, " to a woman—a woman *he loved very
dearly*, Herbert."

There was a moment or two of silence, and then Major
Erlton went to the entrance, raised the curtain, and
looked out. A flood of moonlight streamed into the
tent.

"It's about time I was off," he said after a bit, and there was a queer constraint in his voice. Then he came over and stood by Kate again.

"It isn't any use talking over—over things to-night, Kate," he said quietly. "There's a lot to think of and I haven't thought of it at all. I never knew, you see—if this would happen. But I dare say you have; you were always a oner at thinking. So—so you had better do it for both of us. I don't care, *now*. It will be what you wish, of course."

"We will talk it over to-morrow," she said in a low voice. She would not look in his face. She knew she would find it soft with the memory held in that one word —now. Ah! how much easier it would have been if she had never come back! And yet she shrank from the same thought on his lips.

"There was always the chance of my getting potted," he said almost apologetically. "But I'm not. So— well! let's leave it for to-morrow."

"Yes," she replied steadily, "for to-morrow."

He gathered some of his things together, and then held out his hand. "Good-night, Kate. I wouldn't lie awake thinking, if I were you. What's the good if it? We will just have to make the best of it for the boy. But I'd like you to know two things——"

"Yes——"

"That I couldn't forget, of course; and that——" he paused. "Well! that doesn't matter; it's only about my-self and it doesn't mean much after all. So, good-night."

As she moved to the door also, forced into following him by the ache in her heart for him, more than for her-self, the jingle of her anklets made him turn with an easy laugh.

"It doesn't sound respectable," he said; then, with a sudden compunction, added: "But the dress is much prettier than those dancing girls', and—by Heaven, Kate! you've always been miles too good for me; and that's the fact. Well!—let us leave it for to-morrow."

Yes! for to-morrow, she told herself, with a determina-tion not to think as, dressed as she was, she nestled down into the strange softness of the camp bed, too weary of the pain and pity of this coming back even for tears. Yet she thought of one thing; not that she was safe, not that she would see the boy again. Only of the thing he had been going to tell her about himself. What was it? She wanted to know; she wanted to know all—everything. " Herbert!" she whispered to the pillow, " I wish you had told me—I want to know—I want to make it easier— for—for us all."

And so, not even grateful for her escape, she fell asleep dreamlessly.

It was dawn when she woke with the sound of someone talking outside. He had come back. No! that was not his voice. She sat up listening.

" The servants say she is asleep. Someone had better go in and wake her. The Doctor——"

" He's behind with the dhooli. Ah! there's More-combe; he knows her."

But there was no need to call her. Kate was already at the door, her eyes wide with the certainty of evil. There was no need even to tell her what had happened; for in the first rays of the rising sun, seen almost star-like behind a dip in the rocky ridge, she saw a little pro-cession making for the tent.

" He—he is dead," she said quietly. There was hardly a question in her tone. She knew it must be so. Had he not begged her to leave it till to-morrow? and this was to-morrow. Were not her eyes full of its rising sun, and what its beams held in their bright clasp?

" It seems impossible," said someone in a low voice, breaking in on the pitiful silence. " He always seemed to have a charmed life, and then, in an instant, when nothing was going on, the chance bullet."

It did not seem impossible to her.

" Please don't make a fuss about me, Doctor," she pleaded in a tone which went to his heart when he pro-posed the conventional solaces. " Remember I have been through so—so much already. I can bear it. I can, indeed, if I'm left alone with him—while it is possi-ble. Yes! I know there is another lady, but I only want to be alone, with him."

So they left her there beside the little camp-bed with

its new burden.   There was no sign of strife upon him.
Only that blue mark behind his ear among his hair,
and his face showed no pain.   Kate covered it with a
little fine handkerchief she found folded away in a scented
case she had made for him before they were married.   It
had Alice Gissing's monogram on it.   It was better so,
she told herself; he would have liked it.   She had no
flowers except the faded henna blossom, but it smelled
sweet as she tucked it under the hand which she had
left half clasped upon his sword.   She might at least tell
him so, she thought half bitterly, that the lesson was
learned, that he might go in peace.

Then she sat down at the table and looked over their
boy's letters mechanically; for there was nothing to think
of now.   The morrow had settled the problem.   Captain Morecombe came in once or twice to say a word or
two, or bring in other men, who saluted briefly to her as
they passed to stand beside the dead man for a second,
and then go out again.   She was glad they cared to
come; had begged that any might come who chose, as if
she were not there.   But at one visitor she looked curiously, for he came in alone.   A tall man—as tall as
Herbert, she thought—with a dark beard and keen,
kindly eyes.   She saw them, for he turned to her with the
air of one who has a right to speak, and she stood up
involuntarily.

" His name was up for the Victoria Cross, madam,"
said a clear, resonant voice, " as you may know; but that
is nothing.   He was a fine soldier—a soldier such as I—
I am John Nicholson, madam—can ill spare.   For the
rest—he leaves a good name to his son."

The sunlight streamed in for an instant on to the
little bed and its burden as he passed out, and glittered
on the sword and tassels.   Kate knelt down beside it and
kissed the dead hand.

" That was what you meant, wasn't it, Herbert?" she
whispered.   " I wish you had told it me yourself, dear."

She wished it often.   Thinking over it all in the long
days that followed, it came to be almost her only regret.
If he had told her, if he had heard her say how glad she
was, she felt that she would have asked no more.   And

so, as she went down every evening to lay the white rosebuds the gardener brought her on his grave she used to
repeat, as if he could hear them, his own words: " It is
the finish that is the win or the lose of a race."

That was what many a man was saying to himself upon
the Ridge in the first week of September. For the siege
train had come at last. The winning post lay close
ahead, they must ride all they knew. But those in command said it anxiously; for day by day the hospitals became more crowded, and cholera, reappearing, helped
to swell the rear-guard of graves, when the time had
come for vanguards only.

But some men—among them Baird Smith and John
Nicholson—took no heed of sickness or death. And
these two, especially, looked into each other's eyes and
said, " When you are ready I'm ready." Their seniors
might say that an assault would be thrown on the hazard
of a die. What of that; if men are prepared to throw
sixes, as these two were? They had to be thrown, if
India was to be kept, if this bubble of sovereignty was to
be pricked, the gas let out.

In the city and the Palace also, men, feeling the struggle close, put hand and foot to whip and spur. But there
was no one within the walls who had the seeing single
eye, quick to seize the salient point of a position. Baird
Smith saw it fast enough. Saw the thickets and walls of
the Koodsia Gardens in front of him, the river guarding
his left, a sinuous ravine—cleaving the hillside into cover
creeping down from the Ridge on his right to within two
hundred yards of the city wall. And that bit of the wall,
between the Moree gate and the Water Bastion, was its
weakest portion. The curtain walls long, mere parapets,
only wide enough for defense by muskets. So said the
spies, though it seemed almost incredible to English
engineers that the defense had not been strengthened by
pulling down the adjacent houses and building a rampart for guns.

In truth there was no one to suggest it, and if it had
been suggested there was no one to carry it out, for even
now, at the last, the Palace seethed with dissension and
intrigue. Yet still the sham went on inconceivably.

Jim Douglas, indeed, walking through the bazaars in his Afghan dress, very nearly met his fate through it.   For he was seized incontinently and made to figure as one of the retinue of the Amir of Cabul's ambassador, who, about the beginning of September, was introduced to the private Hall of Audience as a sedative to doubtful dreamers, and a tonic to brocaded bags.   Luckily for him, however, the men called upon to play the other part in the farce—chiefly cloth-merchants from Peshawur and elsewhere, whom Jim Douglas had dodged successfully so far—had been in such abject fear of being discovered themselves that they had no thought of discovering others.   For Bahâdur Shâh had the dust and ashes of a Moghul in him still.   Jim Douglas recognized the fact in the very obstinacy of delusion in the wax-like, haggard old face looking with glazed, tremulous-lidded eyes at the mock mission; and in the faded voice, accepting his vassal of Cabul's promise of help.   It was an almost incredible scene, Jim Douglas thought.   Given it, there was no limit to possibilities in this phantasmagoria of kingship.   The white shadows of the marble arches with their tale of boundless power and wealth in the past, the wide plains beyond, the embroidered curtain of the sunlit garden, the curves of courtiers, most of them in the secret, no doubt; and below the throne these tag-rag and bob-tail of the bazaars, one of them at least a hell-doomed infidel, figuring away in borrowed finery!   All this was as unreal as a magic lantern picture, and like it was followed hap-hazard, without rhyme or reason, by the next on the slide; for, as he passed out of the Presence he heard the question of appointing a Governor to Bombay brought up and discussed gravely; that province being reported to have sent in its allegiance *en bloc* to the Great Moghul.   The slides, however, were not always so dignified, so decorous.   One came, a day or two afterward, showing a miserable old pantaloon driven to despair because six hundred hungry sepoys would not behave according to strict etiquette, but, invading his privacy with threats, reduced him to taking his beautiful new cushion from the Peacock Throne and casting it among them.

"Take it," he cried passionately, "it is all I have left. Take it, and let me go in peace!"

But the lesson was not learned by him as yet; so he had to remain; for once more the sepoys sent out word that there was to be no skulking. To do the Royal family justice, however, they seem by this time to have given up the idea of flight. To be sure they had no place to which they could fly, since the dream required that background of rose-red wall and marble arches. So even Abool-Bukr, forsaking drunkenness as well as that kind, detaining hand, clung to his kinsfolk bravely, behaving in all ways as a newly married young prince should who looked toward filling the throne itself at some future time.*

The sepoys themselves had given up blustering, and many, like Soma, had taken to bhang instead; drugging themselves deliberately into indifference. The latter had recovered from the blow on the back of his head, which, however, as is so often the case, had for the time at any rate deprived him of all recollection of the events immediately preceding it. So, as Tara had restored his uniform before he was able to miss it, he treated her as if nothing had occurred; greatly to her relief. The fact had its disadvantages, however, by depriving her of all corroborative evidence of the mem having really left the city. Thus Jim Douglas, warned by past experience, and made doubtful by Tara's strange reticences, refused to believe it. Her whole story, indeed, marred, as it was, by the endless reserves and exaggerations, seemed incredible; the more so because Tiddu—who lied wildly as to his constant sojourn in Delhi—professed utter disbelief in it. So, after a few days' unavailing attempt to get at the truth, Jim Douglas sent the old man off with a letter of inquiry to the Ridge, and waited for the answer.

Waited, like all Delhi, under the shadow of the lifted sword which hung above the city. A sword, held behind a simulacrum of many, by one arm, sent for that purpose; for John Lawrence, being wise, knew that the shadow of that arm meant more even than the sword it held to

* His widow died last year, having spent thirty-eight years of her fifty-four in cherishing the memory of a saint upon earth.

the wildest half of the province under his control, a province trembling in the balance between allegiance and revolt; a province ready to catch fire if the extinguisher were not put upon the beacon light. And all India waited too. Waited to see that sword fall.

But a hatchet fell first. Fell in the lemon thickets and pomegranates of the walled old gardens, so that men who worked at the batteries still remember the sweet smell that went up from the crushed leaves. A welcome change; for the Ridge, crowded now with eleven thousand troops, was not a pleasant abode. It was on Sunday, the 6th of September, that the final reinforcements came in, and on the 7th the men, reading General Wilson's order for the appointing of prize agents in each corps, and his assurance that all plunder would be divided fairly, felt as if they were already within the walls. The hospitals, too, were giving up their sick; those who could not be of use going to the rear, Meerut-ward, those fit for work to the front. And that night the first siege battery was traced and almost finished below the Sammy-House, while, under cover of this distraction on the right, the Koodsia Gardens and Ludlow Castle on the left were occupied by strong pickets.

But that first battery—only seven hundred yards from the Moree Bastion—had a struggle for dear life. The dawn showed but one gun in position against all the concentrated fire of the bastion which, during the night, had been lured into a useless duel with the old defense batteries above. Only one gun at dawn; but by noon—despite assault and battery—there were five, answering roar for roar. Then for the first time began that welcome echo: the sound of crumbling walls, the grumbling roll of falling stones and mortar. By sunset the gradually diminishing fire from the bastion had ceased, and the bastion itself was a heap of ruins. By this time the four guns in the left section of the battery were keeping down the fire from the Cashmere gate, and so protecting the real advance through the gardens. That was the first day of the siege, and Kate Erlton, sitting in her little tent, which had been moved into a quiet spot, as she had begged to be allowed to stay on the Ridge until some news came of the man to whom she owed so much, thought with a shudder she could not help, of what it must mean to many an innocent soul shut up within those walls. It was bad enough here, where the very tent seemed to shake. It must be terrible down there beside the heating guns, in the roar and the rattle, the grime and the ache and strain of muscle. But in the city—even in Sri Anunda's garden——!

So, naturally enough, she wondered once more what could have become of the man who had gone back to find her nearly ten days before.

"May I come in? John Nicholson."

She would have recognized the voice even without the name, for it was not one to be forgotten. Nor was the owner, as he stood before her, a letter in his hand.

"I have heard from Mr. Douglas, Mrs. Erlton," he said. "It is in the Persian character, so I presume it is no use showing it to you. But it concerns you chiefly. He wants to know if you are safe. I have to answer it immediately. Have you any message you would like to send?"

"Any message?" she echoed. "Only that he must come back at once, of course."

John Nicholson looked at her calmly.

"I shall say nothing of the kind," he replied. "It is best for a man to decide such matters for himself."

She flushed up hotly. "I had not the slightest intention of dictating to Mr.—Mr. Douglas, General Nicholson; but considering how much he has already sacrificed for my sake——"

"You had better let him do as he likes, my dear madam," interrupted the General, with a sudden kindly smile, which, however, faded as quickly as it came, leaving his face stern. "He, like many another man, has sacrificed too much for women, Mrs. Erlton; so if ever you can make up to him for some of the pain, do so—he is worth it. Good-by. I'll tell him that you are safe; but that in spite of that, he has my permission to go ahead and kill—the more the better."

She had not the faintest idea why he made this last remark; but it did not puzzle her, for she was occupied

with his previous one.   Sacrificed too much!   That was
true.   He carried the scars of the knife upon him clearly.
And the man who had just left her presence, who, for all
his courtesy, had treated her so cavalierly?   She was
rather vexed with herself for feeling it, but a sudden
sense of being a poor creature came over her.   It flashed
upon her that she could imagine a world without women
—she was in one, almost, at that very moment—but not
a world without men.   Yet that ceaseless roar filling the
air had more to do with women than men; it went more
as a challenge of revenge than a stern recall to duty.

It was true.   The men, working night and day in the
batteries, thought little of men's rights, only of women's
wrongs.   Even General Wilson in his order had appealed
to those under him on that ground only, urging them to
spend life and strength freely in vengeance on murderers.

And they did.   Down in the scented Koodsia Gardens
the men never seemed to tire, never to shrink, though
the shot from the city—not two hundred and fifty yards
away—flew pinging through the trees above them.   But
the high wall gave cover, and so those off duty slept
peacefully in the cool shade, or sat smoking on the river-
terrace.

Thus, while the first battery, pounding away from the
right at the Moree and Cashmere bastions, diverted attention, and the enemy, deceived by the feint, lavished
a dogged courage in trying to keep up some kind of
reply, a second siege battery in two sections was traced
and made in front of Ludlow Castle, five hundred yards
from the Cashmere gate.   By dawn on the 11th both sections were at work destroying the defenses of the gate;
and pounding away to breach the curtain wall beside it.
So the roar was doubled, and the vibrations of the air
began to quiver on the wearied ear almost painfully.   Yet
they were soon trebled, quadrupled.   Trebled by a party
of wide-mouthed mortars in the garden itself.   Quadrupled by a wicked, dare-devil, impertinent little company
of six eighteen-pounders and twelve small mortars,
which, with Medley of the Engineers as a guide, took advantage of a half ruined house to creep within a hundred

and sixty yards of the doomed walls despite the shower of shell and bullets from it. For by this time the murderers in the city had found out that the men were at work at something in the scented thickets to the left. Not that the discovery hindered the work. The native pioneers, who bore the brunt of it, digging and piling for the wicked little intruder, were working with the master, working with volunteers—officers and men alike—from the 9th Lancers and the Carabineers. So, when one of their number toppled over, they looked to see if he were dead or alive in order to sort him out properly. And if he was dead they would weep a few tears as they laid him in the row beside the others of his kind, before they went on with their work quietly; for, having to decide whether a comrade belonged to the dead or the living thirty-nine times one night, they began to get expert at it. So by the 12th, fifty guns and mortars flashed and roared, and the rumble of falling stones became almost continuous. Sometimes a shell would just crest the parapet, burst, and bring away yards of it at a time.

Up on the Ridge behind the siege batteries, when the cool of the evening came on, every post was filled with sightseers watching the salvos, watching the game. And one, at least, going back to get ready for mess, wrote and told his wife at Meerut, that if she were at the top of Flagstaff Tower, she would remain there till the siege was over—it was so fascinating. But they were merry on the Ridge in these days, and the messes were so full that guests had to be limited at one, till they got a new leaf in the table! Yet on the other slope of the Ridge, men were tumbling over like the stones in the walls. Tumbling over one after another in the batteries, all through the night of the 12th, and the day of the 13th.

Then at ten o'clock in the evening, men, sitting in the mess-tents, looked at each other joyfully, yet with a thrill in their veins, as the firing ceased suddenly. For they knew what that meant; they knew that down under the very walls of the city, friends and comrades were creeping, sword in one hand, their lives in the other, through the starlight, to see if the breaches were practicable.

But the city knew them to be so; and already the last order sent by the Palace to Delhi was being proclaimed by beat of drum through the streets.

So, monotonously, the cry rang from alley to alley.

" Intelligence having just been brought that the infidels intend an assault to-night, it is incumbent on all, Hindoo and Mohammedan, from due regard to their faith, to assemble directly by the Cashmere gate, bringing iron picks and shovels with them. This order is imperative."

Newâsi Begum, among others, heard it as she sat reading. She stood up suddenly, overturning the bookrest and the Holy Word in her haste; for she felt that the crisis was at hand. She had never seen Abool-Bukr since the night, now a whole month past, when he had taunted her with being one more woman ready for kisses. Her pride had kept her from seeking him, and he had not returned. But now her resentment gave way before her fears. She *must* see him—since God only knew what might be going to happen!

True in a way. But up on the Ridge one man felt certain of one thing. John Nicholson, with the order for an assault at dawn safe in his hand, knew that he would be in Delhi on the 14th of September—a day earlier than he had expected.

CHAPTER V.

THROUGH THE WALLS.

I⊤ was a full hour past dawn on the 14th of September ere that sudden silence fell once more upon the echoing rocks of the Ridge and the scented gardens. So, for a second, the twittering birds in the thickets behind them might have been heard by the men who, with fixed bayonets, were jostling the roses and the jasmines. But they were holding their breath—waiting, listening, for something very different; while in the ears of many, excluding all other sounds, lingered the cadence of the text read by the chaplain before dawn in the church lesson for the day.

"Woe to the bloody city—the sword shall cut thee off."

For to many the coming struggle meant neither justice nor revenge, but religion. It was Christ against Anti-Christ. So, whether for revenge or faith they waited. A thousand down by the river opposite the Water Bastion. A thousand in the Koodsia facing the main breach, with John Nicholson, first as ever, to lead it. A thousand more on the broad white road fronting the Cashmere Bastion, with an explosion party ahead to blow in the gate, and a reserve of fifteen hundred to the rear waiting for success. Briefly, four thousand five hundred men—more than half natives—for the assault, facing that half mile or so of northern wall; thus within touch of each other. Beyond, on the western trend, two thousand more—mostly untried troops from Jumoo and a general muster of casuals—to sweep through the suburbs and be ready to enter by the Cabul gate when it was opened to them.

Above, on the Ridge, six hundred sabers awaiting orders. Behind it three thousand sick in hospital, a weak defense, and that rear-guard of graves.

And in front of all stood that tall figure with the keen eyes. "Are you ready, Jones?" asked Nicholson, laying his hand on the last leader's shoulder. His voice and face were calm, almost cold.

"Ready, sir!"

Then, startling ·that momentary silence, came the bugle.

"Advance!"

With a cheer the rifles skirmished ahead joyfully. The engineers posted in the furthest cover long before dawn —who had waited for hours, knowing that each minute made their task harder—rose, waving their swords to guide the stormers toward the breach! Then, calmly, as if it had been dark, not daylight, crested the glacis at a swift walk, followed by the laddermen in line. Behind, with a steady tramp, the two columns bound for the breaches. But the third, upon the road, had to wait a while, as, like greyhounds from a leash, a little company slipped forward at the double.

Home of the Engineers first with two sergeants, a native havildar, and ten Punjâb sappers, running lightly, despite the twenty-five pound powder bags they carried. Behind them, led by Salkeld, the firing party and a bugler. Running under the hail of bullets, faster as they fell faster, as men run to escape a storm; but these courted it, though the task had been set for night, and it was now broad daylight.

What then? They could see better. See the outer gateway open, the footway of the drawbridge destroyed, the inner door closed save for the wicket.

"Come on," shouted Home, and was across the bare beams like a boy, followed by the others.

Incredible daring! What did it mean? The doubt made the scared enemy close the wicket hastily. So against it, at the rebels' very feet, the powder bags were laid. True, one sergeant fell dead with his; but as it fell against the gates his task was done.

"Ready, Salkeld!—your turn," sang out young Home from the ditch, into which, the bags laid, the fuse set, he dropped unhurt. So across the scant foothold came the firing party, its leader holding the portfire. But the paralysis of amazement had passed; the enemy, realizing what the audacity meant, had set the wicket wide. It bristled now with muskets; so did the parapet.

"Burgess!—your turn," called Salkeld as he fell, and passed the portfire to the corporal behind him. Burgess, alias Grierson,—someone perchance retrieving a past under a new name,—took it, stooped, then with a half articulate cry either that it was "right" or "out," fell back into the ditch dead. Smith, of the powder party, lingering to see the deed done, thought the latter, and, matchbox in hand, sprang forward, cuddling the gate for safety as he struck a light. But it was not needed. As he stooped to use it, the port-fire of the fuse exploded in his face, and, half blinded, he turned to plunge headlong for escape into the ditch. A second after the gate was in fragments.

"Your turn, Hawthorne!" came that voice from the

ditch. So the bugler, who had braved death to sound it, gave the advance. Once, twice, thrice, carefully lest the din from the breaches should drown it. Vain precaution, not needed either; for the sound of the explosion was enough. That thousand on the road was hungering to be no whit behind the others, and with a wild cheer the stormers made for the gate.

But Nicholson was already in Delhi, though ten minutes had gone in a fierce struggle to place a single ladder against an avalanche of shot and stone. But that one had been the signal for him to slip into the ditch, and, calling on the 1st Bengal Fusiliers to follow, escalade the bastion, first as ever.

Even so, others were before him. Down at the Water Bastion, though three-quarters of the laddermen had fallen and but a third of the storming party remained, those twenty-five men of the 8th had gained the breach, and, followed by the whole column, were clearing the ramparts toward the Cashmere gate. Hence, again, without a check, joined by the left half of Nicholson's column, they swept the enemy before them like frightened sheep to the Moree gate; though in the bastion itself the gunners stood to their guns and were bayoneted beside them. There, with a whoop, some of the wilder ones leaped to the parapet to wave their caps in exultation to the cavalry below, which, in obedience to orders, was now drawn up, ready to receive, guarding the flank of the assault, despite the murderous fire from the Cabul gate, and the Burn Bastion beyond it. Sitting in their saddles, motionless, doing nothing, a mark for the enemy, yet still a wall of defense. So, leaving them to that hardest task of all—the courage of inaction—the victorious rush swept on to take the Cabul gate, to sweep past it up to the Burn Bastion itself—the last bastion which commanded the position.

And then? Then the order came to retire and await orders at the Cabul gate. The fourth column, after clearing the suburbs, was to have been there ready for admittance, ready to support. It was not. And Nicholson was not there also, to dare and do all. He had had to pause at the Cashmere gate to arrange that the column which had entered through it should push on into the city, leaving the reserve to hold the points already won. And now, with the 1st Fusiliers behind him, he was fighting his way through the streets to the Cabul gate. So, fearing to lose touch with those behind, over-rating the danger, under-estimating the incalculable gain of unchecked advance with an eastern foe, the leader of that victorious sweeping of the ramparts was content to set the English flag flying on the Cabul gate and await orders. But the men had to do something. So they filled up the time plundering. And there were liquor shops about. Europe shops, full of wine and brandy.

The flag had been flying over an hour when Nicholson came up. But by that time the enemy—who had been flying too—flying as far as the boat bridge in sheer conviction that the day was lost—had recovered some courage and were back, crowding the bastion and some tall houses beside it. And in the lane, three hundred yards long, not ten feet wide, leading to it, two brass guns had been posted before bullet proof screens ready to mow down the intruders.

Yet once more John Nicholson saw but one thing— the Burn Bastion. Built by Englishmen, it was one of the strongest—the only remaining one, in fact, likely to give trouble. With it untaken a thorough hold on the city was impossible. Besides, with his vast knowledge of native character, he knew that the enemy had expected us to take it, and would construe caution into cowardice. Then he had the 1st Bengal Fusiliers behind him. He had led them in Delhi, they had fallen in his track in tens and fifties, and still they had come on—they would do this thing for him now.

" We will do what we can, sir," said their commandant, Major Jacob—but his face was grave.

" We will do what men can do, sir," said the commandant of that left half of the column; " but honestly, I don't think it can be done. We have tried it once." His face was graver still.

" Nor I," said Nicholson's Brigade-major.

Nicholson, as he stood by the houses around the Cabul gate, which had been occupied and plundered by the

troops, looked down the straight lane again. It hugged
the city wall on its right, its scanty width narrowed here
and there by buttresses to some three feet. About a
third of the way down was the first gun, placed beside a
feathery kikar tree which sent a lace-like tracery of
shadow upon the screen. As far behind was the second.
Beyond, again, was the bastion jutting out, and so forcing the lane to bend between it and some tall houses.
Both were crowded with the enemy—the screens held
bayonets and marksmen. There was a gun close to the
bastion in the wall, but to the left, cityward, in the low,
flat-roofed mud houses there seemed no trace of flanking foes.

" I think it can be done," he said. He knew it must
be done ere the Palace could be taken. So he gave the
orders. Fusiliers forward; officers to the front!

And to the front they went, with a cheer and a rush,
overwhelming the first gun, within ten yards of the other.
And one man was closer still, for Lieutenant Butler,
pinned against that second bullet-proof screen by two
bayonets thrust through the loopholes at him, had to
fire his revolver through them also, ere he could escape
this two-pronged fork.

But the fire of every musket on the bastion and the
tall houses was centered on that second gun. Grape,
canister, raked the narrow lane—made narrower by fallen Fusiliers—and forced those who remained to fall back
upon the first gun—beyond that even. Yet only for a
moment. Reformed afresh, they carried it a second time,
spiked it and pressed on. Officers still to the front!

Just beyond the gun the commandant fell wounded to
death. "Go on, men, go on!" he shouted to those who
would have paused to help him. " Forward, Fusiliers!"

And they went forward; though at dawn two hundred
and fifty men had dashed for the breach, and now there
were not a hundred and fifty left to obey orders. Less!
For fifty men and seven officers lay in that lane itself.
Surely it was time now for others to step in—and there
were others!

Nicholson saw the waver, knew what it meant, and
sprang forward sword in hand, calling on those others to

follow. But he asked too much. Where the 1st Fusiliers had failed, none cared to try. That is the simple truth. The limit had been reached.

So for a minute or two he stood, a figure instinct with passion, energy, vitality, before men who, God knows with reason, had lost all three for the moment. A colossal figure beyond them, ahead of them, asking more than mere ordinary men could do. So a pitiful figure—a failure at the last!

"Come on, men! Come on, you fools—come on, you —you——"

What the word was, which that bullet full in the chest arrested between heart and lips, those who knew John Nicholson's wild temper, his indomitable will, his fierce resentment at everything which fell short of his ideals, can easily guess.

"Lay me under that tree," he gasped, as they raised him. "I will not leave till the lane is carried. My God! Don't mind me! Forward, men, forward! It *can* be done."

An hour or two afterward a subaltern coming out of the Cashmere gate saw a dhooli, deserted by its bearers. In it lay John Nicholson in dire agony; but he asked nothing of his fellows then save to be taken to hospital. He had learned his lesson. He had done what others had set him to do. He had entered Delhi. He had pricked the bubble, and the gas was leaking out. But he had failed in the task he had set himself. The Burn Bastion was still unwon, and the English force in Delhi, instead of holding its northern half up to the very walls of the Palace, secure from flanking foes, had to retire on the strip of open ground behind the assaulted wall—if, indeed, it had not to retire further still. Had one man had his way it would have retired to the Ridge. Late in the afternoon, when fighting was over for the day, General Wilson rode round the new-won position, and, map in hand, looked despairingly toward the network of narrow lanes and alleys beyond. And he looked at something close at hand with even greater forebodings; for he stood in the European quarter of the town among shops still holding vast stores of wine and spirits which had been left untouched by that other army of occupation.

But what of this one? This product of civilization, and culture, and Christianity; these men who could give points to those others in so many ways, but might barter their very birthright for a bottle of rum. Yet even so, the position must be held. So said Baird Smith at the chief's elbow, so wrote Neville Chamberlain, unable to leave his post on the Ridge. And another man in hospital, thinking of the Burn Bastion, thinking with a strange wonder of men who could refuse to follow, muttered under his breath, "Thank God! I have still strength left to shoot a coward."

And yet General Wilson in a way was right. Five days afterward Major Hodson wrote in his diary: "The troops are utterly demoralized by hard work and hard drink. For the first time in my life I have had to see English soldiers refuse repeatedly to follow their officers. Jacob, Nicholson, Greville, Speke were all sacrificed to this."

A terrible indictment indeed, against brave men.

Yet not worse than that underlying the chief's order of the 15th, directing the Provost-marshal to search for and smash every bottle and barrel to be found, and let the beer and wine, so urgently needed by the sick, run into the gutters; or his admission three days later that another attempt to take the Lahore gate had failed from " the refusal of the European soldiers to follow their officers. One rush and it could have been done easily— we are still, therefore, in the same position to-day as we were yesterday."

So much for drink.

But the enemy luckily was demoralized also. It was still full of defense; empty of attack.

For one thing, attack would have admitted a reverse; and over on that eastern wall of the Palace, in the fretted marble balcony overlooking the river, there was no mention, even now, of such a word. Reverse! Had not the fourth column been killed to a man? Had not Nikalseyn himself fallen a victim to valor? But Soma, and many a man of his sort, gave up the pretense with bitter curses at themselves. They had seen from their own posts that victorious escalade, that swift, unchecked herding of the frightened sheep. And they—intolerable thought!—were sheep also. They saw men with dark faces, no whit better than they—better!—the Rajpoot had at least a longer record than the Sikh!—led to victory while they were not led at all. So brought face to face once more with the old familiar glory and honor, the old familiar sight of the master first—uncompromisingly, indubitably first to snatch success from the grasp of Fate, and hand it back to them—they thought of the past three months with loathing.

And as for Nikalseyn's rebuff. Soma, hearing of it from a comrade, hot at heart as he, went to the place, and looked down the lane as John Nicholson had done. By all the Pandâvas! a place for heroes indeed! Ah! if he had been there, he would have stayed there somehow. He walked up and down it moodily, picturing the struggle to himself; thinking with a curious anger of those men on the housetops, in the bastion, taking potshots at the unsheltered men below. That was all there would be now. They might drive the masters back for a time, they might inveigle them into lanes and reduce their numbers by tens and fifties, they, men of his sort, might make a brave defense.

Defense! Soma wanted to attack. Attracted by the faint shade of the kikar tree he sat down beneath it, resting against the trunk, looking along the lane once more, just as, a day or two before, John Nicholson had rested for a space. And the iron of failure entered into this man's heart also, because there was none to lead. And with the master there had been none to follow.

Suddenly he rose, his mind made up. If that was so, let him go back to the plow. That also was a hereditary trade.

That night, without a word to anyone, leaving his uniform behind him, he started along the Rohtuck road for his ancestral village. But he had to make a detour round the suburbs, for, despite that annihilation spoken of in the Palace, they were now occupied by the English.

Yet but little headway had been made in securing a firmer hold within the city itself.

"You can't, till the Burn Bastion is taken and the Lahore gate secured," said Nicholson from his dying bed, whence, growing perceptibly weaker day by day, yet with mind clear and unclouded, he watched and warned. The single eye was not closed yet, was not even made dim by death. It saw still, what it had seen on the day of the assault; what it had coveted then and failed to reach.

But it was not for five days after this failure that even Baird Smith recognized the absolute accuracy of this judgment, and, against the Chief's will, obtained permission to sap through the shelter of the intervening houses till they could tackle the bastion at close and commanding quarters without asking the troops to face another lane. So on the morning of the 19th, after a night of storm and rain cooling the air incredibly, the pick-ax began what rifles and swords had failed to do. By nightfall a tall house was reached, whence the bastion could be raked fore and aft. Its occupants, recognizing this, took advantage of the growing darkness to evacuate it. Half an hour afterward the master-key of the position was in English hands.

Rather unsteady ones, for here again the troops—once more the 8th, the 75th, the Sikh Infantry, and that balance of the Fusiliers—had found more brandy.

"*Poisoned, sir?*" said one thirsty trooper, flourishing a bottle of Exshaw's Number One before the eyes of his Captain, who, as a last inducement to sobriety, was suggesting danger. "Not a bit of it. Capsules all right."

But this time England could afford a few drunk men. The bastion was gone, and by the Turkoman and Delhi gates half the town was going. And not only the town. Down in the Palace men and women, with fumbling hands and dazed eyes, like those new roused from dreams, were snatching at something to carry with them in their flight. Bukht Khân stood facing the Queen in her favorite summer-house, alone, save for Hâfzan, the scribe, who lingered, watching them with a certain malice in her eyes. She had been right. Vengeance had been coming. Now it had come.

"All is not lost, my Queen," said Bukht Khân, with

hand on sword. "The open country lies before us, Lucknow is ours—come!"

"And the King, and my son," she faltered. The dull glitter of her tarnished jewelry seemed in keeping with the look on her face. There was something sordid in it. Sordid, indeed, for behind that mask of wifely solicitude and maternal care lay the thought of her hidden treasure.

"Let them come too. Naught hinders it."

True. But the gold, the gold!

After he had left her, impatient of her hesitation, a sudden terror seized her, lest he might have sought the King, lest he might persuade him.

"My bearers—woman! Quick!" she called to Hâfzan. "Quick, fool! my dhooli!"

But even dhooli bearers have to fly when vengeance shadows the horizon; and in that secluded corner none remained. Everyone was busy elsewhere; or from sheer terror clustered together where soldiers were to be found.

"The Ornament-of-Palaces can walk," said Hâfzan, still with that faint malice in her face. "There is none to see, and it is not far."

So, for the last time, Zeenut Maihl left the summer-house whence she had watched the Meerut road. Left it on foot, as many a better woman as unused to walking as she was leaving Delhi with babies on their breasts and little children toddling beside them. Past the faint outline of the Pearl Mosque, through the cool damp of the watered garden with the moon shining overhead, she stumbled laboriously. Up the steps of the Audience Hall toward a faint light by the Throne. The King sat on it, almost in the dark; for the oil cressets on a trefoil stand only seemed to make the shadows blacker. They lay thick upon the roof, blotting out that circling boast. Before him stood Bukht Khân, his hand still on his sword, broad, contemptuously bold. But on either side of the shrunken figure, half lost in the shadows also, were other counselors. Ahsan-Oolah, wily as ever, Elahi Buksh, the time-server, who saw the only hope of safety in prompt surrender.

"Let the Pillar-of-Faith claim time for thought," the

latter was saying. " There is no hurry. If the souba-dar-sahib is in one, let him go———"

Bukht Khân broke in with an ugly laugh, " Yea, Mirza-sahib, I can go, but if I go the army goes with me. Remember that. The King can keep the rabble. I have the soldiers."

Bahadur Shah looked from one to the other help-lessly. Whether to go, risk all, endure a life of unknown discomfort at his age, or remain, alone, unprotected, he knew not.

" Yea! that is true. Still there is no need for hurry," put in the physician, with a glance at Elahi Buksh. " Let my master bid the soubadar and the army meet him at the Tomb of Humayon· to-morrow morning. 'Twill be more seemly time to leave than now, like a thief in the night."

Bukht Khân gave a sharp look at the speaker, then laughed again. He saw the game. He scarcely cared to check it.

" So be it. But let it be before noon. I will wait no longer."

As he passed out hastily he almost ran into a half-veiled figure, which, with another behind it, was hugging one of the pillars, peering forward, listening. He guessed it for the Queen, and paused instantly.

" 'Tis thy last chance, Zeenut Màihl," he whispered in her ear. " Come if thou art wise."

The last. No! not that. The last for sovereignty perhaps, but not for hidden treasure. Half an hour afterward, a little procession of Royal dhoolies passed out of the Palace on their way to Elahi Buksh's house beside the Delhi gate, and Ahsan-Oolah walked beside the Queen's. He had gold also to save, and he was wise; so she listened, and as she listened she told herself that it would be best to stay. Her life was safe, and her son was too young for the punishment of death. As for the King, he was too old for the future to hold anything else.

Hâfzan watched her go, still with that half-jeering smile, then turned back into the empty Palace. Even in the outer court it was empty, indeed, save for a few fanatics muttering texts; and within the precincts, deserted utterly, silent as the grave. Until, suddenly, from the Pearl Mosque a voice came, giving the call to prayer; for it was not far from dawn.

She paused, recognizing it, and leaving the marble terrace where she had been standing, looking riverward, walked over to the bronze-studded door, and peered in among the white arches of the mosque for what she sought.

And there it was, a tall white figure looking westward, its back toward her, its arms spread skyward. A fanatic of fanatics.

" Thou art not wise to linger here, Moulvie sahib," she called. " Hast not heard? The Burn Bastion is taken. The King and Queen have fled. The English will be here in an hour or so, and then——"

" And then there comes judgment," answered Mohammed Ismail, turning to look at her sternly. " Doth not it lie within these walls? I stay here, woman, as I have stayed."

" Nay, not here," she argued in conciliatory tones. "It lies yonder, in the outer court, by the trees shadowing the little tank. Thou canst see it from the window of my uncle's room. And he hath gone—like the others. 'Twere better to await it there."

She spoke as she would have spoken to a madman. And, indeed, she held him to be little else. Here was a man who had saved forty infidels, whose reward was sure. And who must needs imperil it by lingering where death was certain; must needs think of his battered soul instead of his body. Mohammed Ismail came and stood beside her, with a curious acquiesence in regard to details which is so often seen in men mastered by one idea.

" It may be better so, sister," he said dreamily. " 'Tis as well to be prepared."

Hâfzan's hard eyes melted a little, for she had a real pity for this man who had haunted the Palace persistently, and lost his reason over his conscience.

If she could once get him into her uncle's room, she would find some method of locking him in, of keeping him out of mischief. For herself, being a woman, the Huzoors were not to be feared.

"Yea! 'tis as well to be near," she said as she led the way.

And the time drew near also; for the dawn of the 20th of September had broken ere, with the key of the outer door in her bosom, she retired into an inner room, leaving the Moulvie saying his prayers in the other. Already the troops, recovered from their unsteadiness, had carried the Lahore gate and were bearing down on the mosque. They found it almost undefended. The circling flight of purple pigeons, which at the first volley flew westward, the sun glistening on their iridescent plumage, was scarcely more swift than the flight of those who attempted a feeble resistance. And now the Palace lay close by. With it captured, Delhi was taken. Its walls, it is true, rose unharmed, secure as ever, hemming in those few acres of God's earth from the march of time; but they were strangely silent. Only now and again a puff of white smoke and an unavailing roar told that someone, who cared not even for success, remained within.

So powder bags were brought. Home of the Engineers sent for, that he might light the fuse which gave entry to the last stronghold; for there was no hurry now. No racing now under hailstorms, and over tight-ropes. Calmly, quietly, the fuse was lit, the gate shivered to atoms, and the long red tunnel with the gleam of sunlight at its end lay before the men, who entered it with a cheer. Then, here and there rose guttural Arabic texts, ending in a groan. Here and there the clash of arms. But not enough to rouse Hâfzan, who, long ere this, had fallen asleep after her wakeful night. It needed a touch on her shoulder for that, and the Moulvie's eager voice in her ear.

"The key, woman! The key—give it! I need the key."

Half-dazed by sleep, deceived by the silence, she put her hand mechanically to her bosom. His followed hers; he had what he sought, and was off. She sprang to her feet, recognizing some danger, and followed him.

"He is mad! He is mad!" she cried, as her halting steps lingered behind the tall white figure which made straight for a crowd of soldiers gathered round the little tank. There were other soldiers here, there, everywhere in the rose-red arcades around the sun-lit court. Soldiers with dark faces and white ones seeking victims, seeking plunder. But these in the center were all white men, and they were standing, as men stand to look at a holy shrine, upon the place where, as the spies had told them, English women and children had been murdered.

So toward them, while curses were in all hearts and on some lips, came the tall white figure with its arms outspread, its wild eyes aflame.

"O God of Might and Right! Give judgment now, give judgment now."

The cry rolled and echoed through the arcades to alien ears even as other cries.

"He is mad—he saved them—he is mad!" gasped the maimed woman behind; but her cry seemed no different to those unheeding ears.

The tall white figure lay on its face, half a dozen bayonets in its back, and half a dozen more were after Hâfzan.

"Stick him! Stick him! A man in disguise. Remember the women and children. Stick the coward!"

She fled shrieking—shrill, feminine shrieks; but the men's blood was up. They could not hear, they would not hear; and yet the awkwardness of that flying figure made them laugh horribly.

"Don't 'ustle 'im! Give 'im time! There's plenty o' run in 'im yet, mates. Lord! 'e'd get first prize at Lillie Bridge 'e would."

Someone else, however, had got it at Harrow not a year before, and was after the reckless crew. Almost too late—not quite. Hâfzan, run to earth against a red wall, felt something on her back, and gave a wild yell. But it was only a boy's hand.

"My God! sir, I've stuck you!" faltered a voice behind, as a man stood rigid, arrested in mid-thrust.

"You d——d fool!" said the boy. "Couldn't you hear it was a woman? I'll—I'll have you shot. Oh,

hang it all! Drag the creature away, someone. Get
out, do!"

For Hâfzan, as he stood stanching the blood from
the slight wound, had fallen at his feet and was kissing
them frantically.

But even that indignity was forgotten as the stained
handkerchief answered the flutter of something which at
that moment caught the breeze above him.

It was the English flag.

The men, forgetting everything else, cheered themselves hoarse—cheered again when an orderly rode past
waving a slip of paper sent back to the General with the
laconic report:

"Blown open the gates! Got the Palace!"

But Hâfzan, her veil up to prevent mistakes, limped
over to where the Moulvie lay, turned him gently on his
back, straightened his limbs and closed his eyes. She
would have liked to tell the truth to someone, but there
was no one to listen. So she left him there before the
tribunal to which he had appealed.

CHAPTER VI.

REWARDS AND PUNISHMENTS.

So the strain of months was over on the Ridge. Delhi
was taken; the Queen's health was being drunk night
after night in the Palace of the Moghuls. But there was
one person to whom the passing days brought a growing
anxiety. This was Kate Erlton; for there were no tidings of Jim Douglas. None.

At first she had comforted herself with the idea that he
was still, for some reason or another, keeping to the yet
unconquered part of the city; that he was obliged to do
so being impossible, the long files of women and children
seeking safety and passing through the Ridge fearlessly
precluding that consolation. Still it was conceivable
he might be busy, though it seemed strange he should
have sent no word. So, like many another in India at

that time, she waited, hoping against hope, possessing her soul in patience. She had no lack of occupation to distract her. How could there be for a woman, when close on twelve hundred men had come back from the city dead or wounded?

But now the 21st of September was upon them. The city was occupied, the work was over. Yet Captain Morecombe, coming back from it, shook his head. He had spent time and trouble in the search, but had failed—failed even, from Kate's limited ideas of their locality, to find either Tara's lodging or the roof in the Mufti's quarter. She could have found them herself, she said almost pathetically; but of course that was impossible now, and would be so for some time to come.

"I'm afraid it is no use, Mrs. Erlton," said the Captain kindly. "There is not a trace to be found, even by Hodson's spies. Unless he is shut up somewhere, he—he must be dead. It is so likely that he should be; you must see that. Possibly before the siege began. Let us hope so."

"Why?" she asked quickly. "You mean that there have been horrible things done of late?—things like that poor soldier who was found chained outside the Cashmere gate as a target for his fellows? Have there? I would so much rather know the worst,—I used always to tell Mr. Douglas so,—it prevents one dreaming at night." She shivered as she spoke, and the man watching her felt his heart go out toward her with a throb of pity. How long, he wondered irrelevantly, would it take her to forget the miserable tragedy, to be ready for consolation?

"Yes, there have been terrible things on both sides. There always are. You can't help it when you sack cities," he replied, interrupting himself hastily with a sort of shame. "The Ghoorkhas had the devil in them when I was down in the Mufti's quarter. They shot dozens of helpless learned people in the Chelon-ke-kucha—one who coached me up for my exams. And about twelve women in the house of a 'Professor of Arabic'—so he styled himself—jumped down the wall to escape—their own fears chiefly. For the men wanted loot, nothing else. That is the worst of it. The whole story from beginning to end seems so needless. It is as if Fate——"

She interrupted him quietly, "It has been Fate. Fate from beginning to end."

He sat for an instant with a grave face, then looked up with a smile. "Perhaps. It's rather *apropos des bottes*, Mrs. Erlton, but I wanted to ask you a question. Hadn't you a white cockatoo, once? When you first came here. I seem to recollect the bird making a row in the veranda when I used to drive up."

Her face grew suddenly pale, she sat staring at him with dread in her eyes. "Yes!" she replied with a manifest effort, "I gave it to Sonny Seymour because—because it loved him——" She broke off, then added swiftly, eagerly, "What then?"

"Only that I found one in the Palace to-day. There is a jolly marble latticed balcony overlooking the river. The King used to write his poetry there, they say. Well! I saw a brass cage hanging high up on a hook—there has been no loot in the precincts, you know, for the Staff has annexed them; I thought the cage was empty till I took it down from sheer curiosity, and there was a dead cockatoo."

"Dead!" echoed Kate, with a quick smile of relief. "Oh! how glad I am it was dead."

Captain Morecombe stared at her. "Poor brute!" he said under his breath. "It was skin and bone. Starved to death. I expect they forgot all about it when they got really frightened. They are cruel devils, Mrs. Erlton."

The Major had used the self-same words to Alice Gissing eighteen months before, and in the same connection. But, perhaps fortunately for Kate in her present state of nervous strain, that knowledge was denied to her. Even so the coincidence of the bird itself absorbed her.

"It had a yellow crest," she began.

"Oh! then it couldn't have been yours," interrupted Captain Morecombe, rather relieved, for he saw that he had somehow touched on a hidden wound. "This one was green; yellowish green. I dare say the King kept pets like the Oude man——"

" It is dead anyhow," said Kate hurriedly.

And the knowledge gave her an unreasoning comfort. To begin with, it seemed to her as if those fateful white wings, which had begun to overshadow her world on that sunny evening down by the Goomtee river, had ceased to hover over it. And then this rounding of the tale—for that the bird was little Sonny's favorite she did not doubt—made her feel that Fate would not leave that other portion of it unfinished. The inevitable sequence would be worked out somehow. She would hear something. So once more she waited like many another; waiting with eyes strained past the last known deed of gallantry for the end which surely must have been nobler still. When that knowledge came, she told herself, she would be content.

Yet there was another thing which held her to hope even more than this; it was the remembrance of John Nicholson's words, " If ever you have a chance of making up." They seemed prophetic; for he who spoke them was so often right. Men talking of him as he lingered, watching, advising, warning, despite dire agony of pain and drowsiness of morphia, said there was none like him for clear insight into the very heart of things.

Yet he, as he lay without a complaint, was telling himself he had been blind. He had sought more from his world than there was in it. And so, though the news of the capture of the Burn Bastion brought a brief rally, he sank steadily.

But Hodson, coming into his tent to tell him of the safe capture of the King and Queen upon the 21st at Humayon's Tomb, found him eager to hear all particulars. So eager, that when the Sirdars of the Mooltanee Horse (a regiment he had practically raised), who sat outside in dozens waiting for every breath of news about their fetish, would not keep quiet, he emphasized his third order by a revolver bullet through the wall of the tent. Greatly to their delight since, as they retired further off, they agreed that Nikalseyn was Nikalseyn still; and surely death dare not claim one so full of life?

Even Hodson smiled in the swift silence in which the laboring breath of the dying man could be heard.

" Well, sir," he went on, " as I was saying, I got permission, thanks to you, to utilize my information——"

" You mean Rujjub Ali's and that sneak Elahi Buksh's, I suppose," put in Nicholson. " It was sharp work. The King only went to Humayon's Tomb yesterday. They must have had it all cut and dried before, surely? "

" The Queen has been trying to surrender on terms some time back, sir," replied Hodson hastily. " She has a lot of treasure—eight lakhs, the spies tell me—and is anxious to keep it. However, to go on. After stopping with Elahi Buksh that night—no doubt, as you say, pressure was put on them then—they went off, as agreed, to meet Bukht Khân, but refused to go with him. Of course the promise of their lives——"

" Then you were negotiating already? " *

" Not exactly—but—but I couldn't have done without the promise unless Wilson had agreed to send out troops, and he wouldn't. So I had to give in, though personally I would a deal rather have brought the old man in dead, than alive. Well, I set off this morning with fifty of my horse and sent in the two messengers while I waited outside. It was nearly two hours before they came back, for the old man was hard to move. Zeenut Maihl was the screw, and when Bahâdur Shâh talked of his ancestors and wept, told him he should have thought of that before he let Bukht Khân and the army go. In fact she did the business for me; but she stipulated for a promise of life from my own lips. So I rode out alone to the causeway by the big gate—it is a splendid place, sir; more like a mosque than a tomb, and drew up to attention. Zeenut Maihl came out first, swinging along in her curtained dhooli, and Rujjub, who was beside me, called out her name and titles decorously. I couldn't help feeling it was a bit of a scene, you know;

---

* (Hodson in his diary says that the promise was virtually given *two* days before the capture. This was the 21st. It must therefore have been given on the 19th. *Most likely* in Elahi Buksh's house. If so, on Hodson's own authority. Query. Was he there in person ?)

my being there, alone, and all that. Then the King came in his palkee; so I rode up, and demanded his sword. He asked if I were Hodson-sahib bahâdur and if I would ratify the promise? So I had to choke over it, for there were two or three thousand of a crowd by this time. Then we came away. It was a long five miles at a footpace, with that crowd following us until we neared the city. Then they funked. Besides I had said openly I'd shoot the King like a dog despite the promise at the first sign of rescue. And that's all, except that you should have seen the officer's face at the Lahore gate when he asked me what I'd got in tow, and I said calmly, 'Only the King of Delhi.' So that is done."

"And well done," said Nicholson briefly, reaching out a parched right hand. "Well done, from the beginning to the end."

Hodson flushed up like a girl. "I'm glad to hear you say so, sir," he replied as nonchalantly as he could, "but personally, of course, I would rather have brought him in dead."

Even that slight action, however, had left Nicholson breathless, and the only comment for a time came from his eyes; bright, questioning eyes, seeking now with a sort of pathetic patience to grasp the world they were leaving, and make allowances for all shortcomings.

"And now for the Princes," said Hodson. "Did you write to Wilson, sir?"

Nicholson nodded, "I think he'll consent. Only—only don't make any more promises, Hodson. Some of them must be hung; they deserve death."

His hearer gave rather an uneasy look at the clear eyes, and remarked sharply: "You thought they deserved more than hanging once, sir."

The old imperious frown of quick displeasure at all challenge came to John Nicholson's face, then faded into a half-smile. "I was not so near death myself. It makes a difference. So good-by, Hodson. I mayn't see you again." He paused, and his smile grew clearer, and strangely soft. "No news, I suppose, of that poor fellow Douglas, who didn't agree with us?"

"None, sir; I warned him it was useless and foolhardy to go back when my information——"

"No doubt," interrupted the dying man gently. "Still, I'd have gone in his place." He lay still for a moment, then murmured to himself. "So he is on the way before me. Well! I don't think we can be unhappy after death. And, as for that poor lady—when you see her, Hodson, tell her I am sorry—sorry she hadn't her chance." The last words were once more murmured to himself and ended in silence.

Kate Erlton, however, did not get the message which would, perhaps, have ended her lingering hope. Major Hodson was too busy to deliver it. Permission to capture the Princes was given him that very night, and early the next morning he set off to Humayon's Tomb once more, with his two spies, his second in command, and about a hundred troopers. A small party indeed, to face the four or five thousand Palace refugees who were known to be in hiding about the tomb, waiting to see if the Princes could make terms like the King had done. But Hodson's orders were strict. He was to bring in Mirza Moghul and Khair Sultân, ex-Commanders-in-Chief, and Abool-Bukr, heir presumptive, unconditionally, or not at all.

The morning was deliciously cool and crisp, full of that promise of winter, which in its perfection of climate consoles the Punjabee for six months of purgatory. The sun sent a yellow flood of light over the endless ruins of ancient Delhi, which here extend for miles on miles. A nasty country for skulking enemies; but Hodson's pluck and dash were equal to anything, and he rode along with a heart joyous at his chance; full of determination to avail himself of it and gain renown.

Someone else, however, was early astir on this the 22d of September, so as to reach Humayon's Tomb in time to press on to the Kutb, if needs be. This was the Princess Farkhoonda Zamâni. Ever since that day, now more than a week past, when the last message to the city had warned her that the supreme moment for the House of Timoor was at hand, and she had started from her study of Holy Writ, telling herself piteously that she must find Prince Abool-Bukr—must, at all sacrifice to pride, seek him, since he would not seek her—

must warn him and keep his hand in hers again—she
had been distracted by the impossibility of carrying out
her decision.   For, expecting an immediate sack of the
town, the Mufti's people had barricaded the only exit
bazaar-ward, and when, after a day or two, she did succeed in creeping out, it was to find the streets unsafe, the
Palace itself closed against all.   But now, at least, there
was a chance.   Like all the royal family, she knew of
these two spies, Rujjub-Ali and Mirza Elahi Buksh, who
was saving his skin by turning Queen's evidence.   She
knew of Hodson sahib's promise to the King and Queen.
She knew that Abool-Bukr was still in hiding with the
arch-offenders, Mirza Moghul and Khair Sultân, at
Humayon's Tomb.   Such an association was fatal; but
if she could persuade him to throw over his uncles, and
go with her, and if, afterward, she could open negotiations with the Englishmen, and prove that Abool-Bukr
had been dismissed from office on the very day of the
death challenge, had been in disgrace ever since—had
even been condemned to death by the King; surely she
might yet drag her dearest from the net into which
Zeenut Maihl had lured him—with what bait she scarcely
trusted herself to think!   The first thing to be done,
therefore, was to persuade Abool to come with her to
some safer hiding.   She would risk all; her pride, her
reputation, his very opinion of her, for this.   And surely
a man of his nature was to be tempted.   So she put on
her finest clothes, her discarded jewels, and set off about
noon in a ruth—a sort of curtain-dhoolie on wheels
drawn by oxen, gay with trappings, and set with jingling
bells.   They let her pass at the Delhi gate, after a brief
look through the curtains, during which she cowered
into a corner without covering her face, lest they might
think her a man, and stop her.

" By George! that was a pretty woman," said the
English subaltern who passed her, as he came back to the
guard-room.   " Never saw such eyes in my life.   They
were as soft, as soft as—well! I don't know what.   And
they looked, somehow, as if they have been crying for
years, and—and as if they saw—saw something, you
know."

" They saw you—you sentimental idiot—that's enough to make any woman cry," retorted his companion. And then the two, mere boys, wild with success and high spirits, fell to horse-play over the insult.

Yet the first boy was right. Newâsi's eyes had seen something day and night, night and day, ever since they had strained into the darkness after Prince Abool-Bukr when he broke from the kind detaining hand and disappeared from the Mufti's quarter. And that something was a flood of sunlight holding a figure, as she had seen it more than once, in a wild unreasoning paroxysm of sheer terror. It seemed to her as if she could hear those white lips gasping once more over the cry which brought the vision. " Why didst not let me live mine own life, die mine own death? but to die—to die needlessly—to die in the sunlight perhaps."

There was a flood of it now outside the ruth as it lumbered along by the jail, not a quarter of a mile yet from the city gate. Half-shivering she peeped through the gay patchwork curtains to assure herself it held no horror.

God and his Holy Prophet! What was that crowd on the road ahead? No, not ahead, she was in it, now, so that the oxen paused, unable to go on. A crowd, a cluster of spear-points, and then, against the jail wall, an open space round another ruth, an Englishman on foot, three figures stripped. No; not three! only two, for one had fallen as the crack of a carbine rang through the startled air. Two? But one, now, and that, oh! saints have mercy! the vision! the vision! It was Abool, dodging like a hare, begging for bare life; seeking it, at last, out of the sunshine, under the shadow of the ruth wheels.

" Abool! Abool! " she screamed. " I am here. Come! I am here."

Did he hear the kind voice? He may have, for it echoed clear before the third and final crack of the carbine. So clear that the driver, terrified lest it should bring like punishment on him, drove his goad into the oxen; and the next instant they were careering madly down a side road, bumping over watercourses and ditches. But Newâsi felt no more buffetings. She lay huddled up inside, as unconscious as that other figure which, by Major Hodson's orders, was being dragged out from under the wheels and placed upon it beside the two other corpses for conveyance to the city. And none of all the crowd, ready—so the tale runs—to rescue the Princes lest death should be their portion in the future, raised voice or hand to avenge them now that it had come so ruthlessly, so wantonly. Perhaps the English guard at the Delhi gate cowed them, as it had cowed those who the day before had followed the King so far, then slunk away.

So the little *cortège* moved on peacefully; far more peacefully than the other ruth, which, with *its* unconscious burden, was racing Kutb-ward as if it was afraid of the very sunshine. But the Princess Farkhoonda, huddled up in all her jewels and fineries, had forgotten even that; forgotten even that vision seen in it.

But Hodson as he rode at ease behind the dead Princes seemed to court the light. He gloried in the deed, telling himself that " in less than twenty-four hours he had disposed of the principal members of the House of Timoor "; so fulfilling his own words written weeks before, " If I get into the Palace, the House of Timoor will not be worth five minutes' purchase, I ween." Telling himself also, that in shooting down with his own hand men who had surrendered without stipulations to his generosity and clemency, surrendered to a hundred troopers when they had five thousand men behind them, he " had rid the earth of ruffians." Telling himself that he was " glad to have had the opportunity, and was game to face the moral risk of praise or blame."

He got the former unstintingly from most of his fellows as, in triumphant procession, the bodies were taken to the chief police station, there to be exposed, so say eye-witnesses, " In the very spot where, four months before, Englishwomen had been outraged and murdered, in the very place where their helpless victims had lain."

A strange perversion of the truth, responsible, perhaps, not only for the praise, but for the very deed itself; so Mohammed Ismail's barter of his truth and soul for the lives of the forty prisoners at the Kolwâb counted for nothing in the judgment of this world.

But Hodson lacked either praise or blame from one man. John Nicholson lay too near the judgment of another world to be disturbed by vexed questions in this; and when the next morning came, men, meeting each other, said sadly, " He is dead."

The news, brought to Kate Erlton by Captain Morecombe when he came over to report another failure, took the heart out of even her hope.

" There is no use in my staying longer, I'm afraid," she said quietly. " I'm only in the way. I will go back to Meerut; and then home—to the boy."

" I think it would be best," he replied kindly. " I can arrange for you to start to-morrow morning. You will be the better for a change; it will help you to forget."

She smiled a little bitterly; but when he had gone she set to work, packing up such of her husband's things as she wished the boy to have with calm deliberation; and early in the afternoon went over to the garden of her old house to get some fresh flowers for what would be her last visit to that rear-guard of graves. To take, also, her last look at the city, and watch it grow mysterious in the glamour of sunset. Seen from afar it seemed unchanged. A mass of rosy light and lilac shadow, with the great white dome of the mosque hanging airily above the smoke wreaths.

Yet the end had come to its four months' dream as it had come to hers. Rebellion would linger long, but its stronghold, its very *raison d'être*, was gone. And Memory would last longer still; yet surely it would not be all bitter. Hers was not. Then with a rush of real regret she thought of the peaceful roof, of old Tiddu, of the Princess Farkhoonda—Tara—Soma—of Sri Anunda in his garden. Was she to go home to safe, snug England, live in a suburb, and forget? Forget all but the tragedy! Yet even that held beautiful memories. Alice Gissing under young Mainwaring's scarf, while he lay at her feet. Her husband leaving a good name to his son. Did not these things help to make the story perfect? No! not perfect. And with the remembrance her eyes filled

with sudden tears.   There would always be a blank for
her in the record.   The Spirit which had moved on the
Face of the Waters, bringing their chance of Healing and
Atonement to so many, had left hers in the shadow.   She
had learned her lesson.   Ah! yes; she had learned it.
But the chance of using it?

As she sat on the plinth of the ruined veranda, watching the city growing dim through the mist of her tears,
John Nicholson's words came back to her once more,
" If ever you have the chance "; but it would never come
now—never!

She started up wildly at the clutch of a brown hand
on her wrist—a brown hand with a circlet of dead gold
above it.

" Come! " said a voice behind her; " come quick! he
needs you."

" Tara! " she gasped—" Tara!   Is—is he alive then? "

" He would not need the mem if he were dead," came
the swift reply.   Then with her wild eyes fixed on
another gold circlet upon the wrist she held, Tara laughed
shrilly.   " So the mem wears it still.   She has not forgotten.   Women do not forget, white or black "—with
a strange stamp of her foot she interrupted herself
fiercely—" come, I say, come! "

If there had been doubts as to the Rajpootni's
sanity at times in past days, there was none now.   A
glance at her face was sufficient.   It was utterly distraught, the clutch on Kate's arm utterly uncontrolled;
so that, involuntarily, the latter shrank back.

" The mem is afraid," cried Tara exultantly.   " So be
it!   I will go back and tell the master.   Tell him I was
right and he wrong, for all the English he chattered.   I
will tell him the mem is not suttee—how could she
be——"

The old taunt roused many memories, and made Kate
ready to risk anything.   " I am coming, Tara—but
where? "   She stood facing the tall figure in crimson,
a tall figure also, in white, her hands full of the roses
she had gathered.

Tara looked at her with that old mingling of regret and

approbation, jealousy and pride. " Then she must come at once. He is dying—may be dead ere we get back."

" Dead! " echoed Kate faintly. " Is he wounded then? "

A sort of somber sullenness dulled the excitement of Tara's face. " He is ill," she replied laconically. Suddenly, however, she burst out again: " The mem need not look so! I have done all—all she could have done. It is his fault. He will not take things. The mem can do no more; but I have come to her, so that none shall say, ' Tara killed the master.' So come. Come quick! "

Five minutes after Kate was swinging cityward in a curtained dhooli which Tara had left waiting on the road below, and trying to piece out a consecutive story from the odd jumble of facts and fancies and explanations which Tara poured into her ear between her swift abuse of the bearers for not going faster, and her assertion that there was no need to hurry. The mem need not hope to save the Huzoor, since everything had been done. It seemed, however, that Tiddu had taken back the letter telling of Kate's safety, and that in consequence of this the master had arranged to leave the city in a day or two, and Tiddu—born liar and gold grubber, so the Rajpootni styled him—had gone off at once to make more money. But on the very eve of his going back to the Ridge, Jim Douglas had been struck down with the Great Sickness, and after two or three days, instead of getting better, had fallen—as Tara put it—into the old way. So far Kate made out clearly; but from this point it became difficult to understand the reproaches, excuses, pathetic assertions of helplessness, and fierce declarations that no one could have done more. But what was the use of the Huzoor's talking English all night? she said; even a suttee could not go out when everyone was being shot in the streets. Besides, it was all obstinacy. The master could have got well if he had tried. And who was to know where to find the mem? Indeed, if it had not been for Sri Anunda's gardener, who knew all the gardener folk, of course, she would not have found the mem even now; for she would never have known which house to inquire at. Not that it would have mattered, since the mem could do nothing—nothing—nothing——

Kate, looking down on the bunch of white flowers which she had literally been too hurried to think of laying aside, felt her heart shrink.   They were rather a fateful gift to be in her hands now.   Had they come there of set purpose, and would the man who had done so much for her be beyond all care save those pitiful offices of the dead?   Still, even that was better than that he should lie alone, untended.   So, urged by Tara's vehement upbraidings, the dhooli-bearers lurched along, to stop at last.   It seemed to Kate as if her heart stopped also.   She could not think of what might lie before her as she followed Tara up the dark, strangely familiar stair.   Surely, she thought, she would have known it among a thousand.   And there was the step on which she had once crouched terror-stricken, because she was shut out from shelter within.   But now Tara's fingers were at the padlock, Tara's hand set the door wide.

Kate paused on the threshold, feeling, in truth, dazed once more at the strange familiarity of all things.   It seemed to her as if she had but just left that strip of roof aglow with the setting sun, the bubble dome of the mosque beginning to flush like a cloud upon the sky.   But Tara, watching her with resentful eyes, put a different interpretation on the pause, and said quickly:

"He is within.   The mem was away, and it was quieter.   But the rest is all the same—there is nothing forgotten—nothing."

Kate, however, heard only the first words, and was already across the outer roof to gain the inner one.   Tara, still beyond the threshold, watched her disappear, then stood listening for a minute, with a face tragic in its intensity.   Suddenly a faint voice broke the silence, and her hands, which had been tightly clenched, relaxed.   She closed the door silently, and went downstairs.

Meanwhile Kate, on the inner roof, had paused beside the low string bed set in its middle, scarcely daring to look at its burden, and so put hope and fear to the touchstone of truth.   But as she stood hesitating, a voice, querulous in its extreme weakness, said in Hindustani:

" It is too soon, Tara; I don't want anything; and— and you needn't wait—thank you."

He lay with his face turned from her, so she could stand, wondering how best to break her presence to him, noting with a failing heart the curious slackness, the lack of contour even on that hard string bed. He seemed lost, sunk in it; and she had seen that sign so often of late that she knew what it meant. One thing was certain, he must have food—stimulants if possible—before she startled him. So she stole back to the outer roof, expecting to find Tara there, and Tara's help. But the roof lay empty, and a sudden fear lest, after all, she had only come to see him die, while she was powerless to fight that death from sheer exhaustion, which seemed so perilously near, made her put down the bunch of flowers she held with an impatient gesture. What a fool she had been not to think of other things!

But as she glanced round, her eye fell on a familiar earthenware basin kept warm in a pan of water over the ashes. It was full of *chikkcn-brât*, and excellent of its kind, too. Then in a niche stood milk and eggs—a bottle of brandy, arrow-root—everything a nurse could wish for. And in another, evidently in case the brew should be condemned, was a fresh chicken ready for use. Strange sights these to bring tears of pity to a woman's eyes; but they did. For Kate, reading between the lines of poor Tara's confusion, began to understand the tragedy underlying those words she had just heard:

" I don't want anything, Tara. And you needn't wait, thank you." She seemed to see, with a flash, the long, long days which had passed, with that patient, polite negative coming to chill the half distraught devotion.

He must take something now, for all that. So, armed with a cup and spoon, she went back, going round the bed so that he could see her.

" It is time for your food, Mr. Greyman," she said quietly; " when you have taken some, I'll tell you everything. Only you must take this first." As she slipped her hand under him, pillow and all, to raise his head slightly, she could see the pained, puzzled expression

narrow his eyes as he swallowed a spoonful. Then with
a frown he turned his head from her impatiently.

"You must take three," she insisted; "you must,
indeed, Mr. Greyman. Then I will tell you—everything."

His face came back to hers with the faintest shadow
of his old mutinous sarcasm upon it, and he lay looking
at her deliberately for a second or two. "I thought you
were a ghost," he said feebly at last; "only they don't
bully. Well! let's get it over."

The memory of many such a bantering reply to her
insistence in the past sent a lump to her throat and kept
her silent. The little low stool on which she had been
wont to sit beside him was in its old place, and half-
mechanically she drew it closer, and, resting her elbow
on the bed as she used to do, looked round her, feeling
as if the last six weeks were a dream. Tara had told
truth. Everything was in its place. There were flowers
in a glass, a spotless fringed cloth on the brass platter.
The pity held in these trivial signs brought a fresh pang
to her heart for that other woman.

But Jim Douglas, lying almost in the arms of death,
was not thinking of such things.

"Then Delhi must have fallen," he said suddenly in
a stronger voice. "Did Nicholson take it?"

"Yes," she replied quietly, thinking it best to be con-
cise and give him, as it were, a fresh grip on facts. "It
has fallen. The King is a prisoner, the Princes have
been shot, and most of the troops move on to-morrow
toward Agra."

It epitomized the situation beyond the possibility of
doubt, and he gave a faint sigh. "Then it is all over.
I'm glad to hear it. Tara never knew anything; and it
seemed so long."

Had she known and refused to tell, Kate wondered?
or in her insane absorption had she really thought of
nothing but the chance Fate had thrown in her way
of saving this man's life? Yes! it must have been very
long. Kate realized this as she watched the spent and
weary face before her, its bright, hollow eyes fixed on
the glow which was now fast fading from the dome.

" All over! " he murmured to himself. " Well! I suppose it couldn't be helped."

She followed his thought unerringly; and a great pity for this man who had done nothing, where others had done so much, surged up in her and made her seek to show his fate no worse than others. Besides, this discouragement was fatal, for it pointed to a lack of that desire for life which is the best weapon against death. She might fail to rouse him, as those had failed who, but a day or two before, had sent a bit of red ribbon representing the Victoria Cross to the dying Salkeld—the hero of the Cashmere gate—and only gained in reply a faint smile and the words, " They will like it at home." Still she would try.

" Yes, it is over! " she echoed, " and it has cost so many lives uselessly. General Nicholson lost his trying to do the impossible—so people say."   •

Jim Douglas still lay staring at the fading glow. " Dead! " he murmured. " That is a pity. But he took Delhi first. He said he would."

" And my husband——" she began.

He turned then, with curiously patient courtesy. " I know. Nicholson wrote that in his letter. And I have been glad—glad he had his chance, and—and—made so much of it."

Once more she followed his thought; knew that, though he was too proud to confess it, he was saying to himself that he had had his chance too and had done nothing. So she answered it as if he had spoken.

" And you had your chance of saving a woman," she said, with a break in her voice, " and you saved her. It isn't much, I suppose. It counts as nothing to you. Why should it? But to me——" She broke off, losing her purpose for him in her own bitter regret and vague resentment. " Why didn't you let them kill me, and then go away? " she went on almost passionately. " It would have been better than saving me to remember always that I stood in your way—better than giving me no chance of repaying you for all—ah! think how much! Better than leaving me alone to a new life—like—like all the others have done."

She buried her face on her arm as it rested on the pillow with a sob.   This, then, was the end, she thought, this bitter unavailing regret for both.

So for a space there was silence while she sat with her face hidden, and he lay staring at that darkening dome. But suddenly she felt his hot hand find hers; so thin, so soft, so curiously strong still in its grip.

"Give me some more wine or something," came his voice consolingly.   "I'll try and stop—if I can."

She made an effort to smile back at him, but it was not very successful.   His, as she fed him, was better; but it did not help Kate Erlton to cheerfulness, for it was accompanied by a murmur that the *chikken-brât* was very different from Tara's stuff.   So she seemed to see a poor ghost glowering at them from the shadows, asking her how she dared take all the thanks.   And the ghost remained long after Jim Douglas had dozed off; remained to ask, so it seemed to Kate Erlton, every question that could be asked about the mystery of womanhood and manhood.

But Tara herself asked none when in the first gray glimmer of dawn she crept up the stairs again and stood beside the sleepers.   For Kate, wearied out, had fallen asleep crouched up on the stool, her head resting on the pillow, her arm flung over the bed to keep that touch on his hand which seemed to bring him rest.   Tara, once more in her widow's dress, looked down on them silently, then threw her bare arms upward.   So for a second she stood, a white-shrouded appealing figure against that dark shadow of the dome which blocked the paling eastern sky.   Then stooping, her long, lissome fingers busied themselves stealthily with the thin gold chain about the sick man's neck; for there was something in the locket attached to it which was hers by right now. Hers, if she could have nothing else; for she was suttee—suttee!

The unuttered cry was surging through her heart and brain, rousing a mad exultation in her, when half an hour afterward she re-entered the narrow lane leading to the arcaded courtyard with the black old shrine

hiding under the tall peepul tree. And what was that
hanging over the congeries of roofs and stairs, the
rabbit warren of rooms and passages where her pigeon-
nest was perched? A canopy of smoke, and below it
leaping flames. There were many wanton fires in Delhi
during those first few days of license, and this was one of
them; but already, in the dawn, English officers were at
work giving orders, limiting the danger as much as possible.

"We can't save that top bit," said one at last, then
turned to one of his fatigue party. "Have you cleared
everybody out, sergeant, as I told you?"

"Yes, sir! it's quite empty."

It *had* been so five minutes before. It was not now;
for that canopy of smoke, those licking tongues of flame,
had given the last touch to Tara's unstable mind. She
had crept up and up, blindly, and was now on her knees
in that bare room set round with her one scrap of culture,
ransacking an old basket for something which had not
seen the light for years, her scarlet tinsel-set wedding
dress. Her hands were trembling, her wild eyes blazed
like fires themselves.

And below, men waited calmly for the flames to claim
this, their last prize; for the turret stood separated from
the next house.

"My God!" came an English voice, as something
showed suddenly upon the roof. "I thought you said
it was empty—and that's a woman!"

It was. A woman in a scarlet, tinsel-set dress, and all
the poor ornaments she possessed upon her widespread
arms. So, outlined against the first sun-ray she stood,
her shrill chanting voice rising above the roar and rush
of the flames.

"Oh! Guardians eight, of this world and the next.
Sun, Moon, and Air, Earth, Ether, Water, and my own
poor soul bear witness! Oh! Lord of death, bear witness that I come. Day, Night, and Twilight say I am
suttee."

There was a louder roar, a sudden leaping of the
flames, and the turret sank inwardly. But the chanting

voice could be heard for a second in the increasing silence which followed.

" Shive-jee hath saved His own," said the crowd, looking toward the unharmed shrine.

And over on the other side of the city, Kate Erlton, roused by that same first ray of sunlight, was looking down with a smile upon Jim Douglas before waking him. The sky was clear as a topaz, the purple pigeons were cooing and sidling on the copings. And in the bright, fresh light she saw the gold locket lying open on the sleeper's breast. She had often wondered what it held, and now—thinking he might not care to find it at her mercy—stooped to close it.

But it was empty.

The snap, slight as it was, roused him. Not, however, to a knowledge of the cause, for he lay looking up at her in his turn.

" So it is all over," he said softly, but he said it with a smile.

Yes! It was all over. Down on the parade ground behind the Ridge the bugles were sounding, and the men who had clung to the red rocks for so long were preparing to leave them for assault elsewhere.

But one man was taking an eternal hold upon them; for John Nicholson was being laid in his grave. Not in the rear-guard, however, but in the van, on the outermost spur of the Ridge abutting on the city wall, within touch almost of the Cashmere gate. Being laid in his grave—by his own request—without escort, without salute; for he knew that he had failed.

So he lies there facing the city he took. But his real grave was in that narrow lane within the walls where those who dream can see him still, alone, ahead, with yards of sheer sunlight between him and his fellow-men.

Yards of sheer sunlight between that face with its confident glance forward, that voice with its clear cry, " Come on, men! Come on!" and those—the mass of men—who with timorous look backward hear in that call to go forward nothing but the vain regret for things familiar that must be left behind. " Going! Going! Gone! "

So, in a way, John Nicholson stands symbol of the many lives lost uselessly in the vain attempt to go forward too fast.

Yet his voice echoed still to the dark faces and the light alike:

" Come on, men!   Come on! "

BOOK VI.

APPENDIX A.

From A. DASHE, *Collector and Magistrate of Kujabpore, to* R. TAPE, Esq., *Commissioner and Superintendent of Kwâbabad.*

Fol. No. O.

Dated 11th May, 1858.

SIR: In reply to your No. 103 of the 20th April requesting me to report on the course of the Mutiny in my district, the measures taken to suppress it, and its effects, if any, on the judicial, executive, and financial work under my charge, I have the honor to inclose a brief statement, which for convenience' sake I have drafted under the usual headings of the annual report which I was unable to send in till last week. I regret the delay, but the pressure of work in the English office due to the revising of forfeiture and pension lists made it unavoidable.

I have the honor, etc., etc.,

A. DASHE, *Coll. and Magte.*

*Introductory Remarks.**—So far as my district is concerned, the late disturbances have simply been a military mutiny. At no time could they be truthfully called a rebellion. In the outlying posts, indeed, the people knew little or nothing of what was going on around them, and even in the towns resistance was not thought of until the prospect of any immediate suppression of the mutiny disappeared.

The small force of soldiers in my district of course followed the example of their brethren. Nothing else could be expected from our position midway between two large cantonments; indeed the continuous stream of mutinous troops which passed up and down the main road during the summer had a decidedly bad effect.

I commenced to disperse the disturbers of the public peace on

---

* Every statement in this supposed report has been gleaned from a real one, or from official papers published at the time. I am responsible for nothing but occasionally the wording.

the 21st May. These were largely escaped felons from the Meerut jail ; and the fact that they were quite indiscriminate in their lawlessness enabled me to rally most of the well-doing people on my side. I hanged a few of the offenders, and having enlisted a small corps with the aid of some native gentlemen (whose names I append for reference), sent it out under charge of my assistant (I myself being forced throughout the whole business to remain at headquarters and keep a grip on things) to put down some Goojurs and other predatory tribes who took occasion to resort to their ancestral habits of life.

No real opposition, however, was ever met with; but in June (after our failure to take Delhi by a *coup de main* became known) there was an organized attempt to seize the Treasury. Fortunately I had some twenty or thirty of my new levy in headquarters at the time, so that the attempt failed, and I was able to bring one or two of the ringleaders (one, I regret to say, a man of considerable importance in my district) to justice.

I subsequently made several applications to the nearest cantonment for a few European soldiers to escort my treasure—some two lakhs—to safer quarters. But this, unfortunately, could not be granted to me, so I had to keep a strong guard of men over the money who might have been more useful elsewhere.

Until the fall of Delhi matters remained much the same. Isolated bands of marauders ravaged portions of my district, often, I regret to say, escaping before punishment could be meted out to them. The general feeling was one of disquiet and alarm to both Europeans and natives. My table attendant, for instance, absented himself from dinner one day, sending a substitute to do his work, under the belief that I had given orders for a general slaughter of Mohammedans that evening. I had done nothing of the kind.

After the fall of Delhi, as you are aware, the mutinous fugitives, some fifty or sixty thousand strong, marched southward in a compact body and caused much alarm. But after camping on the outskirts of my district for a few days, they suddenly disappeared. I am told they dispersed during one night, each to his own home. Anyhow they literally melted away, and the public mind seemed to become aware that the contest was over, and that the struggle to subvert British rule had ignominiously failed. Matters therefore assumed a normal aspect, but I believe that there is more shame, sorrow, and regret in the hearts of many than we shall probably ever have full cognizance of, and that it will take years for the one race to regain its confidence, the other its self-respect.

Civil Judicature.—The courts were temporarily suspended for a week or two ; after that original work went on much as usual, but the appellate work suffered. There was an indisposition both to institute and hear appeals, possibly due to the total eclipse of the higher appellate courts. I myself had little leisure for civil cases.

Criminal Justice.—There has been far less crime than usual during the past year. Possibly because much of it had necessarily to be treated summarily and so did not come on the record. I am inclined to believe, however, that petty offenses really are fewer when serious crime is being properly dealt with.

Police.—The less said about the behavior of the police the better. The force simply melted away; but as it was always inefficient its absence had little effect, save, perhaps, in a failure to bring up those trivial offenses mentioned in the last para.

Jails.—The jail was happily preserved throughout; for the addition of four or five hundred felons to the bad characters of my district might have complicated matters. I was peculiarly fortunate in this, since I learn that only nine out of the forty-three jails in the Province were so held.

Revenue (Sub-head, Land).—The arrears under this head are less than usual, and there seems no reason to apprehend serious loss to Government.

(Opium).—There has, I regret to say, been considerable detriment to our revenue under this head, due to the fact that the smuggling of the drug is extremely easy, owing to its small bulk, and that the demand was greater than usual.

(Stamps).—The revenue here shows an increase of Rs. 72,000. I am unable to account for this, unless the prevailing uncertainty made the public mind incline toward what security it could compass in the matter of bonds, agreements, etc.

(Salt and Customs).—This department shows a very creditable record. My subordinates, with the help of a few volunteers, were able to maintain the Customs line throughout the whole disturbances. Its value as a preventative of roving lawlessness cannot be over-estimated. Four hundred and eighty-two smugglers were punished, and the Customs brought in Rs. 33,770 more than in '56. But the work done by this handful of isolated European patrols, with only a few natives under them, to the cause of law and order, cannot be estimated in money.

Education.—The higher education went on as usual. Primary instruction suffered. Female schools disappeared altogether.

Public Works.—Many things combined to stop anything like a vigorous prosecution of new public works, and those in hand were greatly retarded.

Post-Office.—The work in this department suffered occasional lapses owing to the murder of solitary runners by lawless ruffians, but the service continued fairly efficient. An attempt was made, by the confiscation of sepoys' letters, to discover if any organized plan of attack or resistance was in circulation, but nothing incriminatory was found, the correspondence consisting chiefly of love-letters.

Financial.—At one time the necessary cash for the pay of establishments ran short, but this was met by bills upon native bankers, who have since been repaid.

Hospitals.—The dispensaries were in full working order throughout the year, and the number of cases treated—especially for wounds and hurts, many of them grievous—above the average.

Health and Population.—Both were normal, and the supply of food grains ample. Markets strong, and well supplied throughout. Some grain stores were burned, some plundered; but, as a rule, if A robbed B, B in his turn robbed C. So the matter adjusted itself. In many cases also, the booty was restored amicably when it became evident that Government could hold its own.

Agriculture.—Notwithstanding the violence of contest, the many instances of plundered and burned villages, the necessary impressment of labor and cattle, and the license of mutineers consorting with felons, agricultural interests did not suffer. Plowing and sowing went on steadily, and the land was well covered with a full winter crop.

General Remarks.—Beyond these plundered and burned villages, which are still somewhat of an eyesore, though they are recovering themselves rapidly, the only result of the Mutiny to be observed in my district is that money seems scarcer, and so the cultivators have to pay a higher rate of interest on loans.

There are, of course, some empty chairs in the district durbar. I append a list of their late occupants also, and suggest that the vacancies might be filled from the other list, as some of those gentlemen who helped to raise the levy have not yet got chairs.

In regard to future punishments, however, I venture to suggest that orders should be issued limiting the period during which mutineers can be brought to justice. If some such check on malicious accusation be not laid down we shall have a fine crop of false cases, perjuries, etc., since the late disturbances have, naturally, caused a good many family differences. In view of this also, I believe it would be safest, in the event of such accusations in the future, to punish the whole village to which the alleged mutineer belongs by a heavy fine, rather than to single out individuals as examples. In a case like the present it is extremely difficult to measure the exact proportion of guilt attachable to each member of the community, and, even with the very greatest care, I find it is not always possible to hang the right man. And this is a difficulty which will increase as time goes on.

¶

APPENDIX B.

DELHI, Christmas Day, 1858.

DEAR MRS. ERLTON : I can scarcely believe that two whole years have passed since I helped you to decorate a Christmas-tree in the Government college here. Those long months before the walls, and those others of wild chase after vanishing mutineers over half India seem to belong to someone else's existence now that I—and the world around me—are back in the commonplaces of life. I was down to-day helping the chaplain's wife with another tree—she has a very pretty sister, by the way, just out from England—and I almost fancied as I looked into the dim screened veranda where we are going to have an entertainment, that I could see you sitting there with little Sonny Seymour on your lap as I found you that afternoon half asleep—that interminable play about the Lord of Life and Death (wasn't it ?) had been too much for you.

Well, I can only hope that Mr. Douglas' health and the pleasures of that Scotch home, of which you wrote me such a delightful description, will allow of your returning to India sometime and giving me a sight of you again.

Meanwhile I am reminded that I sent you off a small parcel by last mail which I trust may arrive before the wedding, as this should do, and convey to you the kindly remembrances of friends many thousand miles away. Not that you will need to be reminded. I fancy that few who went through the Indian Mutiny will ever need to have the faces and places they saw there recalled to their memory. Terrible as it was at the time, I myself feel that I would not willingly forget a single detail. So, being certain that it holds your interest, your imagination also, I am inclosing something for you to read. Can you not imagine the Silent and Diffident Dashe writing it ? I can, and the careful way in which he would order the gallows to be removed and lay down his sword in favor of his pen at the earliest opportunity. You see he favors clemency Canning. So do most of us out here except those who have not yet recovered their nerves. I remember hearing Hodson—sad, wasn't it ? his death over a needless piece of dare-devilry—very angry over something Mr. Douglas said about our all being in a blind funk. I am afraid it was true of a good many. Not Dashe, however, he kept his district together by sheer absence of fear, and so did many another. This report, then, will carry you on in

the story, as it were, since you left us. For the rest, there is not
much to tell. You remember our old mess khânsaman Numgal
Khân? He turned up, with his bill, and out of pure delight
insisted on feasting us so lavishly that we had to make him moder-
ate his transports. Even with *batta* and prize money we should
all have been bankrupt, like the royal family. I can't help pitying
it. Of course we have pensioned the lot, but I expect precious
little hard cash gets to some of those wretched women. One of
them, no less a person than the Princess Farkhoonda Zamâni,
that beast Abool-bukr's ally, has set up a girls' school in the city.
If she had only befriended you instead of turning you out to find
your own fate, she would have done better for herself. Talking
of friends and foes, it is rather amusing to find the villages full of
men busy at their plows with a suspiciously military set about
the shoulders, who, according to their own showing, never wore
uniform, or doffed it before the Mutiny began.   I was much struck
with one of these defaulters the other day; a big Rajpoot, who,
but for his name, might have stood for the Laodicean sepoy you
told me about.   But names can be changed, so can faces ; and
that reminds me that I had a petition from that old scoundrel
Tiddu the other day—you know I have been put on to civil work
lately, and shall end, I suppose, by being a Commissioner as well
as a Colonel. He has had a grant of land given him for life, and
he now wants the tenure extended in favor of one Jhungi, who, he
declares, helped you in your marvelous escape. It seems there
was another brother, one Bhungi, who—but I own to being a little
confused in the matter.   Perhaps you can set me straight.   Meanwhile, I have pigeon-hôled the Jhungi-Bhungi claim until I hear
from you. The old man was well, and asked fervently after
Sonny, who, by the way, goes home from Lucknow in the spring.
I expect the Seymours are about the only family in India which came
out of the business unscathed ; yet they were in the thick of it.
Truly the whole thing was a mystery from beginning to end.   I
asked a native yesterday if he could explain it, but he only shook his
head and said the Lord had sent a " breath into the land." But the
most remarkable thing to my mind about the whole affair is the
rapidity with which it proved the stuff a man was made of. You
can see that by looking into the cemeteries. India is a dead level
for the present; all the heads that towered above their fellows laid
low. Think of them all ! Havelock, Lawrence, Outram. The
names crowd to one's lips ; but they seem to begin and end with
one—Nicholson !
Well, good-by ! I have not wished you luck—that goes without saying ; but tell Douglas I'm glad he had his chance.
Ever yours truly,
CHARLES MORECOMBE.

www.ingramcontent.com/pod-product-compliance
Lightning Source LLC
Chambersburg PA
CBHW052333110726
47901CB00005B/1227